9 - W
9 - 1

The
Beauty
Bride

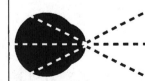

This Large Print Book carries the
Seal of Approval of N.A.V.H.

The Jewels of Kinfairlie Trilogy I

The
Beauty
Bride

Claire Delacroix

Thorndike Press • Waterville, Maine

Published in 2005 by arrangement with Warner Books, Inc.

Thorndike Press® Large Print Basic.

The tree indicium is a trademark of Thorndike Press.

The text of this Large Print edition is unabridged.
Other aspects of the book may vary from the original edition.

Set in 16 pt. Plantin.

Printed in the United States on permanent paper.

Library of Congress Cataloging-in-Publication Data

Delacroix, Claire.
    The beauty bride / by Claire Delacroix.
      p. cm.
    ISBN 0-7862-7841-2 (lg. print : hc : alk. paper)
    1. Brothers and sisters — Fiction. 2. Arranged marriage
— Fiction. 3. Scotland — Fiction. 4. Large type books.
I. Title.
PS3604.E413B43 2005
  811'.6—dc22   2005011901

This trilogy is dedicated
to my readers, with heartfelt
thanks for your loyalty and support.
May you enjoy reading about
the Jewels of Kinfairlie as much
as I have enjoyed recounting their tales.

As the Founder/CEO of NAVH, the only national health agency solely devoted to those who, although not totally blind, have an eye disease which could lead to serious visual impairment, I am pleased to recognize Thorndike Press★ as one of the leading publishers in the large print field.

Founded in 1954 in San Francisco to prepare large print textbooks for partially seeing children, NAVH became the pioneer and standard setting agency in the preparation of large type.

Today, those publishers who meet our standards carry the prestigious "Seal of Approval" indicating high quality large print. We are delighted that Thorndike Press is one of the publishers whose titles meet these standards. We are also pleased to recognize the significant contribution Thorndike Press is making in this important and growing field.

Lorraine H. Marchi, L.H.D.
Founder/CEO
NAVH

★ Thorndike Press encompasses the following imprints: Thorndike, Wheeler, Walker and Large Print Press.

Prologue

Kinfairlie, on the east coast of Scotland — April 1421

Alexander, newly made Laird of Kinfairlie, glowered at his sister.

There was no immediate effect. In fact, Madeline granted him a charming smile. She was a beautiful woman, dark of hair and blue of eye, her coloring and comeliness so striking that men oft stared at her in awe. She was fiercely clever and charming as well. All of these traits, along with the score of men anxious to win her hand, only made Madeline's refusal to wed more irksome.

"You need not look so annoyed, Alexander," she said, her tone teasing. "My suggestion is wrought of good sense."

"It is no good sense for a woman of three and twenty summers to remain unwed," he grumbled. "I cannot imagine what Papa was thinking not to have seen you safely wed a decade ago."

Madeline's eyes flashed. "Papa was

thinking that I loved James and that I would wed James in time."

"James is dead," Alexander retorted, speaking more harshly than was his wont. They had had this argument a dozen times and he tired of his sister's stubborn refusal to accept the obvious truth. "And dead the better part of a year."

A shadow touched Madeline's features and she lifted her chin. "We have no certainty of that."

"Every man was killed in that assault upon the English at Rougemont — that no man survived to tell the tale does not change the truth of it." Alexander softened his tone when Madeline glanced away, blinking back her tears. "We both would have preferred that James's fate had been otherwise, but you must accept that he will not return."

He was pleased to note how Madeline straightened and how the fire returned to her eyes. If she was spirited enough to argue with him, that could only be a good sign. "Though I appreciate a wound to the heart takes long to heal, you grow no younger, Madeline."

Madeline arched a brow. "Nor do any of us, brother mine. Why do you not wed first?"

"Because it is not necessary." Alexander glared at her, again to no avail. He knew that he sounded like a man fifty years older than he was, but he could not help himself — Madeline's refusal to be biddable was annoying. "I ask only that you wed, that you do so out of regard for your four younger sisters, that they too might wed."

"I do not halt their nuptials."

"They will not wed before you and you know it well. So Vivienne and Annelise and Isabella and Elizabeth have *all* informed me. I try only to do what is best for you, but you are all in league against me!" Alexander flung out his hands then rose to his feet, pacing the chamber in his frustration.

Madeline — curse her! — regarded him with dawning amusement. Trust her to be consoled by teasing him!

"It is no small burden to become laird of the keep," she noted, the expression in her eyes knowing when he spun to face her. "No less to be burdened with the lot of us. You were much more merry a year ago, Alexander."

"And no wonder that! This is hell!" he shouted, feeling better for it. "Not a one of you makes this newfound duty any easier for me to bear! I am not mad to demand that you wed! I am trying to assure your future, yet you all defy me at every step!"

Madeline tilted her head, her eyes beginning to sparkle and a smile lifting the corner of her lips. "Can you not imagine that it is a sweet kind of vengeance for all the pranks you have played upon us over the years? How delicious it is to foil you, Alexander, now that you are suddenly stern and proper! Think of all the frogs in my linens and snakes in my slippers for which I can now have vengeance."

"I will not be foiled!" he roared and thudded his fist upon the table between them.

Madeline clucked her tongue, chiding him for his show of temper. "And I will not be wed," she said, her soft tone belying the determination in her gaze. "Not so readily as that. At any rate, you have not the coin in the treasury to offer a dowry, so there is no need to discuss the matter before the tithes are collected in the autumn."

Alexander spun to look out the window, hoping to hide his expression from his confident sister. There might have been a steel band drawn tight around his chest, for he knew a detail that Madeline did not. The tithes would be low this year, so the castellan had confided in him. There had been torrential rains this spring and what seed had not been washed away had rotted in the ground. He marvelled that he had never thought of such matters until this past year and marvelled again at how much he had yet to learn.

How had Papa managed all these concerns? How had he laughed and been so merry with such a weight upon his shoulders? Alexander felt nearly crushed beneath this unfamiliar burden of responsibility.

His gaze trailed over the sea that lapped beneath Kinfairlie's towers and he mourned the loss of their parents anew. He knew that his siblings defied him as a way of denying the cruel truth of their parents' sudden death, but he also knew that he could not feed all those currently resident in this keep in the winter to come. The castellan had told him so, and in no uncertain terms.

His sisters had to be wed, and at least the two eldest had to be wed this summer. They were all of an age to be married, ranging as they did from twenty-three summers to twelve, but Madeline was the sole obstacle to his scheme.

He pivoted to regard her, noting the concern that she quickly hid. She must guess what it cost him to so change his own nature, to abandon his recklessness in favor of responsibility; she must know that he assumed this task for the sake of all of them.

Yet still she defied him.

"You could at least feign compliance," he suggested, anger thrumming beneath his words. "You could try to make my task lighter, Madeline, instead of encouraging our sisters to defy me."

She leaned closer. "You could at least *ask*," she retorted, the sapphire flash of her eyes showing that this would be no easy victory. "In truth, Alexander, you are so demanding these days that a saint would defy you, and do so simply for the pleasure of thwarting your schemes. You have become a different man since you were made laird, and one who is difficult to like."

"I am making choices for the best of all of us," he insisted, "and you only vex me."

Madeline smiled with cursed confidence. "You are not vexed. You are irked, perhaps."

"Annoyed," contributed another feminine voice. Vivienne tipped her head around the corner, revealing that she had been listening to the entire exchange. Vivienne's hair was of a russet hue and her eyes were a dark green. Otherwise, she shared Madeline's virtues and not a few of her faults, including the fact that she also must be wed before the harvest.

Alexander ground his teeth at the slender prospect of succeeding twice in this challenge.

Three shorter women peeked around the edge of the portal, their eyes bright with curiosity. Annelise was sixteen with auburn tresses and eyes as blue as cornflowers; Isabella was fourteen with eyes of vivid green, orange-red hair and freckles across her nose; Elizabeth was ebony-haired like himself and Madeline, her eyes an uncanny green. The sight of all those uncovered tresses — the mark of unmarried maidens — made Alexander's innards clench.

They were no longer merely his sisters, his comrades, or even the victims of his jests — they and their futures were his responsibility.

"But you are certainly not vexed, Alexander," Vivienne continued with a smile.

Madeline nodded agreement. "When Alexander is vexed in truth, he shouts. So know this, Annelise, Isabella, and Elizabeth, you have not truly angered Alexander until he roars fit to lift the roof." The five women giggled and that was enough.

"I am indeed vexed!" Alexander bellowed. The sole result of his outburst was that the three younger women nodded.

"Now he *is* vexed," said Annelise.

"You can tell by the way he shouts," Elizabeth agreed.

"Indeed," said Madeline, that teasing smile curving her lips again. "But still he is a man of honor, upon that we can all rely." She rose and gave a simmering Alexander a peck of a kiss upon each of his cheeks.

She smiled at him with a surety that made him long to throttle her, for she was right.

"Still he will not raise a hand against a woman." Madeline patted his shoulder, as if he were no more threatening than a kitten. "I shall wed when I so choose, Alexander, and not one day before. Fear not — all will be resolved well enough in the end."

With that, Madeline left the chamber, easily gathering their sisters about her. They chattered of kirtles and chemises and new shoes. Elizabeth demanded a story, and as Vivienne complied, their voices faded to naught.

Alexander sat down heavily and put his head in his hands. What was he going to do?

In this same moment, beneath the neighboring keep of Ravensmuir, there was a

14

ruckus in the caverns.

Ravensmuir perched on the coast, and the network of natural caves beneath its high walls had been augmented by men over the eons. In recent centuries, a family named Lammergeier, who trafficked in religious relics, had claimed Ravensmuir and filled the caverns with their hoard. It was said that no soul could invade the caverns, much less steal from them, without the knowledge of the Laird of Ravensmuir.

Which explained the presence of one small fairy — a spriggan, in fact — sleeping contentedly in the hoard, for fairies are well known to have no souls. As for spriggans, in case you have never seen one (and it is doubtful that you have) they are quite small, small enough to sleep in one's hand. They are also quite unattractive, although Darg — for that was the spriggan's name — was even more plain than most.

Darg was dark all over, as if covered by the bark of a gnarled old tree; and her head was like nothing more than a teasle, with the long pointed part forming her nose and the bristles being what passed for her hair. She had small beady dark eyes, and quick little fingers, and even given how strange her appearance, any thinking person would conclude with a glimpse that Darg was a greedy little thief (and that person would have been right). You could not have guessed her gender, not that it mattered much, and indeed, you likely would never glimpse her.

Nonetheless, she was there, in Ravensmuir's caverns.

Darg had claimed a reliquary for her bed, some years ago. Though she had initially resented the intrusion of these foreign spoils in her nice dark cave, this golden reliquary had a comely glitter about it. It also had a nest of soft golden hair coiled carefully within it. (Darg did not know, nor did she care, that these were said to be three sacred hairs from Saint Ursula herself, who had saved ten thousand virgins and whose flaxen tresses had fallen to her very ankles.)

Darg particularly liked the round crystals on the sides of the reliquary, through which she could peek out, mostly because their curve distorted all into nonsensical shapes. As a fairy, albeit a small one with a penchant for making trouble, Darg liked fantastical shapes and illusions.

She could make some pretty impressive ones herself. Spriggans are known for their ability to become enormous phantasms when angered or surprised. In this manifestation, unfortunately, most mortals can see them and often confuse them with vengeful ghosts.

Spriggans are vengeful, to be sure, but not ghosts.

This new noise was enough to wake Darg, who had slept contentedly for several decades. In fact, it had been quiet in the caves for so long — since one laird named Merlyn had foregone the family trade — that Darg had come to think of the glittering hoard as her own. There was one mortal who came to raid the treasure, a woman with long red hair and a bold manner who Darg had never managed to halt.

At the sound of mortal voices, Darg awakened with a yawn and a stretch and a grimace, then peeked through the big clear rock crystal. She was certain that the woman would be responsible, perhaps that Darg would have vengeance this time. Indeed, she was considering which particular large and frightening form would be most effective when she saw the shocking truth.

The intruders were *men*. A good dozen men. What did they scheme? Darg squinted to watch.

"Aye, the better part of it must be

brought to the hall," said a swarthy one who looked somewhat familiar. "Rosamunde will sort what will be sold once it is there."

"But there is so much!"

"You cannot see the half of it," said the first man, then pointed into the darkness unilluminated by their flickering lanterns. "There are said to be hidden caverns stacked with it. I suspect that these caves will never be fully cleared, for much has probably been forgotten."

The three men with him whistled appreciatively. The assessment in their expressions was a familiar expression to Darg, but one she resented when they looked upon *her* treasure.

"We had best begin," said the first man. The other men grunted and began to fill baskets and boxes with golden trinkets. Each man worked with haste, gathering fistfuls of goods, uncaring what was jumbled together. Darg was indignant.

But not so indignant as she became when they lifted the boxes and turned back to the stairs that led to the keep. They were removing the relics.

They were stealing Darg's treasure!

"Aiiiii!" Darg leapt from her hiding place and screeched with all her power.

Without a plan, she transformed into an enormous red angry cloud. The cloud glowed in its midst, it screamed, it was the height of six men. It seemed to push at the walls and ceiling of the cavern, it extinguished the lanterns the men had brought.

And then it screamed some more.

This was the most amusement Darg had had in centuries.

The men, however, were terrified. Some dropped their boxes. They ran for the stairs, bumping into each other in their frenzy to begone.

"Halt! Be calm!" the first man shouted, but no one heeded him. "What manner of men are you to be afraid of the dark?" he roared, his words barely discernible over the thunder of the men's boots on the stairs.

Left alone, he lit his lantern again, his expression one of disgust. He swore, then bent to lift a box of relics. Darg screamed again, thinking him uncommonly valiant, but he paid her no heed. He frowned, then carefully fitted another two gold pieces into his box. Darg spun into his very face, surrounding him with angry red, then screamed again. He tested the weight of his burden, then straightened to leave.

Darg fell back in astonishment. He could

not see her, not in either form. She shrank then to her usual form, for there was no point in expending herself for no purpose. In truth, she felt somewhat disappointed, a bit cheated of his terror. She watched the swarthy man, trying to discern what was different about this mortal. She came to no conclusions, because she knew very little about mortals.

Then he lifted the box and turned toward the stairs.

Nay! He could not flee with her treasure! Darg scampered across the chamber and leapt onto the thief's shoulder. She fit herself into the swinging hoop of his golden earring, and rode to the root of the trouble.

She would wager that the red-headed one was behind this mischief. Darg would also have wagered that the red-headed one knew little of the kind of mischief Darg could make. Darg found herself anticipating the havoc she could wreak with that certain malicious glee which is unique to spriggans.

The defense of her hoard could prove to be amusing, indeed.

Fortunately, she was well rested.

Alexander was still sitting with his head in his hands at Kinfairlie, though the sky was darker, when his visitors arrived.

"He does indeed look glum enough," a familiar voice said, laughter beneath her tone. "So we were warned."

Alexander looked up as his Aunt Rosamunde cast herself upon the bench Madeline had abandoned. She shook the pins from her hair with characteristic impatience. The sunlit tresses fell loose over her shoulders and she sighed with relief.

His spirits rose at the very sight of her, for he and Rosamunde had plotted many a jest together over the years. Hers was a mischievous soul and she was not averse to defying convention or taking a risk.

She winked at him now, though addressed the other visitor. "I would wager that sisters are his woe, Tynan."

"That is not much of a wager," Uncle Tynan said grimly, shaking out his cloak before he leaned upon the lip of the window. He was a sober man, always weighing costs and counselling caution. "They are too merry not to have recently triumphed over Alexander." The older man smiled slightly at his beleaguered nephew. "You are outnumbered and further encumbered by honor. Those five will use any means against you."

This pair had made an unlikely alliance these past years, since it had been revealed that they were not blood cousins. Rosamunde had been adopted by Gawain and Evangeline, which all knew, but was not Gawain's bastard daughter, as everyone had long believed. Tynan was the son of Gawain's brother, Merlyn. Though sparks had long flown between this pair, they had kept their distance, believing themselves to be kin. None had been more surprised than they by the revelation that they shared no blood.

There was a new awareness between them in recent years, and one that Alexander did not wish to explore. Who knew what happened at his uncle's keep of Ravensmuir when Rosamunde's ship was docked in its bay? Rosamunde's labor as a broker of religious relics, both genuine and somewhat less genuine, meant Alexander knew better than to ask questions.

He shook his head now and grimaced. "I could strangle Madeline."

Rosamunde was dismissive of the notion. "But then you would have to face a court and the king's justice, and some misery of incarceration."

"Not to mention purgatory, if not hell itself," Tynan added.

"Hardly worth it," Rosamunde said sagely, then winked at him again. "What has Madeline done — or refused to do — this time?"

"She refuses to wed. She thinks she does me a favor, by saving coin in the treasury." Alexander sighed, then lowered his voice. "But there is no coin and there will be none soon. The castellan says the harvest will be bad, and I fear I will not be able to feed all within these walls this winter."

"The others?" Tynan demanded, leaning forward in his interest.

"I would guess that they refuse to wed afore Madeline," Rosamunde suggested softly.

Alexander nodded glumly. His guests exchanged a glance, then Rosamunde cleared her throat. "Do you not miss the old days, Alexander, when your deeds were the most outrageous of all?"

"I have duties now, and an obligation to Papa's trust," Alexander said, his very tone dutiful beyond belief.

"And so all the spark has gone from your days and your deeds." Rosamunde sat back and shook her head, her eyes dancing wickedly. "I think you should surprise Madeline. You have tried to reason with her, after all, and without success."

"Rosamunde . . ." Tynan said, the single word filled with warning.

Rosamunde leaned toward Alexander, undeterred. "We came this day to tell you of our agreement to be rid of all the relics at Ravensmuir. Tynan will not suffer them beneath the roof any longer, for he tires of my nocturnal visits to plunder his treasure."

Tynan snorted, but said nothing.

"Surely you cannot mean to abandon your trade?" Alexander asked in surprise. "I thought you most successful in this endeavor."

Rosamunde shrugged, her gaze sliding to Tynan. A beguiling color touched her cheeks, then she met Alexander's gaze again. "I grow no younger, Alexander, and the risk of the seas holds less allure than once it did. Perhaps I shall become a nun."

Both men laughed uproariously at this prospect, and Rosamunde chuckled in her turn.

"We are agreed that the family trade will finally halt," she continued more soberly. "And also that the last of the relics must leave Ravensmuir to ensure Tynan has his peace."

"But what will you do with them?" Alexander asked. "Surely you do not mean to grant them as gifts?"

Tynan chuckled darkly. "I would be a generous donor indeed."

"We intend to auction them, in the midst of May, when all are anxious for a diversion," Rosamunde declared, her eyes bright. "We will invite noblemen, bishops and knights from all of Christendom to bid against each other for these prizes. It will be a grand fête and a fitting end to my trade."

"Madeline might find a spouse there," Alexander mused, but his aunt laughed aloud.

"Be more bold than that, Alexander!" she declared. "You sound like a man three times your age."

"Rosamunde," Tynan warned again, but was heeded no more closely than the first time.

Indeed, Rosamunde's voice dropped low and she tapped a finger upon Alexander's knee. Mischief emanated from her every pore. "Perhaps, Alexander, you should auction the Jewel of Kinfairlie. You said you were in need of coin."

Alexander glanced between the pair of them. Tynan had dropped his brow to his hand and shook his head in apparent despair. Rosamunde looked so delighted with herself that Alexander knew he had missed some critical detail.

"But there is no Jewel of Kinfairlie," he began cautiously. Rosamunde laughed and understanding dawned. "Oh! But Madeline would loathe me forever if I auctioned her hand!"

"Shhhh!" counselled Rosamunde. Tynan, with obvious resignation, closed the portal and leaned against it.

Alexander looked between the pair of them, his blood quickening at the prospect. Oh, he could well imagine how infuriated Madeline would be — and truly the prospect gave him some pleasure. "I should not dare," he said carefully.

Rosamunde laughed. "There was a time when you would have dared far more than this to best Madeline." She braced her elbows upon her knees. "Do not tell me that I have to *dare* you to do this deed? Alexander, what has become of you? Surely the ruffian we knew and loved is yet within your heart?"

And that was all it took.

Alexander raised a finger. "We will do this upon one condition. I will compile a list of those I deem suitable matches, and only those men will be advised that the Jewel of Kinfairlie is for sale."

"There is nothing amiss with a private auction, provided all those invited have weighty purses," Rosamunde conceded.

"I cannot believe that I am a part of this

26

foolery," Tynan grumbled.

"Of course you are a part of it," Rosamunde said crisply. "It is you who must pass the word along." She patted his arm and a spark danced between the two of them, one so hot that Alexander felt obliged to glance away. "Who better to quietly and competently ensure that our niece's needs are met?"

A ghost of a smile touched Tynan's lips. "I came also with a proposition for you, Alexander, and one you may find timely. It is fitting for an uncle to train his nephews for knighthood. If you are desirous of it, I will take your brother Malcolm to Ravensmuir, for he is old enough to be so groomed."

"You are too kind, Uncle. And I know that Malcolm would welcome this trust. He has great fondness for you and is most eager to begin his military training."

"And should you desire it," Tynan continued, "I could send word to the Hawk of Inverfyre. I do not doubt that he would take Ross beneath his care, and train him. It might be a good scheme, for the Hawk has so many sons of his own with whom Ross could practice."

"It would see another mouth from your board this winter," Rosamunde said quietly.

Alexander felt his burden lighten. "You are too kind to aid me in this."

"We are family," Rosamunde said firmly. "It is our solemn duty to aid each other, and you have need of more aid than most in these times."

"I thank you for your counsel and your aid," Alexander said, knowing his gratitude showed.

"You must contrive to bring Madeline to Ravensmuir for the auction," Rosamunde said with resolve. "For if she guesses the truth afore the nuptials are complete, there will be trouble. We must act with haste and daring to succeed."

"Woe will come of this particular scheme," Tynan said darkly.

Rosamunde laughed. "You always say as much. I have a feeling, though, that Madeline might well meet her match."

"It has long been said that you see more than most," Tynan acknowledged.

"Yet I do not see what is evident to all," Rosamunde admitted with a laugh. "Given a choice, I am not certain which I would choose, but the choice was made for me."

Their banter made all seem aright. For the first time in many months, Alexander felt himself begin to smile. With such a plan, much could be resolved, and truly a mischievous part of him looked forward to irking Madeline as he had for decades. He would not have been her elder brother otherwise.

"I mean to ensure that she does meet her match." Alexander imagined Madeline's outrage and chuckled, even as he compiled a list of suitors he knew would treat her well. Within a year, Madeline would forget about her lost betrothed James and the wound in her heart would heal. He knew with utter certainty that she would be happy once she was wed and had a babe in her belly. Within a year, Madeline would thank him mightily for his daring deed.

Truly, this was the best possible solution.

"But I have been remiss," Alexander said with a heartiness he could not have imagined he would soon feel again. "You are my guests, yet you have neither wine nor ale in your hand. Come to the hall, come and make merry with all of us. Your presence at Kinfairlie is welcome. I thank you, Aunt and Uncle, for you have brought good tidings and welcome counsel indeed."

Meanwhile, some miles down the coast that faces the North Sea, a warrior met with a priest. The warrior was a stranger to all at Kinfairlie and at Ravensmuir, though his quest would soon bring him to those gates. He sought another Madeline — Madeline Arundel — who should have been twice the age of the Madeline Lammergeier at Kinfairlie. Alnwyck was the keep where priest and warrior met, and this was the day that a mystery would be solved for the warrior.

Rhys FitzHenry touched a fingertip to the name inscribed in the ledger. After many months of searching, he had finally found his cousin Madeline Arundel.

She had died in the winter of 1398, some twenty-three years before.

Rhys looked out the window of the chapel, blind to the windswept shore beyond these stone walls. It rained, a steady patter upon the roof that cast silver across the sea and coast. But in Rhys's mind's eye, he saw his cousin on a summer's day, daisies woven into her raven hair, her hand clasped in the firm grip of Edward Arundel. They had been young, handsome, and vigorously happy.

His uncle Dafydd had called Madeline a tribute bride, a woman exchanged in matrimony to seal a treaty between new allies, but no one would have believed that Madeline wed Edward out of duty alone. There were stars in her eyes and laughter in her voice: even those two old warriors responsible for the nuptials, Dafydd and Owain Glyn Dŵr himself, had smiled at her merriment. Rhys had only been a boy, but he remembered the jubilation of that day well.

Madeline had lived a mere year after that. It was impossible to believe, though no surprise that no one had known, given the chaos that had claimed Wales in those years. Rhys's heart clenched in recollection of the couple's laughter as they left to rejoin the knight's family in Northumberland.

One year they had savored together. It seemed far too little for the happiness they had found.

"God bless her soul," the priest murmured and Rhys echoed the blessing.

He was disappointed, he realized, though logically he should not have been. Though he remembered Madeline only vaguely, though she alone could have thwarted his ambitions, he wished his search might have ended differently.

It would not have been all bad to have found some kin left breathing in these sorry times. The rebellion in Wales against the English crown had plucked the ripest fruit from their family tree, and there were precious few of the multitudes of Rhys's childhood left living.

With Madeline deceased, he would possess Caerwyn himself. Rhys closed his eyes for a moment, the vigor of his desire weakening his knees. He had grown up at Caerwyn, he had learned to wield a blade there, he had joined the ranks to defend her walls when he had been yet a youth. He loved that keep more than life itself, he had dreamed of possessing her, he had despaired that such fortune could ever come to him.

But against all odds, Caerwyn would be his.

Rhys gave Madeline's name a last caress of farewell, then noted a word he had not seen before.

"In childbirth?" he asked of the priest, fear stirring within him. "Madeline died in childbirth?"

The priest nodded. "I am sorry, my son, but it is not uncommon for women to be lost this way. It was said that her husband, Edward, was devoted to her, and I have no doubt that he procured the services of the best midwife . . ."

"But what happened to the child?" Rhys dreaded that his search was but partly completed. The child would be a direct descendant of Dafydd. The child could inherit Caerwyn in Rhys's stead.

He must know the whereabouts of the child!

The priest smiled. "You have uncommon charity for a mere cousin, my son. How kind of you to have a care for your kinswoman's child."

Rhys spoke through gritted teeth. "What happened to the child?"

"Perhaps it died as well." The priest shrugged. "Perhaps the father raised it alone, or wed again."

"I must know the truth of it!" Rhys shouted and the priest flinched at his vigor. He was immediately contrite. "I am sorry, Father, but the matter is of utmost importance to me." Rhys swallowed. "This child would be the last living soul of my kin."

"Of course, of course. Your devotion is most admirable, my son." The priest ran a fingertip down the ledger and frowned. "No other death is recorded here in that year. I cannot imagine that the babe would have died unshriven if the priest recorded the mother's demise. There is no mention of a christening, but my predecessor was not always complete in his records. No child was returned to Lady Madeline's kin?"

"Nay." Rhys was certain of it.

"How curious. Perhaps it remained here, with the father . . ." The priest mused as he unfurled the scroll, and Rhys barely restrained himself from snatching the vellum from the old priest's hands.

"Ah!" The priest granted Rhys a smile. "There is a note here in 1403 that might be of interest. Lady Catherine of Kinfairlie attended the funeral mass for the knight Edward Arundel, who died in battle with Henry Percy." The priest glanced up. "It is writ that the old Earl of Northumberland wept a thousand tears for the untimely demise of his son and heir, Henry Hotspur."

"So it is told in the tales I know, as well."

"But the account states that this Lady Catherine then took the babe of Edward to be her ward, the child's blood parents both being deceased." He nodded. "One would assume that the two ladies had been friends, for Lady Catherine to take on Lady Madeline's young child." He removed his spectacles and considered Rhys. "Perhaps your kin can be found at Kinfairlie, my son."

"Perhaps so." Rhys donned his gloves, knowing his quest was not yet complete. "Where lies this Kinfairlie, Father?"

Chapter One

The auction of Ravensmuir's relics promised to be the event of the decade. Madeline and her sisters had spent the short interval between the announcement and the event ensuring that they would look their best. Uncle Tynan had declared it imperative that they appear to not need the coin, and his nieces did their best to comply.

It was beyond convenient that they could pass kirtles from one to the next, though inevitably there were alterations to be made. They might be sisters, but they were scarcely of the same shape! Hems had to be taken up or let down, seams gathered tighter or let out, and bits of embroidery were required to make each garment "new" for its latest recipient.

There were disagreements invariably between each one and her younger sibling, for their taste in ornamentation varied enormously. Madeline preferred her garments plain, while Vivienne savored lavish embroidery upon the hems, preferably of golden thread. These two did not argue any longer — though once they had done so heatedly, for Madeline sorely disliked to embroider and had been convinced as a young girl that it was unfair for her to endure a hateful task simply to please her sister.

Now, they bent their heads together to make Madeline's discarded kirtles better suit Vivienne, while Vivienne's quick needle made short work of any new garb destined for Madeline. Vivienne was also taller than Madeline, even though she was younger, so the hems had to be let out.

Annelise was shorter even than Madeline, so those hems had to be double-folded when a kirtle passed to her. This often meant that the finest embroidery was hidden from view, though this suited Annelise's more austere taste. Isabella, sadly, was nigh as tall as Vivienne, but could not abide golden embroidery. Her hair was the brightest hue of red of all the sisters and she was convinced that the gold of the thread made her hair appear unattractively fiery. When kirtles passed to her, the sisters would couch the gold with silver and other hues, and the kirtles would be resplendent indeed.

Finally, Elizabeth had the last wearing of each kirtle. This had never been an issue, for she seemed wrought to match the height of Isabella perfectly and was not overly particular of taste. Elizabeth was a girl inclined to dreaming, and was oft teased that she gave more merit to what she could not see than what was directly before her.

But there was a new challenge this year, for Elizabeth was twelve summers of age and her courses had begun. With her courses, her figure had changed radically. Suddenly, she had a much more generous bust than her elder sisters — which meant that she turned crimson when any male so much as glanced her way, as well as that Isabella's kirtles did not begin to fit her. There proved to be insufficient fabric even with the laces let out fully to grant Elizabeth an appearance of grace.

Tears ensued, until Madeline and Vivienne contrived an embroidered panel that could be added down each side of the kirtles in question. Isabella, who was the most clever with a needle, embroidered patterns along their length that so matched the embroidery already on the hem that the panel appeared to have been a part of the kirtle all along.

Shoes and stockings and girdles took their own time to be arranged, but by the time the sisters arrived at Ravensmuir and were summoned to the chamber of the auction, no one could have faulted their splendor. They had even wrought new tabards for their brothers, with Alexander's bearing the glowing orb of Kinfairlie's crest on its front, as was now his right.

So they rode beneath the gates of Ravensmuir, attired in their finest garb. A rider came fast behind them, a single man upon a dappled destrier. He was darkly garbed and his hood was drawn over his helm. Madeline noted him, because he rode a knight's horse but had no squire. He did not appear to be as rough as a mercenary.

Oddly, Rosamunde answered some summons sent by him into the hall. She cried a greeting to this mysterious arrival, then leaned close to hear whatsoever he murmured. Madeline was curious, for she could not imagine what messenger would seek her aunt here, no less what manner of messenger would ride a destrier instead of a horse more fleet of foot. He had but a dog as companion.

"The colors of Kinfairlie suit you well," Vivienne said, giving Alexander's tabard an affectionate tug.

"This work is a marvel!" Alexander declared, sparing his sisters a bright smile. "You all spoil me overmuch, by sharing the labors of your needles." He kissed each of them on both cheeks, behaving more like an elderly gentleman than the rogue they knew and loved. His fulsome manner left the sisters discomfited and suspicious.

"You were not so thrilled at Kinfairlie, when we granted it to you," Vivienne noted.

"But here there are many to appreciate the rare skills of my beauteous sisters."

Years of pranks played by this very brother made all five sisters look over their shoulders.

"I thought you would tickle us," Elizabeth complained.

"Or make faces," Isabella added.

"Or tell us that we had erred in some detail of the insignia," Annelise contributed.

"To grant compliments is most unlike you," Vivienne concluded.

Alexander smiled like an angel. "How could I complain when you have been so blessedly kind?" The sisters stepped back as one, all of them prepared for the worst.

"Do not trust him," Madeline counselled. The two elder sisters shared a nod.

"Alexander is only so merry at the expense of another," Vivienne agreed.

"Me?" Alexander asked, all false innocence and charm.

"Well, at least you are not garbed like a duchess," Malcolm complained. He gestured to the embroidery on his tabard. "This is too lavish for a man training to be a knight."

"At least you do have not to wear this horrendous green," Ross said, shaking his own tabard. "I would not venture to name this hue."

"It matches your eyes, fool," Annelise informed him archly.

"We spent days choosing the perfect cloth," Isabella added.

"I surrendered this length of wool for you, Ross," Vivienne said. "And I will not take kindly to any suggestion now that it would make a finer kirtle than a tabard."

Ross grimaced and tugged at the hem of his tabard, looking as if he itched to cast it aside. "The other squires at Inverfyre will mock me for garbing myself more prettily than any vain maiden." He tugged at the tabard in vexation. "What if the Hawk will not take me to his court?"

"You need fear nothing. Our uncle is most fair, and Tynan has sent him a missive already," Madeline said soothingly. Her gaze followed the stranger and

Rosamunde as they entered the keep, her curiosity unsated by what she had seen.

"A maiden might take note of you, Ross, if you look your best," Elizabeth suggested shyly. Ross flushed scarlet, which did little to flatter the fiery hue of his hair.

"Our fingers are bleeding, our eyes are aching," Vivienne said with a toss of her tresses. "And this is the gratitude we receive! I expected a boon from my grateful brothers."

"A rose in winter," Annelise demanded.

"There is no such thing!" Malcolm scoffed.

"You should pledge to depart on a quest," Elizabeth suggested. "A pledge to seek a treasure for each of us."

"Sisters," Ross said with a roll of his eyes, then marched toward the nearest ostler.

Madeline had no further time to wonder about the stranger who had summoned Rosamunde. There was the usual bustle of arrival, of horses to be stabled and ostlers running, of squires and pages underfoot, of introductions being made and acquaintances being renewed. The stirrup cup had to be passed, sisters had to dress, and the company had to be gathered.

Soon, the moment would be upon them.

The auction that all awaited, the auction that made the very air tingle at Ravensmuir!

"Every soul in Christendom must be here!" Vivienne whispered to Madeline as they entered the chamber behind Alexander. Dozens of men watched their entry, standing politely aside as the family proceeded to the front of the chamber.

"Not quite so many souls as that," Madeline said. She had felt awkward since their arrival, for men seemed to be taking an uncommon interest in her.

"Perhaps you will find a husband here," Vivienne said with a merry wink. "Alexander is most determined that you choose soon."

"I shall choose in my own time and not before," Madeline said mildly, then knew a way to distract her sister. "Perhaps Nicholas Sinclair will be here," she added, her tone teasing.

Vivienne tossed her hair at the mention of her former suitor. "*Him!* He has not the coin for this."

Alexander stood aside and gestured that Madeline and Vivienne should precede him. He seemed stiff, and uncommonly serious.

"Smile, brother," Madeline whispered to him as she passed. "You will never catch the eye of a merry maid with so sour a countenance."

"The Laird of Kinfairlie must have need of an heir!" Vivienne teased with a laugh.

Alexander only averted his gaze.

"He never remains somber for long," Vivienne said as they sat upon the bench. "Look! There is Reginald Neville."

Madeline spared no more than a glance to the vain boy who imagined himself to be besotted with her. As usual, his garb was not only very fine, but he labored overhard to ensure that all noticed it. Even as he waved to her, he held his cloak open with his other hand, the better that its embroidery might be admired.

"I have only rejected him a dozen times." Madeline's tone was wry. "There might yet be hope for his suit."

"What a nightmare his wife's life will be!"

"And what will he do once he has exhausted the treasury he has inherited?"

"You are always so practical, Madeline." Vivienne edged closer, her voice dropping to a conspiratorial whisper. "There is Gerald of York." The elder sisters exchanged a glance, for that somber and steady man's endless tales put them both to sleep without fail.

"His bride will be well-rested, that

much is beyond doubt."

Vivienne giggled. "Oh, you are too wicked."

"Am I? Alexander will turn his gaze upon you next, and demand that you wed soon."

"Not before you, surely?"

"Whyever not? He seems determined to wed all of us in haste."

Vivienne nibbled her lip, her merry mood dispelled. "There is Andrew, that ally of our uncle."

"He is nigh as old as the Hawk of Inverfyre, as well."

"Ancient!" Vivienne agreed with horror. She jabbed her elbow into Madeline's side. "You might be widowed soon, if you wed him though."

"That is hardly an attribute one should seek in a spouse. And I will wed none of them, at any rate."

The Red Douglas men and the Black Douglas men arrived and took to opposite sides of the hall, all the better to glower at each other from a distance. Madeline knew that Alexander preferred to ally with the Black Douglases, as their father had done, but she could not bear the sight of Alan Douglas, their sole remaining unwed get. He was so fair as to be unnatural. He fairly leered at her, the rogue, and she averted her gaze. Roger Douglas, on the other side of the hall, as swarthy as his cousin was fair, found this amusing and granted her a courtly bow.

Madeline glanced away from both of them. Her heart leapt when she found the steady gaze of a man in the corner fixed upon her. He was tall and tanned, quiet of manner and heavily armed. His hair was dark, as were his eyes. He stood so motionless that her eye could have easily danced past him.

But now that she had looked, Madeline could not readily tear her gaze away. He was the stranger from the bailey, she was certain of it.

And he was watching her. Madeline's mouth went dry.

His hair looked damp, for it curled against his brow, as if he had ridden hard to arrive here. He leaned against the wall, his garb so dark that she could not tell where his cloak ended and the shadows began. His gaze darted over the company at intervals, missing no detail and returning always to her. He stood and watched the proceedings, his stillness making Madeline think of a predator at hunt. The sole bright spot upon his garb was the red dragon rampant emblazoned across the chest of his tabard.

She felt his gaze upon her as surely as a touch and she knew her color rose.

"Look!" Elizabeth said, suddenly between Madeline and Vivienne. "There is a little person!"

"The chamber is full of persons of all size," Madeline said, glad of some diversion to make her look away from the dark stranger.

"No, a very small person." Elizabeth dropped her voice. "Like a fairy, almost."

Vivienne shook her head. "Elizabeth, you are too fanciful. There are fairies only in old tales."

"There is one in this chamber," Elizabeth insisted with rare vigor. "It is sitting on Madeline's shoulder."

Madeline glanced from one shoulder to the other, both of which were devoid of fairies, then smiled at her youngest sister. "Are you not becoming too old to believe in such tales?" she asked.

"It is there," Elizabeth said hotly. "It is there, and it is giggling, though not in a very nice way."

The elder sisters exchanged a glance. "What else is it doing?" Vivienne asked, evidently intent upon humoring Elizabeth.

"It is tying a ribbon." Elizabeth glanced across the chamber, as if she truly did see something that the others did not. "There is a golden ribbon, Madeline, one all unfurled around you, though I do not remember that we put it upon your kirtle."

"We did not," Vivienne whispered, dropping her voice as their Uncle Tynan raised his hand for silence. "Madeline does not like gold ribbons on her kirtle."

Elizabeth frowned. "It is twining the golden ribbon with a silver one," she said, her manner dreamy. "Spinning the two ribbons together so that they make a spiral, a spiral that is gold on one side and silver on the other."

"Ladies and gentlemen, knights and dukes, duchesses and maidens," Tynan began.

"A silver ribbon?" Madeline asked softly.

Elizabeth nodded and pointed across the chamber. "It comes from him."

Madeline followed her sister's gesture and found her gaze locking with that of the man in the shadows again. Her heart thumped in a most uncommon fashion, though she knew nothing of him.

"You should not speak nonsense, Elizabeth," she counselled quietly, then turned her attention to her uncle. Elizabeth made a sound of disgust and Madeline's heart pounded with the conviction that the stranger watched her even as she turned away.

"As all of you are aware, the majority of the treasures will be auctioned on the morrow," Tynan said after he had extended greetings and introduced the family. Rosamunde stood at his side, radiant in her rich garb. "You will have the opportunity in the morning to examine such items as are of interest to you, before the bidding begins at noon. Of course, there will be many more arrivals in the morning." The company stirred restlessly and the sisters exchanged a glance of confusion. "You gentlemen have been specifically invited this night for a special auction, an auction of the Jewel of Kinfairlie."

"I did not know there was a Jewel of Kinfairlie," Vivienne whispered with a frown.

"Nor did I." Madeline looked at Alexander, who steadfastly ignored them both.

"I thank you, Uncle," he said, clearly uncomfortable with the weight of the company's attention upon him. "As you all have doubtless ascertained, the Jewel of Kinfairlie is flawless."

"Where is it?" Vivienne demanded and

Madeline shrugged that she did not know. A few men leered and she began to have a foul feeling in the pit of her belly.

How could there be such a gem and the sisters know nothing of it?

Alexander turned to face Madeline, and gestured toward her. "A beauty beyond compromise, a character beyond complaint, a lineage impeccable, my sister Madeline will grace the hall of whichever nobleman is so fortunate as to claim her hand this night."

Vivienne gasped. Madeline felt the color drain from her face. The sisters clutched each other's hands.

Alexander turned to the company, and Madeline suspected he could not hold her gaze any longer. "I urge you gentlemen, selected with care and gathered this night, to consider the merits of the Jewel of Kinfairlie and bid accordingly."

"Surely this is but one of his pranks," Vivienne whispered.

Madeline felt cold beyond cold, however. If this was a prank, it required the complicity of many souls. If this was a mere jest, it was difficult to see how it would not compromise Alexander's repute with his neighbors.

But it was beyond belief that he would

49

truly auction her. To Madeline's dismay, Reginald made the first bid with undisguised enthusiasm.

"Alexander!" Madeline cried in horror.

But her brother granted her a glance so cool as to chill her blood, then nodded to the company that the bidding should continue. He stood so straight that Madeline knew he would not rescind his words.

But to sell her? Madeline's gaze flicked over the company in terror. What if one of these men actually bought her hand?

They seemed intent upon trying to do so. Reginald countered every bid, raising the price with such reckless abandon that his purse must be fat indeed.

The bidding was heated, so heated that it was not long before Gerald of York bowed to Madeline and stepped back into the assembly, flushed with his embarrassment that he could not continue. Madeline sat like a woman struck to stone, shocked at her brother's deed.

Reginald Neville bid again with gusto. Was there a man within this company who could match Neville's wealth? The older Andrew grimaced, bid again, then was swiftly countered by Reginald.

He glared at the boy and shook his head.

"Is that the sum of it?" Reginald cried,

clearly savoring this moment. He spun in place, his embroidered cloak flaring out behind him. "Will none of you pay a penny more for this fair prize of a bride?"

The men shuffled their feet, but not a one raised his voice.

"Reginald Neville," Vivienne whispered, her tone incredulous. Her cold fingers gave Madeline's a tight squeeze of sympathy. Madeline still could not believe that this madness was occurring.

"Last chance to bid, gentlemen!" Alexander cried. "Or the Jewel will be wed to Reginald Neville."

Madeline had to do something! She rose to her feet and every man turned to face her. "This would be the moment in which you declare your jest to be what it is, Alexander." She spoke with a calm grace that did not come easily, for her heart was racing.

"It would have been," Alexander said, "had this been a mere jest. I assure you that it is not."

Madeline's heart sank to her very toes, then anger flooded through her with new vigor. She straightened, knowing her anger showed, and saw the dark stranger smile slightly. There was something secretive and alluring about his smile, something that made her pulse quicken and heat rise in her cheeks. "How dare you show me such dishonor! You will not shame our family like this for no good reason!"

Alexander met her gaze and she saw now the steel in his resolve. "I have good reason. You had the choice to wed of your own volition and you refused to take it. Your own caprice brings us to this deed."

"I asked only for time!"

"I do not have it to grant."

"This is beyond belief! This is an outrage!"

"You will learn to do as you must, just as I have learned to do as I must." Alexander lowered his voice. "It will not be so arduous a fate, Madeline, you will see."

But Madeline was not reassured. She would be wed to the highest bidder, like a milk cow at the Wednesday market. Worse, they all found it to be merry entertainment.

Worse again, the highest bidder was Reginald Neville. Madeline could not decide whether she would prefer to murder her brother or her ardent suitor.

She swore with inelegant vigor, thinking it might dissuade Reginald, but the men in the company only laughed. "You are all barbarians!" she cried.

"Oh, I like a woman with spirit," said Alan Douglas, fingering his coins. He offered another bid which was swiftly countered by Reginald.

"No marriage of merit will be wrought of this travesty!" Madeline declared, but not a one of them heeded her. The bidding rose higher even as she stood, trembling with anger. She could hear Vivienne praying softly beside her, for doubtless Vivienne feared that she would face a similar scene soon.

Could matters be worse?

Reginald bid again, to Madeline's dismay. She felt the weight of the stranger's gaze upon her and her very flesh seemed to prickle with that awareness.

No matter who bid, Reginald countered every offer. He urged the price higher with giddy abandon and as the company became slower to respond, he began to wink boldly at Madeline.

"You are worth every *denier* to me, Madeline," he cried. "Fear not, my beloved, I shall be stalwart to the end."

"So long as victory can be achieved with his father's coin," Vivienne said softly.

There were but five men bidding now, the counterbids coming more slowly each time. Madeline could scarce take a breath.

"Out of coin?" Reginald demanded cheerfully as one man reddened and bowed his head, leaving the fray.

Four men. Madeline's mouth was as dry as salted fish.

Roger Douglas thumbed his purse, then outbid Reginald.

Reginald pivoted and upped the bid, fairly daring Roger to counter. That man bowed his head in defeat.

Three men. Reginald's manner became effusive, his gestures more sweeping as he became persuaded of his certain victory. "Come now," he cried. "Is there not a one of you willing to pay such a paltry sum for the Jewel of Kinfairlie?"

Then two men were left, only Reginald and the uncommonly pale Alan Douglas. As much as she loathed Reginald, it was a sign of her desperation that Madeline began to wish that Reginald would triumph. At least Reginald did not frighten her, as Alan did.

Every bid Alan made, Reginald defeated with gusto. He did so quickly, flamboyantly, clearly not caring how much he paid.

But then, Vivienne had spoken aright. It was his father's coin and though there would be no more once it was spent, Reginald showed no restraint in ridding himself of its burden.

Alan frowned, stepped forward and bid again. The company held its collective breath.

Reginald laughed, then topped the bid, his tone triumphant.

There was a heavy pause. Alan glared at Reginald, then his shoulders dropped. He stepped away in defeat, his pose saying all that needed to be said.

"I win! I win, I win, I win!" Reginald shouted like a young boy who had won at draughts. He skipped around the floor, hugging himself with delight.

Madeline watched him with disgust. This was the man she would be compelled to wed.

There had to be some means of escape from Alexander's mad scheme.

Reginald chortled. "Me, me, *me!* I win!"

"You have not won yet," a man said, his voice low and filled with a seductive rhythm. "The winner can only claim his prize when the auction is complete."

Madeline's heart fairly stopped as the dark stranger stepped out of the shadows. Though he was not much older than Alexander, he seemed experienced in a way that Madeline's brother was not. She did not doubt that he would win any duel, that his blade had tasted blood. He moved with a warrior's confidence and the other men created a path for him, as if they could do nothing else.

"He is a fool to wear such an insignia openly," muttered one man.

"Who is he?" Madeline asked. She jumped when Rosamunde spoke from behind her. Her aunt had moved while Madeline had been distracted by the auction.

"The King of England has set a price upon his head for treason," Rosamunde said. "Every bounty hunter in England knows the name of Rhys FitzHenry."

"I daresay every man in Christendom knows of me, Rosamunde," the man in question said with confidence. "Grant credit where it is deserved, at least." He spared Madeline a glance, as if daring her to show fear of him. She held his gaze deliberately, though her heart fluttered like a caged bird.

Rhys then doubled Reginald's bid with an ease that indicated he had coin and to spare.

The lady Madeline was perfect.

She was the proper age to be the surviving child of Rhys's cousin Madeline Arundel. She shared her mother's coloring and her mother's name. Her supposed family were so anxious to be rid of her without a dowry that they resorted to this vulgar practice of an auction, something no man would do to his blood sister.

And Rhys had to admit that he liked the fire in this Madeline's eyes. She was tall and slender, though not without womanly curves. Her hair was as dark as ebony and hung unbound over her shoulders, her eyes flashed with fury. Rhys had seen many women, but he had never seen one as beguiling as this angry beauty.

A single glimpse of her had been all it had taken to persuade Rhys that buying Madeline's hand was the most effective solution to his woes.

After all, with Caerwyn beneath his authority, he would have need of a bride to have an heir. And wedding this woman, if she indeed proved to be Madeline's daughter and the sole competing heir for Caerwyn, would ensure that no one could challenge his claim to the holding. He did not fool himself that he had sufficient charm to win the hand of such a bride any other way. Rhys had no qualms about wedding his cousin's daughter, if Madeline proved to be that woman. In Wales, it was not uncommon for cousins to wed, so he barely spared the prospect of their common blood a thought.

Indeed, she would be compelled to wed

some man this night, and Rhys doubted that any would grant her the evenhanded wager that he was prepared to offer to his bride. Rhys had to believe that he could grant a woman a better life than that offered by her family or this irksome boy, Reginald.

Marriage was a perfect solution for both of them. And so he bid.

And so the chamber fell silent.

It was as simple as that. Madeline would be his.

Rhys strode forward to pay his due, well content with what he had wrought.

The young Laird of Kinfairlie responsible for this foolery spoke finally with vigor. "I protest your bid. You were not invited to this auction and I will not surrender my sister to your hand."

Before Rhys could argue, Tynan granted the younger man a poisonous glance. "Did I not warn you that matters might not proceed as you had schemed, Alexander?"

Alexander flushed. "But still . . ."

"The matter has passed from your grasp," Tynan said with finality. Rhys knew that Tynan would indeed have cast him out if Rosamunde had not vouched for his character. The lady Madeline had some souls concerned for her future, at least.

"You cannot claim her!" Alexander cried. "I will not permit it."

Rhys smiled a chilly smile and let his gaze drift over the younger man. "You cannot stop me. And you cannot afford to exceed my bid."

The young laird flushed crimson and stepped back with a murmured apology to his sister, which Rhys thought long overdue.

Rhys then turned to the huffing Reginald Neville. "Have you no more coin?"

Reginald's face turned red and he threw his gloves onto the floor. "You cannot have that much coin!"

Rhys arched a brow. "Because you do not?"

Anger flashed in the boy's eyes. "Show your coin before we continue. I insist upon it!" Reginald flung out his hands and turned to the assembly. "Can we trust a man of such poor repute to honor his debts?"

A murmur passed through the company and Rhys shrugged. He sauntered to the high table, removing a chamois sack from within his leather jerkin. The lady caught her breath when he paused beside her and Rhys studied her for a heartbeat. Her eyes were wide, a glorious simmering blue, and though he sensed her uncertainty of him, she held her ground.

It was not all bad that she was as aware of him as this. He liked the glitter of intelligence in her eyes, as well as the fact that she had tried to halt this folly. He was accustomed to women who spoke their minds and a bride who did as much would suit him well.

He smiled slightly at her, hoping to reassure her, and she swallowed visibly. His gaze lingered upon the ruddy fullness of her lips and he thought of tasting her, knowing then how he would seal their agreement.

But first, the agreement had to be confirmed.

"You need not fear, sir," Rhys said coolly. "I will owe no debt for the lady's hand." There were more than enough gold coins in his sack, but Rhys was not anxious to flaunt his wealth. He cautiously removed only the amount necessary, and stacked the coins upon the board with care. Tynan bent and bit each one of them to test their quality, then nodded approval.

"Then, have her!" Reginald spat in the rushes with poor grace and stormed from the room. His gallantry, in Rhys's opinion, was somewhat lacking.

There was utter silence in the chamber as Rhys reached out and laid claim to Madeline's hand, such silence that he heard her catch her breath. His hand was much larger than hers and her fingers trembled within his grasp.

But she did not pull her hand from his and she held his gaze steadily. Again, he admired that she was stalwart in standing by the terms of agreement. He bent and brushed his lips across her knuckles, feeling her shiver slightly.

Alexander placed a hand upon Rhys's arm. "I do not care for convention or broken agreements. You cannot wed my sister — you are charged with treason!"

Rhys spoke softly, not relinquishing the lady's hand. "Do not tell me that the Laird of Kinfairlie is not a man of his word?"

Alexander flushed scarlet. His gaze fell upon the stack of coins and Rhys knew that he had desperate need of those funds.

He leaned closer to the boy, the lady's hand yet firmly clasped in his own, and dared the new heir of Kinfairlie. He would show the lady, at least, what manner of man her brother was. "I will grant you a chance to rescind your offer, though it is more than you deserve. Reject my coin, but solely upon the condition that the lady shall not be sold to *any* man."

It was clear that the younger man struggled with this decision. He appealed to his sister with a glance. "Madeline, you must know that I would not do this without cause."

And he reached for the coin.

"Cur!" she cried, her scorn matching Rhys's own. Rhys turned to her, his breath catching at the fury that lit her expression. "Take it then, Alexander! Take it, for whatever debts you have, and reject whatsoever loyalty Papa might have thought you owed to your siblings."

Alexander's hand shook slightly as he claimed the coins. "Madeline, you do not understand. I must think of the others . . ."

"I understand as much as I need to understand," she said, her words as cold as ice. "God save my sisters if you think of them as you have thought of me."

"Madeline!"

But the lady turned her back upon her sibling, her bearing as regal as that of a queen, her gaze locking with Rhys's own. He saw the hurt that she fought to hide and felt a kinship with her, for he too had been betrayed by those he had believed held him in regard.

"I believe there is a meal laid to celebrate our pending nuptials, sir," she said, her words carrying clearly over the hall.

Aye, this bride would suit him well. Rhys lifted her hand in his grip and bent to brush his lips across her knuckles in salute. She shivered and he smiled, knowing their nuptial night would be a lusty one.

"Well done, my lady," he murmured, liking that she was not readily daunted. "Perhaps our agreement should be sealed in a more fitting way."

A beguiling flush launched over the lady's face and her lips parted as if in invitation. Rhys gave her hand a minute tug as the company hooted, and she took a pace closer. He could fairly feel the heat of her breath upon his cheek and her cheeks flushed. Still she did not look away, though her breath came quickly in her uncertainty.

Rhys entwined their fingers, then lifted his other hand to her face. He moved slowly, so as not to alarm her, well aware of her uncertainty. She would be a maiden, without doubt. It would not do to make her fearful of his touch. Rhys tipped Madeline's chin upward with his fingertip. Her flesh was soft beyond belief, her valor admirable. He smiled slightly, saw a spark in her eyes that reassured him as little else might have done. This was no fragile maiden who would fear her own shadow.

Rhys bent and captured Madeline's sweet lips beneath his own. To his satisfaction, the lady did not flinch, nor did she pull away.

Aye, this was a wife who would suit him well.

Chapter Two

Rhys's kiss was more gentle than Madeline had anticipated.

Indeed, his kiss fairly melted her bones. An intoxicating heat rolled through her, the pressure of his lips against hers making her yearn for more. He smelled of wind and rain and leather, altogether masculine and alluring.

Yet he was gentle with her. And patient. Madeline knew that he coaxed her caress, that he believed her to be innocent, and though she guessed it to be his intent, her fear of him faded like night at the dawn.

Truly, the man could addle the wits of any woman with a kiss like this. Madeline had never guessed that such pleasure could be launched from such a gentle caress, nor had she imagined that she might become a willing participant in this embrace.

But then, circumstances were most uncommon. She was angry and hurt and knew not which way to turn. That she should be consoled by a complete stranger, a stranger she would be compelled to wed against her own volition, was beyond belief.

No less that he would console her with a kiss.

Her heart had nigh stopped when she had guessed what he would do, then it had raced when he touched her chin. A measure of her resistance had melted with the softening of his expression, and she did not doubt that he knew as much.

Then his lips had claimed hers and she found herself beguiled. Her anger with Alexander was forgotten in a trio of heartbeats, her curiosity about his sudden need for coin faded to nothing.

The sole thing of import was Rhys's gently persuasive kiss. Madeline would never have guessed that a man so stern of appearance could grant such a seductive caress. The very fact of it made her wonder what manner of man he was truly, whether his garb and manner belied his true nature.

When Rhys lifted his head, there was a twinkle in his dark eyes, a twinkle as alluring as his kiss. His grip was tight upon her fingers and he seemed to be drawn taut, waiting for her response as the arrow waits to be loosed from the bow.

As if he cared whether she was pleased.

Madeline was breathless and dishevelled. She found her hand upon the breadth of his chest, her fingers knotted in the lace of his leather jerkin, and she did not know what had overcome her.

Then she met his bemused gaze and understood the danger of this man. Rhys had undermined her objections to this unconventional match, and he had done so with a mere kiss. The threat of this man was not in his repute but in his ability to make her ignore what she knew.

He was a traitor wanted by the king. He was a man of dark deeds and considerable coin, which Madeline doubted had been earned with honest labor. Madeline dared not cede again to the passion he conjured so readily as she had done just this moment.

She had need of time. Somehow, she had to escape both Alexander's scheme and Rhys's intent. But she could not think when her wits were so addled as this.

Madeline forced a smile. "I would have the nuptials on the morrow," she said, hoping her calm tone hid her intent to evade those marital vows. She let her lashes flutter to her cheeks, as if she were far more demure than she was. "I would have a night to prepare myself."

"It is reasonable enough," Tynan said firmly when Alexander might have protested. "Madeline has confronted more surprises this day than any soul could expect."

Madeline, for her part, could scarce draw a breath, so aware was she of Rhys's avid gaze upon her. He seemed to peer into her very thoughts, to guess at the root of her hesitation, and she felt a strange compulsion to confess that she had no desire to wed him.

She would have refused to wed him outright, had she known why Alexander had such need of this coin, had she known that he would not then promptly offer Vivienne's hand for auction. After all, there was a willing company already gathered.

"I invite you all to celebrate this agreement at the board!" Tynan declared. The men cheered and began to make their way to the hall, the smell of roasting meat tempting them to hasten. Madeline heard barrels of wine being rolled into the hall, and a woman from the kitchens shouted that there was ale aplenty for all.

"Do not do that!" Elizabeth cried suddenly. She pointed over the heads of Madeline and Rhys. There was nothing there that anyone else could discern.

"Elizabeth, that is enough about such nonsense," Madeline said firmly, having no patience in this moment for her sister's ridiculous talk about fairies.

"It is not nonsense!" Elizabeth swatted with such vigor that she nearly hit Madeline. "That fairy is knotting your ribbons!"

"What ribbons would those be?" Rhys asked.

"The ones it wove together earlier, of course," Elizabeth said impatiently. "Your silver one and Madeline's golden one. But now it knots the ribbons into a most fearsome tangle, and it laughs." She gave Rhys a somber look. "It is not a nice laugh."

"I would expect not," he agreed with equal solemnity and Madeline knew that he must think her sister mad.

"Halt!" Elizabeth swung her fist again at the invisible foe and Rhys ducked in the nick of time. "Cease your mischief, little fairy! I do not know what those ribbons mean, but your deed cannot be a good one."

"Elizabeth, cease *your* mischief!" Vivienne retorted, seizing her youngest sister by the arm. Other people were beginning to look askance at Elizabeth and more than one couple whispered, undoubtedly about the girl's odd behavior.

Madeline parted her lips to agree with Vivienne, then had a thought. Would Rhys insist upon wedding her if he thought her mad, as well? No man could desire a wife who might give him tainted children.

Perfect! Here was her means of breaking this agreement.

"Indeed," Madeline said, without another moment's consideration. "You will injure the fairy with such gestures, and that would scarce be wise. They are said to be vengeful if wounded."

Elizabeth gaped at her, clearly astonished that someone took her cause. "You can see it?"

"Do you feel well, Madeline?" Vivienne asked.

"Of course I feel well. And of course I can see it!" Madeline smiled at her astonished family. Rhys watched her with care, his eyes narrowed. "What is amiss with the eyes of all of you? It is right there." And she pointed to the right, high over their heads. All turned to look, then glanced back at Madeline.

"No, it is over there," Elizabeth corrected with scorn, pointing in the opposite direction. The family turned again, then considered the two sisters with open skepticism.

"So it is, it moves so quickly for such a small creature." Madeline laughed merrily, then patted Elizabeth's shoulder as if they two shared a jest. "It must be those golden wings that grant it such speed."

"It has no wings," Elizabeth fairly growled. "I would wager that you cannot see it at all."

Truly, Elizabeth could have been of more aid in this! Madeline gripped her sister's shoulder. "Perhaps you have not looked closely enough to see its wings," she said with resolve. "I see that it has little golden wings. And bells upon its toes. Indeed, it is quite a beauteous little fairy. It might befriend you, Elizabeth, if you ceased trying to strike it."

Elizabeth granted Madeline a dark glance. "It is the most ugly creature that ever I have seen, and it is cruel besides. You should understand as much, seeing as it is knotting *your* ribbon with such malice." With that, the younger sister put her nose in the air and marched toward the great hall.

Madeline watched her go for a moment, then summoned a bright smile. "Of course, I had forgotten the ribbons," she said gaily to her family.

"Perhaps because you cannot see them?" Vivienne suggested.

"Is it not said that the fey appear differently to the eyes of each mortal?" Madeline said, wishing someone who shared blood with her might be of assistance on this day. "Who can say what scheme this one has to appear so loathsome to Elizabeth?"

"Who indeed?" Rhys murmured, then laid claim to her elbow. "Shall we proceed to the hall, my lady?"

"Look! The little fairy is on the end of your nose!" Madeline laughed and pointed at Rhys's nose. "Can you not see it?"

"Nay, I cannot," he said. "But perhaps I am merely hungry."

"Oh, there it flies, its little wings flashing!" Madeline laughed like a lunatic, and all but Rhys quickly put some distance between themselves and her. "Oh, it is entangled in the ribbons. How amusing!"

Rhys made to lead her from the hall, apparently untroubled by her manner.

Madeline pulled back from his grip to meet his gaze. "Are you not concerned that I see creatures that you do not?"

He shook his head. "The fey show themselves where they will. Indeed, it has been said that it is a gift to see them. Perhaps you will bring fortune to my days, my lady."

Madeline gritted her teeth, irked that he could find merit in her ploy. "I have never heard of madwomen bringing good fortune to their spouses — quite the opposite, in fact."

"That may well be," he agreed easily. "But you are no more mad than me."

"But my sister . . ."

"Has an uncommon gift, it is clear, as might you. I have no concerns with kin who can see the fey — quite the contrary, in fact. Come, the meal awaits."

Madeline gaped at her betrothed, uncertain what to make of his manner. This warrior believed in fairies?

He spared her a sudden glance, his eyes twinkling so merrily that he might have been another man than the stern one who had won her hand, and her heart skipped again. How much else did she not know about Rhys FitzHenry?

Madeline's sisters closed ranks around her as they made their way noisily to the great hall, and she was separated from Rhys. Vivienne gripped her right hand, her characteristic merriment dispelled. Annelise held fast to Madeline's other hand, and was uncommonly quiet even for one known to be quiet. Madeline assumed that Rhys had gone on to the hall and indeed, she was glad to have a moment with her sisters.

"We shall ensure that your dress is absolutely perfect," Vivienne said with such false cheer that Madeline knew she spoke for the benefit of the younger girls. "Do you think the blue samite needs another row of pearls upon the hem?"

"A wedding should be rich indeed," Isabella said. "And you will be the first of us wed, Madeline. Can we come to your new abode to visit?"

"Of course," Madeline said, then wondered where that abode might be. Did Rhys even have claim to a keep or a hut, or did he travel all the time? Where would her home be? Had Alexander behaved responsibly, they would all know this critical detail.

"Will you have babies of your own?" Annelise asked shyly.

"I suppose that I will," Madeline said.

"We could persuade Uncle Tynan to open his treasury and spare more gems for you," Isabella said. "To ensure that you will be a glorious bride."

Rosamunde laughed beneath her breath, her hand landing again on Madeline's shoulder. "That would be a fair triumph."

"But what of you, Aunt Rosamunde?" demanded Isabella. "Will you not shower Madeline with rubies and sapphires on the night before her wedding? She could be as radiant as the sun!"

"Indeed, Aunt Rosamunde," Tynan said darkly. "There are treasures aplenty in your stores that you might spare a few."

Rosamunde granted him a telling glance. "Madeline will be radiant with or without more gems. I would share with her something more enduring."

"Like what?" The girls clustered around Rosamunde, their eyes wide.

"It will be a secret between Madeline and me," Rosamunde said mysteriously, which did little to sate the curiosity of Madeline's sisters. Madeline could not be certain what her aunt meant, though she suspected Rosamunde's gift would be counsel.

Madeline knew something of what happened between men and women — she had been in the fields in the spring, when the animals mated, after all — but felt in need of a little more information. She had no doubt that Rosamunde knew much more about such deeds.

"Nonetheless, we will stay awake all the night long!" Isabella said, happy at the prospect of a celebration. She raced after Tynan, while quiet Annelise hung close to Madeline. Madeline could fairly smell the concern of her next two sisters, the fear for their own futures.

She had to do something to ensure that Alexander did not repeat this folly.

To his credit, Alexander looked somewhat uneasy with what he had wrought. "I am sorry, Madeline," he said. "You must know that this was not the outcome I anticipated."

If he thought matters could be repaired with a pretty apology — after he had recklessly shaped the rest of Madeline's life! — he was mistaken. "You took his coin amiably enough," she observed, not troubling to hide her displeasure.

Alexander flushed. "You would not wed of your own volition and I had to make a choice. You will be happy enough in a year, when your belly is round with a child."

"You think the matter is as simple as that?" Madeline was aghast.

Alexander's lips set stubbornly. "I had little choice. You do not understand the challenges before me."

"No, I do not." Madeline held his gaze with no small measure of determination herself. "You might tell me of them."

"I cannot." Alexander cast a glance over the watchful sisters. "Not here. Not now."

His reticence made Madeline believe that he had little reason for this foolery — or that his reason was not one flattering to himself. "You merely thought it a jest," she accused. "But I would have you pledge to me, brother mine, that you will not so shame our sisters as you have me."

"I meant well, Madeline. You have to know that!"

"Your intent is of less import than your deeds. You always were too besotted with your own ideas, however wild they were." Madeline spoke as sternly as their father oft had. "All the world is not so readily charmed by you and your schemes as Maman and Papa were. Take greater care with our sisters' lives than you have with mine."

Alexander's mouth set into the relentless line that Madeline knew all too well. "You cannot command me to do your will, not when I am Laird of Kinfairlie."

"Swear it!" Madeline cried, her vigor so uncharacteristic that her siblings looked at her in alarm. "I will not suffer you to repeat this foolery! You have coin aplenty to pay any debt as a result of this day's folly. Swear it, Alexander."

Alexander looked disinclined to do as much, and her sisters' grips tightened on Madeline's hand.

"I would suggest you do so as the lady suggests," Rhys said from unexpected proximity. "Your sister speaks with greater sense than you have shown thus far."

"I thought myself among kin," Alexander complained as he scowled at Rhys. "You should have declared your presence afore this!"

"And you should look about yourself afore you speak." Rhys captured Madeline's hand in his once again, easing Annelise aside. "A man must keep his wits about him better than you have done this night if he means to survive as lord of a holding. He must also guard his treasures more closely than you have guarded the Jewel of Kinfairlie. We will be kin soon enough, Laird of Kinfairlie."

Alexander flushed scarlet at this, obviously discerning some truth in Rhys's words. Madeline was astonished that her new betrothed was the one to champion her demand. Her sisters regarded Rhys with admiration.

Rhys drew Madeline closer to his side, as if they spoke as one. "Grant my lady the pledge she requests of you and grant it to her immediately."

His lady. That treacherous shiver began deep within Madeline's belly. She was stirred by Rhys's touch and so surprised by his endorsement that she could not summon a word to her lips.

Alexander regarded the pair of them sullenly. "I swear it, Madeline. I shall not auction our sisters."

And there, the pledge she had requested was hers as readily as that. Madeline had the uncommon sense that Rhys would ensure the promise was kept. She was relieved, yet felt a debt to Rhys that she would have preferred not to owe.

"Does that suit you well enough?" Rhys demanded of Madeline.

"It does."

"Then what was begun poorly has ended well." Rhys tucked Madeline's hand into his elbow. "Come, my lady. Our betrothal feast awaits."

Madeline turned at his bidding, as if she would indeed be a dutiful wife to this renegade. She dared not let him see the defiance that roiled within her. She matched her step to his and even managed to grant him a small smile. Though she was glad of Rhys's intercession, she was wary of his reasons for doing so.

Her sisters thanked him prettily for his intervention, their estimation of his character obviously improving by the moment. Madeline did not doubt that Rhys cultivated their approval deliberately — and she did not trust that he did so.

Any man could be charming for one evening.

Any man of dark repute might find that one evening of such charm served him well, if it gained him the bride he desired for all eternity.

It was Madeline who would have to live with the result.

Rhys seemed so determined to eliminate her misgivings — and to think well of her — that he roused her suspicions. That he was a traitor to the crown made Madeline doubly determined to not pledge herself forevermore to an utter stranger. But no matter, for by the morning, Madeline would be gone from Ravensmuir, leaving no trace of her destination behind.

That would be simple to do, for she as yet had no idea where she would go.

Rhys could fairly smell the defiance of his intended. In truth, he could not blame her for being reluctant to wed under such strange circumstance, no less to a man she did not know.

No less to a man reputed to be a villain.

But wed they would be, and wed they would be on the morrow. Rhys would suffer no further delay in his claiming of Caerwyn.

The sole solution was to reassure the lady, in what little time remained between this meal and the exchange of nuptial vows. He had begun with reassuring her sisters, and so he would continue. Indeed, their merry presence awakened a yearning in Rhys, a memory of his own lost sisters and the way they had tormented their only and much younger brother. He felt an uncommon tenderness in the midst of these sisters, for their bickering was evocative of his own half-forgotten past.

The company were seated at the high board under the direction of Tynan's castellan. Tynan claimed the central seat, with Rosamunde upon his left and a young boy upon his right. The boy shared the dark hair of Madeline and Alexander, though his eyes were a vivid green, so Rhys guessed him to be another sibling. Further to Tynan's right was Alexander, then two of the younger sisters.

Rhys was seated to the left of Rosamunde, Madeline to his left and her sister Vivienne to her left. The sister, Elizabeth, who had seen the fairy, had the end place at the table and seemed despondent that no one had believed her earlier. She cast covert glances down the table, often in strange directions, and Rhys wondered what she saw.

81

At the first table facing the high table were seated various bishops and dukes and lords in their finery, their wives and consorts at their sides. They were all seated roughly by rank, though the ale had already flowed with sufficient vigor that none were in the mood to take offense at any inevitable slight.

Rhys saw the women settled and their cups filled, then winked at the dejected Elizabeth. Her color rose and she toyed with her cup, even as she cast him a glare.

"Do not mock me," she said.

"I would not dream of doing as much. You must have a fearsome power to be able to see the fey so clearly."

"Do you think so?"

"Yours is a rare gift."

The girl brightened at Rhys's nod, and Rhys felt Madeline stiffen beside him. He had a thought then that the lady's resistance could be softened through her siblings.

"It is pulling your ear and making fearsome faces," Elizabeth confided.

"Then it is a mercy that I cannot see it, much less feel the pain."

Elizabeth laughed. "Why do you believe in fairies?"

"Because they exist, of course."

"But how can you know as much, if you cannot see them?"

"My mother and her kin are reputed to be descended from a water fairy, who wed a mortal man, my own forebear." Rhys watched the girl's eyes widen and felt Vivienne turn to listen to his words. "Do you know the tale of the Gwraggedd Annwn?"

Both girls shook their heads, while Madeline took a studied interest in the arrival of the venison. Rhys did not doubt that she listened to him as well, and he was glad to have chosen this tale to recount.

In fact, it described his own response to the lady beside him perfectly, and he hoped that she would discern the morsel of truth in his words. He was aware of her presence, of the spill of her kirtle so close to his leg, of the soft scent of her flesh, of her thigh beside his own. Her hand rested on the board, soft and finely wrought, and though he yearned to capture it within his own, he feared to frighten her.

A tale might soften her resistance to him.

He cleared his throat and began. "There are many lakes in Wales, where I was born, and most of them have a mysterious air. It is said that there are fairies living beneath the surface, in splendid palaces that mortal men can only glimpse once in a long while. It is said that their daughters are beauteous beyond belief, and immortal, and wise. And it is told that one such lake maiden liked to sit on a certain rock on the shore and comb her hair in the sunlight."

"I would wager that a mortal man spied her there," Vivienne said, her eyes glowing.

"Indeed, one such man did," Rhys agreed. "And as you might anticipate, he was smitten at the sight of this rare beauty. Some say that she was singing and that her voice was such a marvel that he was enchanted. Others recount that it was her beauty alone that snared him. I heard that she had hair as dark as a raven's wing, and eyes that flashed like sapphires. I have heard that he had only to see her once to lose his heart completely."

Madeline cast him a glance at this description, which so nearly matched her own, and Rhys held her gaze as he continued. "She was a beauty beyond beauties, that much is for certain, and her character was no less attractive than her face. And so, the mortal man was smitten, and in the hope of winning her attention, he offered to share his bread with her."

Rhys glanced down at the table, knowing

Madeline's gaze would follow his own, and considered the trencher cut of bread that they were to share. Madeline's cheeks were stained with sudden color and she looked across the hall.

"And what happened?" Elizabeth demanded.

"The fairy maiden said that his bread was too hard. She may have laughed at his dismay, then she disappeared beneath the water, scarcely leaving a ripple on its surface."

"Oh." Elizabeth was clearly disappointed, thinking the tale finished, but Vivienne spoke up.

"He probably did not give up easily."

"Indeed he did not, for love is a fearsome power. He knew that he had to win this maiden's favor, and he did not care how difficult the task might prove to be. No man of merit surrenders readily to the challenge of his lady's desire."

A page placed meat upon the trencher and Rhys nudged the choice morsels toward Madeline. She glanced down, took nothing, and looked away again, her back straight.

Rhys was not deterred.

"The man returned home and sought his mother's counsel, and that woman gave him bread the following morning which had not been baked. He went back to the same place, and was thrilled to find the lake maiden there again. He offered to share this bread, but she laughed and said it was too soft for her. With that, she disappeared into the lake once more."

"And the third day?" Elizabeth prompted.

"On the third day, he brought bread that was half-baked, and the fairy maiden liked it very well. Indeed, I suspect that she liked that he labored so determinedly to win her favor." Vivienne laughed at this, though Madeline drew slightly away from Rhys. Did she find herself susceptible to his meager charm, or was she repulsed by him? He could not guess, but continued on. "No sooner had she eaten of the bread, though, than she disappeared again into the lake. The man was disappointed by this, for he thought the fairy maiden spurned him."

The girls were rapt, and even Madeline glanced over her shoulder at Rhys. "Did he abandon his quest, then?" she asked and Rhys let himself smile.

"Did I not mention that love had a hold upon him? No sooner had he begun to fret than three resplendent figures rose from the depths of the lake. They walked across its surface to him, their garb and jewels glittering in the sunlight. There were two maidens, each as beautiful as the other, both so similar as to have been the same woman in two places. They stood on either side of an older gentleman in fine garb, who informed the mortal man that he was the king of the fairies beneath the lake. The king offered one of his daughters in marriage to the mortal man, if that man could identify which daughter had accepted his bread."

Rhys pursed his lips. "This was no easy task. The man looked between them and feared that he would fail, for he could discern no difference between the sisters. And just when he thought all to be lost, the one on the right slid her foot slightly forward. For you see, the fairy maiden had fallen in love with the mortal man, and she did not desire to lose him."

He captured Madeline's hand and let his thumb slide over her skin. She shivered and her eyes turned a more fervid blue, though she did not pull her hand from his grasp. "He recognized the slipper of his lady love immediately, and was overjoyed that she too was willing to make this match. Thus he spoke out and chose his bride correctly."

"And so they were wed," Vivienne prompted.

"And so they were wed, though the fairy king granted an injunction. If the mortal man struck his fairy wife three times, then he would lose her forever, for she would be compelled to return to her father's kingdom beneath the lake."

"And he agreed to this?" Madeline asked.

"Of course." Rhys held her gaze. "No man of merit strikes his lady wife, for any reason." A little of the stiffness seemed to ease from her shoulders. "The mortal man agreed to the father's demand, seeing no reason why he would so abuse his beautiful bride. And so they were wed, and so they had sons, and good fortune, bountiful crops, and many sheep to call their own. It was said by all his neighbors that the man had been blessed indeed on the day that he wed this bride."

Rhys sipped of his ale, aware that Madeline had eaten nothing and had had little to drink. Her hand seemed to tremble within his own, as if he had snared a wild bird, and when she pulled her hand this time, he released his grip. Did she understand that he meant to reassure her with this tale?

"That cannot be the end of their tale," Vivienne charged.

"Far from it, for there was an oddity about the man's fairy wife. Perhaps because she was immortal, perhaps because she had a touch of the Sight, they tended to disagree on occasion. First, she laughed at a funeral, laughed with such gusto that her husband felt compelled to tap her on the shoulder and demand that she be quiet. She fell silent for a moment, and then she said 'That would be the first strike'. The man was appalled by what he had done, and he resolved to be more careful in the future."

"But he was not," Elizabeth guessed.

"She wept at a wedding," Rhys agreed with a nod. "Wept as if all the merit of the world were lost in the forming of this union. And the people gathered there looked askance at her manner, and the man finally lost his temper. He tapped his wife on the shoulder and bade her be quiet. She fell silent for a moment, and then she said 'That would be the second strike'. And she did not speak to him for days, for she loved him as much as he loved her, and she feared that he would compel them to separate for all eternity. Matters went well for a number of years, their sons grew ever taller, and their sheep more numerous."

"And then?" Vivienne demanded.

"And then?" Elizabeth asked.

"And then a child was drowned in the very lake from which the fairy woman had come. It was a child known well by the couple, a lovely child greeted with fondness at every door. But when the truth was learned, and the people gathered at the shore of the lake where the child's body had been found, the fairy wife sang. She did not sing a funeral dirge, she sang a song of joy, as if there was a matter to celebrate instead of one to mourn.

"As the people turned from her in disgust, her husband grew impatient yet again. He tapped her on the shoulder, told her that the song was not fitting, and bade her be quiet. She fell silent for a moment, and then she said 'That would be the third strike'. She kissed her sons and caressed her husband's cheek, and then she walked into the water. She disappeared beneath the surface, lost to him for all time, deaf apparently to his weeping entreaties. And so they were parted, just as the fairy king had foretold."

Both girls looked disappointed with this ending, but Rhys lifted a finger, for he was not done. "But it is said that she never forgot her sons or her beloved. Some people say that she would return to that stone on moonlit nights, that she would meet her husband there, and they would sit, an arm's length apart, and talk. Others say that she visited her sons in their dreams, and that she imparted all her knowledge of healing herbs to them. They became a family of famed physicians, who still can be found beside that lake, to this very day."

Vivienne sighed with satisfaction. "What fortune you have, Madeline, to wed a man who can tell a tale so well."

"And one descended from fairies!" Elizabeth enthused.

Rhys glanced down the table and thought he could supply the endorsements of the other two sisters. Annelise had been reassured by his insistence that Alexander not repeat this foolery of an auction, while Isabella seemed content that Rhys and his bid had been responsible for a wedding.

Madeline alone remained unpersuaded of his merit. Rhys had charmed the sisters, but not his bride.

"I think it a sad tale," she said with disapproval, her hands folded tightly together in her lap.

His bad fortune, it appeared, had not fully changed. But Rhys, like the man in his own tale, did not surrender the challenge of winning his lady's desire so readily as that.

Chapter Three

Madeline thought she might scream in her impatience to be gone. It seemed to take the assembly half the night to tire of Tynan's wine and ale. Madeline contrived to hide every sign of her desire to flee.

Rhys did not speak to her directly again, but the heat of his thigh was close to her own and she could fairly hear him listening to her breath. Though he glanced across the hall, apparently unconcerned with her, Madeline knew that she held his complete attention.

It was more than disconcerting.

Worse, since his tale of the water fairy, Elizabeth and Vivienne appeared to be charmed by Rhys. Isabella, who always favored a celebration over quieter moments, anticipated the wedding with glee. Even Annelise, who was slow to take a liking to strangers, looked upon Rhys with favor since he had insisted that Alexander not auction more of the sisters.

Only Madeline seemed to have eyes left in her head, or wits between her ears. She would flee so far away that they would never hear tell of her again.

"Are you well, Madeline?" Vivienne asked for what must have been the seventh time. "You are so quiet this night."

Knowing full well that Rhys listened to their conversation, Madeline wished her sister could have let the matter be. "I am always so demure," she said with a sweetness that should have warned her sister.

Instead, Vivienne laughed. "You? I should think not!"

Madeline gritted her teeth and kicked her sister beneath the table. Vivienne kicked her back, hard enough to leave a bruise upon her shin.

"How amusing you are, Vivienne," Madeline said firmly. "We all know that I am the quiet one of the family."

Vivienne, blissfully oblivious to the message Madeline was trying to send, giggled so hard that she could barely speak. "You? You talk more than all of us put together! Remember how our old nursemaid used to say as much?"

"I have forgotten the chatter of that madwoman," Madeline said firmly.

"How could you? She was the one who said that you had boldness enough for all eight of us and to spare!"

Elizabeth hooted. "Remember when she tried to gag you to make you silent for a morning?"

Madeline felt her color rise at Rhys's sidelong glance. "I do not recall."

"How could you forget? Truly, Madeline, you are not yourself this night." To Madeline's disgust, her sister tapped Rhys upon the arm as if they were old comrades. "She must be simply astonished, sir."

"This night's circumstance is certainly an uncommon one," Rhys acknowledged.

Vivienne smiled. "Oh, but I assure you that my sister is always more vivacious than this. She is practical, but also outspoken. You can rely upon Madeline, sir, to tell you her thoughts but also to be of aid."

"Vivienne!"

Rhys sipped of his ale and Madeline could have sworn that he smiled. "There is nothing akin to the teasing of a sister," he said so softly that Vivienne could not hear him.

Madeline was surprised to find his tone of rueful affection such a perfect echo of her thoughts. "You must have sisters yourself."

A shadow touched his face and Madeline found herself intrigued. "Four I had, once," he admitted and looked away.

"How can you not have such sisters any longer?"

Rhys stared across the hall for a long moment, as if he had not heard her. "They are all dead, my lady."

Madeline was shocked. He said nothing more, but his grim countenance was enough to tear at her heart. "I am sorry."

"As am I." He brushed his fingertips across her hand and Madeline felt a warmth in her belly, though whether it was due to his gentle touch or his confession, she could not say. She felt a flush stain her cheeks and dropped her gaze to hide her awareness of him.

Then she wondered whether his confession was truth, or a falsehood intended to soften her resistance to him.

Vivienne was suddenly attentive again, as if sensing that she had missed something.

"Perhaps I am *slightly* more quiet than usual," Madeline said, "because I have never experienced the eve of my own wedding afore."

Vivienne sobered at that. "Oh, but you must not fret about the morrow, Madeline. You will be the most beauteous bride that Ravensmuir has ever seen. I know it well, even if Uncle Tynan does not see fit to surrender more pearls for the hem of your kirtle. The blue samite suits you so well. Rosamunde speaks rightly when she says all will be perfect."

Madeline bit her tongue lest she comment that the appearance of her wedding day was not uppermost in her concerns. It was her intent, after all, to let Rhys believe her amenable to this folly.

"Then I am reassured," she said stiffly. She took a sip of her ale lest she say more.

"You, the quiet one," Vivienne murmured, then shook her head. "I should tell Alexander of that jest."

"Perhaps it is concern with wedding a stranger that has stolen the lady's tongue," Rhys suggested.

Madeline felt her color rise that her fear had been so clearly identified, no less that it had been so named by the one who should have known her least of all.

"No less a stranger of such dark repute," Rhys amended and Madeline knew she flushed crimson.

Vivienne's eyes widened. "Is there truly a price upon your head?" she asked with an admiration that was certainly undeserved.

Rhys only nodded.

"Of course, you are unjustly condemned," Vivienne said with conviction. "And the king will pardon you and beg your forgiveness and it will be as romantic as an old tale. Rosamunde knows you, after all!"

That Rosamunde knew all manner of scoundrels and rogues made this endorsement less compelling than Madeline would have preferred.

Vivienne chattered on, much enamored of the tale she wove. "Perhaps Madeline will even have to ride to the king's court to beg his clemency."

Elizabeth shivered in delight. "Would that not be a marvel?"

Rhys seemed to be fighting that smile again.

"It might be folly." Madeline could not keep silent any longer.

Vivienne frowned. "How so?"

"Perhaps the king has named the crime rightly."

"Perhaps he has," Rhys agreed so easily that the matter could not particularly concern him.

"Then it would scarcely be sensible to *not* feel some trepidation in wedding such a man," Madeline said more sharply than she had intended, then struggled to compose herself. "Might we discuss some other matter? The rain, perhaps?"

"It rains, as always it does in spring," Vivienne said dismissively, then leaned toward Rhys again. "Are you guilty of treason, sir?"

"Vivienne!"

"Surely you desire to know the truth of it?" Vivienne asked with the scorn that one sister reserves solely for another. "You are to wed the man, after all."

Madeline bit her tongue so that she did not insult her spouse. She felt him watching her and feigned a fascination with her napkin. His gaze was so intent that she feared he had guessed her plan to flee.

"Perhaps the lady is unconvinced that I will surrender the truth," Rhys said with care. "To tell a falsehood would be a much lesser crime than treason, after all."

Vivienne looked much impressed by this reasoning, though Madeline fought to hide her surprise. How could this stranger guess her thoughts so readily, when her entire family seemed unable to comprehend her?

"A traitor in our very ranks," Vivienne said, again showing unnecessary awe. "But why was the charge made against you? Do you mean to unseat the king? Will you be captured in the night and dragged to the gallows?"

Rhys's eyes narrowed slightly. "You need not fear for your sister's safety in my company. As for the accusations against me, I have found that a dangerous repute keeps wolves from one's door."

"How reassuring," Madeline said, and took a quaff of ale. Vivienne turned to answer some query from Alexander and Madeline bristled beneath the full weight of Rhys's attention.

"Are you fearful?" Rhys asked so quietly that none could hear him save Madeline herself. She was irked that he should be the one to show her compassion and found anger claiming her tongue, despite her intent to be demure.

"What of it? A man who buys a bride at auction cannot be concerned with that lady's fears." She turned to glare at him and was surprised to catch his smile. She stared, for the expression transformed him, making him look younger and more handsome.

"Finally, the lady deigns to speak her thoughts," he mused, that smile lighting the darkness of his eyes. He lifted his cup as if in tribute to her. He sipped of his wine, his gaze unswerving from her own.

Madeline stared at him, for she had always been rebuked for speaking her thoughts clearly. "And what is that to mean?"

Rhys, though, did not appear to mind. "That I would have expected to be singed by the fire of your anger afore this."

Madeline forced herself to recall that she meant to win his trust. She summoned a smile with an effort.

"There, you disguise your thoughts again," he said softly. Madeline straightened.

"Perhaps I am more pleased at the prospect of finally being wedded than fearful."

"To a traitor? Your family must be a deceitful lot indeed." Rhys's smile still curved his lips and took the sting from his words. Madeline had the sense that he provoked her, and she was indeed provoked, but newly determined to hide her thoughts.

"Oh, a man's repute is not the same as his truth," she said so sweetly that her teeth fairly ached. "Doubtless your deeds have been misunderstood or misrepresented by your foes."

Rhys leaned on the board, bending toward her so that he was dangerously close. Madeline could smell his very flesh, but worse, she could see the twinkle in his eyes. "You grant me much credit, my lady, considering that I have done little to earn such devotion."

Madeline touched his hand, more fleetingly than she had intended. "You have bought a bride, sir, and there is nothing I can do but be happy about that fact."

He claimed her hand when she would have pulled it away and she quivered at the heat of his flesh pressed against her own. "Is there not?" he asked softly, so softly that Madeline guessed that he knew she lied.

She smiled with gritted teeth, fairly writhing beneath his steady perusal. "I am certain we shall be happy indeed."

"As am I," he murmured. "Though I had no expectation that our thoughts would be as one so very soon. Let us celebrate our agreement with vigor, then."

There was a dangerous glint in his eye that warned Madeline. Before she could respond, he had caught her nape in his hand with gentle resolve and his mouth had closed determinedly over hers once again. The company hooted with delight and began to pound their cups upon the board.

Madeline had the sense that Rhys tried to provoke her again, to prod her into showing some response to him. She was tempted to push him away, to slap him before the entire company in retaliation for his boldness.

He deserved no less and doubtless he knew it. Even Vivienne gasped in awe beside them.

Madeline just barely recalled her plan to allay his suspicions. She sighed, as if well content, and let her hands land upon his shoulders. It was not so difficult to do.

Rhys needed no more encouragement than that. He deepened his kiss, pulling her closer with the ease of one more accustomed to sharing such bold embraces than she. He was gentle, though, for all the surprise of his amorous assault.

And then it was too late to retreat. This kiss was different from his first salute. It was no less thrilling, and awakened no less heat in her belly. But this kiss was possessive and demanding. It called for her, not to surrender, but to join him in the pursuit of pleasure. Her very blood quickened and her lips parted. She heard herself gasp as his tongue darted between her lips, teasing and tasting her.

And she wanted more.

In the midst of Rhys's kiss, Madeline realized a shocking truth. James had kissed her, to be sure, but never had he claimed her mouth with such possessive ardor. Never had he slipped his tongue between her lips, never had he locked his hands around her waist and pulled her so close that her breasts were crushed against his chest.

Never had she liked his kiss so much as she liked this one from Rhys. And never had her pulse raced so madly in the circle of James' embrace. It was not so difficult to pretend to enjoy Rhys' caress, for every fiber of Madeline responded to his sure touch.

She pulled away with an effort, aware that she was only able to do so because Rhys released her. She flushed furiously when the company burst into applause and took a long draught of her ale to hide her discomfiture.

It was solely the fact that this would be the last kiss Rhys ever granted her that had persuaded her to make the most of it. That was the truth of it, Madeline assured herself. It was solely that Alexander squirmed to see her handled like a whore before her nuptials and she yearned to pay her brother back for his scheme.

Despite her ready explanation, Madeline felt flustered as she never had before. Her own body called her a liar. She was no less aware of the way Rhys watched her.

Satisfaction gleamed in his eyes.

Madeline caught her breath and squared her shoulders as the company hollered for more. She certainly felt no yearning to kiss Rhys FitzHenry again. That would not have been sensible.

Even though her pulse yet raced and her very blood simmered.

Rhys smiled wickedly, seemingly aware of his effect upon her. His warm fingertip slid across her cheek as he tucked a tendril of hair behind her ear. "That is more like the wife I expect to meet," he murmured.

Madeline glanced his way, not entirely understanding him. "The wife or the whore?"

"You are not so meek as to accept this fate as you would have me believe," he said, his gaze shrewd. "You are too passionate to readily accept such indignity as you have endured this day. Do not lie to me, my lady, and our match will fare well. All I ask of you is loyalty."

"All?"

"And sons, of course."

Madeline could not look away from the intensity of his gaze. She was half-persuaded that he tried to compel a confession from her lips of her scheme to escape. His eyes were bright, his manner sure.

But he could not know. He could not

have read her thoughts.

Madeline granted him a smile. "There is no merit in anger, my lord, when one cannot change one's fate. I am simply accepting of what will be mine, as a woman should be."

Rhys snorted. "You know as well as I do that one can always change one's fate."

"But not necessarily to a better end." Madeline saw that she had his attention. "You should know the root of my argument with my brother. I refused to wed any man, because my heart is no longer mine to grant."

Rhys stilled then, though he did not look away.

"My betrothed died."

To Madeline's surprise, that compassion again shone in Rhys's eyes. "I am sorry, my lady."

Madeline smiled ruefully. "I thank you for the sentiment, though you cannot be so sorry as I am," she said, forcing herself to sound demure. "James is gone, though my heart is his forever. I would have chosen not to wed, rather than offer less than my all to a spouse." She sighed. "My brother, though, saw matters otherwise."

"It could be argued that he is concerned for your future."

"It could be argued that if he will be rid

of me by such means as an auction, then he cannot be trusted either to leave me be, or to find me a spouse by any more fitting manner."

Madeline spoke more heatedly than she had intended, and she doubted that the watchful man by her side had missed as much. She tried to smile with a great measure of resignation. "I can wed you, or I can await Alexander's next scheme. My choices are few, and wedding you would seem to be the best of them."

"I would wager that all will look better on the morrow," Rhys said with care. "You have endured much indignity this day, after all."

Sympathy was the last honor Madeline desired from this man. Indeed, the man softened her resistance with nigh every word he uttered and every deed he did! She had to be away from Ravensmuir afore they exchanged vows, afore she forgot the truth of his past.

For any man could summon charm for a single night. Madeline desired more than one night's consideration from whatever man she would wed.

"Doubtless you speak aright," she agreed, thinking that she would be far away indeed by then. "A sound night's sleep reduces the most insurmountable challenge."

He fought that smile again, seemingly amused that she implied him to be such a challenge. Before Madeline could repair her error, Rhys lifted his cup and touched it to her own. "To our nuptials on the morrow, my lady. May they mark a new beginning for both of us."

Madeline drank to his toast, feeling more deceitful than she knew she should have done.

The lady had a scheme.

Rhys would have wagered his precious destrier upon it. It was beyond belief that the woman so outraged at her brother's intent to auction her could have made her peace with her fate so readily as that. Indeed, she fought to hide that anger with every comment she made, her flashing eyes revealing that she was not demure in the least.

Rhys knew his charms, such as they were, and knew his reputation well enough that he could be certain no woman would have been hasty to pledge herself to him for all eternity.

Certainly not a woman of such splendid intellect as Madeline.

Indeed, he found his lady even more intriguing for the fact that she tried to disarm him, to deceive him, to persuade him that he could not want her as his wife. Madeline was clever, and not accustomed to matching wits with another as clever as she.

That boded well indeed for their match.

Rhys waited and he watched, drinking little of the ale and finally feigning exhaustion. He was as wide awake as a cat upon the hunt, though there was no need for any other soul in Ravensmuir's hall to guess as much.

Eventually the company grew quiet, their yawns became more lengthy, and the fires burned down to glowing coals. The ladies retired to a chamber in the tower, and Rhys rose and claimed Madeline's hand as she left the high table.

She watched him for a moment, her eyes filled with shadows, then to his astonishment leaned closer. "Are you truly charged with treason against the king?" she whispered.

Rhys wished he could have lied, for he knew that a falsehood alone would settle her fears. Instead he nodded. "I am."

He thought that he could hear the flutter of her heart then, reminding him again of that captive bird, then she spun and left his side. He knew that he did not imagine the fear that shone in her eyes.

But there was not a man alive who could change his past deeds. Rhys reminded himself that it was more admirable to confess the truth, though his heart called him a fool. He noted how Madeline cast a last glance back over the hall as she climbed the stairs, and did not doubt that she believed she would never see him again.

She would flee this night, and he would pursue her, and they would be wed all the same. He could have told her that it was not so easy to be rid of Rhys FitzHenry as that.

Rhys noted that Reginald watched Madeline until she was out of sight, then saw that man's lips thin with displeasure. Reginald cast a poisonous glance in Rhys's direction. Rhys held the other man's gaze steadily, daring him to make an issue of what had transpired.

Reginald turned away, summoning his squires like a hen gathering chicks, insisting that proper arrangements be made for his slumber. Rhys quietly claimed a pallet and gathered his cloak about himself, taking a place where he could watch the stairs. Candles were snuffed and snores began to echo through the hall.

Rhys settled onto his pallet, one eye half open, pretended to sleep and waited. He knew that Madeline's last kiss at the board, and her unexpected surrender to his demanding embrace, would keep his blood simmering all the night.

He did not have to wait long.

Madeline could have respected Rhys's honesty, had he told her a more reassuring truth. Traitors, she well knew, met fearsome fates; their spouses, children, and property faring little better. Her very marrow still hummed from Rhys's tempting kiss, and she knew that he would quickly overcome her good sense with his beguiling touch. Though she was afraid of fleeing alone in the night, she was more afraid of Rhys FitzHenry.

Madeline was surprised when Rosamunde tugged her sleeve, half persuaded that her perceptive aunt had guessed her intent.

"Come with me for a moment," Rosamunde said, her manner mysterious and her voice low. Madeline's sisters continued to the ladies' chamber, unaware that they were unattended.

"No harm will come to them," Rosamunde said when Madeline hesitated.

"I would fulfill my pledge to your mother."

Madeline needed no more persuasion than that to follow her aunt. Rosamunde was garbed in a splendid kirtle of deep sapphire blue, its hem thick with golden embroidery, and its cut favoring the lithe curves of her figure. Her girdle was rich beyond belief and studded with gems; her hair hung loose to her hips like a cascade of rose gold. Although dressed in feminine splendor, there was a determination to Rosamunde's stride that was unfitting for a lady.

Rosamunde led Madeline to the laird's solar with a familiarity unexpected. Madeline's eyes widened, and she fought to hold her silence. She had heard rumors about the intimacy of the older pair, of course, but she had always believed such tales untrue.

Rosamunde turned and smiled. "In here, we can be certain to be alone. This is a responsibility to be discharged in privacy."

Tynan's chamber was richly adorned and a fire had already been kindled in the fireplace for his comfort. It blazed merrily, casting the chamber in a welcoming glow. Maiden and aunt made as one for the pair of stools set close to the hearth.

Rosamunde shivered. "I shall never grow

accustomed to the chill of this country," she muttered, then pulled a velvet sack from her lavish skirts. "This is for you." She smiled at Madeline as she placed the small bag in her hands.

The sack was square, less in each dimension than the first two digits of her finger. Madeline could hide it easily in her palm and she marvelled at the richness of its purple hue. It was embroidered in gold so lavishly that it was a treasure in itself, the gold thread making a radiant star against the velvet. A twisted golden cord fastened the small sack closed, the cord's length sufficient that the sack could be hung around one's neck like a gem. It was light, so light she assumed it empty.

"Is this silken velvet?" Madeline asked with awe.

Rosamunde laughed. "Doubtless, but this is a mere repository. The true gift is inside."

Madeline regarded her aunt for a moment, then loosed the cord.

"Use care!" Rosamunde counselled and bent closer.

Madeline tipped the small sack and a sphere the size of her fingernail spilled into her palm. It might have been a bead of water, but it was hard and gleamed in the firelight.

"It is called the Tear of the Virgin," Rosamunde breathed. "And said to have been shed by Mary at the crucifixion."

Madeline regarded the gem in wonder as her aunt spoke.

"Though Mary knew that Jesus died to save all of mankind, he was yet her only son: she mourned him, as any mother would do. And it is said that God looked down upon this weak vessel of a woman, her tears shedding like gems, and he felt compassion that she endured such loss for the gain of her fellows. It is said that He turned four and twenty of her tears to gems, in tribute to her grief."

"There are more of these marvels?"

Rosamunde shrugged. "I cannot say. This is the only one I have ever seen, and I only heard the tale from your grandfather, Merlyn."

"But I thought Grandfather shunned the relics?"

"He shunned the family trade in them, to be sure, but he had a reverence for those he thought to be genuine." Rosamunde gestured to the gem in Madeline's palm and smiled in recollection. "This was one for which he professed a fondness. Indeed, he gave it to your mother on the night before her nuptials."

Madeline glanced up in surprise, and Rosamunde nodded. "Merlyn told her, she said, that he would have given this to his daughter upon her wedding. Since he had no blood daughter, he hoped that Catherine would accept it. Merlyn and Ysabella considered your mother as their daughter, for she wed their son, Roland."

Madeline's hand closed over the gem, seemingly of its own will, so precious was any link to her mother. She fought against her own tears, so potent was the presence of her grandparents and parents in this chamber. She knew that Merlyn and Ysabella had rebuilt Ravensmuir and occupied this chamber themselves for many years. She knew that it had been granted to her parents for their nuptial night and that Merlyn had oft jested that his grandson, Alexander, had been wrought in his own bed.

She swallowed with an effort, feeling the embrace of ghosts around her. "And now you grant it to me afore my own wedding," she said, her voice husky.

"Your mother desired as much." Rosamunde settled back and stared into the flames. "You will not recall this, for little has been said of it of late, but I was one of your godmothers."

115

"You were?" Madeline was surprised yet again, though the merriment in Rosamunde's eyes made her believe the tale.

"Against all expectation!" Rosamunde chuckled. "Though I was not your mother's first choice, and I was not granted the task alone. Even then, I am the last of your godmothers surviving." She sobered. "Indeed, I am the last of all women charged with your upbringing to survive."

Madeline glanced away, feeling her mother's absence keenly.

Rosamunde's hand fell over her own, its warmth a comfort. Madeline wondered whether she imagined that her aunt's voice was suddenly hoarse. "I have always had a fondness for you, Madeline. Perhaps your mother saw into my own heart when she granted me this precious duty." Rosamunde gave Madeline's hand a minute squeeze. "But the fact remains that at your christening, your mother entrusted this gem to my care. She asked me to grant it to you on the eve afore your nuptials, just as Merlyn had granted it to her, and to tell of the gem. It was the sole duty she expected of me, this she said, and thus I fulfill it in her honor."

Madeline swallowed and looked back at

her aunt. "What of the gem?"

"It is said to possess a kind of power, though I cannot vouch for the truth of it. Your mother confided only the tale to me, that I might deliver it to you with the gem. It is said that the Tear feels the weight of sorrow, in keeping with its origins, and that it will change hue to warn its bearer of ill tidings. Perhaps it is Mary herself who would warn the bearer. I cannot say."

Madeline feared then that her intent to escape Ravensmuir and avoid her wedding ceremony was evident to her perceptive aunt, and that Rosamunde meant to dissuade her.

But Rosamunde frowned at Madeline's closed fist. "It is said that the stone will turn black when ill fortune lies ahead for its bearer, and that it will shine when all will be well."

"Do you believe as much?"

Rosamunde smiled. "There are many things that make little sense to us, many mysteries that may never be solved. Perhaps this is one of them; perhaps it is but a pretty quartz gem with a tale. Either way, you hold a token of goodwill from your mother in your hand, an heirloom passed through your family, and that is of no small merit."

Madeline caressed the gem in her grip.

"Am I to grant it to my first daughter on the eve of her wedding?"

Rosamunde smiled. "I would wager that Merlyn would approve of that."

Madeline glanced away as she blinked back her tears and fingered the cord. "Did Maman wear it?"

Rosamunde nodded. "Catherine wore the gem on her breast on her wedding day. Though I was not here, it was said that the Tear shone with a radiance to rival the sun."

"Then perhaps its power is genuine." Madeline's fingers fairly itched to open and reveal the hue of the stone, but she wanted to view it alone.

"Perhaps. Your parents did possess a great love for each other, one that only grew as the years passed. Remember them merry, Madeline. It is the best remembrance you can grant."

The women sat in silence for a moment as Madeline struggled to do as she was bidden. Their deaths were so recent that she had not begun to remember her mother's joyful laugh, or the way her father's eyes had twinkled when he teased any one of them.

Rosamunde cleared her throat. "Catherine also wrought this sack for the gem, with her own needle, to ensure its safety. Hidden or displayed, she wore it night and day until you were born." Rosamunde pushed to her feet, her eyes shining with unshed tears. "Then she entrusted it to me, though I never imagined I would deliver it without her beside me."

"Rosamunde, you were the sole person in the hall who admitted to knowing Rhys FitzHenry," Madeline said softly.

Rosamunde nodded, and waited, eyes bright.

"Alexander said he was not invited."

"Not by Alexander. He arrived earlier on a mission of his own, and summoned me. He asked for the reason of the gathering, and when I told him of it, he confessed his curiosity." Rosamunde shrugged. "And so I saw him admitted, with no realization that he too had need of a wife. Rhys has always been most solitary."

"But you did not forbid him from participating."

Rosamunde smiled. "It seemed to me, Madeline, that you might die of boredom wed to a man of Alexander's choosing."

"Will I die of some other malady wed to this traitor?"

Rosamunde laughed beneath her breath, a most odd reaction in Madeline's thinking. "A man's repute is not the same as his truth, Madeline." She rose and smoothed her skirts, which surely were in no need of smoothing, then cleared her throat. "I must attend your sisters. With the hall full of men with their bellies full of drink, I would ensure that they are all maidens on the morrow."

"I would sit here for a moment." Madeline raised her fist, tightened around the gem, to her lips. The Tear seemed to throb within her grasp.

Rosamunde touched her shoulder with affection. "Do not put too much stock in old tales, Madeline. A marriage is what man and wife make of it, and Rhys has spent sufficient coin that his attentiveness should be assured."

It was not the most reassuring thing Rosamunde might have said, but she departed in a swirl of silk afore Madeline could ask for more details of Rhys.

Not that it mattered overmuch. Madeline would be gone before the morrow, gone before her nuptials, gone before Rhys could claim her hand forevermore. First she would look into the gem, though, and hope for some assurance. She held her breath, unfurled her fingers and let the firelight touch the gem within her hand.

The Tear might have been wrought of obsidian, so dark was it. The gem was black to its very core, with nary a flicker of light within its depths. Madeline's heart froze, then raced. She pushed the stone back into the small velvet sack with shaking fingers, secured it, then looped the cord around her neck.

She had to flee. She had chosen aright, for even the stone forecast an ill fate if she remained at Ravensmuir and wed Rhys FitzHenry.

Chapter Four

Ravensmuir was silent, save for the snores of men and hounds. Madeline could hear the patter of rain upon the stones, and the lap of the sea against the shore. The wind had died down, though still it rained mightily.

Her sisters slept deeply, their pallets surrounding her own. The younger girls had been excited this night at the prospect of a wedding, and had taken cursedly long to settle onto their pallets. Elizabeth in particular had insisted upon talking to herself, as if she was truly talking to the invisible fairy. Madeline had been certain that the girl would never fall asleep.

But now, in the quiet of the night, the sole obstacle to Madeline's departure was her aunt Rosamunde, who had declared herself sentry over them all.

Madeline rolled over and peered through her lashes in the direction of her aunt. That woman sat on a bench by the portal. Rosamunde yawned fully, then folded her arms across her chest, her eyes gleaming in the darkness.

Madeline bit her lip, considering her course.

Neither of them saw the spriggan Darg, who danced around Rosamunde with vengeful delight. Neither of them saw Darg snarl and knot and tangle the golden ribbon emanating from Rosamunde — which neither of them saw either — and neither of them heard the fairy's spiteful little song.

Perhaps it was just as well. Darg did not have a melodious voice.

Madeline had just decided to lie to her aunt, and claim that she had to go to the privy, when there was a light knock upon the portal. It was so faint a sound that Madeline barely heard it. She saw her aunt turn, saw the heavy wood door open slightly.

"Surely you do not mean to sit here sleepless all the night long?" someone asked in a soft whisper. It was a man's voice, though Madeline could not see who spoke. She watched Rosamunde smile and knew she had seen that smile afore.

It was Uncle Tynan, Madeline would wager.

Unobserved by all of the mortals present, Darg pounced upon Tynan's silver ribbon and began to shred it, as well as put knots in it worthy of a rat's nest.

"And what else would I do?" Rosamunde murmured, her tone mischievous. "I have no other way to fill the hours of the night."

"How tragic," Tynan mused. "I would be a poor host to not offer better circumstance to a guest."

Rosamunde laughed lightly. She reached through the gap of the open portal, her smile broadening. "And what do you offer to me, Laird of Ravensmuir?"

"There is one soft bed that is broad enough to be shared."

"With whom shall I share it?"

Rosamunde gasped as her hand was evidently tugged. She disappeared in a flurry of skirts through the open door and Madeline closed her eyes at the sound of a very affectionate embrace. She thought of Rhys kissing her with such gusto and her face burned.

"But the girls . . ." Rosamunde protested, her voice oddly breathless.

"Can slumber well enough without you."

"But . . ."

Tynan interrupted her with resolve. "While I cannot."

"You do not mean to slumber, sir," Rosamunde said, her laughter undermining her supposed outrage.

"Nor do you," Tynan retorted.

"Trust a man to insist upon his way alone."

"It is a way you have found satisfactory enough in the past."

Rosamunde sighed and more amorous sounds carried to Madeline's ears. She stared at the ceiling, understanding rather more of her aunt's and uncle's relationship than she had before, and uncertain whether she was glad of it.

The door was closed with a firm click, then Tynan's footsteps echoed down the corridor. The sound of Rosamunde's whispers faded, then another portal was closed.

It was locked with a resounding echo of the tumblers.

This was her chance.

Madeline slipped from her pallet and donned her boots, her hands shaking in her haste. She had gone to bed in her stockings and her chemise, complaining that she was cold when her sisters commented. She pulled her thickest wool kirtle over her head, pilfered the purses of her sisters for stray coins, and claimed Vivienne's new fur-lined woolen cloak. She took her own eating knife, shoving it into her belt, and crept to the portal.

Her heart was thundering so loudly that she feared it would awaken all the household. Madeline swallowed and squared her shoulders, blew a farewell kiss to her sisters, then slipped into the shadowed corridor.

She could have taken a maid, or one of her sisters, but Madeline feared to endanger a companion unnecessarily. Alone, she could pretend to be a village lass — having a servant might arouse suspicion. She was deeply afraid, yet excited in a way. She had never travelled alone before, but surely she was keen enough of wit to ensure her own safety. She had always been the practical one, after all.

First, she had to get through the crowded hall.

Then, she had to steal a horse.

Then, she had to get through the closed gates of Ravensmuir without alerting the sentinels to her departure.

Truly, the odds were against her in this endeavor. Madeline said a silent prayer and made her way along the corridor as furtively as she could manage. Fortunately, she would have a good bit of time to consider precisely where she would flee once she was through Ravensmuir's gates.

And even Darg was not witness to Madeline's departure.

Madeline's palms were slick with sweat by the time she reached the stables. She had crept through the hall, heart pounding, stepping over and between the sleeping men. Fortunately, her uncle had been generous with his wine and the men slept soundly.

Every sound though, every man rolling over, every dog's tail wagging in that beast's sleep, had made her jump for the skies. She had not noticed Rhys, had not looked for him, for the men bundled in their cloaks were virtually indistinguishable from each other and she dared not spare the time.

She had been glad to make the deserted corridor, even if the wind from the sea made her shiver. No one had called a warning, no one had awakened and alerted the household.

Rhys FitzHenry, his dangerous reputation and his even more dangerous kisses, were all behind her for good.

Madeline heaved a sigh of relief but did not hesitate on the threshold of the stables. She knew the steed she wanted, the palfrey that she had ridden from Kinfairlie. The mare knew her and would be the least likely to nicker in alarm at what she did.

The horses had been moved, to Madeline's dismay, presumably to make space for the destriers of the arriving men.

She wasted precious moments looking for Tarascon, and finally found her sharing a stall with two other palfreys from Kinfairlie.

"Tarascon!" Madeline whispered, knowing the beast would discern her excitement. The mare's tail swung in recognition of Madeline's voice and she began to turn, her companion horses stirring from sleep as well.

"Tarascon, make not a sound! All of you be still, for I have brought you treats from the hall." Madeline's fingers fumbled with the latch and she hastened into the shadowed stall, intent only on reassuring the horses before the ostler awakened.

They immediately surrounded her, nuzzling her cloak, seeking any treat. Tarascon nipped Madeline's braid with affection and nigh flattened her against the wall of the stalls. Madeline laughed beneath her breath, and offered the trio of apples that she had seized from the food yet littering the hall. So concerned was she in finding Tarascon's saddle that Madeline did not realize that she was no longer alone.

Not until the man cleared his throat.

At the sound, Madeline jumped and bit back a scream.

A fair-haired man smiled amiably as he leaned upon the door of the stall. "Is it customary to feed Ravensmuir's horses in the night? And that without the ostler's awareness?"

"Kerr!" Madeline whispered, her knees weak in her relief. Kerr was a man-at-arms who had served at Kinfairlie for as long as she could remember. "You frightened me beyond belief!"

He scowled with the affection of an older brother. "There should be some soul watching over you, Lady Madeline, for it is not fitting for you to be about the keep while it is filled with fighting men." He shook his head. "Even worse, they are fighting men who have had their fill of drink and then some." He shook a finger at her. "You should be locked in your chamber with your sisters."

Madeline chose to confide in him. "I must flee, Kerr, and I must flee this night."

He pursed his lips. "You mean to avoid your nuptials." It was not a question, though Madeline nodded quickly. She would have explained but Kerr held up his hand. "You need not tell me more of it, Lady Madeline. I have always thought you to be a sensible lass, and in this, you show me to be right. Rhys FitzHenry is a dangerous man, one with a price upon his head for treason. No woman could be blamed for trying to avoid a match with him."

"Indeed, Kerr . . ."

He shook that finger again, his manner scolding. "But you are a fool and then some to consider departing alone. You cannot know what or who you will meet upon the road, nor what dangers you will face. No lady should travel alone in these times."

"But Kerr, I could not ask a maid or one of my sisters to accompany me and Rosamunde would not have agreed to do so." Madeline sighed. "She seems to have an affection for Rhys, which I cannot explain."

"Birds of a feather, no doubt, my lady," Kerr said darkly. "Your aunt has lived outside the bounds of law for so long, if you will forgive my speaking bluntly, that she sees only good in a fellow rogue and not his wickedness."

Madeline turned back to her steed, glad that she was familiar with saddling it herself. "I thank you for your counsel, Kerr, but I must leave afore my absence is noted."

"But you will not go alone," the burly Scotsman insisted.

Madeline glanced up, surprised at his tone.

"If you insist upon going, my lady, then I

will escort you to a safe haven. I owe your father's memory that much, at least."

Madeline smiled, relieved by his offer. "My uncle and brother will not be pleased with you, Kerr."

He shrugged. "They are not the only lairds in Christendom with coin to hire a fighting man." He sobered and granted her a level glance. "And there are times, my lady, when a man must do what he must do, and let the consequences be as they will be."

"I thank you, Kerr."

"Hasten yourself," he said gruffly, glancing over his shoulder with the manner of one uncomfortable with a lady's gratitude. "There are many at Ravensmuir who sleep lightly this night."

Dawn touched the eastern sky before Kerr finally called a halt. Madeline was exhausted, so unaccustomed was she to missing a night of sleep. At least the rain had halted shortly after their departure, and though their course was muddy, she had not been drenched. Kerr indicated a gully and she turned Tarascon in that direction. The palfrey moved with purpose once she heard the hidden stream that flowed there.

Meeting Kerr in the stables had been an uncommon stroke of fortune. Madeline did not know how he had coaxed the gate-keeper to open Ravensmuir's double port-cullis, nor did she know how he had found a path across the wilderness of the moors.

There had been a course though, or at least one visible to any soul who already knew it to be there, and it had avoided the towns and abbeys. The only town they had passed close had been Galashiels, slumbering as it had been.

The rising sun showed hills and little else, hills that were more verdant than the ones near Kinfairlie and of a more gentle inclination. Madeline could no longer smell the sea, and she guessed that they had taken a course southward with a slight inclination to the west.

But she had no quibbles. She realized now that she could never have managed her escape alone, so limited was her experience in such journeying. During the night's ride, it had occurred to her where she might go — she could try to discover the truth of James's demise herself. She wondered if she had coin enough to hire Kerr to aid her in such a quest, for she would have to go to France.

They had ridden in such silence for all

the night that she had not had the opportunity or the will to ask him as much, not as yet. Kerr was not a man who said much, but Madeline trusted his abilities. He could not have been more than a decade older than she, though he had lived more roughly, to be sure.

But she was glad of his competence, and even more glad that they would halt shortly.

Despite the fact that the rain had ceased, Madeline was damp and chilly and filled with aches. She had not complained at this unfamiliar hardship, for there were many miles between herself and Rhys FitzHenry. It was only now that the household of Ravensmuir would be awakening, only now that her absence might be discovered.

Thanks to Kerr, none would find her soon. Madeline granted him a smile. He did not return it, merely flicked a glance her way before his narrowed gaze scanned the horizon again. There was more gorse here, thick along the gully, and Madeline understood his trepidation. There might be all manner of wild creatures taking shelter here, who might take exception to being roused.

Perhaps she was a fool, but Madeline was too tired to care. Let the wolves come upon her, if they dared. She would wash her face. Madeline dismounted, grateful for the change of posture, and stretched her back. She followed Tarascon down the steep bank of the gully, sat upon a rock and bent to lift the cold water in her cupped hands.

It was blessedly cold. Madeline heard Kerr and his destrier descending the slope behind her. Tarascon waded in the stream, drinking noisily of the water as her tail swished. Madeline bent again, but her hands never reached the surface of the stream.

A gloved hand closed over her mouth and Kerr roughly pulled her back against him. The cold blade of his knife touched Madeline's throat.

She tried to scream but Kerr's blade only cut deeper. "Make a sound, lass, and I will cut out your tongue afore I have you."

Madeline whimpered against his glove, so astonished was she. At the press of the blade, she fell silent.

"That is better, lass." Kerr removed his hand from her mouth. He spun her to face him, gripping her bodice and tearing the front of her kirtle in one gesture.

Madeline gasped as the cold air touched her bared breasts. She backed away, biting back her scream lest she vex him further.

"I have wanted to see those for many a year," he said, his gaze devouring the sight of her. A cruel smile claimed his lips. "And I shall have my due, though I could never have paid your brother's price."

"But, but you, my father . . ."

"Your father knew my desires well enough." Kerr laughed. "Why do you think I left Kinfairlie last year? But he was fool enough to not confide in his son, so Alexander was quick to hire me back." Kerr smirked. "You nobles all think you are so clever."

Madeline realized that Kerr's breeches were already unfastened. She could see his prick and could have no doubt of his intent.

"Come here, for I have waited long enough. I will have my due now and I will have it time and again until I am sated." Kerr reached for her and Madeline ran.

Kerr swore and lunged after her. He caught a fistful of her hair, dragging her to a painful halt. Tarascon whinnied and turned to aid her mistress, but Kerr slashed at the steed's flank with his knife. His stroke was brutally effective — the horse fled as the long deep wound began to bleed profusely.

Madeline screamed.

Kerr struck her across the face. "I bade you be quiet!"

"But my horse! You cut her apurpose!"

Kerr tightened his grip upon Madeline's hair, winding the length of it around his fist. "It is but a horse," he said with a sneer.

Madeline feared that she had seen but a small measure of his cruelty. She had no doubt that she would bear the worst of it, and her heart leapt in terror.

She dared not make a sound of protest.

Kerr smiled coldly. "I have waited long enough for this moment that I will bear no interruption." He gave Madeline a shake. "You knew I watched you in your father's abode. You felt the weight of my gaze upon you and tempted me apurpose, for you wanted this as much as I."

"No! I . . ."

"Silence!" He waved the knife beneath her nose. "Now, lift your skirts, wench, and offer yourself to me." He leaned closer, his breath upon her very cheek. "Sweetly, my Madeline."

There was fury and lust in his eyes, as well as a determination that did not bode well for Madeline's fate. Would she leave this creek alive? She did not imagine so.

Anger burned within Madeline, anger

that pushed her fear aside. How dare he blame her for his unholy lust? How dare he declare that she had tempted him? Somehow she had to evade him.

She dared not let Kerr glimpse her intent, so she lowered her gaze as if embarrassed.

"You speak the truth, Kerr," she said meekly. "No other man could have guessed my thoughts so well as you."

"I knew it! Tell me you have dreamed of this moment."

Madeline swallowed her rising bile. "Of course I have dreamed of this moment." She could not summon any conviction to her words, but they seemed to please him. She swallowed, then began to lift her skirts in apparent compliance. "I have dreamed only of you."

Kerr chuckled when he could see her knees and his prick danced with enthusiasm.

Madeline took a shaking breath and raised the hem of her kirtle higher. Her hands were trembling, both with anger and the need to deceive him.

The wool cleared the top of her stockings and her garters. Kerr caught his breath in anticipation when he spied her bare thighs. Madeline guessed that he was as distracted as he would be afore this deed was done. She let one hand trail to her waist, relying upon the fact that the other lifted her skirts yet higher to keep Kerr distracted.

She seized the small knife in her belt, and slashed suddenly at his hand. To her delight, her blade found the increment of bare flesh between his glove and his sleeve, and it bit deeply. Kerr roared, and Madeline kicked him in the crotch as hard as she was able.

He cursed and loosed his grip upon her hair. This was her sole chance! Madeline leapt away from him, landed kneedeep in the cold water of the stream, and ran.

Kerr swore with unholy vigor. Madeline's heart thundered in her chest. She crossed the creek with great bounds, cursing the weight of her full wet skirt.

She scrambled up the opposite bank of the gully on all fours, weeping as her boots slipped in the mud. She was blind to the course she took, needing only to put distance between them.

Kerr was fast behind her, his feet landing heavily on the bank as he muttered curses. Madeline did not look back. She seized a tree and pulled herself up the hill as quickly as possible. Her breath came in pants and there was an ache in her side and she dared not slow down.

"Whore!" Kerr shouted. "Thankless bitch! You will get what you deserve soon enough and it will be all the more bitter for your defiance!"

Madeline reached the summit. She did not pause for a single breath before she raced out onto the moor.

"You will not flee far!" Kerr roared.

Madeline heard him behind her, his every step covering twice as much ground as one of her own. She heard his hard breathing and glanced over her shoulder.

His furious expression fairly made her heart stop. He was close behind her, too close.

He leapt and snatched at her.

Madeline ducked, evading his grasp in the last moment, fairly feeling his fingers slide through her hair. He swore. She redoubled her pace in panic, holding her skirts in fistfuls above her knees.

Then she slipped in the mud and fell.

Madeline knew she could not recover her balance, though she tried. Her flight was ended. Kerr would have her now, he would hold her down. He would take her all the more cruelly because she had fled from him.

She heard Kerr's shout of triumph, heard a curious whistling, then she landed hard against the earth. She winced at the impact, then Kerr landed upon her so heavily that the breath was driven from Madeline's chest. His head was beside hers, his lips fairly against her ear, the weight of him squarely atop her. She was crushed beneath him, but that was the least of her woes.

Madeline hoped his crime was quickly done. She squeezed her eyes closed, for there was nothing else she could do, and waited for the worst.

Rosamunde awakened in Ravensmuir's solar, well content. She did not open her eyes immediately, for it suited her to savor the comfort that surrounded her. Tynan's bed was wide, its mattress plump, its draperies rich enough even to satisfy Rosamunde's discerning tastes. His solar was warm, as so few chambers were in this cursedly northern clime, and she smiled at the possibility that he had stoked the fire particularly for her.

It was not so bad a wager she had made, in trading her life on the seas for a life with Tynan. Though she would miss the journeys to foreign ports, it was a relief to sleep fully, knowing that none came to assault her in the night.

Rosamunde stretched a toe across the expanse of the bed, prepared to celebrate their mutual agreement again, but only found cold linens. She shivered, then opened one eye.

Though she was alone in bed, she was not alone in the chamber. Tynan was fully dressed, in deepest indigo as was his custom. His hair was damp, his back toward her. He faced the leaping flames in the fireplace, arms folded across his chest, his handsome features cast into profile. She saw the silver at his temples, the lines from laughter beside his eyes, and her heart softened with the certainty that he was her love and her mate.

"You should return to bed, that we might finish what was begun." Rosamunde spoke softly, but Tynan jumped all the same.

Almost as if he felt guilt about some matter.

Rosamunde was immediately awake. She sat up, not troubling to cover her bare breasts, and could not fail to note how Tynan simply frowned into the fire.

He cleared his throat, as he oft did when he knew his words would not be welcomed. "If you would be so kind, I would not have you found here when the household awakens."

A chill slipped down Rosamunde's spine, but she feigned misunderstanding. "Oh, there is no reason to worry." She abandoned the warm bed with reluctance, then stretched like a cat. She shook her hair over her shoulders, knowing that he watched her covertly. The desire between them was impossible to ignore, after all. "All know by this time that we are not half-cousins. It is the talk of all that I share no blood with the Lammergeier family who raised me." She laughed under her breath as she donned a gossamer chemise, then a silken robe rich with embroidery. "If only because it rouses such astonishment that Gawain Lammergeier could have shown such compassion as to raise an unknown babe as his own."

"So it is," he agreed coolly. "But I would still have you return to the women's chamber."

Rosamunde held his gaze, hoping she hid her newfound fear from him well. "Of what import if I am found in your bed? Most know that I have shared it many a time in the past twelve years." Rosamunde paused, then named the crux of the matter. "And all will know as soon as our nuptials are announced."

Tynan pivoted to face the fire again, his

shoulders stiff, and Rosamunde knew, she *knew* what he would say.

"There will be no nuptials between the two of us."

Her anger surprised her only by its vehemence. "What is this? All these years we have loved, and understood that the sole obstacle between us was my trade in relics!"

"True."

"And now I have agreed to surrender that trade, to sate you. We will auction the best of the remaining relics, by this agreement."

"True."

"I released my crew. I sold my ship! I relinquished all of the elements of my trade that I might settle at Ravensmuir. With you."

Tynan looked ill at ease. "You have misunderstood my intent. We have no future together, here or elsewhere."

"You cur! You might have mentioned as much last evening!" Rosamunde crossed the floor and seized his shoulder, compelling him to face her. "You might have recalled such a choice afore seeking your pleasure anew!"

He had the grace to color, but she knew from his eyes that he would not change his thinking. "It is true that I served you poorly, Rosamunde." His tenderness took the sting from her temper, and she hated that he possessed this much power over her.

Tynan lifted a tendril of her golden red hair between his finger and thumb and rubbed it. He met her gaze. "You are a madness in my very veins. I could not resist one last night together."

"And you knew I would not grant it to you, had you been man enough to tell me the truth." Rosamunde did not hide her bitterness as she snatched the curl of her hair from his grasp. "We had an agreement!"

He shook his head once. "I never vowed to wed you."

It was true. Rosamunde cast her memory over their discussions and her innards went cold. He had never made such a pledge — she had simply assumed that such a man as he would not continue their torrid lovemaking without the formality of nuptial vows. Neither had she imagined that he would forgo the pleasure they granted each other.

Clearly, she had erred. It was as had oft been said of her — she might be able to see into the future, to see what others could not, but on occasion, she did not discern what was evident to all.

"Then I shall have my part of the legacy in Ravensmuir's caverns," she insisted. "I will withdraw a part of the store offered for auction, afore it is sold this day."

Tynan shook his head. "You have no legacy here at Ravensmuir." His gaze filled with chilly resolve. "You are not kin to the Lammergeier."

Rosamunde gaped at him for a long moment in silence, so great was her fury. "You wretch! How dare you demand the surrender of all of value in my life, then cast me from your gates like so much rubbish?"

"You will fend well enough for yourself. We both know the truth of that." He turned away, and Rosamunde resisted the urge to spit upon him for his faithlessness. "Make haste. Someone will arrive shortly to tend the fires."

"You might at least tell me why. What has changed?"

Tynan glanced over his shoulder. His gaze danced over her and Rosamunde took some satisfaction from the fact that he could not hide the admiration in his gaze. Tynan always regarded her as if she were a rare marvel, and she felt like one beneath his caress.

She *had* felt like one, at least, afore this morning.

"You can never be Lady of Ravensmuir, Rosamunde. It would not be fitting." He turned and walked away from her then, and she wondered if he did not trust himself to keep from touching her.

"Whyever not?"

His quick glance was impatient. "Marriages are made for alliance, not for pleasure. Wedding you would not secure my borders or bind my neighbors to me."

"And now that the relics will be sold that stain your repute by their very presence, I will not bring you wealth." She spoke with heat, letting him see how his decision stung.

"Rosamunde . . ."

She backed away from him, for he knew too well how to make her forget her anger. "Do not try to soften your cruelty with sweet words!" She spoke then on impulse, naming her fear, hoping she was mistaken. "Doubtless your thinking would be different, were I young enough to offer you the prospect of a son."

There was silence between them, silence that told Rosamunde she had guessed aright. She felt sickened then, but she would show him no weakness.

By no fault of her own, she had been cheated of love by a tale told for her own protection. That it was a false tale, one revealed too late for her to offer children to her lover, and withheld out of kindness by her beloved foster parents, made the revelation no more easily borne.

Tynan caught his breath and halted his pursuit of her. He stared at the floor, as if fighting to find the words, then met her gaze anew. His voice was taut, and though she saw that this choice cost him dearly, she would not make matters easier for him. "You should know that I do not mean only to train my nephew Malcolm: I will raise him as my son and make him heir of Ravensmuir."

"So you have no need of a wife at all, let alone one of such sorry repute as me."

Tynan threw out his hands. "Can you not see that it is your own history at root? You admitted Rhys FitzHenry to the auction for Madeline's hand! What seized your wits?"

"I would wager that she will be happier wed to him than to one of those pathetic fools invited by Alexander."

"My niece is to be wed to a man charged with treason! You must appreciate the damage to her reputation, and her very welfare may be endangered." Tynan shoved a hand through his hair and paced the chamber. "I have considered this all the night long . . ."

"Not *all* the night long."

He glared at her. "*Most* of the night, then. I cannot let this wedding proceed. Alexander must return the coin of this Rhys . . ."

"Rhys FitzHenry." Rosamunde's blood simmered. How dare Tynan not ask for her opinion of Rhys? How dare he not ask what she knew of this man, or even why she had admitted him after he had begged a word with her upon his arrival at Ravensmuir? She was the sole person in this hall who knew Rhys. How *dare* Tynan assume that Rosamunde would willingly endanger her own goddaughter, by tethering the girl to a rogue of no repute?

She stubbornly held her tongue, knowing that Tynan did not deserve to know that his conclusions were incorrect. Let him make a fool of himself!

"I shall insist that the wedding be halted. Madeline will wed, but not to a man wanted for treason. I owe more than this to my brother Roland. I owe more to his children than to make such a mockery of their nuptials and futures." Tynan shook his head. "I cannot imagine how you persuaded me to participate in such madness.

148

No man of dignity would auction a niece!"

"Because the neighbors might not approve?"

He turned on her then, furious as he had not been yet. "Do not mock me, Rosamunde! I must live among these people and rely upon their alliances in times of woe."

"You have no such obligation to remain. You only say as much because you love Ravensmuir more than any living soul!"

"I cannot merely sail away to a more friendly port. I cannot treat every challenge of life as a jest. I cannot make my own rules, discarding the law of the land when it does not suit my desires."

"Is that how you believe I live?"

"Is it not evident that you do?"

"At least I am alive! At least I can yet take a risk, or a wager that might result in my favor. Do you claim Ravensmuir or does it claim you?"

"I will never leave Ravensmuir."

"But you will cast away everything and everyone else, if necessary. Who is the fool in this, Tynan?"

He said nothing, which was answer enough.

Rosamunde advanced upon Tynan. "I thought you more than this, Tynan. I thought you a man who did not care for the whisperings of his neighbors." She glared at him. "I thought you were your father's son."

Their gazes locked, each knowing well enough that Tynan's father had claimed an unconventional bride, for the sake of love alone.

Then Tynan sighed and looked away. He looked so discouraged that Rosamunde was tempted to reach for him, to lay a hand upon his shoulder.

"I am a man who learned the price of his father's choices, and do not welcome their burden upon my own shoulders," he said, sounding a thousand years old.

Rosamunde hardened her heart against him. Let Tynan bear his own burdens from this day forth. That, after all, was the choice he had made.

Some sorry soul knocked then upon the portal.

Chapter Five

Tynan gave Rosamunde a sharp look, but she held her ground. "I am here, Laird of Ravensmuir, and I will remain here," she said, scoffing at his evident disapproval. "You are less than I had imagined you to be, if you care so much for rumor in your own hall."

"Rosamunde," he growled, but she did not let him continue.

"You and your expectation that I should shirk from the truth of what I have done are welcome to find the way to hell." She cast herself into the fine chair that he favored. She dangled her legs over one side of it, fairly daring Tynan to comment upon the visibility of her bare shins and feet. The chair was in a beam of sunlight and Rosamunde knew the light would make her hair look afire. "I intend to remain here, in full view of whosoever troubles his lord so early in the day. Let them guess what deeds have been done in this chamber and bed in hours past."

"You cannot."

"I will, unless you forcibly remove me."

"It is sorely tempting," Tynan said, sparing a significant glance to the window.

Rosamunde smiled, her heart as cold as ice. "Be assured, my lord, that dead courtesans arouse more gossip than live ones."

There was a cup of wine left within reach. Rosamunde picked it up with a cavalier gesture, held Tynan's furious gaze, and drank of it lustily. She licked her lips, opened the neckline of her robe so that the curve of her breast was visible, and fluttered her eyelashes at the very vexed man before her. "Do you not mean to answer the door, my lord?"

Tynan's jaw set, and he raised a finger toward her. His eyes flashed and she was glad to see that some fire yet lurked in his veins. But it was not enough for her, not anymore. She wanted all of him, she wanted to be acknowledged openly as his mate, she wanted the security of a permanent abode.

Tynan had offered as much, and he knew full well what she had read between the lines of their agreement. He had offered her heart's desire, then snatched it away for the sake of convention.

Rosamunde would have her vengeance, to be sure. She might not share blood with her foster father, Gawain, but she alone had claimed the legacy of the man who had been the greatest thief in Christendom. She alone had begged Gawain to teach her his cunning tricks, his means of deception, his art of thievery.

Tynan might believe that his legacy was secure, but Rosamunde knew that legacies were as oft stolen as inherited by law.

The prospect of throttling Rosamunde offered more pleasure to Tynan than many responsibilities he had faced of late.

The sole exception was the night they had just spent entangled together. He had known himself to be a knave of the worst order in deceiving her, but Rosamunde possessed an allure he could not resist. He could not sleep, even knowing that she was within the walls of Ravensmuir.

He dared not let her guess how close he had come to swearing off Ravensmuir simply to have her by his side. Had she not invited that traitor to the auction, he might have lost his wits utterly.

The solution was clear: Rosamunde had to leave. Tynan had to think clearly, for matters grew complicated. The Red Douglas family and the Black Douglas family grew ever more aggressive in their pursuit of power — and Ravensmuir was directly in the middle of their ancestral lands. He would have to choose sides soon, and he would probably have to secure that choice with a marriage.

It would best be his own.

Tynan did not have to like the truth of it. Even then, Ravensmuir would likely be assaulted by the side he had not chosen, but at least he would have allies to aid in its defense. He could not permit the destruction of his family abode — Rosamunde would never understand his commitment to what she oft called a pile of old stones, but Tynan could not deny it.

Nor could he deny his sense of responsibility to his forebears. It was not sweet to forgo the desires of his heart. There was a heavy stone in his chest that seemed to grow larger the more vehemently he pushed Rosamunde away from his side.

It would be easier for both of them if she left Ravensmuir and never returned.

The knock came again. Tynan swore, then shouted. "Enter!"

The portal opened slowly. Tynan crossed the floor and hauled open the door so abruptly that Alexander fairly tumbled into the chamber.

The young man's gaze flew from Tynan

to Rosamunde, who had indeed displayed herself like a courtesan, and he flushed scarlet. He stammered in the attempt to say whatsoever he had come to say, his gaze remaining fixed upon Tynan's face as his own face grew more ruddy.

Curse Rosamunde!

"What *is* it? What ails you, Alexander?" Tynan forced himself to recall that Alexander had seen five-and-twenty summers. He seemed so much younger than he was only because Roland had indulged him overmuch.

But then, what man could guess that he would die young? "It is James. He is here!"

Tynan did not recognize the name. "James? Who is James?"

"Madeline's betrothed," Rosamunde said tartly. "How like you to forget such a bond."

Alexander glanced to his aunt and nodded. "James is returned from France and comes to claim Madeline's hand. His father accompanies him, and there is much hustle to make arrangements for the steeds and squires, seeing as the stables are so full."

"It seems matters resolve themselves well." Tynan granted Rosamunde an arch glance, not hiding that he was pleased indeed with these tidings.

"Indeed, what need to worry what Madeline desires," Rosamunde said bitterly, then strolled to the women's chamber. The scent of her perfume lingered in his chamber, tempting Tynan and doubtless informing any who might enter of her presence the previous night. There was not a soul with perfume as exotic as Rosamunde.

"But what of the coin, Uncle Tynan?" Alexander demanded with some anxiety. "I shall have to return Rhys FitzHenry's coin to him if he does not wed Madeline, and the castellan yet insists that Kinfairlie's harvest will be poor."

"You will have one less to feed in the hall next winter, if nothing else," Tynan said. "And James's family might be persuaded to pay a bride price. He has, after all, taken overlong to return to wed Madeline and some compense could well be expected for the insult." He laid a hand upon Alexander's shoulder. "I shall see what can be done."

Of course, Tynan should have guessed that with Rosamunde involved, nothing would be simply resolved. She returned slowly, swinging her hips as she strolled down the corridor and he had a feeling that she brought unwelcome news.

"Madeline is gone," she said with no small pleasure.

Tynan almost made an accusation he would have regretted, for Rosamunde had appointed herself to guard the maidenly virtues of her nieces the night before. Rosamunde's sharp glance reminded him that he alone was responsible for her abandoning her vigil.

Alexander glanced between them. "But where could she have gone?"

"She might be in the hall, or the kitchen," Tynan suggested.

"Madeline never would descend alone to a hall full of men," Alexander said.

"Not while they were awake, at least," Rosamunde said. "She might well have fled. She is a woman of uncommon confidence, after all, and she had cause to be displeased with both of you last evening."

"Fled?" Alexander stepped back. "She has never travelled alone! She has no weapons. She could be in peril!"

"If she is gone, we will pursue her, of course," Rosamunde said.

"Begin a search of the entire keep," Tynan instructed his castellan, who arrived just then. "My niece Madeline is not in her bed." The castellan nodded and darted to his task.

"You will not find her." Rosamunde cast off her robe as she crossed the chamber. The silk chemise clung lovingly to her curves, though her manner was far from seductive. "Tell this James to be prepared to ride within moments. I shall lead the hunt."

"You?" Tynan asked.

She granted him a contemptuous glance that he knew he deserved. "Of course. *You* could not be expected to leave Ravensmuir."

"But what about me?" Alexander demanded. "I will go! It would be my fault if any harm came to her."

"You may come if you desire. I will pursue Madeline either way." Rosamunde sat on the far side of the pillared bed and donned chausses that had been made for her in the manner of men's garb. Few men, though, had chausses wrought of such fine leather as these.

"Perhaps you should go," Tynan said, his thoughts upon Rosamunde's safety as well. "You began this trouble, and it makes sense to me that the two of you should see it resolved. I will ensure Kinfairlie's security in your absence."

Alexander straightened. "We shall need fast horses."

"We will have six black destriers, the finest stallions from Ravensmuir's stables," Rosamunde interjected crisply. She laced a fur-lined black tabard over her chemise, its surface graced with golden embroidery. She had donned her black boots and hefted her fur-lined cloak over her arm.

Tynan regarded her in astonishment at this command, no less when she smiled sadly.

"That is the price of being rid of me forever, Tynan, and we know you desire no less," she said. She brushed past him without another word, without a parting caress, without a backward glance.

The stone in his chest became so heavy that it fairly took him to his knees. Tynan understood then that Rosamunde would never return to Ravensmuir, that she would never grace his bed or laugh in his hall again. Though he had demanded as much of her, the prospect was more grim than ever he might have imagined. He supposed that he would have years to grow accustomed to her absence.

"Is something amiss, uncle?" Alexander asked.

Tynan gripped the younger man's shoulder. "Prepare yourself to ride, Alexander, for I doubt that Rosamunde will delay her departure for any man."

In the end, they were six, upon those stallions Rosamunde had demanded. Rosamunde led the company, and was joined by the sole remaining man of her crew, one Padraig who wore a golden earring and said little. Alexander rode with them, as did James. Vivienne demanded that she be permitted to ensure the welfare of her closest sister — though Tynan suspected the girl wished solely to participate in a quest reminiscent of an old tale.

There remained but one steed without a rider when Elizabeth insisted that she be allowed to be the sixth. Tynan was inclined to deny her, though he had always had a weakness for the girl's charm. He argued that she was too young, at only twelve summers.

Elizabeth flushed crimson but lifted her chin and informed him that she was old enough to be wedded and bear babes of her own, a detail he would have preferred to have lived without but one whose truth could not be denied. She also declared that the spriggan accompanied them, dangling as it did in the horses' tails, and that she was the sole one who could see the creature.

Even Tynan could not find an argument

against that, though he bade Alexander take great care with his sisters.

In a trice, the party was gone, the steeds fairly flying through Ravensmuir's gates, their ebony tails flowing like dark banners. Tynan watched until the dust of the road swallowed their silhouettes, but his beloved never so much as glanced back.

In the same moment that Ravensmuir was roused to seek Madeline, she lay on the moor far to the south of that keep. The mercenary atop her did not move.

Indeed, Kerr did not make a sound.

His was a curious manner of assault. Madeline opened her eyes cautiously, for still she was trapped beneath him, cold mud against her cheek and chest. She listened, but Kerr did not seem to breathe.

Something warm trickled onto her throat. Madeline touched it and found vivid red blood smeared across her flesh. She yelped and recoiled and Kerr shifted. She glanced over her shoulder in fear of his retaliation.

Kerr's eyes were wide open. He stared into the distance unblinkingly. There was a knife lodged in his throat, a knife clearly responsible for the blood that flowed over her.

Kerr had not assaulted her, because he was dead.

There was a *dead* man atop her, and it was his warm blood that flowed over her own skin.

Madeline's composure abandoned her utterly. A horrible choking sound came from her throat. She struggled beneath the weight of the corpse in a panic, wanting only to flee as far as possible. She began to weep when she could not dislodge Kerr's body from atop her, though her frenzy seemed only to embed her more deeply in the mud.

"Do not scream," Rhys commanded. His words were so stern and her astonishment at his presence so complete that Madeline froze, trembling. "We shall never find the horses if you do, my lady. They are sufficiently frightened already."

Madeline gasped as Kerr was hauled from her back. Rhys removed the knife from the man's throat and matter-of-factly slit Kerr's throat more thoroughly. He kicked the corpse aside, wiped his blade and replaced it in its scabbard, then offered Madeline his gloved hand. All of this he achieved with a familiar competence that Madeline found both reassuring and somewhat troubling.

She swallowed her scream with an effort, though she could barely summon a word to her lips in her shock. "You, you . . ."

"I can throw a knife well enough, it appears." Rhys spoke so calmly that he might have been admitting an affection for ale. He reached down and seized her hand when she did not immediately accept his aid. He pulled her to her feet with a sure gesture and held her hands fast within his own.

He was dressed as afore all in garb of darkest midnight and his manner was stern. The leather of his gloves was thick but had softened with use and taken the shape of his hand, a strong hand that she could feel gripping her own. Madeline found herself grateful for his steady support.

Rhys gave her a hard look. "Are you injured?"

Madeline's mouth worked, and she realized that she was quivering to her very marrow. She shook her head when words failed her and Rhys appeared to be relieved. She fought to compose herself.

Surely the man deserved no less for aiding her in such a timely fashion?

Her gaze fell upon the dead man, and she shuddered again even as she looked away. "How oft have you slit a man's throat?"

163

Rhys gave her a hard look. "A man must do what must be done. Would you have preferred that I had let him live?"

Madeline's knees shook with such vigor at the very prospect that she feared they would not hold her weight.

"Bear up, my lady." Rhys held her hand with a firmer grip, though he did not touch her otherwise. He offered her a cloth to wipe the blood from her throat.

"He meant to rape me." Madeline knew it was an unnecessary comment but she could not keep the words from spilling forth. She felt her color deepen. "I should never have trusted him. You must think me a fool." She should never have left Ravensmuir, much less with a man about whom she knew so little.

To her astonishment, Rhys simply held her hand more tightly, as if he understood his grip to be precisely what she needed. He was like a rock to which she clung as her terror subsided.

"I think you a woman of uncommon resource. It is a mark of your valor that he did not succeed so readily." Rhys spoke with such resolve that she did not doubt he meant every word. "I applaud your quick thinking and your fortitude. Are you unscathed?"

"I am frightened, to be sure." She took a deep breath and glanced over herself. Her gown was mired and ripped, and there were scratches aplenty upon her skin. She had torn three fingernails and was thoroughly adorned with mud. She realized with horror that her shredded kirtle hung open and her breasts were bared.

Madeline seized the torn fabric to clutch it closed and flushed crimson. Rhys, she noted, did not look below her face. His gallantry encouraged her to summon a tremulous smile. "But otherwise I am well enough, I suppose."

"It is a rare woman who can stand upon her own feet after such an assault." Rhys granted her a brief flicker of a smile, the sight of which warmed Madeline's heart. "In Wales, we have great regard for stalwart women. Have ever you heard of Gwenllian?"

Madeline shook her head, even while the rest of her trembled.

"She was the mother of Lord Rhys, the last king of Wales. He rose in rebellion against the Normans in 1136. Gwenllian was his mother, and so great was her valor that she raised her own army, and led it against the enemy in aid of her son. Even when she witnessed one of her sons killed and another taken prisoner, she fought on so valiantly that still that field of battle, in Cydweli in Dyfed, bears her name in honor."

While he spoke, Madeline found herself drawing vigor from his words and his grip. "I did not know. I had never heard of a woman leading an army to war."

"And now you have." Rhys became solemn again. "I apologize for the tardiness of my aid. There was no assistance I could grant while you were in the gorse, for I was not close enough to have a clear sight of the villain. Your attempt to flee offered me the necessary opportunity."

"Had I not been such a fool, I would not have had need of it." She drew a shuddering breath.

"Do not judge yourself so harshly." A smile touched Rhys's lips. "I understand that the prospect of wedding me must have been daunting for you to have taken such a risk."

Madeline flushed. Not only had he perceived her fears but he must have anticipated her flight. How else could he have followed her and Kerr?

"My father employed Kerr's services for years," she said, needing to explain herself. "I trusted him because of that, though he clearly had a darker scheme than I realized."

"I trust that you have learned something about using more caution in your choice of companions." Rather than lingering upon his lesson, Rhys turned as soon as Madeline nodded. He released her hand and Madeline felt bereft.

Then he whistled. His destrier appeared, apparently having been hidden in the gorse, and trotted toward its master. It was a fine dapple grey beast, its mane and tail as dark as charcoal. A shaggy hound trotted beside the steed, and proved to be a dog of formidable size. It surveyed Madeline with shrewd eyes and its tail wagged as it leaned against Rhys.

"This is Gelert," he said, and gestured the dog toward Madeline. She reached out a hand, liking the hound's friendly manner. Its tousled fur looked like shaggy silver brows over its eyes, and those brows moved most expressively. It sniffed her hand, then sat beside her, leaning heavily against her leg. Madeline sank her fingers into the thick warmth of fur at the scruff of the dog's neck and found its presence reassuring. Indeed, the heat of it against her and its appearance made her want to smile.

"And this is Gwynt Arian," Rhys said as

he seized the destrier's reins. The beast tossed its head and flared its nostrils, as if in recognition of its name.

"Is that a Welsh name?"

Rhys nodded as he rubbed the beast's nose. "It means 'silver wind'."

"It is a fine name for a steed so regal as he," Madeline said, taking comfort in their mundane conversation. "But you travel with no squire?"

Rhys shook his head. "These two bear witness, but tell no tales."

Madeline wondered who had betrayed him in the past, but Rhys clearly had no interest in sharing confidences.

"Fasten your cloak tightly about yourself," he advised as he led his horse closer.

Madeline complied with his instruction, grateful to have no need to make decisions herself for the moment. Rhys lifted her into his saddle with a single smooth gesture. He murmured to the steed, then rummaged in his saddlebag. Gelert stood diligently beside the stirrup, as if guarding Madeline.

Rhys offered a leather flask to Madeline along with a sharp glance. "Sip of this."

"What is it?"

"Eau-de-vie." Again that teasing smile curved his lips for just a heartbeat.

Madeline wished Rhys would smile more often, for he was less fearsome then. "It will persuade you that you have not joined the dead as yet. Drink."

Madeline sipped cautiously. The flask's contents burned her throat like fire and forged a course to her innards. Her eyes watered and she choked as if she would cough up her very liver.

When her vision cleared, Rhys nodded, amusement in his eyes. "Take another."

Madeline did as she was bidden, though the second draught was scarcely easier to down than the first.

"Better?"

To her astonishment, Madeline did feel better. The liquid had awakened a heat in her flesh and driven the shivers away. She nodded, and Rhys lifted the flask from her hand. Their fingers brushed in the transaction, reminding Madeline of his possessive kisses and awakening another warmth within her.

"Two small draughts is a sufficient measure for a lady," he said, then took a long draught himself. For the first time, Madeline wondered whether he had been troubled by Kerr's assault.

Rhys seemed so unconcerned, as if he routinely aided women attacked upon the moors, as if he often killed mercenaries for the greater good. His desire for the *eau-de-vie* hinted that he might have shared at least a measure of her fear.

Madeline shook her head, certain she saw a vulnerability in this warrior that was not there. Undoubtedly, he felt a responsibility toward her.

He had bought her, after all.

Perhaps he was a man who protected all of his possessions with such vigor. Madeline did not know, but she was clever enough to admit herself glad in this moment of his sense of obligation.

Rhys winced at the liquor's vigor but did not cough. He turned to scan the moors with narrowed eyes, then nodded at the distant silhouette of a palfrey. "Your steed?"

Madeline nodded. "Tarascon. Kerr cut her flank to make her run away from us. I do not know the depth of her injury." Her fingers tightened on the pommel. "I hope she is not sorely wounded."

"She runs yet, so it cannot be so dire a wound." Rhys spoke such good sense that Madeline wished she had realized as much herself. She seemed fated to show herself poorly in this man's presence.

Rhys took the reins and led the destrier toward the mare. He whistled softly.

Tarascon turned to watch their progress, her ears twitching nervously.

"The blood will have frightened her," Rhys said, the very tone of his voice reassuring. "Do you ride her often?"

"Almost daily."

"Then she will have smelled your fear, as well, and been troubled by that."

"I can call her. She always comes to me." The palfrey took but one step closer when Madeline called, then retreated four paces, her tail swishing nervously.

"Does she then?" There was humor in Rhys' tone.

Madeline sat straighter, wishing she could do something right in this man's company. "Usually she does."

"These are uncommon circumstances, my lady. Do not take her uncertainty to heart. Wait until we are closer and she can be certain that it is you."

"She might flee afore then." Madeline called again, then watched in horror as her horse danced in the opposite direction.

Rhys halted and still Tarascon fled another trio of steps. She was anxious as Madeline had never seen her, though she could not blame the mare for her fear of men.

"Look in the saddlebag," Rhys said softly. "See if a pair of apples are yet there."

Madeline was glad to comply and to be of aid. The apples were there, but Tarascon was not as readily tempted by the treat as she might have been just hours before.

The sun was approaching midheaven by the time they coaxed the palfrey to let them approach her. Madeline was impressed by the gentle persistence Rhys showed in pursuing the frightened steed. They had steadily drawn closer to Tarascon, Rhys's murmur obviously calming the horse's fears.

That Gelert had finally run behind the palfrey at Rhys's signal and barked aggressively, urging her toward Rhys, also had not hurt.

Madeline held the palfrey's reins once Rhys had captured her, spoke to the horse softly and stroked her nose. Meanwhile, Rhys examined the creature's wound with careful fingers. There was kindness in this man, though much else that Madeline could not name. The horse fidgeted but Madeline whispered to her, trusting Rhys to give good counsel.

"Mercifully, it is not as brutal as it might have been. I believe that the damage will heal readily enough," he said as he straightened. "I would have liked to have a better ostler than myself look upon it to be sure."

"We could return to Ravensmuir."

Rhys granted Madeline a steady glance and she could not guess his thoughts. "I think it too far for your mare," he said with care. "There is an abbey to the north of here that we could reach by mid-afternoon, if you are willing. They have granted me aid in the past, for my aunt is abbess there."

Madeline's heart quailed that they would have to ride together, for her mare was too injured to bear her weight. She could not imagine being pressed against any man's heat on this day, much less Rhys who kindled that unfamiliar fire within her. Their gazes caught and held, an awareness crackling between them that frightened Madeline to her core.

Rhys turned away before she could protest and methodically tied Tarascon's reins to the back of the saddle. He whispered to his steed then strode away, with nary a word of explanation. Gelert sat beside her, as bidden. Puzzled, Madeline watched Rhys disappear into the gorse.

Was he leaving her here?

Did he prepare for whatever reward he would demand of her? She knew he desired her, she had tasted as much in his kisses. In his absence, Madeline's suspicions seemed to feed upon themselves and multiply. Though Rhys had been kind, Kerr had been kind until he thought she had no hope of summoning aid.

Had she leapt from the fat to the fire?

Had she only delayed her rape? What would compel a man of such dangerous repute as Rhys to treat her with honor, now that they were alone upon the moors?

This might well be her sole chance to escape! Madeline dug her heels into the destrier's sides, urging it onward.

The beast did not so much as flinch, let alone move. It nibbled at a wildflower, supremely indifferent to Madeline's attempt to flee. The dog spared her a glance, as if chiding her, then returned to its vigil.

Madeline panicked. Had Rhys himself not advised her to choose her companions with care? She whispered to the horse, commanded it, patted its flank, pulled the reins. She did everything she could think of doing to persuade it to take a step.

All to no avail. The feet of the beast might have taken root. She might have tried to encourage a stone to move with better results. She made to dismount and run, just as Rhys's voice carried to her ears.

"Arian heeds none but me, my lady." He was striding from the gorse toward her, leading Kerr's destrier. Again, he seemed amused but unsurprised.

Madeline felt a twinge of irritation. Did nothing astonish the man? Was Rhys never taken unawares?

"Truly?" she replied as if she had not discovered the very same fact herself. "It is uncommon to find a steed so loyal."

"Indeed it is. A man can count himself fortunate to have any soul serve him with such loyalty, be it man or beast."

Madeline watched him, curious despite herself. He made yet another reference to betrayal. What had happened to Rhys? And what was at root of the king's charge against him?

She did not imagine that Rhys would answer her questions. Indeed, he frowned in concentration as he removed Kerr's saddlebag. He solemnly sifted through its contents and ultimately removed only the coins from the dead man's purse. Rhys then flung the saddlebag and the rest of its contents across the moor.

Madeline regarded him with surprise.

"Any who find his corpse will think he was attacked by bandits," Rhys said simply, then swung into the other steed's saddle.

He lifted the reins of his destrier from Madeline's numb fingertips. "Shall we go to the ostler, then?"

Madeline only nodded, and Rhys studied her for a moment before he urged the horse to a walk. "You look to have need of a tale," he said. "And I know the very one."

Madeline thought she needed many things in this moment, the last of which would have been a tale, but it seemed rude to say as much. She let him lead the horse and resigned herself to listen.

She did not expect to be entertained, no less to be charmed, but she was quickly proven wrong.

Rhys cleared his throat. "There is a place in Wales known as Pen Dinas, a place where it is said by those who know such things that the fairies hold their high court. Pen Dinas is a high flat rock near a river and its summit is uncommonly level. The turf there is a rich green, beyond the hue of any other place, as if it has been blessed by the feet of many magical dancers."

Madeline found the tightness easing in her shoulders. Rhys's voice was easy to attend and indeed, the unfamiliar rhythm of his speech was beguiling. This reminded her of the tales her father would tell the family when she and her siblings had been very small, and it was reassuring for that.

"So it was that a boy came there to hide. It is said that his name was Elidorus, but that is no Welsh name. Let us call him Llewelyn ap Alan."

Madeline laughed despite herself. His substitution was so different that it caught her by surprise, and it was such an uncommon name. "You cannot say that name a dozen times quickly!"

Rhys granted her a wry glance and did precisely that, making it sound like music as he did so. She wondered whether she imagined the mischievous twinkle in his eye, so abruptly did he sober and resume his tale.

"So it was that Llewelyn ap Alan decided to flee his tutor, for he did not like to learn his meter, and he liked less to be chided for his inattention."

"His meter?"

"The meter of poetry. It is what a boy learns from a tutor, how the rhymes must be made and the repetitions be calculated."

Madeline knew nothing of this, but she nodded as if she understood. She was loathe to interrupt Rhys's tale, and he thought the matter of meter so obvious that she did not want him to think her simple.

"So Llewelyn ap Alan hid himself near this very place, Pen Dinas, so that none might find him. That very night, when the moon waxed round and bright, he heard music. As slovenly as Llewelyn ap Alan might have been, he was no fool. He knew to avoid the music of the fairies and never to join them in their circles, lest he be lost to the mortal world for a hundred years. He put his fingers in his ears and he stayed hidden until the morning came and the fairy music ceased.

"Yet in the early light of dawn, when he might have allowed himself to sleep, Llewelyn ap Alan was confronted by two small men. They invited him to their abode, to show him marvels, and after having their pledge that he would be allowed to leave at his very request, the curious boy accompanied them.

"They led him to a secret passage, one cleverly concealed behind a trio of stones, and into a kingdom hidden beneath the hill of Pen Dinas. Although it was cloudy there, for no sun shone under the hill, the land was beautiful and the people yet more so. Every one of them was blessed with hair as fair as his own was dark, every one of them seemed on the verge of laughter. They had wealth beyond measure — goblets of gold and gems upon every finger. Their horses were swift and lovely, their hounds were graceful. It was a veritable paradise.

"Llewelyn ap Alan was greeted by the king himself. The king explained the manners of his people, and bade Llewelyn ap Alan not to demand a pledge again. The fairies made few vows, far fewer than men, for they would keep each and every one of them to the letter. The king told Llewelyn ap Alan that he and his people despised deception and faithlessness beyond all."

Madeline watched her companion, noting again a reference to betrayal. She was beginning to have a good measure of curiosity about this man, though she suspected it was a dangerous inquisitiveness.

"Llewelyn ap Alan professed this to be most admirable and was granted leave to play with the king's son. He did not forget himself, as he had feared, and it was not overlong before he asked permission to leave. His guides showed him a way home and he quickly made his way to his mother's abode, half-fearing that time would have slipped away.

"But there had been no deception. The

fairies had kept their bargain with him and he had been gone but three days, just as he had expected. Some weeks later, he sought the secret portal and found it, much to the delight of the king's son. So it was that Llewelyn ap Alan became accustomed to spending time in both worlds and enjoyed the merits of both."

Rhys glanced over his shoulder and Madeline did not trouble to hide how enchanted she was by his tale. She smiled, hoping to urge him to continue, and Rhys turned away so abruptly that she feared she had somehow insulted him.

But he merely continued on. "The secret began to itch Llewelyn ap Alan, as secrets are wont to do, and increasingly it saddened him that no one knew what he knew. He confided one day in his mother, who seemed as delighted with his adventure as he. For a while, this confidence sufficed and he told her each time he returned what new marvels he had seen.

"Now, the marvels of that kingdom were not finite, and it seemed that each time he visited, Llewelyn ap Alan saw something yet more wondrous. And in time, as his tales seemed to grow more fanciful, and as his recounting of the wealth in the kingdom of the fairies grew more magnificent, his mother became impatient. She began to think that he played a trick upon her, as young boys will do, and she demanded some evidence that his journeys occurred in truth.

"So it was that the next time Llewelyn ap Alan visited the kingdom, he stole the golden ball with which he and the king's son played. He made for the portal, but was pursued with a hue and a cry. He reached the door, but it was closed fast against him . . . until he surrendered the ball to the very pair who had led him to this place. They frowned at him, and turned a deaf ear to his apologies.

"When Llewelyn ap Alan blinked, he found himself upon the bare turf of Pen Dinas. Alone. He never did find the entry to the fairy kingdom again, though it was said that he wandered long and far in search of it. And though he oft heard their music at a distance, on a night when the moon shone bright, he never could spy their dancing, nor could he approach their merrymaking." Rhys paused, seemingly to draw attention to the end of his tale. "Llewelyn ap Alan had shown himself faithless and a poor guest, and in that, he lost what he should have valued in the first place."

The moral was a potent one. Madeline wondered if Rhys had chosen this tale apurpose, but she had no time to ask him before he raised a finger to point to the horizon.

"There! See the curl of smoke from the abbey's chimney? It is not far, my lady. You will be among women and behind high walls soon enough. I daresay they will have a hot *potage* over the fire, as well."

Madeline looked, saw the plume of smoke, and was ashamed of her earlier suspicions of his motives. Rhys was going to take her to an abbey where she would be safe.

No, she had been safe ever since she left Ravensmuir, safe because Rhys had ridden close behind her and kept a vigilant eye upon her, despite her own mistake.

And she had been doubly safe since he had saved her from Kerr.

Madeline smiled at Rhys, smiled genuinely for the first time since they had met. "Thank you, Rhys. I have done little to deserve your aid and courtesy of this day, but I grant you my heartfelt thanks."

Curiously, the man did not return her smile.

Indeed, he blinked, as if he had looked into the center of the sun, then frowned. He turned away, his entire being apparently focused upon making a course to the abbey.

"We had best make haste," he said gruffly. "A wound heals better when it is tended sooner." He whistled to Gelert and the hound trotted at the quickened pace of the destrier. Rhys did not speak to Madeline again — indeed, his concentration was so complete that he might have been riding alone.

And Madeline was surprised by how much Rhys's silence — and his indifference to her presence — troubled her.

Chapter Six

In fact, Rhys was far from indifferent to the presence of the lady close behind him.

Rhys was aware of Madeline's beauty as he had never been aware of a woman before. It had been with considerable effort that he had kept himself from reassuring her with his touch. It had taken a fortitude he had not known he possessed to restrain himself from kissing her soundly in his relief that she was unscathed.

He had been afraid when Kerr took to the gorse. He had been terrified that the wily mercenary would rape Madeline before he could come to the lady's aid. He had left too much distance between them in his determination not to be observed and he had been certain that his lady would pay the price of his miscalculation.

He had not overstated his relief that she had attempted to escape.

The *eau-de-vie* had not truly settled Rhys's worries. Indeed, it curdled in his gut. A resounding kiss would have served him better, no less the lady's hands curling in his hair. But Rhys had glimpsed Madeline's terror and he did not want to redouble it.

The lady had endured sufficient insult and trial of late.

Rhys particularly respected that she blamed herself for making a foolish choice. It was a rare soul who admitted his or her own part in subsequent misfortunes. To be sure, it was partly Rhys's fault as well. Fear of meeting him at the altar was behind Madeline's flight and he blamed himself for not doing a better task of eliminating her uncertainties.

It was not the lady's fault that she had been protected from knowledge of wickedness in the world, especially the kind of wickedness Kerr had shown. He could well understand why she would trust a man who had been in her father's employ.

He resisted the urge to steal a glimpse of her, for fear that she would smile at him again and addle his wits completely. The lady had an admirable valor, to be sure. Most women would have wept by this time, but Madeline sat straight in the saddle.

Even dishevelled, she possessed a beauty that could make a man forget himself. Her braid had become unfastened and her dark hair hung loose over her shoulders. There was a scratch upon her cheek and more upon her hands, none of which Rhys dared to offer to tend. He did not doubt that the smeared mud hid bruises upon her flesh. The lady was too soft, too temptingly sweet, and the mere glimpse he had had of the curve of her breast had nigh been enough to make him forget any chivalrous intent he possessed.

Yet he had not been so entangled in his lust that he had not seen the truth of it. Madeline had been so frightened that his merest touch might have made her bolt like her palfrey. He would not take advantage of her fear to sate his own desires.

That was not the way to earn her trust, to make a match that would endure.

It was most unlike Rhys to feel such a potent yearning for any woman, and he had never expected he would feel it for the woman he ultimately took to wife. Rhys was certain that his response was a result of little sleep, or perhaps of a fear that Caerwyn could have been lost to him. Both he and Madeline would be restored by the morrow.

For, by then, they would be wed in truth, the lady's future would be secured, and Caerwyn would be his forevermore.

★ ★ ★

When they reached the walled community, the abbey gates were closed. Rhys seemed untroubled by this, and Madeline said nothing, guessing that he must prefer her silence. These were heavy wooden gates, boasting no expensive portcullis or ornamental details, their sole virtue being their size and weight. Madeline could see the cross on the roof of the chapel, smell a *potage* of vegetables, and discern little else.

Rhys dismounted, then seized the rope beside the gate and pulled it. A sonorous pealing echoed behind the walls, the sound prompting Madeline to smile. It was a merry sequence of notes, a glorious ringing that made her heart soar. The music was sufficient that she almost forgot what she had endured this day.

"How delightful!" she whispered. Tears clouded her vision, for she recalled all too keenly how music had bound her and James together. She remembered him bent over his lute, composing a ballad. She recalled the play of light on his fair hair, and grief caught her by the throat.

Surely he could not be dead?

Surely she would have known if the man she loved with all her heart and soul had died?

Yet if James were alive, surely he would have sent word to her in ten long months? Madeline brushed aside her tears, wishing she were bold enough to ask for more of the *eau-de-vie*.

Rhys was watching her, and his expression had become wary once again.

Madeline did not care what he thought of her in this moment. "Could you ring it once more?" she asked, her words uneven. "It is so joyous a sound, as if angels themselves announce our arrival."

Rhys said nothing. He pulled the cord again, his expression impassive.

Madeline listened, eyes closed, hands clasped together as the healing balm of the pealing bells rolled over her. The sound was so beautiful that the ache of her loss diminished slightly. She felt the fullness of her lost love while the bells sounded and it shook her to realize how much her life had changed.

Only when the bells fell silent did Madeline become aware that Rhys had watched her, transfixed, all the while.

"It is a community of women," he said roughly, pivoting to stare at the wooden gate, "although there are several priests who live separately and offer the sacraments, as well as an excellent ostler."

Madeline was surprised by his manner. Perhaps she had offended him, taking pleasure from something so inconsequential when he had granted her more considerable aid. She leaned forward and touched Rhys' arm, knowing she owed him a heartfelt thanks. He jumped at her touch but did not look at her.

He *was* irked, then.

Before Madeline could try again to ease his mood with gratitude, a small portal in the gate was opened. She glimpsed a face peering through the grille. "Who comes to our gate?"

Gelert barked joyously and leapt at the gate, apparently recognizing the monk's voice and anxious to make his acquaintance again.

"Brother Thomas, it is Rhys FitzHenry." Rhys straightened and took a step closer to the gate that he might be seen. "I regret that I must beg your hospitality yet again."

"Rhys! You old dog!" The portal was flung open with a creak of its ancient hinges. Thomas proved to be a burly monk whose girth was too great for his robe. The garment was tight around his ample belly and thus rode short in the front, revealing his hairy shins and sturdy sandals. "And you, Gelert!" He bent to pat the dog, which leapt with happiness and licked his ears. "I wager I can find a soup bone for you."

"No wonder the beast loves you more than life itself," Rhys grumbled amiably.

"You could feed the creature once in a while, and you might earn such affection for yourself," Thomas retorted, and the two men grinned at each other.

The monk's joy at seeing Rhys was unmistakable, for he caught the reluctant warrior in a tight hug of welcome. Madeline was surprised, both at the warmth of the monk's greeting and the fact that Rhys endured it.

Finally, the monk stood back and gave Rhys a friendly cuff on the shoulder. "You old sinner. Are you in need of sanctuary again so soon? Is there no end to your wickedness?"

This charge was made without malice, as if the pair commonly jested about such things. It reminded Madeline of how her brothers teased each other, though she was fascinated that any soul would tease Rhys FitzHenry.

And curious as to what he would do about the matter.

The color rose on the back of Rhys's neck, and his manner became even more stern than usual. "It is the lady in need of your aid on this day. I only accompany her."

"A lady!" Thomas sobered and straightened, tugging futilely at the front of his robe as he turned to Madeline. "Good day, my lady, and welcome to our humble gates." He bowed, the effort such that the bald top of his head framed by his tonsure turned crimson.

"This is Lady Madeline of Kinfairlie." Rhys spoke with care and Madeline guessed that he meant to present a slightly altered version of their adventure. She held his gaze, willing him to understand that she would not deny his tale. "She was beset upon the road by bandits. Mercifully, I arrived in time to be of aid."

"God in Heaven!" Thomas crossed himself. "What times we live in! How fortunate that you came upon her and recognized her plight."

"Not so fortunate as that, old friend." Rhys smiled slightly and Madeline felt suddenly warm beneath his gaze. "The lady and I are betrothed, and I thought I recognized her steed at a distance."

"Merciful heavens! God is great indeed that he granted you such keen vision!" Thomas looked between the pair of them with astonishment. "But why did we not know of your betrothal sooner, Rhys? That you of all men should take a bride is a tale worth hearing, and you were here but a fortnight past."

Madeline blinked. She had only heard of Ravensmuir's auction a fortnight past. Rhys must have ridden from Wales for some other purpose — what might it have been? And why had he chosen to attend the auction, no less to buy her hand?

Rhys cleared his throat pointedly. "I did not share this news, for I thought you unconcerned with the ways of the mortal world."

Thomas flushed and grinned. "That does not mean that we have no interest in gossip. Rhys FitzHenry to be wed!" He laughed and shook a finger at Madeline. "You must be an intrepid lady to take such a ruffian as this to your side!"

"Thomas . . ." Rhys growled, but the monk ignored him.

Thomas leaned closer to Madeline, his manner conspiratorial. "Or are you, Lady Madeline, that uncommon manner of woman who sees the gold that the careless eye will perceive as dross?" Thomas winked mischievously and Madeline fought a smile, even as she considered Rhys anew.

What did the monk mean?

"There is little of merit in this world that reveals all of its value to a cursory glance," she said.

Thomas hooted with delight. "Indeed, indeed! I should have known that Rhys would be unafraid to wed a woman with her wits about her."

"He told me a fine tale while we rode here, and I am much appreciative of his kindness."

"A tale? Where did you find such a glib tongue, Rhys?" Thomas nudged Rhys, then said something that Madeline did not understand. He winked at her puzzled glance. "An old Welsh proverb, it was. 'The best Welshman is the one away from home.' That fits you well enough, does it not, Rhys? It is not often that you loose a measure of your meager charm."

Rhys glared at his friend and seemed at a loss for words.

Thomas leaned closer to Madeline, his manner that of a man practiced in selling goods to those who have no need or desire of them. "Truly, Lady Madeline, this one has tales of his own to tell, though he never does. Discretion is the second name of our Rhys . . ."

"As opposed to your own second name,

which is garrulous," Rhys muttered.

Madeline laughed, for their banter lightened her heart.

Thomas huffed, though his eyes yet sparkled. "Well, there is not a soul alive who will mistake me for a man struck to stone, as you are pretending to be this day."

"Much less a man struck dumb," Rhys retorted. "I thought you offered hospitality at these gates to those in need of it."

"Indeed, indeed." Thomas threw up his hands and laughed. "Forgive me! Come, Lady Madeline, come within the circle of our gates." Thomas claimed the reins of Rhys's destrier and spoke to it.

The creature immediately followed his bidding.

"How curious," Madeline said. "I thought Arian followed only Rhys's bidding."

Rhys said nothing, though his lips seemed to tighten.

"Is that the tale you were told?" Thomas demanded with glee. "What nonsense!" He gave Rhys a playful shove, then strode onward.

"How delightful it is to know when a man's word can be trusted," Madeline said, her voice so low that only Rhys heard her.

To her satisfaction, he seemed to avoid her gaze and the back of his neck turned ruddy. "The fiends even attacked her palfrey," he said to Thomas, indicating Tarascon's wound.

"Ah! Such wickedness!" Thomas was immediately concerned with the horse, talking to her and stroking her back as he murmured.

"Thomas is the ostler I mentioned," Rhys said to Madeline without glancing her way. "His talent is widely reputed."

Thomas led the palfrey toward the stables, his focus on the steed so complete that he might have forgotten the rest of the party. Tarascon seemed to understand that she had encountered one who would care for her. Her ears flicked less vigorously as Thomas spoke to her, and one last ripple passed over her flesh as she settled.

His seemed so uncommon an ability in such a place that Madeline could not hold her tongue. Indeed, there was not another horse to be seen, or any sign of one, in the abbey's courtyard. "But surely an abbey has little coin for the expense of horses?"

Rhys's smile flashed, the sight making Madeline's heart leap. "Our Thomas was a horse thief afore he took his vows."

"And you knew him then?"

Rhys nodded, his attention upon the other man. "We wasted our youths together, it is true."

Madeline was intrigued by the affection in his tone. She might have asked for more detail, but Rhys raised his voice. "There are more of us, Thomas, than simply one steed," he called. "And I do not think that wound so grievous."

Thomas jumped with guilt. "It is her fear which is the greater injury," he agreed. He smiled reassuringly for Madeline. "In a week or so, my lady, she will be hale again."

"I thank you for your assistance. She is a faithful steed and I was much distressed to see her injured, let alone so willfully."

"You speak aright, my lady. It is a wicked man who can inflict a wound upon a horse." Thomas called for a boy to aid him. That boy continued to stroke Tarascon as he led her toward the small empty stable.

The palfrey favored her leg, but her terror had been dismissed. Madeline realized that her own fears were similarly gone. She considered Rhys, as he watched the palfrey being led away, and admitted herself intrigued.

It might not be so foul a fate to wed so protective and competent a man as Rhys FitzHenry.

Or was that precisely what he wished her to believe?

Satisfied with the boy's efforts, Thomas turned his gaze upon the rest of the party. He frowned at the other destrier. "But what of this other steed? What need have you of a second stallion, Rhys?" Thomas asked, his hand landing upon Kerr's destrier. "I have never seen this beast before."

Madeline said nothing, for she was uncertain what Rhys meant to do about the beast. He clearly had a scheme for he stood more stiffly, his manner more alert. Had Thomas noted the difference in Rhys's posture?

Rhys shrugged, feigning indifference. "No need, to be sure."

"You did not buy it?"

Rhys shook his head. "It must have belonged to one of the bandits. We found it wandering where the lady was assaulted."

Madeline shivered. "That villain will have no need of it any longer."

"And I would not leave the beast to wander the moor, lest it become fodder for wolves."

Thomas nodded in understanding and ran his hands over the horse. "It is not a bad steed. Not poorly tended or fed." He granted Rhys a shrewd look over the steed's back. "A bit of a rich mount for a bandit, one would think. A destrier is a better mount for a warrior than a thief, given the thief's need for speed."

Madeline straightened, certain the truth would come out, but Rhys did not so much as blink. "He must have stolen it from another victim then."

"Indeed." Thomas watched Rhys, his eyes bright. "Do you mean to keep it?"

Rhys shook his head. "I owe you a boon, Thomas, for this visit and the last one. Sell it and put the coin in your community's coffers."

Madeline was astonished by his act of generosity. A destrier was worth a considerable measure of coin.

Thomas pursed his lips. "We could keep it for the abbess. She has a fondness for a good mount."

"Sell it," Rhys said, steel in his tone. "And the trap, as well."

Thomas straightened. Consideration lurked in his own gaze. "There is a good market for horses in Newcastle," he said with care, still stroking the beast, still watching Rhys. "And I must go to the moneylenders there at month-end for the abbess."

Rhys spoke in the same deliberate manner. "I hear the market is better in Carlisle."

"Oh no!" Madeline protested, wanting only to be of aid. Rhys was not from these parts, after all, and she knew he would want the abbey to fetch the best price for Kerr's steed. They must make the most of his generous gift! "I know that destriers fetch a far better price in Newcastle than in Carlisle. The king himself sends men there to acquire steeds and the market is most competitive."

Rhys appeared to be gritting his teeth. He granted Madeline a dark glance, then spoke with vigor. "Nonetheless, a beast of this size and hue will garner a better price in Carlisle."

Madeline shook her head, certain of her facts. "No, Rhys. I beg your pardon but you are not from these parts. My father bought only palfreys and ponies in Carlisle, for he said the stallion stock was poor there."

Rhys glared at her. "Perhaps your father erred, my lady."

Madeline parted her lips to argue but Rhys held her gaze with such heat that she knew he warned her to be silent. She closed her mouth with annoyance and glared at him in her turn.

What ailed the man? Did he not want the most made of his gift?

"I know Carlisle to be a better market for this beast," Rhys repeated firmly.

"Carlisle 'twill be, then," Thomas said, looking between the pair of them with interest. "Your counsel is always good, Rhys, though Carlisle *is* less convenient."

"I think it would be well worth the journey." Rhys seemed to be fighting his exasperation with the pair of them. What vexed him about Newcastle?

Then Madeline realized the truth. Newcastle was closer to Ravensmuir and Kinfairlie. Rhys did not want the horse recognized, for then retribution for Kerr's death could fall upon this abbey. It was entirely possible that no one would believe the mercenary had been killed by thieves, equally possible that Kerr's comrades might question that conclusion if his horse was spied.

If suspicion fell upon the abbey for having some involvement in the mercenary's death — or worse, if Kerr's fellow mercenaries demanded a vengeance of their own — that would be a poor reward to the abbey and its occupants for any favor they had shown to Rhys. His aunt was abbess, after all.

And she had nearly foiled his protective intent. Even now, Thomas was suspicious of the horse's origin, suspicious as he might not have been if she had kept her counsel to herself.

Rhys must think her a witless fool, so thoroughly did she err in his presence!

Rhys frowned. "The trap, however, might sell for a better price in York."

"A horse with trap always fetches a better price," Thomas said, amusement in his tone.

Rhys bent toward the older man, his manner intent. "Perhaps even Lincoln or Winchester would be good."

Thomas grinned. Mischief danced openly in his gaze now. "Why do you not save the horse, Rhys, and take it all the way to Wales to be sold? Surely the price will be better there?"

"Perhaps the gain would not be worth the risk."

Thomas chuckled and clapped the other man on the shoulder. "I welcome your advice, Rhys. Fear not, old friend, all shall be done as you counsel. I shall ensure that this horse is not recognized."

Madeline saw that Thomas had understood Rhys's intent all along, and had only teased him.

"Can you tell me more of who might recognize it?"

"It is better that you know less." Rhys spoke with such resolve that Thomas nodded.

Then the monk smiled. "Aye, you are protective of those you call your friends, of that no man can have a doubt. I hope you have espied this man's true nature, Lady Madeline, and not been deceived by his poor manners."

Madeline nodded. She had seen much of merit in her companion on this day.

Rhys folded his arms across his chest. "Perhaps the abbess might be summoned, that the lady could be aided as well."

"My lady, are you injured?" Thomas demanded with horror.

"She is stalwart, but has had a shock," Rhys said when Madeline might have demurred. "Summon the abbess if you will." He held Madeline's gaze with sudden determination. "I would ask another favor of the abbey, for I would have our nuptials celebrated here this very day."

Madeline blinked. Rhys still intended to wed her?

On this day?

"Here?" Thomas echoed in astonishment. "But what of the lady's family?"

"We cannot continue to Ravensmuir until the steed is healed."

"But they could come here," Madeline suggested. "Surely we could wait until they arrived from Ravensmuir?"

Rhys shook his head. "Surely, events of this day have shown that we dare wait no longer. We will be wed before nightfall, my lady, and send word to Ravensmuir in the morning, after our match is consummated."

With that, Rhys pivoted and strode toward the stables, leaving Madeline fuming at his commanding tone. He might have asked her opinion on the matter, instead of ordering her to do his bidding like a trained hound! Her anger must have shown, for Thomas touched a fingertip to her arm.

"I would remind you, Lady Madeline, that it is ill-advised to murder a man within the walls of a community pledged to God's work."

"Then I shall have to wait until we depart," Madeline said with sweet ferocity. "Doubtless the road is long and quiet to my lord husband's home."

Thomas laughed. "I have oft thought murder too fine a fate for some rogues, my lady. Let him live long, the better that you might plague him with your wit."

Madeline found herself smiling at the monk's counsel.

"There," Thomas said. "It is always a better omen if the bride is merry."

That reminder sobered Madeline utterly. She would be wed. And Rhys had made it clear that their match would be consummated this night. Given her experience of this day, that prospect filled her with a goodly quantity of dread.

It had not, perhaps, been the best way for Rhys to declare his desire and intent to wed Madeline.

Rhys brushed down his steed, cursing the fact that he had no abilities to summon sweet words for this woman's ears. Why could he not have been blessed with a silver tongue? Why was he so incapable of saying what nonsense a woman wished to hear? He could have eased Madeline's fears, but no, he had redoubled them. It had been brilliantly done.

So engrossed was Rhys in his task and his recriminations, that he did not notice Thomas's arrival until that man cleared his throat.

Rhys jumped and pivoted to find the other man leaning against the door of the stall. Gelert watched with interest, though the dog had already flattened himself a bed in the straw. The hound had become accustomed to this stable of late.

"Do you mean to change her thinking, then?" Thomas asked.

"I do not need your reminder that I know little of courting a noblewoman," Rhys said and turned back to his task.

"Perhaps you need a reminder that she can spurn you until the vows are exchanged." At Rhys's glance of alarm, Thomas smiled. "She could take the veil here, and you know it well."

The prospect sent a new thread of fear through Rhys. He had not considered that possibility. "My betrothed will never become a bride of Christ. It is not her nature." Rhys was not as convinced as his words might have sounded. Indeed, the lady had already shown her desire to evade wedding him by fleeing Ravensmuir.

The abbey had to offer a more alluring option than Kerr had presented. A cold hand closed around Rhys's heart and he brushed the horse down with renewed vigor.

Surely Madeline would not do as much?

But Rhys did not know and he dared not hope.

"Do not be so certain of your suit, old friend," Thomas said, offering no reassurance at all. "Women are a fickle and unpredictable lot. The abbess would be delighted to claim another noblewoman's soul for her community." Thomas nodded, making the prospect sound dangerously plausible to Rhys. "It can never hurt to have more coin in the coffers and more influence at court."

"Perhaps I should tell the abbess that the lady's family has neither coin nor influence." That was not strictly true, Rhys realized, for the Kinfairlie clan now had the coin he had paid for Madeline's hand.

"Kinfairlie have no coin? Are you mad?" Thomas gave a low whistle. "They are kin with the lot at Ravensmuir, who are auctioning a considerable cache of religious relics this week, are they not?"

"Indeed they are," Rhys agreed, seeing where this argument led.

Thomas amiably plucked the brush from Rhys's hand. "Leave the beast some flesh, Rhys." He shook the brush at Rhys. "Do you know what your aunt would do for a larger relic than the one currently in our chapel?"

Rhys stared at the stable floor grimly. "I dare not think about it." His aunt had taken the veil when widowed for the third time. She had survived not only those three husbands, but the bearing of eleven children and a civil war. Miriam had always been kind to him, but she had never had to choose between her own objectives and his own.

Rhys did not doubt that she would gladly trade his desires, if she knew that Caerwyn was in the balance, for her own ambitions.

"I would suggest that you do think about the matter, and do so quickly, or your bride may be traded for a fingerbone!" Thomas chided, then flung out his hands. "Why did you even bring the woman here? You should have ridden onward!"

But Madeline had been frightened and her palfrey had been wounded. Rhys had known that she had needed solace and the chance to recover from her ordeal — and he had thought no further than that.

It was unlike him to underestimate a threat like the one the abbey offered to a woman who did not desire to wed. Rhys exhaled and paced the length of the stable, admitting only to himself how Madeline's needs seemed to have overwhelmed all other details in his thoughts.

In truth, she had not been the sole one in need of a moment to recover after Kerr's assault.

"Your aunt will twist the lady to her will," Thomas insisted. "If you truly wish to wed her, then no good can come of your arrival here."

Rhys knew that well enough. "Perhaps I too should greet the abbess," he said, his tone revealing his lack of enthusiasm.

"If she lets you into her chambers."

Rhys looked up, angered at the prospect. "She will not stop me, not this day."

"There is the spirit you need!" Thomas grinned and brushed off Rhys's jerkin, like a squire preparing his knight for a battle. Rhys could not help but note that Thomas showed an overabundance of cheer, as if he anticipated that Rhys might lose this particular battle. "You should have a squire, Rhys, to ensure that you do not look like a ruffian," he chided.

"Squires talk overmuch. I would have my secrets be my own."

"Perhaps so, but I would advise you not to keep any desire you have for this bride a secret any longer. Women like sweet confessions, Rhys. One such might serve you well in this case."

Rhys frowned and glanced away from his friend. "And I am to take counsel in courting a woman from a monk."

Thomas laughed. "I was not tonsured from the cradle. You, of all men, should know as much."

"Aye, you took your vows to avoid the claims of all your bastard children."

Thomas laughed again, though Rhys's comment was not that far from the truth. "You can show a certain rough charm when you so desire, Rhys," the monk insisted. "If wedding this woman is of import to you, then you might summon a bit of that charm. You will need the lady's endorsement if you mean to thwart the ambitions of our abbess."

That, Rhys knew, was true enough.

"Tell her a tale of love redeemed, or one thwarted and reclaimed. You are better with a tale than a compliment."

That was also true.

But Rhys knew that there was no love betwixt himself and Madeline. He had bought her hand, no more than that, and if he confessed to having tender feelings for her, the lady would not believe him. Madeline was no fool.

Regrettably, his aunt Miriam's eye was cursedly sharp, and she too would note the lack of affection between them. He scowled at the floor, uncertain what he could say in his own defense.

"Tell her of Caerwyn," Thomas suggested, ever helpful. "Women like to know a man's intent for them."

Caerwyn! If Miriam guessed the truth of it, if Madeline truly was his cousin's daughter and thus the potential heir of Caerwyn in her own right, there was far more than a fingerbone at stake.

Miriam could demand Caerwyn as a donation, and that castle would be lost to Rhys forevermore. Rhys's blood ran cold. He cursed, shoved a hand through his hair, and strode to the abbess's chamber with new purpose.

For Caerwyn, he would utter whatever words were necessary to make Madeline his bride. He would find them, somehow.

He dared do no less.

Chapter Seven

The silence of the abbey closed around Madeline like a shroud.

Everything within the abbey was wrought in hues of white: the walls were whitewashed and the nuns wore identical garb of undyed linen. Veils covered their hair and wimples covered their throats, only their hands and faces — which were all pale — were revealed, even to each other. A faint melodic chant from the chapel carried through the tranquil corridors, the sound muted and bleak instead of celebratory. Even the sunlight that slanted through the high windows seemed as pale as milk.

The bells at the gate would seem to be out of character. Madeline wondered whether Thomas was responsible for their very presence.

As she followed a nun to a small chamber where she could refresh herself, Madeline had the eerie sense that she walked among the dead. And truly, these women were dead to their families and to the mortal world beyond these walls. They had entered divine service to become closer to God and were thus cloistered from the many distractions of the mortal world.

When first Madeline had left the courtyard, the tranquility of this place had soothed her annoyance with Rhys. But by the time she had washed the filth from her skin and trimmed her nails, combed and braided her hair, the silence had begun to annoy her.

Madeline was accustomed to the barely contained chaos of Kinfairlie and the volume of seven boisterous siblings. Silence was not to be trusted, for it made her suspect that someone plotted a jest against her. So it had always been at Kinfairlie; silence warned a soul to be wary.

At any moment, Malcolm might leap from some unanticipated hiding place to make her yelp in surprise. Or Ross would sneak up behind her while she donned her kirtle and drop some slithering creature down her chemise. Madeline pulled this undyed kirtle hastily over her head then glanced over her shoulder, but Ross was not there.

The meek nun who was evidently her custodian stared into space, with no curiosity about Madeline or her manner at all. She might have been a corpse, standing at the portal. Madeline turned her back upon the girl.

Alexander had always planned more elaborate jests, like the time he had fanned smoke into the chamber that his sisters shared, then shouted "FIRE!". Madeline smiled at the sight they must have made, all five of them screaming as they fled into the bailey in no more than their chemises. The entire prank had delighted the squires and stableboys of Kinfairlie, while Alexander had been too convulsed with laughter to fully appreciate what he had wrought.

At least until their father had heard tell of his deeds. Alexander had sat gingerly for a week.

Madeline laced the sides of the plain kirtle, her smile fading. Those had been happy days indeed, but now her parents were dead. Malcolm and Ross had been dispatched to train as knights, her beloved James was lost, and Alexander had played the cruelest jest upon her of all.

Madeline was alone as she had never been alone in all her days and nights, and she did not care a whit for it.

The wooden comb clattered as Madeline

put it down. No, Madeline decided, she did not merely distrust silence. She loathed it. It was unnatural for people to live in such quietude. She decided not to don the wimple and veil left for her, for she was not a member of this community. As a maiden, she had the right to wear her hair uncovered.

Madeline recalled suddenly the weight upon her neck and realized that she was not utterly alone. She still had the token left to her by her mother, the Tear of the Virgin.

She lifted the velvet sack out of the front of her chemise. She picked a bit of dried mud from it, and unknotted the cord with some trepidation. She did not know what to expect of it, not after it had been so dark the night before.

But its prediction was less clear to her now than it had been last evening. Had the Tear of the Virgin anticipated her flight, and predicted only the woe she had endured at Kerr's hand? Or had its warning been a prediction for her match with Rhys?

There was but one way to know. Madeline let the stone slip into her palm, though she quickly closed her fingers over it. She kissed her clenched fist, whispered a prayer, then opened her hand.

At first she thought the gem was as dark as before, but then she spied a gleam of light deep within it. Madeline lifted her hand so that she could see the stone better. A small golden star seemed trapped within the stone, much as she was trapped by the few choices before her. She turned the gem this way and that: Though the star remained, it neither grew larger nor smaller.

The fact that it was present meant that there was hope.

Or at least, that there was more hope for Madeline than there had been last evening.

She put the gem back into the velvet sack with a frown and supposed she would have to content herself with that.

The young nun who accompanied Madeline to the abbess seemed to be at peace with her choice to enter the cloister. Indeed, she exuded a tranquility that Madeline knew she would never feel herself. The nun halted at the portal to the chamber occupied by the abbess, then stood silently, waiting for the abbess to note their presence.

The abbess was an older woman, in the midst of writing. The only sound was the scratch of her nib against the vellum. She seemed blissfully unaware of the two women awaiting her attention.

Madeline looked between the pair of them and realized that the young nun would wait quite contentedly forever, if it took that long for the abbess to become aware of them. Madeline was not so submissive as her companion. She cleared her throat, and stepped forward when the abbess glanced up in surprise.

She felt the shock of the girl beside her and did not care.

"Good day. I greet you and thank you for your hospitality this day," she said, advancing into the chamber. "I am Madeline Lammergeier of Kinfairlie. Doubtless you have already heard of my arrival here."

The abbess's smile was not immediate. In fact, the older woman seemed to take the measure of Madeline at her leisure before she spoke.

"I have indeed heard the tale," she said finally, then rose to her feet with the grace of a duchess. She flicked the barest glance at the young nun behind Madeline. "That will suffice, Sister Theresa. I bid you return to your prayers."

There was a whisper of leather slippers against the stone floor as the young nun slipped away, then that cursed silence assailed Madeline's ears once more.

The abbess surveyed Madeline, her gaze so shrewd that Madeline doubted there was much news this woman did not hear. The slender angles of her figure were evident despite the full cut of her gown and the wimple and veil that framed her face. Her eyes were a faded blue, though her avid gaze undoubtedly missed no detail, however trivial.

Madeline would not like to be a foe of this woman.

"You are far from Kinfairlie, child," the abbess said, crossing the room with the leisure of a cat stalking its prey. She halted before Madeline, that incisive gaze all the more forceful at such close proximity.

"Indeed I am." Madeline fought the urge to blink.

She started when the abbess abruptly flicked the cloth of her kirtle away from her throat. "Did Rhys FitzHenry do this to you?" The abbess flicked a finger across Madeline's throat, the tingle telling her that there was a bruise upon her flesh.

"Quite the opposite. I was attacked by a bandit." Madeline was certain that it was better to say less to this woman than more. "I survived the villain's assault because Rhys FitzHenry killed him."

The abbess was clearly unsurprised by

this detail, though she arched a silver brow. "And the price of Rhys's intervention is marriage?"

Madeline felt herself flush. "We were betrothed afore."

"How curious that I did not know of it."

"We were betrothed but yesterday."

A faint smile of triumph touched the abbess's lips before she pivoted to stroll across the chamber. "Yet this very morn, you were far from Kinfairlie and either alone or so poorly defended that a bandit could threaten your life." She glanced over her shoulder, eyes glinting. "The Rhys I know takes better care of what he holds to be of value."

Madeline's face heated yet more, for she was a poor liar. "The details of my woes are surely not of import."

The abbess considered her for a moment, then gestured that Madeline should take a seat. She trailed her fingertips across the top of the table, then spoke so idly that Madeline knew her question would be of import. "Do you know Rhys well?"

"Not at all." Madeline smiled politely. "Though that is hardly uncommon for a betrothed maiden."

The abbess inclined her head in agreement. "Of course not. Though I do know

Rhys rather well, as he is my nephew. It is curious to me that Rhys would choose to wed with such . . . impatience. He is, in my experience, a man who considers his every deed with great care."

"Nonetheless, I tell no falsehood about our agreement."

The abbess studied Madeline, who resolutely said no more. "There were rumors of a strange auction at Ravensmuir yesterday. Are those at Ravensmuir not the kin of your family at Kinfairlie?"

"My uncle is the Laird of Ravensmuir."

The abbess nodded. "The same laird who permitted the auction of one of his nieces as a bride, the same laird whose niece sits afore me, telling me that she does not know the man she is abruptly pledged to wed."

Madeline said nothing, for she could not guess the older woman's intent. She knew solely that she did not trust her.

The abbess seemed to find her response — or lack of it — amusing. "You may keep your secrets, child, but I shall make you a wager." She braced her hands on the table, her eyes bright. "You surely know that you have come to the one place that might offer you sanctuary. You cannot wish to wed a stranger, no less one charged with treason by the king himself."

The abbess's eyes shone as she leaned closer. "Pledge to join this abbey and you need not exchange vows with Rhys FitzHenry. Become a bride of Christ, Madeline, instead of the wife of a warrior, and save your immortal soul."

Madeline was not tempted by the prospect of coming beneath this woman's authority, but she could not quickly think of a way to diplomatically decline. She marvelled instead that she was more afraid of this abbess than she was of Rhys.

"Aunt Miriam, is it not impolite for you to try to dissuade my betrothed from wedding me?"

Madeline spun to find Rhys leaning against the portal. Her heart leapt with a strange joy at the very sight of him. His eyes were darker than they had been and his mood seemed foul. He looked larger in this sanctuary, darker and more dangerous amidst the white walls and undyed cloth. His hands were propped upon his hips, his demeanor formidable, and Madeline had a sudden urge to taste his demanding kiss once more.

It was more than the hue of his garb, or even his gender, that made him look out of place. Rhys's very presence shattered the tranquility here. He brought a whiff of the outside world, of war and death and passion, that enlivened the chamber more than the serene music and rays of sunlight could.

Madeline knew that this was why his presence was so very welcome. She thought of his demand for sons and knew that he would not be sated with one or two. Rhys's home would be filled with the noise to which she was accustomed.

Madeline knew in that moment what her choice would be. She could not imagine a worse fate than being sealed within these walls for all of her remaining days and nights. She would rather live each moment to the fullest, even if that meant accepting uncertainty, than pass her days in such tranquil seclusion.

If she put her hand in that of Rhys FitzHenry, Madeline wagered that she would have adventure and passion aplenty, as well as the protection of a formidable man. Perhaps Vivienne's notion had not been such folly; perhaps Madeline might clear the stain from her husband's name. From what she had seen of Rhys, she could not imagine that he had betrayed his liege lord, for faithlessness seemed a crime beyond all to him.

The abbess smiled briefly. "You should not feel so welcome as to come to my chamber, nephew. I have indulged you overmuch in this place."

"I would have come in this moment with your indulgence or nay. My betrothed and her welfare is of greater import to me than any condemnation you might utter." Rhys smiled at Madeline, the very sight making her pulse race. "How do you fare, my lady fair? Have you sufficiently recovered from events of this morn?"

He was suddenly so courteous and charismatic that Madeline did not know what to say.

"Are *you* well?" she whispered.

Rhys chuckled, claimed her hand and laid a kiss upon her knuckles. "Better now that I see you again."

Who was this man? Had Rhys been struck in the head? He watched her over her knuckles, and she frowned at him. Why did he not simply tell her what was amiss?

He tightened his grip upon her fingers and his lips tightened with what might have been displeasure. "Is it so difficult to believe that I have yearned for the sight of your smile in your absence?"

Madeline parted her lips to confess that

it was, then realized that the abbess watched their exchange with keen interest. She put her hand over Rhys's and smiled. "I am but surprised that you make such sweet confessions in the presence of another."

Rhys straightened and pulled Madeline closer to him. She fairly stood within the circle of his arms, though he continued to merely hold her hands. "It is charming that you are so shy, though our affection cannot always remain a private matter between us." Rhys caressed her hand with his fingertips. "Once we are wed, all will expect to witness our joy in each other's company."

He bent and inexplicably brushed his lips across her brow. Madeline did not know what to say or do, she was so astonished by his courtly manner.

The abbess spoke firmly to Madeline, though her gaze did not waver from Rhys. "Do not let Rhys force you into a match you do not desire, child. You have fled him once and come to a haven. I do not deny that he is a forceful man and I do not deny that men have their allure."

The abbess looked then at Madeline. "But earthly temptation and its satisfactions are fleeting, and I can be as vigilant in defending those beneath my care as any man. Choose the veil and I will defend you even from my own nephew."

"And all this you would do for the reward of the smallest relic from Ravensmuir's hoard," Rhys added quietly. His eyes were narrowed, his usual skeptical manner restored, though still he did not release Madeline's hand.

The abbess's eyes flashed. "Do not place a price upon good will!"

"Not even when it has one?"

The abbess's nostrils flared and Madeline spoke with care. "You would not be the first to offer some favor in exchange for a relic from Ravensmuir's hoard. Perhaps you should know that access to its treasures is not mine to grant."

The abbess scoffed. "Surely you could persuade your uncle to make a donation for the good of his immortal soul?"

"And the sustenance of you in this abbey in this life," Rhys amended wryly.

"Whatsoever my uncle does with his inheritance is his choice, not mine."

"Well spoken, my lady."

The abbess flushed as she lost her temper. "You are impertinent, Rhys, as always you have been! I bid you begone from this abbey!"

"I will begone on the morrow," he said

calmly. "After my bride and I exchange our vows and consummate our match."

"Not within the walls of this abbey!"

"You have a priest and a chapel, which suits me well."

The abbess shook a finger at her nephew. "You are a rogue and a man who finds trouble whether he seeks it or nay. You will lead this woman to woe; I know the truth of it."

Rhys shook his head, untroubled by his aunt's condemnation. "And you forget, Aunt, that I know you save your harshest words for those who defy your will." He granted Madeline a piercing glance. "Prepare yourself for an onslaught of cruel words, my lady, afore you decline her offer."

"No woman of sense would deny me!" The abbess flung out her hand. "What have you to offer a bride, Rhys? A life at the side of a man with no abode, a man hunted by the king himself?"

"Caerwyn," Rhys said softly, his grip on Madeline's hand tightening anew. He uttered the word with all the reverence of a benediction. "My bride will be the Lady of Caerwyn, as I am its lord."

"Caerwyn!" the abbess retorted. "You may dream all you choose, but you do not hold that fortress as your own!"

Rhys might have been wrought of stone. He spoke with quiet vigor, though his eyes snapped with fire. "Aye, I do. And thus I have need of a bride, and thus I have chosen one."

"You do not have to accept this," the abbess said angrily to Madeline. "You do not have to believe this fanciful tale. Choose, child! Choose sin or the veil."

But Rhys's words gave Madeline an inkling of how he could have been named a traitor by England's land-hungry king. "Is this holding yours in truth?" she asked.

Rhys nodded. "By Welsh law and custom, it comes fully to my hands upon our nuptials."

The abbess frowned, her manner becoming intent. "But . . ."

Madeline interrupted her firmly, not trusting whatsoever the older woman might say. She understood the choice before her, and understood that it truly was not a choice. It was not within her to retire from the mortal world and become a bride of Christ. She could not return to Kinfairlie, given that she had been alone with Kerr and Rhys this day. Rumor would destroy her reputation. And she could not wed the man she had chosen herself.

Rhys had paid the price for her hand and proven his intent to defend her. He had a home and a title. She would judge him by his deeds, not his shadowed repute.

"I will make an agreement with you, Rhys."

He inclined his head to hers. "Name it."

"You say you have need only of sons." Madeline was well aware of the abbess's gaze flicking between them. "There must be more between us than that. I offer you my loyalty in exchange for your honesty. Whatsoever occurs, Rhys, I will never betray your trust. I ask only that you keep no secrets from me."

"And sons?"

Madeline nodded, her mouth dry. "As many as God has the grace to grant to us."

Rhys's smile flashed with such sudden brilliance that Madeline blinked. "There is a wager no man could refuse." Before she could speak, he cupped the back of her head in his hand and bent to kiss her so thoroughly that she was left dizzy.

His kiss teased and tempted, it cajoled her to join him. Madeline closed her eyes and surrendered to his touch, wondering whether his passion was wrought of relief or a desire to reassure her about their wedding night.

In truth, she did not care.

When he finally lifted his head, the abbess made a sound of disgust. Madeline could not look away from Rhys, though, nor could she seem to draw a full breath. His eyes glimmered with satisfaction and humor, and that smile lifted the corner of his firm lips.

"Call your priest, Aunt," Rhys said with purpose.

"This will not be done in my abbey!"

"Aye, it will." Rhys granted the abbess a grim glance. "There will be no questions, Aunt, and no suspicions. Our marriage will be consummated this very night, with your blessing, and you will witness the mark upon the linens."

He was so determined that Madeline wondered. Why was it of such import to Rhys that their match have no chance of being annulled?

Something had changed; Miriam knew it well. She had seen enough of the world before retiring to this convent to know that men like her nephew did not suddenly rechart their course. A mere fortnight past, Rhys had had no intent of wedding. It made no sense that he now professed such a vigorous desire for this bride.

Even if he had bought her hand at that auction, Miriam could not understand why he had even offered a bid. To be sure, Madeline was a beauty, but Rhys was not the manner of man swayed by a pretty smile — and he had not known the woman long enough to be certain of her character.

And Caerwyn! If Rhys had secured his claim to Caerwyn a fortnight past, he would have crowed his triumph from the rooftops. She knew how much he desired that holding, knew how often his attempt to secure it had been foiled.

What could have changed in his days here, near Scotland's borders? What had he sought here?

And what had he found?

The puzzle missed a piece. Miriam liked to understand how matters fit together, why people made the choices that they did. She told herself that she had need of this knowledge to better guide her charges, but the truth was that the only element of the mortal world that she missed was gossip.

She watched the sun set, tapping her fingertips upon the window sill. The wedding ceremony had been unremarkable, as barren an exchange of pledges as she could have offered to this pair. It had dissuaded neither of them from their course, but then, Miriam had not expected it to do so.

They were stubborn, both of them. She shook her head, recalling this Madeline's outspoken manner. She would have made a poor nun, at any rate. Perhaps she and Rhys deserved each other.

Had Rhys fallen in love, as abruptly as some fool in a troubador's tale? Knowing him as the stern warrior he was, Miriam could not imagine as much.

She drummed her fingers again, knowing she missed some detail that might grant her a clue. Thomas undoubtedly knew more than he had confessed to her, but that wily monk was cursedly difficult to interrogate. He would tease her with his more fulsome knowledge but surrender no crumb of information in the end.

Miriam's fingers halted suddenly. Why had Rhys been here a fortnight past? She had offered him sanctuary in the hope of gaining news, but he had had a mission of some kind, and he had been characteristically close with the details.

He and Thomas were of a kind, that was for certain.

But Miriam's sister would either know or she could be prompted to unearth the truth. They did not have a strong bond beyond blood, Rhys's mother and Miriam, for there were too many years between them, but they shared a taste for knowing other people's concerns. Adele would pry the truth from Rhys, one way or the other, if she did not know it already.

Miriam smiled, anticipating that her sister probably did not know that her son was a wedded man — how could she? — and that Miriam could be the one to offer this delicious tidbit of news to her sibling. It could not hurt to put Adele in her debt in terms of information shared.

Miriam chose a relatively unused sheet of vellum, dipped her quill and began to write a missive to her sister. A runner could leave with the dawn and soon, soon she would know the truth.

Whatever store of charm Rhys might have possessed had obviously been exhausted during that interview in his aunt's presence. The exchange of their nuptial vows had been cursory, at best, the priest distracted, and Rhys feared that Madeline might be sorely disappointed in the ritual they had been granted.

Afterward, Rhys stood in the chamber he and Madeline had been allotted, astounded that she truly had pledged to be his wife, and was completely uncertain how to proceed.

He knew what had to happen, of course, and he knew how to do the deed itself, but he had never met a virgin abed. To be sure, he had never coupled with a woman when there was so much at stake.

Madeline could still spurn him. She could refuse his affections or dislike his touch. She could be fearful or cold. She could find him rough and unsavory, ill-mannered or coarse. This amorous encounter could proceed very badly.

That Rhys was so anxious that all go well did little to ease his trepidation. How much did Madeline know of such matters? What had she been told? He watched Madeline light the candles and found her composed manner difficult to interpret. He thought that she carried the flame from one candle to the next with unnecessary care, and wondered whether she too was uncertain.

She lit every candle in the chamber, then extinguished the piece of kindling she had used to light them with the same thoroughness. She blew out the flame, dipped the kindling in a pail of water, then plunged it into sand. She looked about the chamber, as if seeking some other duty to perform, but it was sparsely furnished.

Madeline turned to face Rhys only then,

only when she had no choice. She clasped her hands together before herself, but not so quickly that Rhys did not see them tremble. She seemed to take a deep breath before she offered him a thin smile.

And then Rhys knew what he must do.

He gave a deliberate glance over the contents of the whitewashed chamber, hoping his manner was that of a man utterly at ease. There was but a narrow pallet on the floor, the candles and a wooden carving of Christ in agony hanging upon the wall. The artist had shown a particular interest in the more grisly details, and Rhys did not doubt that his aunt had deliberately chosen this room for them with the crucifix in mind.

He would not be deterred by so obvious a ploy.

He shook his head, as if bemused. "I never imagined that I would be wed in an abbey."

Madeline laughed, her merriment of short duration. "Nor I," she said, her eyes widening as she stared at him. She swallowed visibly and began to twist the plain silver ring he had so recently moved from his finger to her own. It was as if its newfound weight plagued her, as if its burden upon her finger only now reminded her of what she had sworn to do.

Rhys felt protective of his new wife then, and doubly determined to ensure that this night was one of pleasure for her. He crossed the chamber and stood before the crucifix. "Truth be told, I would feel less like a man sinning in church if we had no audience." He glanced at Madeline for approval. "It but hangs on a nail, my lady, and can be laid upon the sill for a while, if you share my thought."

Madeline nodded hastily. "I would prefer that." She crossed herself as Rhys lifted the sculpture from the wall and seemed to heave a sigh of relief when it was laid aside. "Rhys, I know that you have the right to do whatsoever you will this night, but . . ."

He crossed the floor, watching how her breath hastened as he drew near, and laid a finger across her lips to silence her. "My right is of less import on this night than my duty."

She regarded him quizzically. "I do not understand."

"A man has many duties to his bride, the most important of which is not writ in the law of any land."

"What duty is this?"

Rhys lifted the end of her braid in his

hand and concentrated fully upon loosening the knot in the tie that held it bound. "I owe you pleasure abed on this night of nights. We will have no other nuptial night together, so memories must be wrought of this one." He met her gaze. "I would have them be fond memories."

"As would I."

He worked his fingers through the dark silk of her hair, delighted that it curled around his fingers like the tendrils of a possessive vine. He spread it across her shoulders with care and she did not seem to breathe. He kept his voice low and even, for he knew she had need of reassurance. "What do you know of this deed, my lady? I would not surprise you."

"Little enough," she admitted with a shrug. "Save the lewd tales one hears in the kitchens. And I have seen horses, of course."

He eased the last of the braid from the hair at her nape, then pressed a kiss to the soft flesh beneath her ear. She caught her breath, but did not move away. Rhys ran a fingertip down her throat in a gentle caress, then turned his attention to the laces on the sides of her kirtle.

"I heard it oft hurts the first time," Madeline said suddenly.

Rhys nodded. "I have heard the same." He unfastened the lace and drew it from the eyelets, pondering his course. He could not pledge to halt if she was hurt, not on this night. "We shall have to endeavor to ensure otherwise," he said, then removed the second lace as he had the first. Her kirtle hung open on the sides now, and he slipped his hands beneath it, lifting it over her head and casting it aside.

The rough garment, even though some-what fitted, had not begun to do her justice. He could discern her curves beneath the sheer linen chemise and her beauty left him speechless. She was tall, his lady wife, and wrought with slender strength. Her breasts were full, her nipples dark through the linen and pertly erect.

"You are beautiful," he whispered, hearing the awe in his voice. He cupped one of her breasts in his hand, the linen an irksome barrier to her flesh. He loosed the tie at the neck of the garment, then eased the linen aside. She wore some token around her neck, trapped as it was in a velvet sack, and he did not risk removing it. Who knew what it might be?

Instead, he slipped his hand beneath the chemise and could not believe her softness. "Softer than a rose petal," he murmured, then bent and kissed her nipple.

Madeline caught her breath. He proceeded with gentle determination until she sighed, until she softened, until she clutched at his hair.

Rhys halted with an effort and leaned his brow upon her shoulder. "I would not hasten you. I would not remind you of Kerr," he said thickly.

"I doubt that you could," she whispered.

He looked and noted the stars glittering in her eyes.

"You are so gentle, Rhys." She smiled at him. "You ask, you do not demand, and it makes all the difference."

They shared a smile that heated his blood and he resolved to continue asking, to ask all the night long if she would let him do so. He bent and kissed her other nipple, liking well how she caught her breath again, as if surprised by the pleasure he granted. Madeline arched her back and moaned softly, that sound and the taut peak of her nipple telling Rhys that she was pleased.

She whispered his name. He chose to take that as an invitation and trailed slow kisses up her throat. He encircled her ear with tiny kisses, taking a thousand years to reach her lips. She gasped and began to rub her breasts against him. He loved how she wound her fingers into his hair, how she made little sounds of pleasure. He slipped his thumb over the fluttering pulse in her throat and held her fast against him.

When he finally captured her lips, she opened her mouth immediately to him. To his delight and astonishment, her tongue touched his, tentatively at first, then with increasing demand. Her fingers locked into his hair, she pulled him closer and Rhys was lost.

His restraint was banished by her willing participation, by her sweet softness matched with passion. His intent to be cautious was vanquished and he drew her hard against his chest. Madeline met him touch for touch, her kisses as fervid as his own. He caught her buttocks in his hands and drew her heat against him, lifting her off her feet and letting her feel her effect upon him.

Madeline broke her kiss suddenly and Rhys was ashamed to realize that he had been close to simply claiming her. She did not seem to be disgusted with him, though. Her cheeks were flushed and her eyes sparkling, her breath came quickly. "I never knew that kissing could give such pleasure."

"You have seen but the half of it." He set

her upon her feet and took a deep breath.

Madeline poked his boiled leather jerkin playfully. "And I have seen none of you, sir. Do you mean to meet me abed in your armor?"

"Is that an invitation?"

She lifted her chin with admirable spirit. "I am curious, Rhys, and we are wedded in truth. Surely you intend to sate my curiosity?" The proposition in her sapphire gaze was one that no man with blood in his veins could refuse.

Rhys FitzHenry had blood in his veins.

Chapter Eight

Rhys undressed with unholy haste, holding Madeline's gaze all the while. He hoped that she did not change her thinking on this matter. He unbuckled his belt and laid his sword upon the floor with care, then unlaced his jerkin and cast it aside.

Madeline's cheeks grew pinker with every item of clothing he discarded, though she did not look away. Indeed, she surveyed him with such curiosity that he dared to hope events might proceed well. Rhys shed his tall boots, pulled his shirt and then his chemise over his head, and paused only when he stood before his wife in no more than his chausses.

She arched a brow, looking suddenly mischievous. "I would wager that you will have to shed those, as well."

"It is time enough that I had assistance."

She flushed scarlet, but as he anticipated, she did not shy away. His heart fairly burst with pride when she closed the distance between them and her hand landed upon the lace of his chausses. She was intrepid, this bride he had claimed; she faced her fears with a valor he could appreciate.

"There are those who do not like bold women," Madeline said.

"There are those who value women who are courageous." Rhys smiled at her. "I count myself in their ranks."

She smiled though the redness of her cheeks did not diminish. "Then perhaps we have wed well, Rhys FitzHenry. My forthright manner was oft considered a liability, until now."

She stepped closer and he caught his breath when she claimed the end of one lace. She held his gaze, her own a violent sapphire, and slowly pulled the laces out of his chausses. His erection pushed the heavy wool aside, so desirous was he of this tempting woman. She glanced down and her valor seemed to desert her.

"There is no need for haste." Rhys eased her hair behind her ear with a gentle fingertip. Madeline swallowed and summoned a smile, then slipped her hands into his chausses and eased them over his hips. The feel of her fingertips on his flesh coaxed the heat beneath Rhys's flesh to a raging flame. He impatiently kicked the garment aside and stood nude before her, half certain he would lose control beneath her gaze.

He thought she might flee then, for it seemed to cost her dearly to hold her ground. He wondered how far matters had proceeded with Kerr and feared it had been too much for her, but his lady squared her shoulders. Her eyes snapped with such determination that he knew he did not have to tell her that this deed was of import.

"I choose this," she said with vigor and looked him in the eye. "I choose you, Rhys, to be my lawfully wedded spouse."

He was proud of her, but had no chance to tell her as much.

For the lady, against all expectation, touched him.

Rhys's blood thundered in his ears, so astonished and aroused was he. He stood like a man turned to stone, not daring to move lest she be frightened. Her fingers explored him timidly, then with greater boldness, teasing and caressing. He did not know whether she knew how she tormented him, but he knew that he would spill his seed in her hands if this continued.

"Madeline," he said, fairly growling her name.

"This gives you pleasure," she said, that wicked glint in her eye again. "I shall have to remember as much."

Rhys could resist her no longer. "With good fortune, there will be much to remember of this night." He claimed the end of the tie holding the neck of her chemise.

She trembled suddenly, not so bold as she had appeared, and he deliberately slowed his pace. He tugged the tie from the chemise one increment at a time. She held her breath, her eyes wide as she stared at him.

Time seemed to halt and there was nothing beyond this chamber, nothing beyond the blue of Madeline's eyes and the soft curve of her lips.

The tie slipped loose from the chemise and the garment fluttered over Madeline's shoulders. She did not try to halt its descent, merely let it fall to pool around her ankles in a gossamer puddle. She straightened, aware of her nudity and his gaze, and Rhys did not hide his admiration.

"Beautiful," he whispered, and when she smiled, he caught her close. He kissed her, waiting for her to join his embrace, then deepened his kiss when she did so. When she twined her arms around his neck and opened her mouth to him with a soft sigh, he lifted her in his arms and laid her down on the pallet without breaking his embrace.

Only then did he slip his fingers between

her thighs, his heart leaping at the slick heat he found there. He caressed her, holding her captive beneath his kiss and his teasing fingers. He coaxed her to a tide of pleasure and Madeline followed his lead without hesitation.

Indeed, Rhys's chest tightened at the trust she showed in him. It was not long before Madeline writhed, she gasped, she pulled his weight partly over her. He felt her breasts pressed against his chest, that small velvet sack caressing his skin when it was trapped between them. He felt her flesh heat as he summoned the climax from deep within her.

"Rhys!" She parted her legs further and he slipped one thigh between her own. Her hips began to buck, her kiss grew more frenzied and then the lady Madeline convulsed beneath his hand.

She broke their kiss and shouted fit to wake the dead, her nails digging into his back. Her hair was wild against the linens, her lips were swollen from his kisses and her eyes were filled with stars.

When she caught her breath, she regarded him with amazement and whispered his name with awe. There were tears upon her cheeks, and he eased them away with his thumb.

"That did not hurt," she finally managed to say.

"We are not yet finished." Rhys eased his weight between her thighs and saw her eyes widen when she felt his heat against her softness. He let his thumb caress her again and the tension eased from her shoulders.

She smiled at him and took a deep breath. "Show me, Rhys. I would learn of all the deed this night."

Rhys moved with care, fighting his desire to bury himself in her sweet heat. Madeline caught her breath as he entered her, and he paused to caress her again. He was fairly bursting with the need to possess her, yet aware that this night could poison all the others they would share.

Rhys fought for restraint. He struggled to be worthy of her sweet trust. He closed his eyes and leaned his brow upon the pillow beside her, welcoming the calming stroke of her hand upon the back of his neck. He eased a little deeper and she caught her breath, her kiss landing upon his ear.

"Finish what we have begun, Rhys," she whispered, her other hand landing upon his buttocks. He turned his head, knowing he was large enough to injure her, and kissed her. His kiss was gentle, an attempt to express an admiration that he could not fully explain in words. He swallowed her gasp, her welcoming heat and sweet kiss making him dizzy.

And he kept his thumb between them, coaxing her response anew even as he sought his own release. She quickened beneath him, as he had guessed that she would, and he resolved to wait for her to find her release again.

Though he knew it might well kill him. He watched her pleasure mount, felt her pulse race, and the sight of her arousal nigh undid him.

And when she cried out, he felt like a champion. No sooner had Madeline clutched his shoulders again than Rhys fairly exploded within her heat. Satisfaction swelled his heart that he had claimed Madeline as his bride for all eternity.

It was some time before Rhys recalled that with this deed, he had also secured his suzerainty of Caerwyn.

Madeline had never guessed that people found such pleasure abed. To be sure, there had been some pain, but the delight Rhys had summoned with his fingertips had made it easy to endure.

And in future, she hoped that she would have no pain.

Indeed, this coupling left her with a splendid sense of contentment. She smiled as she stroked Rhys's dark hair. He yet lay partly atop her as he dozed against her shoulder. His release had exhausted him, it was clear, though Madeline did not mind. She liked having the opportunity to study him, and found him far less daunting while he slept.

To be sure, Rhys was wrought more formidably than she had imagined. It was not armor alone that made his chest look so broad, nor was it his boots that made him stand so tall. His skin was tanned and covered in places with a dark tangle of curly hair; his muscled strength was considerable. There were scars upon his flesh, scars from battle wounds long healed. He was vigorous and virile.

And he was her wedded spouse. He had been tender with her, despite his evident desire, and he had pursued her pleasure as diligently as his own. Though she had initially been fearful that Kerr's way was the sole way, she was glad beyond all that she had found the fortitude to learn the truth. Rhys did not mind that she was curious, nor that she touched him of her own volition, nor that she welcomed his passion with her own. And he had not been censo-rious in those moments when her valor abandoned her.

Rhys was not James, to be sure, and he would never be the gentle-mannered man that James had been, but there was merit in this man she had wed. Madeline watched her fingers slip through his hair and considered that her match was made well enough.

She might never love Rhys as she had loved James, and Rhys might never love her, but she already felt a certain affection for her gruff spouse. It was no small thing that he appreciated her as she was, that he ensured her safety with such vigor, that he courted mutual pleasure abed with such enthusiasm.

Madeline might even find a certain con-tentment with this warrior. The prospect made her smile broaden just as Rhys opened his eyes. He regarded her for a mo-ment with the same reverence that had lit his eyes when he had removed her kirtle, then his lips curved slightly.

"You are pleased?"

Madeline nodded, feeling herself flush.

He propped himself upon on his elbow, removing his weight from her with an apology. He was yet close beside her, seeming larger and warmer now that he had awakened. He looked disheveled as she had never seen him, almost boyish. The slow smile that kindled a heat in his gaze was not boyish, however, and made her tingle in recollection of what they had just done. "And did it hurt?"

Madeline shrugged. "A little, though the pleasure was worth the price." She touched the marks her nails had left upon his back. "Did this hurt?"

He spared the marks no more than the barest glance, then granted her a smile so wicked that her breath was stolen away. "The pleasure was worth the price," he echoed, then claimed her lips anew. He kissed her with leisure, his fingertips sliding lightly over her flesh, and reawakened her ardor with astonishing ease.

One touch from Rhys and her blood fairly simmered, one caress and she yearned to feel his strength within her again. His kisses at Ravensmuir had been a mere portent of the pleasure he could grant her. She returned his embrace, liking that his erection grew against her thigh.

Perhaps she had a power to please him, as well.

Rhys broke their kiss and rolled to his back, folding his hands behind his neck, as if to keep himself from touching her. "Once this night will suffice for you, I think," he said, his tone so rueful that Madeline laughed.

She liked that she already had the confidence in his nature to tease him. She touched his erection with a fingertip and it lifted beneath her caress. "But not for you?"

He gave her a glance so lustful that her mouth went dry. "I suspect that once with you will never suffice for me, *anwylaf*," he said, his words low and his eyes dark.

She assumed the Welsh word meant "wife", for it sounded so similar, and she did not mind the sound of it upon his lips. "Then my caress is a cruel one," she whispered.

Rhys shrugged, a slow smile claiming his lips again. "Perhaps the pleasure is worth the price."

Madeline laughed and laid her hand upon his chest. Rhys rolled to his side, facing her, and snared her hand within his own. His thumb slid across her palm in a slow caress and she smiled at him, feeling a contentment beyond expectation.

"Perhaps we have wrought a son already," he said.

"As quickly as that?"

"It is possible." His gaze dropped to their entwined hands and his words slowed. "My father always said that sons were wrought in passion, while daughters were wrought in dutiful coupling."

Madeline felt herself flush, for they had met with passion indeed this night. "What a notion! I should like to think myself wrought in passion, not duty."

"Perhaps he only said as much to encourage me."

Madeline was puzzled. "Why would that encourage you?"

"Because I am bastard-born, but a son nonetheless." Rhys lifted a fingertip to her cheek, stroking her as if she were wrought of fine silk. "My father only had daughters by his lady wife."

Madeline frowned and put an increment of space between them. She was more troubled by this confession than she could have believed. "Your father took a whore to ensure that he had a son?"

"Aye, he did. And it was a successful ploy, clearly."

That Rhys could endorse such infidelity, and do so with such calm, infuriated Madeline.

All the same, it was more difficult to shun Rhys's heat and his touch than she would have liked. She donned her chemise with hasty gestures and gathered her thoughts with an effort, well aware of the weight of his perceptive gaze.

"What is amiss?" he asked.

Madeline put the width of the chamber between them, considering her course. She did not want secrets between them, nor fears, so she pivoted to confront him. "How quickly will you turn to another woman to have the sons you desire?"

"What do you mean?"

Madeline heard her voice rise. "How much time do you grant me to conjure your son, Rhys? How long will you frequent my bed afore you take a whore?"

Rhys sat up and folded his arms across his chest. His eyes narrowed, but Madeline did not care if he was irked. "You are vexed by this prospect."

"My parents found pleasure solely with each other for the duration of their match. I expect no less of my marriage, howsoever it was wrought."

Rhys shook his head. "But that is unreasonable. With Caerwyn beneath my hand, I have need of sons to ensure the preservation and protection of my legacy."

"And you have greater need of the loyalty of your wife." When Rhys did not agree, Madeline continued in haste. "What gain was made by your father taking other women to his bed? He had a son, to be sure, but I doubt that your place in his household was an easy one."

Rhys's lips set in a stubborn line. "It is a question of the law of inheritance."

"You know as well as I that a daughter can inherit through her spouse, if necessary."

Rhys looked grim. "I will not have it. Strife comes of such uncertainty; strife and war and waste. It is irresponsible for a man to not ensure that he provides an heir who is a son."

Madeline regarded him in astonishment. On the very night of her nuptials, her husband was vowing to be unfaithful to her! How could she have imagined she might find contentment with him? "Swear to me that you will come to my bed alone."

He shook his head, impatient with the very notion. "You ask too much in this. I will have a son, if not two. And if they do not come from you, they shall come from another woman's womb." He rose and donned his chemise, apparently untroubled that she was so furious with him. "Under Welsh law, their mother's name is of less import than their father's seed."

"I care nothing for the law! I will not be mocked in my own household!" Madeline fairly shouted. Never had her concerns been so casually dismissed. "I will not be compelled to show courtesy to a whore who has usurped my place."

There was silence in the chamber then, a silence broken solely by the quickness of Madeline's breath. Rhys donned his chausses as if he had not a care in the world, then donned his boots and fastened his belt about his waist.

Only once he had checked his weapons did he meet her gaze steadily. "Then I would suggest that you conceive a son with all haste, my lady." With that, he bent to pick up his cloak.

His dismissive attitude infuriated Madeline as little else could have done.

"You faithless wretch! I should abandon this travesty of a marriage now!"

Rhys spared a telling glance at the ruby stain of her lost maidenhead upon the linens. "And who would welcome you?" he asked, as if curious to know her answer. "Your brother will not surrender my coin, nor will he find another willing suitor for you after last night. I will not tell a falsehood about what has happened between us this night, upon that you may rely."

Madeline glared at him, disliking the truth in his words. Indeed, her fury made her shake. "I should deny you access to my bed!"

That dangerous gleam lit Rhys's eye, though still he spoke with studied calm. "And how will that ensure that you conceive a son? How will it compel me to not take another woman to my bed? You are too keen of wit to not see the flaw in that scheme, my lady."

Rhys was right and they both knew it, though that did little to soothe Madeline's temper. His eyes shone, so certain was he that she was cornered, and Madeline yearned to prove him wrong. But any reluctance she showed abed would persuade him that they would not conceive a son, as he believed his father's edict about passion.

She glared across the chamber at the evidence of what they had done. He spoke aright about her lost maidenhead. Her sole path forward was as Rhys FitzHenry's wife.

Madeline drew herself to her full height and spoke with all the frost she could muster. "I salute your cunning, sir, for you have ensured that I have no choice but to grant your will to you. But your triumph is won at great cost."

"I see no cost in ensuring that matters will be between us as they should be."

"Oh! You are a barbarian indeed!" she cried. "You have lost my good will, which should be of import to you! What manner

255

of Christian pledges to be unfaithful to his bride upon the night of their nuptials?"

Rhys's lips thinned. "An *honest* man in need of a son."

"You will not blame me for your cruel confession."

"Nay?" For the first time, Rhys showed annoyance. He jabbed a finger through the air at Madeline as he crossed the chamber, his eyes flashing. "You were the one to demand honesty of me, but you complain at your first taste of the truth." He shoved a hand through his hair and glowered at her. "Would you prefer that I lie to you about my intent? Would you prefer to be deceived?"

"I would prefer that you be faithful!"

He donned his tabard with curt gestures. "The remedy for that is within your own womb."

Of course, no woman had control over her womb. Madeline could not choose when to become pregnant, let alone which gender of child she bore. It was scarce the same as choosing between red or green samite for a kirtle.

And Rhys knew it, curse him. Madeline clenched her fists and drew a fortifying breath, the urge to murder this man growing stronger by the moment.

"I would ask you to return the crucifix to its rightful place, husband," she said with heat, "for I have need of a witness to my prayers."

"While you pray for that son?" It was as much a statement as a question. Apparently as untroubled by her mood as he could possibly be, Rhys retrieved the sculpture and hung it again.

"Perhaps I mean to pray for widowhood," Madeline said sweetly. "For that would solve all of the woes come to me this night." She saw the flash of alarm in Rhys's eyes, but she did not care. She fell to her knees and prayed with fervor, acknowledging her husband's hovering presence no more.

Let Rhys worry what she asked of the Almighty. He deserved no less than that measure of uncertainty.

Rhys had always found women somewhat incomprehensible and a goodly amount of trouble. It was small consolation that his new wife proved his earlier conclusions to be valid.

No less that she did so with such gusto.

He watched her pray, well aware that she was deliberately ignoring him. He was certain her mood would pass, but the night retreated and Madeline did not rise from her knees. Her lips worked and her eyes remained closed, and he realized that she was no longer ignoring him.

She was oblivious to his presence.

And she prayed, as if expecting results.

Rhys had never troubled overmuch with prayer. He was of the opinion — taught to him by his indomitable mother — that God aided those who aided themselves. Anything he had ever desired, he had labored to make his own, instead of demanding divine intervention to see his desire fulfilled. Indeed, he was skeptical that God would even lend an ear to the prayers of a man like him: mortal men of power became deaf when bastards spoke, and he could see no reason why an immortal lord should be different.

Madeline, however, appeared to have expectations. Was she accustomed to having her prayers answered? And if that were true, what might she ask of God?

Surely she had jested about requesting widowhood?

Rhys was not so certain. It was clear enough that Madeline might have regrets about the nuptial vows they had exchanged just the day before. It would have taken a less perceptive man than he to miss the fact that she had not taken well to his determination to have a son.

The prospect of losing her troubled Rhys more than he would have liked to admit, though he knew his marriage was of strategic import alone. He was more concerned about losing Caerwyn than Madeline — or so he told himself as he watched her lips move silently in appeal.

All the same, it would not have been all bad for matters to have remained amiable between them. Their mating had gone well enough, at least in his view, and he had been fairly certain she had been pleased as well. She knew he needed a son, so why did his determination to have one trouble her so much? Bastards were common in Wales and great lords commonly had concubines living openly alongside their wives.

Perhaps matters were different in Scotland.

Barbarian. Rhys had been called many things in his day, worse things by far, but his new wife's accusation had stung.

Rhys shuffled his feet, but Madeline showed no awareness of his movement. He donned his cloak and noisily resettled his blades in their scabbards. She remained as immobile as a statue, except for her lips which worked in silent fury. He began to wonder what request would require such a protracted appeal and a new restlessness dawned upon him.

It was then that a whisper carried through the small window. "Rhys!"

It was Thomas, Rhys was certain of it.

"Rhys, are you there?" The monk spoke in Welsh, which made Rhys's blood quicken. Something was amiss.

He hastened to the window and peered over the high sill. Thomas huddled beneath the window. That the monk tried to hide his bulk in the meager shadow there would have been amusing had his manner not been so troubled.

"I am here, Thomas. Tell me what news you bring."

"They are coming for you, Rhys, six riders on great steeds." Thomas glanced from the gate to Rhys repeatedly, his anxiety clear. "They ride directly for our gates. I will not be able to halt them, but they must not find you here."

Rhys clutched the sill. "Whose insignia do they wear?"

Thomas granted him a glance filled with concern. "They wear no markings, though their steeds are too impressive for their riders to be of no import at all. Great black destriers, they are, their coats gleaming like a raven's plumage."

This was no good news.

"I fear you speak aright, Thomas." Rhys pivoted and found Madeline watching him with wide eyes. He cast her kirtle and her boots toward her and spoke so that she would understand. "Garb yourself with haste. We leave immediately."

She held her garments before herself. "But why? Where do we go?"

"There is no time to speak of it now." Rhys had no intent of telling his bride how closely the king's men had come to capturing him when he last had ventured out of Wales. He did not want to frighten her, and in truth, once they reached Caerwyn, he did not intend to leave those protective walls again soon. A trickle of dread slid down his spine, for he did not know what the king's men would do to his new bride.

He feared he could guess, though, for Madeline's beauty could not be denied. His determination to escape was redoubled.

"Make haste!" he said so harshly that she flinched.

She did his bidding, though, at least for the moment.

Rhys turned again to the window, just as the bells pealed from the gate, and spoke in Welsh again. "Thomas? Have you a scheme?"

"Go through the kitchens, Rhys. There

are few awake as yet. And linger in the shadows until this party is shown in to meet the abbess. I will ensure that your steeds are saddled so that you can flee while they await her hospitality."

"It will not give us much of a margin, but it is the sole one we will be granted," Rhys agreed.

"Godspeed to you, old friend, in case I have not the chance again to wish you well."

"And thank you for your aid, Thomas. I am again in your debt."

"You do not know yet what price that destrier will fetch," Thomas teased, then he was gone.

Rhys turned to Madeline again. To his relief, she was fully dressed and she was fastening the end of the plait in her hair.

"I hear horses." She regarded him with curiosity, her fingers working with haste. "Who comes that we must leave so quickly?"

He recalled too well her intent to be rid of him and decided that honesty would have to be sacrificed until they were too far away for her to betray him. "Trouble for my aunt, no doubt," he said. "She is one to pick battles and I have neither the time nor the inclination to become entangled in her woes. Come!"

"But why such haste?"

Rhys granted her a quelling glance — which had no discernible effect — then seized her hand instead. "There is no time for discussion. We must be silent."

Madeline held her ground. "I wish to know what is happening."

"Then I will answer your queries once we are away from here." He drew her closer and held her gaze, feeling like a cur for what he had to do. "Trust me in this, Madeline."

The use of her name seemed to soften her resistance. Though her lips remained thin, she no longer fought his urging. He drew her hood over her hair and opened the portal.

He looked to the left and to the right, saw no other soul, then ducked out into the hall. He decided that the kitchen was to the left, for he could smell bread rising and they had come from the right on the night before. He set a brisk pace, his wife fast behind him and blessedly quiet.

Thus far.

Rhys already knew his lady wife well enough to realize that situation could not last.

Chapter Nine

Madeline remained silent — with an effort — until they reached the stables. Thomas was saddling Rhys's dappled grey destrier. A chestnut palfrey stood beside the large stallion, its bright eye and tendency to fidget showing that it was ready to run. Rhys offered Madeline a hand to lift her into the palfrey's saddle but she stepped away from him.

"This is not Tarascon."

"Nay, it is not," Rhys said, speaking through gritted teeth. "Nor is this steed injured." He offered his hand again, with greater insistence, and his eyes snapped with impatience.

"But I cannot leave without my horse!"

"And you cannot thwart her healing by riding her hard so soon after that injury."

"Then I will not ride hard this day."

Rhys made an exasperated noise. Before he could argue, Madeline anxiously looked around the stable. She could not even spy Tarascon. She feared suddenly that the palfrey had been killed because of the injury and none had told her of it.

She clutched Rhys's arm. "What have you done to her? Where is she? How could you have her killed and not tell me of it?"

"The steed is not dead," Rhys said with such conviction that Madeline almost believed him. He shoved a hand through his hair, glanced to the courtyard, then paced to the end of the stables. His next words were more kindly uttered. "Look here, at this palfrey, and be quick about it."

He gestured to a mare of darker hue than Tarascon and lacking the familiar white star upon her brow. "That is not Tarascon!" Madeline had time to say before the beast nickered and came to bury its nose in her hand.

She stared, astonished that this horse moved in so similar a manner to her own, and indeed, seemed to know her. She glanced up to find Rhys's eyes twinkling.

"Do you not recognize your own steed?" he asked, his words low with laughter. "She knows you well enough."

Madeline stared at the horse nuzzling her palm, then stroked her ears. It *was* Tarascon, albeit disguised. "But what happened to the star on her brow?"

"Soot, my lady," said Thomas. "It rid her of her socks, as well as darkened her hue. Only one who knew her and looked closely would know her now."

Indeed, even Madeline's eye had passed over the beast.

"She will be safe here, my lady, safer than we may be," Rhys said with quiet vigor. "Come."

Even as she formed the question on her lips, voices carried from the bailey to their ears.

Rhys's manner changed immediately. "Now! We must begone."

Thomas peered through the stable doors. "They go into the abbey. This may be your sole chance, Rhys."

Rhys paused beside the palfrey and offered Madeline his hand again. She was torn between her loyalty to her lawful husband and to the steed she had known from its foaling.

"But I cannot leave Tarascon!"

"You must."

"I will ensure her good care, my lady," Thomas interjected.

"But she is my steed. I have ridden her for years. I cannot simply abandon her!" It was more than leaving the steed that she protested, and Madeline knew it well. Tarascon was her last link with Kinfairlie, with all that was familiar to her.

"There is no time for such discussion." Rhys spoke with such fierce precision that Madeline knew he was irked with her. "Mount this steed immediately, my lady, or I will cast you across the saddle with mine own hands and truss you there."

Madeline bristled. "That would hardly be appropriate. You may have the right to do as you will with me, but I do not have to endure it silently."

"I scarce imagine you could do so."

"Oh!"

Thomas seemed to be fighting a smile and losing the battle. "How sweet it is to see two destined lovers seal their fates together for all eternity," he murmured.

"I will thank you to keep your whimsy to yourself," Rhys snapped, then reached for Madeline's waist. His hands closed hard around her, despite her squeal of protest, and she was dropped into the saddle without further ceremony. Rhys glared up at her. "Must I truss you there, or can you be trusted not to leap from the saddle and injure yourself?"

Madeline met his gaze with equal fury. "I am not so foolish as that."

Rhys seized the palfrey's reins, sparing her only a dark glance that spoke volumes, and knotted the reins to the back of his saddle. "Our sole chance of safe departure lies in silence. I recommend you say nothing, my lady, or I will be compelled to gag you to ensure as much."

Madeline did not doubt that he would do it. She set her lips and sat straight in the saddle. She had learned once that fleeing this man could only grant her greater trouble. Though Rhys was rough spoken, he had never injured her.

She supposed she would have to be content with that. No court in Christendom would annul her match, or cede her a divorce: their match was consummated and they shared no kinship. With the spill of her maidenhead, Madeline was tethered to Rhys FitzHenry for life, for better or for worse.

Rhys swung into his own saddle, awaited Thomas's signal, then urged his horse into the bailey at a slow canter. Rhys's dog appeared from some corner of the stables, a shaggy grey shadow that matched its pace to their own. Six steeds were tethered in the shadows on the far side of the bailey, but Madeline barely had a glimpse of them before Rhys hustled her onward.

Thomas had run ahead to open the gate. The two men shook hands as the pair of steeds passed the ostler. "Thank you, Thomas, yet again," Rhys said.

"Ride, my old friend, and ride swiftly," Thomas said with a fervor that surprised Madeline again. "Ride long and hard this day. I will keep them here as long as I can, and I will pray for you." The monk blinked with sudden vigor and his words turned husky. "Be well, both of you, and know that you will always be welcome at my gates."

It seemed a rather fulsome expression of friendship to Madeline and she peered at her spouse with new interest. She doubted she would learn more of their shared past from Rhys, and the sorry fact was that she might never see talkative Thomas again.

Rhys touched his spurs to his destrier's flanks, and the beast needed little encouragement to run. The sky was only faintly touched with the rosy hue of the dawn, the dew heavy on the ground. Madeline pulled her cloak more tightly about herself and held fast to the saddle, shivering slightly in the dampness. She was glad to have the plain woolen garb from the abbey, for though the kirtle was crudely cut, it was thick and warmer than the one she had worn the day before.

The abbey was left behind them with startling speed and only now, Madeline had the chance to speculate upon those arrivals. She did not doubt that their presence had driven Rhys to leave with such haste.

Was it the king's men who had come to capture Rhys as a traitor? That alone could explain Rhys's desire for haste and silence. Madeline glanced back at the abbey, which looked serene and sleepy in the distance.

What would happen to her if Rhys was captured by the crown? Traitors seldom were granted a fair trial or a kind death, that much she knew for certain. As much as Madeline was loathe to admit it, her best protection might be in conceiving that heir to her husband's property.

She studied Rhys as he rode ahead of her, his back straight and uncompromising. Madeline supposed she should become accustomed to not knowing her husband's thoughts, for he clearly preferred to hold them close, though she doubted she was the nature of woman who could readily manage such a feat.

She was simply too curious.

Perhaps she should turn her intellect — which Rhys professed to admire — to the task of uncovering her husband's many secrets. She doubted that a woman could save her husband from the charge of treason, as Vivienne had suggested, but it would not hurt to know the truth of Rhys's deeds and history. She might then be able to protect her child, should she conceive one.

Or even herself.

Madeline smiled, well pleased with the notion of challenging Rhys's expectations of her. She suspected she might be able to learn much more than her husband would prefer.

And truly, if Rhys FitzHenry had wanted a dutiful, obedient wife, he should have bought himself one.

Their best chance — at least to Rhys's thinking — was to avoid the lands of the English king, or of those barons pledged to serve him. For all Rhys knew, there might now be a fat bounty upon his head.

And he had a keen desire to survive somewhat longer.

Rhys found a road that led southwest and wagered that this would be the road his pursuers would anticipate he would follow. He took it, intending to turn aside as soon as possible. Sadly, the hills rose steeply on either side of the path, and their unbroken crest on either side indicated that they would not be surmounted readily or quickly.

He wanted to go west, or even north-west, but for the moment was compelled to choose between riding back past the abbey, or continuing on southward with the hope of not being overtaken.

Madeline must have guessed his thoughts. "Rhys, give me the reins of my steed."

He glanced back, uncertain.

"We will make better time without the horses hobbled together." She smiled slightly, perhaps at his surprise. "You need not fear for me keeping your pace. I have ridden from the time I could reach the stirrup."

"And should I fear for your intent?"

Madeline shrugged. "A live husband suits me better than one drawn and quartered as a traitor." He was not truly surprised that she had guessed the real reason for their sudden departure, but he did not answer her.

Her expression turned wry when he said nothing. "That is true for the moment, at least. You would do well to not labor so stridently to change my thinking. It occurs to me that you might have need of an ally other than Thomas."

Rhys found himself smiling in admiration of her forthright speech. "Fair enough. I could endeavor to vex you less." They shared a tentative smile, all the sweeter for how little he had expected amity between them again. "But in this moment, I have need of counsel. I would make for Glasgow."

"Why?"

Rhys braced himself to deceive her yet again. "I have a friend there, whom I would visit before returning home."

She did not believe him, he saw as much immediately. Indeed, Rhys suspected that there was not another woman in Christendom whose thoughts could be read so easily in her eyes as those of his new wife.

But she did not challenge him upon this detail. Madeline bit her lip and scanned the hills on either side of them. To his relief, she asked no further questions, though it might simply have been that she doubted he would answer them.

"If Moffat lies ahead," she mused, "as I suspect it must, there is a road from there to Glasgow. It goes by Abington and Kirkmuirhill. I have heard my uncles speak of its smooth course."

"Excellent." Rhys cast her the reins. "It will be a long day, my lady. Tell me when you can endure it no longer."

Madeline nodded, but a glint of resolve

lit her eyes, a glint that told Rhys again that his lady wife was forged of stern steel. He could rely upon her to not be the weak link in their escape.

If that was the sole good news of this day, it was good enough. He gave his steed his spurs and the horses galloped down the narrow path, flinging mud from their hooves as the sun climbed over the horizon.

Madeline was relieved that Moffat had indeed proven to be ahead of them, and that they reached it afore the empty growl of her belly became too much to bear. The road coiled around a hill before ap-proaching Moffat's gates and Rhys indi-cated that they should hide themselves in the cluster of trees at the summit. They rode up the hill from the side opposite the village, so that the gatekeeper could not glimpse them.

Rhys tethered the horses there, pausing only to aid Madeline to dismount and to turn his tabard inside-out. The red dragon was hidden thus, the tabard plain black.

"Caerwyn," he whispered. "Say it."

"Caerwyn," Madeline echoed, and he corrected her pronunciation.

He caught her chin between his finger and thumb and met her gaze steadily. "You are the lady there, and let no man tell you otherwise. Go there, alone if you must, and tell them of this truth. Tell them that my son rides in your belly, whether it be true or not. None will dare to raise a hand against you." He brushed his lips across her brow, his words making Madeline's spirit quail.

He feared he might not return.

Before she could speak, Rhys was gone, retracing their steps with long strides. His dog sat vigil beside her, watching avidly as Rhys returned to the road, out of view of the gatekeeper, then strode toward the village as if he had been walking all the while. His kiss burned upon Madeline's forehead and she wondered what he knew, what he suspected, what he anticipated would meet him within those walls.

Little good, that was for certain. Despite herself, despite her annoyance with her vexing new spouse, Madeline feared for him.

Rhys whistled as he walked, weapons tucked around the back of his belt and his cloak pulled against the wind. Without his horse, he looked like a mercenary betrayed by Fortune. He walked to the village gates, his dark figure growing ever smaller. He hailed the gatekeeper with a wave, paused to speak to the man, then disappeared into the village without a backward glance. The hound straightened, its unblinking gaze fixed upon the point where Rhys had disappeared.

Madeline knotted her hands together and was uncommonly glad that she had not prayed for widowhood. Gone were the high walls of Kinfairlie, the certain influence of father and uncles, the defense of armed men. The security she had known for all her days and nights was gone, as was her childish conviction that all must come aright, simply of necessity.

It was not long before Madeline was watching as anxiously as the hound for Rhys's return. In his absence, her thoughts began to race. What if Rhys was a traitor? Guilty or not, what if he was apprehended?

She remembered all too well — and somewhat disconcertingly — the tale of Henry Hotspur, who had challenged the authority of Henry IV, the father of the current English king. Heir to the Percy earldom near Kinfairlie, Henry Hotspur had wrought a bargain with a Welshman and the Mortimer heir who had a competing claim to the English crown. All three had been condemned as traitors, though they had fought on in defense of their union.

Henry Hotspur had been killed in battle and his corpse had been sent home to his grieving wife and father. After his funeral, his body had been exhumed and decapitated, at the command of Henry IV, who intended to wring a lesson from the demise of one of his enemies. Hotspur's head had been displayed at York; his body quartered and displayed at London, Newcastle, Bristol, and Chester. It had been left hanging for a year, as a warning to would-be traitors throughout the king's lands.

Madeline shivered. No man deserved such an indignity, regardless of his deeds. Rhys could not deserve such a fate.

But if his course had been anticipated, and he was seized in Moffat, how would she know? She doubted that Rhys would betray her presence to another living soul, no matter what was done to him.

He was protective of her, if nothing else.

Madeline watched, more concerned for Rhys with every additional moment he was gone. She recalled now that the Neville clan quibbled over suzerainty of Moffat, the same Neville family so burdened with children to wed, the same Neville family so adept at making fortuitous matches. The same Neville family had been granted stewardship of the western Marches by the

English king. They would sell a traitor to the king with nary a second thought.

And their darling son, Reginald Neville, would not beg clemency for the man who had embarrassed him at Ravensmuir's auction.

Madeline bit her lip in trepidation. The sun rose higher, drying the dew and heating the stones. Its golden warmth seemed to coax spring's tendrils to unfurl, but Madeline stared fixedly at the town. The horses grazed behind her, peeling young shoots from the trees, but Madeline spared them no attention.

The sound of approaching hoofbeats made her heart race. She dared not be discovered! She urged Rhys's steed deeper into the forest and held her hand over his dog's snout as she tried to count the steeds. She could see nothing through the dense undergrowth of the forest, though that meant that none could see her. She dared not venture closer to the edge of the forest for a better look.

For there were a number of horses passing her hiding place. At least six. They were large, as large as destriers, for their hoofbeats fell with force. And they made uncommon haste.

Could they be the steeds from the

abbey? Her heart fairly stopped at the prospect.

Surely they would not seize Rhys at Moffat?

Surely she could not lose him so soon?

There were voices at Moffat's gate.

Rhys ducked into an alley in the nick of time, his purchases held fast against his chest. He listened and was startled to hear the sound of a woman's voice.

No less, a familiar woman's voice.

"I seek a young woman," that woman said, her tone authoritative. "She has dark hair and blue eyes, and is fair indeed to look upon. She might travel with a man garbed as a mercenary."

Rhys stifled the urge to peek with difficulty, for he could not believe his own ears. *Rosamunde* led the party in pursuit of Madeline?

Rhys frowned at this conclusion, unable to understand why this might be. It had been Rosamunde who had ensured that he could join the auction. What had changed her thinking? What had happened at Ravensmuir after their departure?

"I have seen no such woman," the gate-keeper said gruffly.

"And the man?"

Rhys caught his breath and flattened himself into the shadow of the wall.

The gatekeeper scoffed. "Who can say? Men come and men go — I do not note them, particularly the mercenaries. If they mean no harm and intend to be gone by sunset, they are welcome to leave coin in our coffers."

"You cannot be so poor of sight and memory as this!" Rosamunde said.

"I cannot be expected to confess all I know to a stranger!" the gatekeeper retorted. "Especially one so oddly garbed and so bold a wench as you."

"Let us pass!" Rosamunde said imperiously. "We will make our own search."

"You will surrender your weapons here, for I do not trust you to be peaceful within these walls."

Rosamunde argued with the gatekeeper but made no progress. Rhys listened as she surrendered her weapons in poor humor, then commanded her company to do the same.

Those six black destriers strode past his hiding place, their tails flicking and their nostrils flaring. Madeline's brother Alexander was within the company. The heir to Kinfairlie looked more a man already, not only because of his armor but because of his somber expression. Beside him rode two of Madeline's sisters, the next eldest who had plagued him with questions at Ravensmuir's board and the youngest, so smitten with fairies.

Two other men comprised the rest of the party, one of whom Rhys had noted at Ravensmuir. He was as flamboyantly garbed as Rosamunde and must have been her comrade. The last man was a stranger. He might have been the same age as Alexander and Rhys studied him with curiosity. He carried a lute slung across his back, and was wrought slender with pale skin and fair hair.

Something pricked at Rhys's memory, though he could not name it in this moment. To be sure, he could not fathom why Rosamunde would bring a musician with her, unless she meant to keep him in her company. Perhaps this one was uncommonly gifted.

Much to Rhys's annoyance, Rosamunde left the musician to guard the gates while she led the others toward the town square.

"We will find hay and water for the horses," she instructed. "Then ale and a hot meal for ourselves. Doubtless there will be a tavern in the main square, and with a full belly, we will search more effectively for Madeline."

Rhys retreated further into the shadows to think. Why did they seek Madeline? This family had auctioned Madeline's hand, so slender was their concern for her, yet within a day, they dispatched a company riding in pursuit. It made little sense.

It made even less sense that Rosamunde led the search. Rhys knew Rosamunde's nature enough to guess that she saw some advantage in this mission to herself, and that she would think little of betraying anyone to serve her own ends. She alone might have the audacity to threaten to deliver Rhys to the king to ensure her terms, whatever they might be.

Even knowing what he knew now, even seeing the concern of Madeline's siblings, Rhys was not anxious to make acquaintance with the daring adventuress Rosamunde just yet. Let her pursue him to Caerwyn, where he had the choice of whether to raise the portcullis or not.

A woman cleared her throat and Rhys jumped, then pretended to have been relieving himself in the alley. She rolled her eyes as he fumbled with his chausses.

"Is there another tavern?" he asked of her, slurring his speech as if besotted. Additionally, such speech would disguise his unfamiliar accent. He gestured toward the town square. "That one would beggar a common man."

"There," she said, pointing in the opposite direction as if glad to be rid of his presence. "Around the corner and to the left is Old Man McGillivray's house. He will sell you a cup of his ale, though I doubt you have much need of another."

"I thank you, good woman!" Rhys bowed, then pretended to lose his balance. He gripped the wall and waved after the woman, thanking her profusely as she made haste to get away from him.

Then he turned in the direction she had indicated, drawing his hood over his head. He dared not be seen, yet he could not attempt to pass through the gates just yet.

The musician needed time to become bored with his task.

And Rhys needed to find some soul who could unwittingly provide him with the means to pass the gates unnoted.

It was nearly midday and still there was no sign of Rhys.

The horses had disappeared into the town and Madeline had returned cautiously to her earlier place. She had seen precious few men come and go from the town since Rhys had disappeared. Moffat's gates seemed to swallow souls and not allow them to depart. She would go mad if she stood vigil, fretting, any longer.

With a start, she realized that she could walk into the town, just as Rhys had done.

Madeline surveyed herself. Her garb was dirty and austere enough that none would grant her a second look — not unless she rode a fine horse and drew every eye to herself. She would leave the horses here, as Rhys had done.

She could pretend to be a farmer's wife. No, she knew no one locally and that alone would prompt suspicion. She must concoct a fitting tale of who she was and how she came to be in Moffat alone.

She could pretend to be the wife of a mercenary seeking news of her lost spouse. Aha! It was unfortunate that she was not round with Rhys's child, as yet. A pregnancy would elicit sympathy as well as ensure that she was not assaulted by some fiend like Kerr.

The thought was too good to abandon. Madeline rummaged in Rhys's saddlebag, feeling like a thief for no good reason, and claimed a pair of his rumpled chemises. They smelled of Rhys and she impulsively buried her nose in them for a moment, breathing deeply of the scent of his flesh, curiously as reassured as if he stood beside her.

She could have done worse for a spouse, that much was certain. Rhys was no courtier, but she fancied that his heart was good.

She knotted his chemises into a round bundle. She tore her own chemise and secured the bundle beneath her skirts as if she was indeed ripe with child. She patted the lump, well pleased with her efforts, and ensured that the horses were well tethered.

"Stay," she bade the hound, which watched her so warily that she could not be certain it would obey.

A farmer's wagon, drawn by a weary plough horse, came through the town gates just as Madeline made to step out of her hiding place. She impatiently settled back into the shadows as she waited for the wagon to pass. It would not do for the horses to be stolen while she retrieved Rhys. She dared not be spied as she left this place, and would have preferred to have no contact with any soul upon the road.

The wagon was cursedly slow, as if its driver meant specifically to try her patience. The farmer seemed merry enough and was obviously chatting with his boy

285

who rode behind him. Madeline heaved a sigh, certain they had savored the ale in town overmuch, for they sang loudly and tunelessly. She wished they would hasten themselves home. The hound watched them as keenly as did Madeline. They rounded the hill, laughing like fools, and she knew she was nearly rid of them.

To her dismay, the wagon halted at the base of the hill on the far side from the village. The boy, who proved to be large enough to be a man, rolled out of the back. He tripped over his own feet, the drunken lout, and landed facedown beside the road. The farmer laughed so hard that his state could hardly be better.

Madeline was less amused, for she knew that dark tabard and dark tousle of hair all too well.

Here she had stood worrying, while Rhys had been drinking himself into a stupor! Her cursed spouse stumbled drunkenly to the woods on the other side of the road. Madeline looked away in disgust as he fumbled with the lacing on his chausses. He tripped anew, fell harder, and did not move again.

Here she had been fearful for the man's very survival! The prospect of throttling him herself grew mightily in appeal.

Madeline simmered, even as she watched the farmer stagger to Rhys's side. The older man gave Rhys a poke in the shoulder, but Rhys did not move. The hound growled at Madeline's feet and she put a hand upon its collar.

The farmer punched Rhys harder, and Rhys took a drunken swing at the other man, rolled to his back and began to snore.

The farmer found this so amusing that he had to sit down on a stone until his laughter subsided.

Oh, Alexander had done well in finding Madeline a husband not only charged with treason, but rough of manner and unable to resist the allure of ale! What need of an auction? He could have abandoned her at the nearest tavern to find such a rare prize of a spouse.

But then, Alexander would not have had Rhys's coin. Madeline gritted her teeth, so heartily displeased was she with the men in her life, and glared at events unfolding below.

The farmer wiped his brow, gave his drinking partner one last salute, then climbed into his cart and whistled to his ancient horse. The cart creaked as it began to move and the farmer started to sing a drunken ditty. Rhys did not move, so deep was his stupor.

Madeline should leave him there to rot! He deserved no less for such selfish folly.

But the sorry fact was that Rhys was little good to her drunk in a ditch. He was her husband: Madeline had pledged herself to him. Though this was worse than she had expected, she was not a woman to forget her pledges.

What to do? She could not carry the man, nor even drag him to his steed. She supposed she should go to him, like the sweet dutiful wife she was not, and see just how badly he was impaired.

And if he was not in pain, she could ensure that he was.

The prospect of such vengeance made Madeline smile despite herself. She knew she could never injure Rhys, so much larger and stronger was he. Still, she could have a word with him. It would not do for him to drink with such gusto with any frequency.

She peered after the wagon, which was well and truly gone, then made to stride down to the road.

But when she turned, Rhys was racing up the hill toward her, looking no more besotted than she.

"We ride!" he declared even as she gaped at him. He pointed across the road. "There is a path that cuts through the hills and joins the road you spoke of . . ."

"But you are not drunk!"

"Of course not." Rhys's glance was scathing. "Only a man of no merit whatsoever drinks himself to a stupor this early in the day. What manner of men are your brothers?"

That they should agree so vehemently on this matter was somewhat astonishing. Rhys did not wait for a reply, which was fortuitous as Madeline could not summon a word to her lips.

"I feigned drunkenness to be ignored. A drunken mercenary is not remembered, my lady, not even by the alemaker who takes the drunkard's coin."

His thinking made splendid sense. "You feign such a state so well that I was fooled," Madeline said. "Should I fret that it is your own extensive practice that grants you such skill?"

Rhys's grin flashed. "I have eyes in my head, no more than that." He lashed the bag he carried behind his saddle. "I have brought food, but we shall have to eat later." He fitted his hands around Madeline's waist to lift her into her saddle and froze at the changed shape of her belly.

His grip tightened around her and he did not lift her higher, holding her so that their gazes were level. "You conceive with uncommon haste, my lady."

Then he smiled a wolfish smile, one that set a thousand stars dancing in his eyes and awakened a fearsome tingle in Madeline's belly. She was very aware of the heat of his chest fairly against her breasts, of their breath mingling between them, of his resolute grip upon her waist.

Madeline found herself flushing furiously. "I meant to follow you. I was concerned that you took so long, and it seemed good sense to disguise myself . . ."

Madeline could not finish her explanation, for Rhys kissed her with an enthusiasm that made her forget her own thoughts. Her hands found their own way around his neck, and he caught her close against his heat. They kissed hungrily and she knew that she was not the sole one relieved by his safe return.

"I like it well that you fret for me, *anwylaf*," he whispered when he finally raised his head. "But I do not mean to die just yet."

"And how bold is a man who believes that choice is his alone?" Madeline demanded sternly, unsettled by the happy gallop of her heart in this man's presence.

Rhys held her gaze for a heady moment,

as if he might make some sweet confession. Madeline held her breath, until Rhys shook his head and turned, leading their steeds back to the road. His manner was watchful and silent once more, and Madeline did not know whether to be relieved or disappointed that he had said no more.

He was safe by her side, and for the moment, that would suffice.

Chapter Ten

Madeline and Rhys spent precious hours winding a path back and forth around Moffat, trying to ensure that their destination appeared to be Carlisle when it was not. Rhys wanted to ensure that many souls saw them upon that road, and only when he was satisfied that there had been enough witnesses did he take to the concealed track that the farmer had mentioned.

"How do you know that he will not tell another what he told you?" Madeline demanded.

"He was drunken enough that he will be asleep himself by the time any other party catches up with him," Rhys said grimly.

"And on the morrow?"

Rhys shrugged. "I doubt he will recall his own name, let alone the nameless mercenary who bought him ale."

"How much ale did you buy for him?"

Rhys chuckled. "Enough to ensure as much, though he had an uncommon thirst."

"You will be impoverished if you continue to waste your coin thus," Madeline chided, having no idea how much coin Rhys possessed.

"Aye, I have dispensed a great deal of coin upon women and ale on this journey." He cast her that beguiling smile. "Though I cannot call the expense a waste, in all fairness."

She could not take offense, not when he looked at her thus. Indeed, her heart thumped with painful vigor beneath his smile, and she felt herself flush.

She would have to steel herself against her husband's unexpected allure, lest she become fond of a man who had wed her solely for the fruit her womb might bear.

To Rhys's relief, the path not only existed, but it was where the farmer had told him. It was also deserted, much as the one Kerr had taken across the moors. Ever cautious, Rhys only chose to halt after they were a goodly distance from Moffat. They dismounted in a small clearing that would be out of clear sight of a rider.

Madeline looked about herself. "You chose this place because you can see the path."

"Without being readily seen ourselves," Rhys agreed, appreciative of her perceptiveness. He laid out the results of his excursion, apologetic that there was so little. A noblewoman would be accustomed to finer fare than he could offer, not only on this day. "Apples and cheese, bread and ale. There was little other than that, as it was not market day."

Madeline, however, seemed untroubled by the simple repast. "How long must it last?"

"Perhaps until Glasgow. Perhaps we shall risk another town before then."

"But you would prefer not to be seen," Madeline concluded, no censure in her tone. She divided the food with quick efficiency, granting him a measure more than herself and putting a good bit back in the sack. "The bread will be hard by the morrow, so we shall eat it today, half now and half this evening. Be sparing with the cheese, for it will keep a while with that good rind upon it. We shall each have an apple or two at each meal, at least until they are gone."

As he stared at her, impressed by her pragmatism, she gave an elaborate shrug. "And the ale is clearly for me, as you must have had your fill of it already this day." She granted him a glance of such mischief that he was tempted to forget the meal in favor of continuing their efforts to conceive a son.

Madeline must have guessed the direction of his thoughts, for she flushed scarlet, then sat down and busied herself with the meal. Her hands shook slightly and Rhys hesitated before joining her.

"Are you so afraid of me as that?" he asked.

She glanced up, her gaze clear. "Are you a traitor?"

"That depends upon who is asked."

She frowned. "That is not an answer."

Rhys shed his tabard and turned it around again, so that the red dragon of Wales was clearly emblazoned again upon his chest.

Madeline watched with interest. "There were those at Ravensmuir who said you tempted Fate by wearing that insignia so openly. Why?"

Rhys sat down beside her and bit into an apple as he considered where to begin. "Eons past, there was a king of Wales who decided to build his court upon a hill in Gwynedd."

"Where is Gwynedd?"

"It is the ancient heart of Wales, the territory within which one finds Eryri, the mountain known as Snowdonia in English.

It is there that the oldest seat of Welsh authority lies, the hill of Dinas Emrys, and it was upon this hill that King Gwrtheyrn vowed to build his hall."

Rhys bit into his apple with vigor, taking his time with the tale. "But something was amiss, for each night whatsoever had been constructed that day disappeared before the sun rose again. The stones were swallowed by the earth, so fully did they disappear, and the king was vexed that so little progress was made."

Madeline listened, rapt. Her hands stilled over the bread.

"And so it was that the king called for a seer to tell him what had gone awry. He summoned Myrddin, a young sorcerer who would be known by the English as Merlin, who conjured a dream. After his dreaming, Myrddin counselled the king to dig beneath the hill, to dig until he found a lake. And beside that lake would be a tent, and within that tent would be two dragons, one red and one white. And so it was done, upon the bidding of the sorcerer's dream."

"And what did they find?"

"It was as Myrddin had predicted, but as the king and his men watched, the dragons awakened. The pair fought a vicious battle through the tent and into the lake, then disappeared. And Myrddin said that it would always be thus, that this pair would battle again and again for all eternity. He said that the white dragon was England and the red was Cymru —"

"Cymru?"

"Wales." Rhys chewed his apple and stared over the hills, savoring that Madeline's attention did not waver. "And he counselled the king to build his abode elsewhere."

"Why?"

"So long as Dinas Emrys remains a wooded hill, the red dragon lives on, to wage war against the white. So long as the hill is unfettered, the red dragon will do battle." Rhys met Madeline's gaze, letting her see his determination. "He will fight to his dying breath, each and every night for all eternity if need be, until the red dragon is ultimately triumphant over the white."

They stared at each other for a potent moment, and Rhys recalled the silk of her skin beneath his hand, the way she gasped when she found her pleasure. Desire stirred within him and he thought of bedding her here, upon this cloth, without regard to whosoever pursued them.

He was startled by the appeal of the notion, a notion that could result in his own demise. What power had this woman over him? And how had she conjured it in so few days? Rhys had the wit to be afraid.

Madeline looked down at the bread in her hands, breaking the heated gaze that had bound them together. "You can tell a tale, husband."

"I am Welsh," Rhys said and looked away from the temptation she offered.

She cleared her throat. "No wonder your insignia was thought to be provocative."

Rhys considered this for a moment. "My insignia declares me to be who I am, which is the task of an insignia. I am not the manner of man to pretend that I am other than I am."

"Except in Moffat."

He smiled at that and let her think what she would. There was more to consider than his own sorry hide, at least until they reached Caerwyn.

"Will you tell me why the king charged you with treason?"

"Nay," Rhys said firmly. He took another apple and bit into it, noting that she was irked with him again. To be sure, the lady was bewitching when her eyes flashed with such vigor. He stared at the road and willed the enthusiasm in his chausses to abandon him.

"Then I shall have to learn the tale from someone else," she said tartly. "You may be certain that there are others who know about the charges against you, Rhys, and they may not be so interested in granting you a fair hearing as you might yourself be."

"Then you should not seek the tale from others," he said, determined to end her curiosity. "It is not comely for a lady to seek gossip, after all." Madeline gasped in indignation but before she could make another demand, he made one of his own. "What of this man who captured your heart? Do you mean to tell me of him?"

Her eyes widened in surprise. "James?"

"If that was his name." Rhys shrugged, trying to give the impression that he was less interested than he knew himself to be. "Your betrothed, who died."

"James." Her lips tightened and she sighed, looking suddenly despondent. She seemed both intent upon cutting her apple with her knife and disinterested in whatsoever she did.

Rhys stretched out in the grass, much happier asking questions than answering them. He watched Madeline, seeking the answers she would not express in words. "What manner of man was he?"

She sighed and a sweet smile touched her lips. That such a smile had nothing to do with him — and never would — tore Rhys's heart with surprising force.

"James was a kind and gentle man. He was filled with such goodness, and he could sing as if he were an angel."

Rhys snorted. "Then they shall be glad of him in their chorus."

Madeline glared at him. "James was a well-mannered and elegant man. He was good and kind and gentle and . . ."

"Your point being that I am as unlike James as ever a man could be."

Her gaze swept over him, and she sniffed. "I would never be so rude as to say as much." Madeline turned her attention to her apple again, twin spots of color burning in her cheeks. "He could play the lute with such skill."

"The lute?" Rhys straightened. "He was a musician?"

Madeline nodded, oblivious to how avid Rhys had become. "He wrote some verse and sang many more composed by others. He played the lute with great cunning."

A poet and lutenist! Rhys looked away, alarmed as he seldom was. The apple was as sawdust in his mouth, for he guessed well enough who the musician was who travelled with Rosamunde, why that party had pursued him from Ravensmuir and what they wanted with him.

How perfect for Rosamunde that she could readily condemn Rhys, and thus ensure that Madeline was widowed. And Madeline could wed the man she vowed to love.

Rhys cast the core into the undergrowth with force, not caring that he had not finished the flesh, and realized that Madeline watched him warily.

He struggled to keep his tone idle, though his interest in his wife's answer was far from idle. "Did you kiss James as you kiss me?" He heard that his effort failed, that he sounded as if he sought an argument.

He found one.

Madeline's glance was positively lethal. "James was too much of a nobleman to force his embrace upon me."

Rhys recalled all too well that she had called him a barbarian. And no wonder, for bards were men of considerable abilities. They were marked for their destiny early, they were granted the best schooling, they were clever and talented and the most exalted men in Welsh society. No wonder she found Rhys a poor substitute for this

James. He would have to remember not to sing in her presence, lest that comparison serve him poorly as well.

"Which means that you did not." Rhys pushed to his feet, disturbed beyond expectation by the impressive credentials of this lost suitor. "So, how did he die? Did he argue a case that he could not win, and thus meet the anger of the losing side?"

Madeline looked up, her bewilderment clear. "I do not understand."

Rhys spoke roughly in his annoyance. "You said he was a poet and a musician, so he must have also been a lawyer. The best poets are lawyers, as well. Do you tell me that he was incompetent as a musician?"

She laughed, the sound bursting from her lips in her surprise. "What madness is this? Poets as lawyers! Surely you jest?"

"Surely I do not!" Her attitude irked Rhys as little else could have done. "It requires eloquence to argue a legal case, and the ability to cast a spell over one's audience. A lawyer is an orator, as is a poet. Any person of sense can see the connection." Madeline blinked, but Rhys could not halt himself. "Bards are well accustomed to remembering long passages of verse, not dissimilar to remembering passages of law. And poets, finally, are clever beyond belief, for they must not only master the ancient twenty-four meters of rhyming verse, but be able to make such compositions as they sing."

"I did not realize . . ."

Rhys shoved a hand through his hair, agitated by his competitor's skills, no less that Madeline did not appear to appreciate them. How galling that he had to explain the other man's copious talents! "Few realize the complexity of the metered verse. In Welsh, we call such harmony *cynghanedd* and it is not easily learned. The syllables must be of the same number within each line of the verse, and each word of each line must begin with the same sound, and the first word of each line must ally with the first words in all the other lines, and the last consonant of each line must allude to the first word of the next!" Rhys flung out his hands and roared. "It is not a pursuit for the simple of intellect, I assure you!"

Madeline simply stared at him, so great was her astonishment.

Rhys exhaled heavily and forced his voice to return to its usual timbre. "Thus, in my uncle's court, the poet who possessed such fearsome abilities was also the man who knew and argued the law."

"I have never heard the like of that." Madeline heaved a sigh in her turn. "James simply could pluck a pretty tune."

Rhys gaped at her. "He could not compose in meter?"

She shook her head.

"Are you certain that he simply did not burden you with the fullness of his abilities?"

Madeline chuckled. "I am certain. He was almost untutored, for his father had no interest in music. He composed little himself and I heartily doubt that he knew near as much of law as you expect. His charm lay in other traits." She smiled at Rhys with bemusement as she peeled an apple with her knife. "You Welshmen are a whimsical lot indeed. Poets as lawyers!"

Though Rhys was relieved that James was not as formidable a foe as he had feared, his mood was not improved by Madeline responding to good sense as if he were mad. He glared at her. "So, how did this esteemed musician of so few talents die? Did he cut his white fingers upon lute strings drawn too taut?"

Madeline cast aside the skin of her apple with annoyance. "His father fairly had him killed."

"Then perhaps this James was not so kind and gentle of a man, if he so enraged his father. Perhaps he was not so clever as you believe."

"His father was not enraged," Madeline asserted with force. "He was simply blind to the manner of man his son was. I told you that he had no interest in music or its merit. He dispatched James to the war in France, despite James's protests."

"Why did this James not defy his father? It can be done." Rhys considered his piece of bread and decided to risk provoking her again. "Unless, of course, one does not want to threaten one's inheritance."

"Oh! You are quick to cast aspersions on those you have not known!" Madeline's eyes flashed. "His father was cruel and unfair! He had James imprisoned in their own keep until James agreed to go to war. And then he sent James with his own warriors, with the command that they were to ensure that James served his father's interests well in France. He ensured that James could not escape, that he had to fight. And so James died. It was wicked and utterly unfitting for a father to treat his son in such a manner."

"He was killed in battle?"

Madeline nodded once. "James was not a man wrought for war. His father should never have sent him to France when he did!"

"You speak aright," Rhys acknowledged. "Had he been a good father, he would have sent him to war sooner."

Madeline dropped knife and apple, outrage bringing her to her feet. "What madness is this? No decent father would see his son killed for no good reason!"

Rhys was fascinated by the sight of his wife. She was so impassioned, so determined to defend a man who could not have been a fitting match for her fiery nature.

As he was. He rose to his feet in turn, unafraid to grant her a measure of the honesty she so admired.

"Your betrothed died because he had not been prepared for what he had to do," Rhys asserted. "*All* men must fight one day for what they would call their own, and it is a father's duty to ensure that his sons are prepared for that duty. By granting your James his freedom from war for so long as he did, the father might as well have driven his own blade into his son's chest."

"But not all men are suited to war!"

"True enough. Some serve better as priests and monks." Rhys watched for her response, knowing there would be one. "But that choice would scarcely have ensured the survival of James as your spouse."

A ruby flush rose from Madeline's throat to suffuse her face. Her eyes gleamed angrily, their vivid hue akin to lightning, and her words were low and hot. "You go too far in this. You did not even know James, you never heard the magic he could wring from a lute, and you have no right to despoil my memories of him."

But Rhys was angry now, and he was fearful of Rosamunde's intent. It seemed suddenly critical that Madeline face the truth that this James was an unsuitable match for her. "I shall wager that you wished to wed your betrothed afore his departure to France," he said curtly. He rose and gathered together the remnants of their meal. "But your father forbade it."

All the color abandoned Madeline's cheeks as she gaped at him. Her voice was almost inaudible. "How could you know this?"

Rhys barely glanced at her, so irked was he that she failed to show her good sense in a matter of such import. "Because your father knew James, obviously, and must have known the truth of James's lack of military ability. No man would willingly wed his daughter to a man who might not be able to ensure her safety. Your father undoubtedly reasoned that James would either die in France, or he would prove himself to be more of a warrior than he had been thus far."

Rhys shrugged. "You were better wedding him after that truth was known or not wedding him at all. Your father fulfilled his responsibility to you, as I will fulfil mine to our daughters, should we be blessed with any."

With that, Rhys began to pack their meal away with savage gestures. Madeline said nothing at all, though he could feel her dismayed gaze upon him. He had not meant to wound her heart, though he had no doubt he had done so. He would not, however, have the repute of the great saintly James thrust upon him each time he faltered in his wife's expectations.

Especially as that man was very likely in pursuit of them. He might not be able to avoid the prospect of Madeline choosing between them, but he would do his best to ensure that she had no illusions if ever she did so.

He glanced back to find her pulling the bundled cloth from beneath her kirtle, her tears falling with such vigor that he felt a knave. She had loved this fool James, and he should not fault her for that.

"Leave it, Madeline," he said softly.

"Your scheme is a good one."

She halted and stared at him, her face streaked with tears. "I love James and that will never change."

"I understand." Rhys was contrite, for he had spoken too harshly to her. "I shall not speak of him again, out of respect for you. Indeed, I apologize that my temper was lost so much as it was."

"I will never love another," she said, her voice hoarse.

Rhys nodded once and turned away, understanding what she was telling him. There was a hollowness within him, a regret that Madeline could not offer him all that she had offered James, but Rhys was accustomed to making do with the remnants of others.

He saddled the horses, then offered her his hand. "Come, my lady. It is time to ride again."

Rhys FitzHenry had no heart at all. Madeline was wed to a man who did not care that she would never love him. She decided that this revelation was not so surprising, after all. Was there not a saying that a woman wed once for duty and thence for love? She supposed she would have to survive Rhys to have a chance of such love in her second marriage.

It seemed a thin prospect. They rode onward in grim silence, only the calls of birds and the occasional rustle in the undergrowth carrying to Madeline's ears.

At least they were not being pursued.

And the weather was not as bad as it might have been.

That seemed a sorry list of Fortune's favor, but there was no changing it. Madeline watched Rhys and wondered about his hidden thoughts.

The man had no shortage of them, it was clear.

Sadly, his indifference to love was evident. Such tender feelings must not be of any import to a man of war such as himself. She had seen the glow in his eyes when he spoke of Caerwyn, and guessed that he loved that keep. Though she knew that she should not have been surprised that he cared only for property, she was deeply disappointed.

Perhaps it was time that she prodded more of his carefully kept secrets into the open. She had precious little to lose.

Madeline eyed her spouse, noting that he was more grim than usual, and urged her steed slightly closer to his. Rhys barely spared her a glance, his own gaze darting restlessly over the shadowed greenery on their every side. It was falling dark, a triumphant smear of pink staining the indigo of the western skies.

"Who do you know in Glasgow?" Madeline asked.

If anything, Rhys grew more grim. "It is of no import."

Madeline had not expected an easy confession from him. Indeed, she could be as stubborn as he was and it was time he confronted the truth of it. "How do you know of any soul in Glasgow? That town is far indeed from Wales."

"It is of no import." Rhys led his destrier from the path and cut a course through the forest, making it impossible for Madeline to continue their conversation. She waited, albeit impatiently, until he halted in a small clearing by a stream. He dismounted, moving with confidence in the shadows, then aided her to dismount.

"Do you simply make a visit, or do you expect aid from this friend in Glasgow?" Madeline asked, keeping her tone deliberately bright. She won a hard look for her trouble, but lifted a finger before he could speak. "I think this *is* of import."

Rhys shrugged. "And I do not." He unfastened his saddlebag, removed something, and strode into the woods. Gelert darted after Rhys, its tail waving like a bedraggled banner in its excitement.

With half a dozen steps, he was gone. Half a dozen more and she could not even hear him.

He had effectively abandoned Madeline to her own questions. Madeline shouted after her spouse, to no avail, and the sounds of the forest closed around her. The horses bent their heads to graze, swishing their tails and amiably bumping alongside each other.

The man had the manners of a boar! Madeline shouted again, not truly expecting any reply. She did not receive one.

Cur! Knave and ruffian! Rhys FitzHenry had the worst manners of any man who ever she had had the misfortune to meet. He yearned for a son, did he? Oh, he could count himself fortunate indeed if ever he found himself between her thighs again. He was welcome to keep a hundred whores, given his attitude.

What manner of man left a woman alone in the forest at night? No man of merit, that was for certain!

Madeline gritted her teeth, then unfastened the saddlebags, casting them to the forest floor. He had no squire, so she must perform the duties of one, or see the steeds suffer.

Wretched man. She unfurled the two blankets she found within Rhys's bag. She could only manage to remove the palfrey's saddle, for that of the destrier was not only too large, but the beast itself stood too tall. She dropped the reins over the horses' heads and let them graze, then found the horse brush in one bag.

Indeed, what need had Rhys of a squire when he had a wife? She brushed down the two horses with vigor, for it was not their fault that their master was a selfish cur. There was no merit in letting them fall ill from the chill of their own sweat.

Madeline soundly cursed her husband's irresponsibility as she worked. Once she was done, she set to gathering wood for a fire. She supposed that the presence of his destrier indicated that Rhys would return, though she would not have wagered her last *denier* upon it. She also would not rely upon his provision of a meal for both of them whenever he did return. For all she knew, he might have sniffed the ale of an inn in the distance, and hied himself off to warmth and a good meal.

If he thought she would let herself freeze to death, or sulk at his absence, he was sorely mistaken. Fortunately, there was a good bit of dry kindling to be found. It must not have rained as diligently in these parts as it had further east.

As her anger ran its course and faded, Madeline's fear began to grow. She kept herself busy, painfully aware that she had never been alone in the forest before. She was accustomed to the security of high walls at night, and she recalled all too readily the tales of ravenous wolves that she had so often heard.

She fed the fire to a tremendous blaze, hoping to dissuade any predators from coming close. Despite her efforts, night fell and a wolf howled in the distance. To her dismay, another answered from the other direction. They sounded close to her inexperienced ears, too close. Even the horses eased closer to each other, their ears flicking.

Madeline told herself to ignore the gleam of watchful eyes in the forest around her — surely the sight of them was no more than her imagination. She wrapped her cloak tightly about herself, cursed her spouse once more, then sat and took a bite out of an apple. She would eat a meal, then she would sleep.

Or at least she would try to do so.

"I had thought you would desire a hot meal on this night," Rhys said with humor.

As usual, the man reappeared at sudden proximity, only his words revealing his presence. When Madeline pivoted to face him, she found him standing in the shadows, the dog fast by his side. He held a trio of fish aloft, as if that and his smile could compensate for his abrupt departure. The confidence in his manner was the last vexation that she needed on this night to lose her temper in truth.

"You faithless wretch!" Madeline cried, more relieved by the sight of Rhys than she cared to admit. She cast her apple at her spouse with all the force she could muster, hoping only that the resulting bruise was large and lasting.

Chapter Eleven

To survive three teasing brothers, Madeline had learned to aim and throw, and she had learned to do it well.

The apple hit Rhys square in the nose, so astonished was he by her assault. He yelped and jumped backward, dropping one fish, then cursing as he searched for it in the leaves.

The apple meanwhile hit the ground and bounced. Gelert darted after it, tail wagging with delight when the apple was discovered. The dog trotted to Madeline, uncommonly proud of itself, apple held high, then lay at her feet to eat its prize.

Rhys was not so happy. He regarded Madeline warily as he came closer, still shaking dried leaves from the retrieved fish. "You are annoyed," he said, as if her response was inexplicable.

"What splendid fortune to be wed to a perceptive man."

"Where did you think I had gone?"

"Perhaps to hell." Madeline folded her arms across her chest, intrigued despite her annoyance at his manner. Did Rhys truly not understand that she had been afraid?

His gaze slipped over her features and she knew he missed no detail. "You cannot have thought that I had abandoned you," he said, as evidently the prospect occurred to him.

"What else was I to think?" Madeline spun to tend to the fire, fairly hearing Rhys think as he watched her.

"I take care of what is mine own," he said.

Madeline snorted. "How welcome it is to know that you count me among your possessions. Like your saddle, or your knife. Perhaps your hound." She jabbed a stick into the fire. "There is a sentiment to warm a woman's heart."

She heard his steps just afore he seized her elbow and spun her to meet the fire in his eyes. "You make accusations without cause! There is a river. Can you not hear it?" He shook his head in irritation. "Could you not guess that I would provide a hot meal for us? You had to know that I would return."

"I knew no such thing."

"Then why did you build a fire?" He spared it a disapproving glance. "No less one as big as a pyre. Those who hunt us will find us without effort, if this continues to burn so high."

That he should criticize her resourcefulness in this moment was too much.

"Then perhaps they will find their prey roasted upon it!" Madeline kicked some of the wood out of the bonfire while Rhys regarded her with astonishment, then stamped upon the burning faggots.

By the time she was done, the fire was much smaller, as was her irritation with Rhys. All the same, she spun to confront him and propped her hands upon her hips. "Does that suit you better, husband? You should leave more precise instructions in future, that I might do your bidding fully!"

The air fairly crackled between them, then Rhys shook his head. "Surely you cannot have been afraid," he said, frowning as he gutted the fish with decisive gestures. "You are too intrepid a woman to be fearful of shadows."

"It was the wolves and their appetites I feared, not the darkness."

Another one howled, as if to emphasize her argument. Rhys cocked his head to listen. "They are not coming closer," he said with a confidence Madeline did not feel.

"All the same, I will not sleep this night."

He spared her a piercing glance. "Have you ever spent a night outside of fortress walls?"

"Only once," Madeline admitted tightly. "A few nights past."

She thought at first that Rhys had not heard her, for he made no acknowledgment of her words. He methodically impaled the cleaned fish upon sticks that he must have peeled and sharpened while he waited for the fish to take his lure. He drove the sticks into the ground so that they made a tripod and ensured that the fish were angled over the flames.

Only then did he apparently take note of her. "Will you watch that they do not burn? You can turn them readily, like this." Rhys spun one stick to demonstrate and Madeline nodded grudgingly. He inclined his head so that she could see the twinkle in his eyes and for a moment she feared that he would mock her.

Instead Rhys spoke gently. "I vow to return, after I leave word for the wolves to let my lady slumber in peace this night."

He strode away and Madeline could not at first guess what he would do. She saw his shadow slide behind one tree and heard the splatter of liquid falling, and then she guessed.

Rhys left a message for the wolves in a manner they would understand. He marked the perimeter of their camp with his urine, as wolves marked their territory.

And he did so to reassure her. How could she stay angry with a man of such rough charm? Her brothers would never have done such a deed to reassure her — they would have simply teased her until she dared not express her fear any longer.

Once again, Rhys had surprised her.

Madeline blinked back unexpected tears and paid undue attention to the fish. She heard the rustle of Rhys's footsteps as he moved all around the circle of their camp, pausing to leave a missive for the wolves every few feet.

There was a pause, then she heard him splashing in the river that she had not noted earlier. Truly, she was not accustomed to heeding the sounds of the forest, for the river's flow was readily discernible now that she listened for it.

And her heart wrung again with the realization of what Rhys did. This exasperating man washed afore he shared a meal with her, as if he meant to show his bride that his manners were not entirely coarse. Madeline would never have expected him to be so concerned for her fears and expectations.

But he was. Though he was not accustomed to sharing his every thought, though he did not always understand or anticipate her concerns, the man had made efforts to make their match a successful one. She owed him more than sniping better suited to an alewife. She watched the fish diligently, her empty stomach beginning to growl in complaint at the tempting smell of the roasting fish.

Rhys returned with his hair wet and his tabard in his hands, his chemise untucked and clinging to his damp skin. Madeline could see the outline of his muscled chest through the wet cloth, and the dark tangle of hair there. Her mouth went dry, her appetite kindled for something other than roasted fish. Rhys shook the water out of his hair as he drew near to the fire, then checked the fish with an experienced eye.

"They will go well with that bread," was all he said, but his tone was amiable. Madeline understood that he wanted their argument behind them.

So did she, so she offered him a tentative smile. "You should stay near the fire, until you are dry. Let me fetch the bread."

He glanced at her smile, blinked, then

frowned at the fish. "I did not mean to frighten you, but I confess that I think poorly with an empty belly."

Madeline nodded at his apology. "I understand that now. I apologize for my anger."

His frown deepened. "It was not undeserved. I am not accustomed to riding with another person, let alone with a noblewoman."

"Or a wife?"

He smiled then, that smile that melted all her reservations. "Or a wife, *anwylaf.*"

Perhaps they could make a good match out of this poor beginning. Perhaps their marriage was not fated to be merely endured. A son in her womb would resolve much of what stood between them.

Madeline dared to hope.

"It seems that we slowly come to understand each other, Rhys," she said, brushing her fingertips across his arm. He impaled her with a glance when she used his name, and that dangerous heat within her was coaxed to a flame. She did not look away as her mouth went dry, nor did he.

Then the fish began to smoke.

Rhys shouted in dismay and Madeline hastened to fetch the bread. She held a slice of bread while Rhys removed each fish from the stake. He deftly removed its head and skin, leaving a steaming fillet upon each piece of bread.

"Ah, for a measure of salt," he said wistfully as they sat down by the fire, then granted Madeline an unexpected wink.

She sat, feeling all ashiver in his presence, thinking of sons and their conceptions, and ate her meal. The fish was delicious, the warmth of the fire a delight. It was not all bad to be alone in the woods like this, night pressing against them on all sides, not now that Rhys sat beside her. The horses dozed, their tails swishing, and Gelert kept a keen watch over the camp.

Rhys cleared his throat. "I owe you a boon, my lady, for it was not my intent to frighten you."

Madeline regarded him with interest. It was unlike Rhys to offer any concession. "No doubt you will name what manner of boon it must be."

A crooked smile touched his lips. "What if I offer you a tale?"

"A tale of fancy, or one of your own history?"

"What do you think?"

"I think you would die before you confessed a morsel of your own history to me," Madeline said, much fortified by a warm meal in her belly. "But I shall risk the asking."

"God save me from this fearless woman I have taken to wife," Rhys muttered, though his tone was warm.

Madeline chuckled, then licked the last of the fish from her fingers. "One must make the most of such a rare offer from you," she teased and Rhys chuckled in his turn. She liked the twinkle in his eyes, the way he looked when he teased her, and that alone tempted her to ask what she really desired to know. "Who betrayed you?"

Rhys froze then, his gaze rising slowly to meet her own. Madeline did not blink, nor did she look away. His eyes were dark, his expression unfathomable, but he hesitated so that she thought he might answer her.

Then he shook his head and turned his attention back to his meal. "You do not know that anyone betrayed me."

"I would wager it."

"You have nothing with which to wager."

"You offered me the boon of a tale."

A muscle worked in his throat and his voice dropped low. "Not that one, Madeline."

She knew him well enough not to push on this matter. "Then tell me of Caerwyn."

His quick glance was piercing. "Why?"

"Because you love it."

"All love it. You shall see it when we arrive there."

Madeline gathered her rapidly diminishing patience with an effort. "My aunt Rosamunde seemed to know you." She wondered whether she imagined that Rhys stiffened at these words. "Does she?"

"Aye." He would not meet her gaze.

"How?"

Rhys shrugged. "It is a long tale."

Madeline gritted her teeth. The boon he offered was not one he would fulfil readily, it was clear! "She said that I should not judge a man by his appearance, or even by his repute. Thomas said much the same thing of you. What do they know of you that I do not?"

"Who can say?" Rhys said. "You should ask them."

"I am not likely to have the opportunity to do so for quite some time!"

He almost smiled. "I doubt you will forget your query, no matter how much time elapses." And he helped himself to another piece of bread.

"Is it your intent to be the most vexing man in Christendom, or do you have an innate talent for keeping your secrets to yourself? I am certain that I have never had so strong an urge to injure another living being as I have had since meeting you!"

Rhys smiled fully then, the expression

driving the shadows from his eyes. "Evasiveness is a learned talent, but one I possess to be sure." He finished his own meal and stretched out upon his cloak. He crossed his booted ankles and leaned his weight upon his elbow as he regarded her warmly. His eyes twinkled in a most beguiling way. "No more questions?"

"What would be the merit?"

"Surely you cannot mean to surrender your boon as readily as that? I thought you a woman of some persistence."

Madeline glanced about herself, not knowing what to ask him that he might deign to answer. The hound rose, shook itself, then fairly pounced upon the discarded skins of the fishes. "Why did you name the dog Gelert?"

Rhys sighed, his gaze landing upon the dog. "It is a name from an old tale, one of which I am fond."

"Tell me of it." To Madeline's relief, Rhys did not argue.

He snapped his fingers and the dog came to his side. He scratched its ears, and the dog's delight made both man and wife smile. "It is said that long ago, there was a knight. He had a castle to his name, as well as a village and some land. Because he had only his steed, his armor and his faithful hound, Gelert, to keep him company, he decided to find a wife. He met a noblewoman who found him as pleasing as he found her, and they were wedded. In time, they had a son."

"Only the hound has a name in this tale?"

Rhys smiled fully, even as he scratched his own dog's ears. "Only the hound is of import in this tale." He smiled at her and Madeline had difficulty thinking clearly. The similarity between this tale and their own was evident, after all. It was easy enough to recall how Rhys's flesh had felt against her own, no less to yearn for his caress again.

They did not, after all, have a son as yet.

"And so, what happened next?" she managed to ask.

"They found a nursemaid to care for the child. When the babe was still in swaddling, the parents went out to hunt, leaving the nursemaid with the care of the child. It was perhaps the first time that the mother had left her infant son. The dog remained beside the child, so diligently did it guard whatsoever its master held dear."

"There is a hound worth the having. It knew the difference between mere possessions and what a man holds dear."

Rhys flicked a glance at Madeline, but continued his tale without further comment. "While the maid slept that afternoon, an enormous snake slithered into the nursery. It had a thousand teeth and was a hundred ells long; its scales were red and black and green, and its eyes were yellow. It was an ancient snake, one which fed solely upon children, and it made its slithering path directly toward the knight's only son."

Madeline's fingers knotted together in her skirt, even as Rhys's own fingers moved in Gelert's fur.

"The faithful dog attacked the snake, though the wicked beast was far larger and more vicious than the hound. The two battled over which should claim the child. The hound was bitten terribly by the snake, and though the dog fought with all its vigor, the loss of blood weakened it sorely. It sank its teeth into the snake in a last bid to save the child, but the snake hit the hound with a mighty thump of its tail. The hound was dazed long enough for the snake to achieve its desire. The snake devoured the child whole, who screamed to no avail as he met his demise."

"How horrible a tale," Madeline whispered.

"It becomes worse. For the maid was roused from sleep by the screams of the child. She ran into the chamber, but arrived after the snake had disappeared back to its hiding place. She saw only the blood of the child upon the linens, and the blood of the snake upon the jowls of the hound, Gelert. She assumed that all the blood was from the same small body, and she screamed that the hound had murdered its master's son."

"Oh!"

"The knight returned from the hunt shortly thereafter, and was told of events. His wife was devastated, while he was furious. He called his hound, which came to him willingly for the beast knew that it had done no wrong. And the knight pulled his sword and killed his own hound with a single stroke. He struck the head from his loyal dog with his own blade in his own hand, he saw justice served for the crime he believed his dog had done."

"Oh no," Madeline whispered.

"And his wife wept, inconsolable at the loss of her son." Rhys licked his lips, his gaze upon his own hound, which stared at him adoringly. This tale seemed to Madeline to be a terrible reason to give a hound such a name. She had no chance to speak before Rhys continued, his words so melodic that the tale seemed to cast a spell.

"But there was a peasant in the bailey, a woman who had come to beg the knight's charity on the day that he was at hunt and who had chosen to await his return. She had seen the snake slither from the window of the nursery, she had seen it disappear into a hole in the wall of the cellar. She had witnessed the knight's return and the anguish that ensued. It was only when she heard the tale of what had happened, that she wondered about the snake. She had her audience with the knight, and instead of making her plea, she told him of what she had glimpsed. He immediately sent men to seek out this uncommon snake."

Madeline shivered and it seemed that the night pressed closer. Rhys rose and put some more wood on the fire. He squatted on the far side of the fire and stared into the flames. The light danced through the linen of his chemise, painting his chest with golden light, and she yearned to run her hands across his warm skin once again.

Then he spoke, even as he seemed fascinated by the fire. "They found the beast sleeping in the cellar, where it had hidden for years between the cobbles and the casks, and they were afraid of its unholy size even while it slumbered. But the knight and his men attacked it all the same, and they cut off its head, though it took three strokes from three different blades to break the snake's unholy armor. It was then, as the blood of the snake stained their boots, that they heard a babe crying."

"Oh!" Madeline raised her clasped hands to her lips. Rhys cast her a smile and came to sit beside her, capturing her clasped fingers within the heat of his own. He rubbed her hands between his, kindling more than one kind of warmth within her. She could smell his skin and she tingled at his proximity.

"When the knight and his men looked within the corpse of the snake, they found the knight's infant son, bloodied and frightened but otherwise unharmed. So, the truth of that day's events was finally known."

"But the hound . . ." Madeline whispered.

Rhys lifted a curl of her hair in his fingers, turning the tendril in the light of the fire as if it was uncommonly fascinating. Madeline held her breath.

"Aye, the hound was dead, and for no good reason. The knight despaired at what he had done," he said softly, "for he had killed his most loyal servant unjustly and he knew the fullness of his sin."

Madeline held his hand tightly, even as this Gelert began to snore in contentment. The hound had spread across the indentation on the cloak that Rhys had left, and had done so with undisguised contentment.

"The nursemaid, whose testimony had condemned the hound, left those lands forever and was never seen again. The knight built a shrine to the memory of Gelert with his own hands and spent his days in penance and mourning. His lands failed beneath God's disfavor, and his keep fell to ruins, save for the shrine which was visited by one and all. Yet he did not complain, for he knew that this was the reward for his haste and faithlessness. His lady returned to her family with their son, abandoning him to his grief, but the knight served his penance tirelessly."

Rhys sighed and entwined his fingers more tightly with those of Madeline. "And so it is told that when the knight died and faced his judgment, it was his hound, Gelert, loyal for all eternity, that he found at the very feet of God, begging clemency for his beloved master."

Madeline wiped her tears with the hem of her kirtle, embarrassed to find her eyes wet while Rhys's were dry. "You have a power with a tale, husband."

"I am Welsh," he said softly, humor touching his tone this time.

Madeline offered him an unsteady smile. "Should I be surprised that it is a tale of loyalty spurned?"

Rhys shrugged and eyed the dog, seemingly startled by her observation. Madeline reached up and touched his jaw. The stubble of his beard prickled her palm as she cupped his face in her hand, and he turned with her urging to look down at her. There were shadows lurking in his eyes, shadows she yearned to push aside.

"Who betrayed you, Rhys?" she asked without ever intending to do so. She bit her lip then, wishing she could call back the question that would only put the wall between them once again.

Rhys parted his lips, then closed them again. Madeline was certain he would deny her an answer once more, but he met her gaze abruptly, solemnly.

"My father," he admitted, the confession hoarse.

"But I thought you were his only son."

"I was." Rhys bent his head and touched his lips to Madeline's fingertips. The firelight danced in the ebony curls of his hair and he spoke into her hand, his gaze hidden from her. "But in the end, a bastard, even a bastard son who served him well, could not suffice."

Madeline had a glimpse of the wound left by that betrayal, a fleeting sight of the hurt that Rhys hid uncommonly well. She bent and kissed his hand, wondering whether the salt upon his flesh was from his tears or her own. She eased closer to him then and touched her lips to the corner of his mouth, feeling him shiver beneath her caress.

How could she expect Rhys to understand her notions of marriage, given his own history? He had never witnessed a loving match, never been able to trust those upon whom he should have been able to rely.

There was but one solution: she would have to teach him to trust her. She would have to teach her husband the merit of a loving, monogamous match.

Madeline did not doubt that it could be done. Indeed, she sensed that Rhys longed to trust her but that he dared not do so, out of fear that what he had endured might repeat itself.

It was fortunate that she was as persistent as the man believed.

She slipped her fingers into his hair, keeping her face close to his own. She could nigh hear his heart begin to pound. "I trust you will not make the same error with this hound, after we conceive a son," she whispered.

Rhys smiled ruefully. "There are no snakes in Caerwyn."

"And there is not yet a babe in my belly." She took his hands and brought them to her waist. She saw the flash of Rhys's dark eyes and knew that she wanted to be with him this night beyond all else. She wanted his heat within her, she wanted to be surrounded by his embrace. "We have sons to conceive, Rhys. This was our wager, and I would see it kept."

Madeline had truly read her husband's desire aright. No sooner had she uttered her invitation than she found herself upon her back, Rhys's heat above her, and his kiss demanding her response.

She knotted her fingers in his hair and drew him closer. She granted the response he demanded of her, and she granted it most willingly indeed.

Madeline found his secrets even when

Rhys thought them well disguised. She seemed to be able to peer directly into his heart, to be capable of retrieving what he would have kept from her at all costs.

And worse, Rhys did not care.

Madeline offered him honesty and loyalty that he knew he had done little to deserve. She offered herself, her passion and her wit, and he would claim each gift with gusto. He would give her sons, he would give her pleasure, he would give her a home of which she could be proud. He would defend her against all threats, with his sword and his life, if need be.

If her heart was not to be his, what she offered him already would more than suffice. It was more than any other soul had ever granted to Rhys FitzHenry and he suspected that it was more than he deserved.

He was a shameless cur, and this caress she granted him might as well have been stolen from her. It was gained by deceit, and though he knew it, Rhys did not confess the truth. He was a scoundrel — for truly, what manner of knave would accept what the lady offered without telling her that her beloved James still drew breath?

Then Madeline kissed Rhys with vigor, driving all such concern from his thoughts. She had learned quickly how pleasure abed was kindled. Her tongue duelled with his own, her hands ran over him, as if she were as impatient as he. He forced himself to slow their lovemaking, to take the time to savor the taste of her. He broke their kiss and traced a path to her ear with his lips, smiling against the softness of her flesh when she whispered his name in complaint.

He stretched out beside her, one hand running over her curves lightly as he kissed her ear. Madeline stirred restlessly, her hand landing upon the lace of his chausses.

"Patience," Rhys counselled softly. "The reward is greater when it is approached slowly."

In response, she turned her head and sealed her lips to his again.

Rhys claimed her busy hands and lifted them over her head, entangling his fingers with her own. Madeline stretched, arching her back as he unlaced the sides of her kirtle with his free hand. He slid his hand beneath the cloth and teased her nipples to peaks. She writhed beside him, the scent of her fairly tormenting him. He was not surprised to find the dampness gathering between her thighs, nor that she parted her legs to his questing fingers.

Still they kissed as if intent upon devouring each other, her hunger growing with every passing moment. He took pride in how he coaxed her response, took pleasure in watching her reach for her own.

There were few gifts he could give her, but he could give her this one. A flush rose over her cheeks, a trembling seized her body, and still he coaxed her onward. And when she cried out, he swallowed the sound of her release with a satisfaction of his own.

He let her catch her breath for a moment, before his fingers moved against her softness again. She gasped his name and he smiled, though he did not cease.

"Again?" she whispered, even as her body responded.

"A woman can seize pleasure repeatedly in one night, as we already know. Shall we not discover how oft it can be done?"

Madeline's eyes sparkled and she nestled closer, her fingers falling upon the erection which strained his chausses. "What of a man?"

"Aye, that too can be done. All the same, we will pursue mine only once this night."

Her smile warmed his heart. "Because you yet fear to hurt me." She pressed her lips to the corner of his mouth, her caress fairly driving him mad. "I would not have you displeased, Rhys."

"There is no cause to fear for that," he grumbled, then moved his fingers against her once again.

Her second release came more quickly, though it was more vehement than the first. Her eyes glittered and her face flushed crimson, yet barely had Madeline cried out than she was pulling at his chemise.

"I can wait no longer, Rhys," she whispered, her urgency like music to his ears. He shed his boots and chausses with haste, but halted her when she would have cast aside her kirtle.

"You will become cold," he counselled, then slid beneath the hem. Their gazes locked and held; her lips parted as he eased himself within her heat. He bent and touched his brow to hers, willing himself to proceed slowly, even as his wife began to move beneath him.

"You are a bold wench," he teased and she laughed.

She locked her hands around his neck and regarded him with such delight that Rhys had an idea.

"Hold fast," he counselled, then rolled quickly to his back. Madeline gasped, though he remained buried within her, then she laughed again to find herself atop him.

She braced her hands upon his shoulders and laughed down at him, her hair in fetching disarray. "What do I do?"

"Whatsoever you desire," he said with a smile. "I am your captive."

Her smile turned wicked then and despite his advice, she cast off her kirtle and chemise. The light of the flames caressed her curves lovingly, gilding her like the treasure she was. Alexander had rightly called his sister a jewel, though she was worth far far more than the price Rhys had paid. He was fascinated by the sight of his wife, enthralled by the way she surveyed him, enchanted by the glimmer of mischief in her gaze.

When she began to move, he knew he would not last. He gripped her hips and watched her, fighting his body's desire for release. She took such pleasure in the torment she granted to him that he wanted to endure it all the night long, though that was not destined to be. With every stroke, he became more taut, he felt more invincible, her web drew a little tighter around him.

Suddenly, Madeline lay upon his chest and kissed him soundly. She trailed kisses to his ear, as he had done to her, and he thought his heart would stop. Rhys caught her close, loving the press of her breasts against him, the tangle of her hair in his mouth. They moved together, in perfect concert, and he felt the deep quiver awaken within her once more.

"Rhys!" she gasped as the tumult claimed her. At the sight of her pleasure, he could restrain himself no longer. His triumphant shout echoed through the forest and Rhys did not care who heard him.

It took him long to even his breathing, even longer to calm the erratic pace of his heart. His wife's eyes closed almost immediately, her dark lashes making crescents against her fair skin. He kissed her temple, affection swelling his heart to bursting.

"Quite definitely a son," Madeline whispered sleepily against his throat and Rhys smiled. He wrapped her protectively in her cloak, then rose to kick out the flames. He dressed while he watched her in the embers' glow, then rejoined her in their makeshift bed. He evicted the hound, then pulled his own cloak over himself and Madeline, cradling her against his chest for the night.

Only then did he sleep, the warmth of his wife curled against him, and truly, he was content.

Chapter Twelve

Madeline awakened to find Rhys's gloved finger against her lips and his lips against her ear. Her eyes flew open and she realized that he had braced his weight upon his elbows over her, shielding her from some threat. He was dressed and wide awake, his watchful gaze flitting across the camp. Gelert was alert, as well, and a faint growl escaped the hound's chest.

Rhys whispered a single command which must have been in Welsh and the dog fell silent. The hair still stood on the back of the hound's neck, though, and the creature was nigh as watchful as Rhys.

It was only then that Madeline heard the sound of hoofbeats echoing through the forest. They were distant but drawing closer, the pace of the horses indicating that they trod the path she and Rhys had followed the day before.

"Destriers," she murmured, knowing the sound of heavy warhorses.

Rhys nodded. "Three."

Madeline listened carefully and realized that the steeds came from the direction of

Moffat. It must be their pursuers!

But if so, they had split forces, for there had been six destriers the day before. Madeline bit her lip, not wanting to consider what would happen to Rhys if they were captured. She struggled to recall what she knew of the road to Glasgow ahead, for her father and uncle had spoken often of such matters.

It proved to be convenient to have a family so engaged in trade. There were times when Tynan delivered relics for Rosamunde — though under protest — and other times when Michael dispatched trained falcons from Inverfyre. All of the men discussed routes when the family met and Madeline was glad she had listened even as much as she had.

The hoofbeats grew in volume, coming dangerously close. Rhys lowered himself further and Madeline buried her face in his shoulder. The horses passed without halting, then faded in the distance of the direction they meant to go this day.

Rhys waited long moments before he finally rose. As soon as he did, Madeline leapt to her feet and dressed with haste, knowing full well what had to be done. She relieved herself and washed with uncommon speed, then returned to find the horses saddled.

She opened one saddlebag and granted Rhys a piece of bread, another chunk of cheese and an apple. He hesitated, eying the low angle of the sun, clearly estimating how far they could ride this day.

"We must eat," she counselled sternly. "And it will serve little to be fast upon their heels."

"I would seek a fork in the road." Rhys accepted the food and counsel with impatience, but at least he ceded to her. "There must be another route, one that they will not anticipate."

"I believe the road does fork, perhaps at Abington." Madeline tried to recall the precise location as Rhys watched her with interest. "The east road goes to Edinburgh, the west to Glasgow."

"And there must be links between them, shortcuts for those travelling in the opposite direction." Rhys bent and seized a handful of ashes from the dead fire, then began to rub them over his destrier's hide. Arian quickly took on a darker hue.

"Once one has consorted with horse thieves, their cunning is not readily forgotten," Madeline said, then took a handful of ash to the horse's other side.

Rhys's grin flashed unexpectedly. "The strategy works so long as there is no rain.

Will you pray for that, my lady?"

"If my husband makes the matter worth my while," she teased, liking the way his eyes gleamed. The bite of the wind was suddenly less, the threat offered by the king's men more remote. She smiled at her husband, a tingle dancing over her very flesh.

Rhys started at some noise in the distance and his merry mood was dispatched. Madeline shivered, reminded of the sun ducking suddenly behind a cloud, leaving a chill where its heat had been.

"They might believe you intent upon begging clemency at the court of the King of Scotland," she suggested.

"And so we could feign that we made a course to Edinburgh," Rhys mused, then regarded her steadily. He began to smile. "You guessed all along that we fled the king's men."

Madeline sniffed. "I would wager that you do not know a single soul in Glasgow."

Rhys shook his head. "And I would wager that you will not agree to patiently wait hidden here while I check the road."

Madeline met his bemused gaze. "For better or for worse, husband, we ride together."

Rhys nodded, apparently not displeased. "Aye, and for better or for worse, *anwylaf,*

345

we come to understand each other." He offered his hand. "Into the saddle, my lady. It will be a long day."

And so it was.

For three days and nights, they gave a merry chase to the party on the black destriers. They hid in barns and lurked in forests; they raced down roads making all the noise they could muster, then crept back along shallow creeks. Rhys dodged and feinted with such abandon that Madeline was oft unsure whether they made any progress toward Glasgow at all.

They heard the great horses, of course. Madeline caught only the barest glimpse of the beasts' dark rumps, for Rhys always hid her fully from the sight of them. Their hoofbeats thundered past hiding places, the sound of their passing making Madeline's heart thump in fear.

On the first day, they came close enough to Glasgow to enter a warren of entangled roads around its perimeter, which pleased her spouse mightily. Rhys seemingly made a random choice at every crossroads, darting this way and that across the countryside. The hoofbeats were fast behind them the first day, through she heard them less frequently with every passing day.

It was only on the third day that Madeline realized they had steadily eased to the northwest, circumnavigating Glasgow on the north side. On that day, too, she heard the party pursuing them less and less frequently. Perhaps their pursuers truly had believed that they had made for Edinburgh. There was no hint of them when she awakened on the fourth morning to the patter of rain.

All was grey around her, and many of the trees were just beginning to come into leaf. The sky was an endless spread of pewter-hued clouds and the rain already began to make mud of the road. Rhys huddled in his cloak, watchful and silent as he had been for days.

"There will be a new moon this night," he said gruffly, as if such news was of great import.

"And what of it?"

"It is time we made haste." He stood then and shook the rain out of his cloak, saddling the horses with quick purpose.

Madeline knew she should be growing accustomed to her husband's manner, but such enigmatic statements still had the power to annoy her. Yet she knew that if she asked him for an explanation, he would not grant her one.

"How old are you, Rhys?" she asked

while assembling the last of their fare. Three apples were the sum of it. She hoped his scheme to make haste included a good meal later this day.

"I have seen thirty summers. Why do you ask?"

"And do you oft consort with women?"

"I have, on occasion." He regarded her with suspicion. "Why?"

"But never for more than a night or two, I would wager."

Rhys nodded, but said no more.

"That answers my question, then."

"What question?"

"How so vexing a man could survive so long, of course. Had you been wed before, you would have been found dead in your own bed years ago! There is not a woman alive who can endure such a meager measure of information as you will surrender." Madeline bit into her apple. "And even that must be coaxed from your lips morsel by morsel."

"Yet every time I have very nearly been found dead in my bed, as you say, it has been because I confessed too much to some soul I should not have trusted." He tightened the harness around the palfrey's belly, unrepentant. "I think you have the wrong end of the tale, my lady."

Madeline stopped eating to regard him in astonishment. "Do you mean that you tell me so little because you still do not trust me? What cause have you to distrust me?"

"What cause have I to trust you?" he answered and held her gaze unswervingly.

"But we meet abed each night in pleasure!"

"That and trust are two different matters."

"I should be insulted."

"You are too clever not to see that I speak the truth. Come, my lady, time it is to ride."

Madeline let him aid her to mount, uncertain what to do about his skepticism. What could she do to encourage his trust? Madeline could imagine no worse fate than spending her life beside a man who did not — or would not — trust her.

She had aided his flight. She had shared what she knew of the countryside. She had wed him, she had bedded him, she had agreed to his demand for sons, she had tried to make their marriage meet her expectations. What else could she do?

Or had she only to continue on her present course to slowly win him to her side? Was Rhys so terse because he softened toward her, and he feared the import of that?

Madeline had plenty of time to consider

the puzzle, for Rhys was disinclined to talk on this day. Each time she tried to speak, he raised an imperious finger, silencing her as he listened intently for any hint of pursuit.

And the weather was not an aid to conversation. Within moments of their riding out of their camp, the gentle patter ended and it began to rain as if the deluge had come again.

The rain fell in sheets; it fell relentlessly, steadily, endlessly. They were sodden to their very bones within moments, and the soot was washed away quickly from Arian's hide.

Fortunately, there did not seem to be anyone interested in identifying the horse or two riders fool enough to be out in such weather. The road was so quiet that Rhys began to ride openly, his pace relentless.

Rhys took a course due west, without explanation, and Madeline watched the plumes of smoke that must be rising from Glasgow slide past them to the south. It was clear he did not make for Glasgow at all. She wondered at his destination, for only the highlands and islands lay ahead of them.

And the sea, of course. She smelled its salt in the wind and tasted it in the rain. She strained her ears and thought she could discern its rhythm on a close shore. That was welcome, at least, for she had missed the sound and sight of the ocean.

She might not know where she was going, or what her husband desired of her beyond those sons, but she would take the lesson from his tales. She would savor whatever small gifts came to her. She would look forward to seeing the sea in all its silver majesty again.

And that, for the moment, would have to suffice.

In contrast, far to the south at Caerwyn keep, the sun shone merrily. The sea glistened beyond the high white walls for which the keep was named, the pennants snapped in the wind from the sea, birds cried overhead and the widow of Henry ap Dafydd was annoyed beyond belief.

Nelwyna supposed that she should have become accustomed to matters not proceeding in her favor, for she had faced obstacle after obstacle since arriving as a new bride at this holding. Nonetheless, each new challenge seemed an insult, an abnegation of all she had suffered and endured in the hope of ultimately achieving her ambition. Thus, each cursed time that something went awry, she was infuriated.

All she had ever desired, all she had ever deserved, was to be the lady of a fief. She did not even care which one, and even Caerwyn, at this point, would suffice. Nelwyna had wed Henry ap Dafydd, believing that she would be his lady upon her marriage, but she had been deceived. Henry had held title to nothing. All the family wealth had passed to his elder brother, Dafydd ap Dafydd. Even when Dafydd had captured Caerwyn, she had hoped he might grant it to Henry, but Dafydd had kept all.

Even now, with Dafydd and Henry both dead, and Dafydd's wife and children also gone, Nelwyna was merely regent in her stepson's stead. Nelwyna chafed with the awareness that her authority could be (and would be) removed with but a moment's notice.

It was unfair!

On this day, to be sure, her mood was already sour, but morning had brought many vexations to test an old woman's humor. Nelwyna had awakened with aches in her joints and her years heavy upon her shoulders. She was painfully aware that she had not much time left to gain her objective.

She made her painful way to the hall, anticipating a good meal to break her fast, at least. Sadly, she would not eat alone this day. The pretty face of her husband's cursed courtesan, and the sparkle of that woman's laughter, did little to brighten the morn.

Indeed, the sight of Adele was enough to make Nelwyna's blood boil. Nelwyna had never become accustomed to the Welsh, with their disregard for the sanctity of marital vows, with their lack of concern with legitimacy. When Henry had returned from a journey with Adele fairly in his lap, almost forty summers before, the entire household had been shocked that Nelwyna was not immediately pleased.

A man needed a son, they told her.

A man must do what must be done.

She should be glad, they told her, that the burden of responsibility had been removed from her, that there would be no shame attached to her name.

Nelwyna, surrounded by mad people, her own womb seemingly intent on producing solely daughters, had feigned acceptance. She had pretended that their scheme made great sense, she had hidden her resentment, she had welcomed the whore to her home with a false smile.

But Nelwyna had never accepted Adele's presence. She had prayed for the whore to die in labor, with no result. She had schemed to ensure the whore had a fateful accident, but the woman had the luck of the angels.

Worse, Adele never seemed to age, a fact that Nelwyna despised when she felt her every year so keenly. Adele's face was nigh as smooth as the day she had arrived here. She was calm and serene and so sweet of nature that she fairly made Nelwyna's teeth ache.

It was uncommonly cruel that Adele had been the one to bear Henry the son he so desired.

"Look, Nelwyna!" Adele cried as the older woman had made her way to the board. "A missive from my sister, Miriam."

That Adele was happier than usual this day was as salt in the wound.

"How delightful. How fortunate you are to have kin who remember you." Nelwyna settled herself at the board and took the largest piece of honeycomb without remorse. It was her right to eat first, at least, and she never refrained from taking the best that was offered. "How wise it was for Miriam to take the veil and retire from secular life, once her husband had died."

It was the broadest hint imaginable, but Adele only smiled. "I had long thought you might so retire. Henry, after all, has been gone these ten years and you have no surviving children to make demands upon you."

The reminder that Adele's child lived, despite Nelwyna's efforts, made the older woman grind her teeth. Nelwyna vowed then to have vengeance upon the courtesan. How vulgar and selfish Adele was! And Nelwyna was the only one who could see it!

Adele, oblivious, unfurled the missive and read with avid interest, her small white teeth nibbling at the fullness of her ruddy bottom lip.

Was it possible that there was not a single silver hair in that ebony mane?

"Oh!" Adele said, and paled. She frowned and read the missive again, then tucked it hastily into her bodice.

"Bad tidings?" Nelwyna asked.

Adele granted her the barest glance. "It is not of import. What fine honey we have this day!"

In that moment Nelwyna decided she must read that missive. She would have wagered that there was news within it that she could use in her own favor.

Tidings she could use against this pretty fool.

★ ★ ★

That objective brought Nelwyna to Adele's chamber, in the midst of a fine afternoon. Adele always retired to rest in the afternoon, a old habit adopted when Henry was alive. He had accompanied his courtesan to her chamber in those days, and the sounds of their lovemaking had been evident to any soul who pressed her ear against the door to listen.

Nelwyna, meanwhile, had been compelled to welcome Henry late at night, after he had drunk his fill of ale, after his prick had already been bathed in his whore's sauces.

She did not miss the old cur. She would have been rid of the whore upon his death, but the choice had not been hers to make. By some folly of her father — or some glib tale of her spouse — she had been wed to the younger son of Dafydd, the man who would only inherit if his elder brother died before him.

Sadly, Dafydd ap Dafydd had been a vigorous old toad, and had only surrendered his grip upon all he owned the previous Yule. It had been a measure of Henry's merit, in Nelwyna's opinion, that he had never cared that he lived in his brother's home, beneath his brother's hand, taking his meals and his ale from his brother's table. The man had not had a drop of jealousy in his veins, nor any measure of ambition. He had been content in Dafydd's shadow, the old fool.

Worse, when Henry had finally died, Dafydd had professed to liking Adele too much to cast her out. Nelwyna had oft wondered if he had partaken of Adele's feast in Henry's absence.

She crept into Adele's chamber, hating that it was so much finer than her own. It was warmer, it was larger, it had a better view and it was more richly appointed. Only an imbecile could have failed to discern the intensity of Henry's affections.

It had been that son that had changed all. Nelwyna could never decide whether she loathed Adele or Rhys the most.

On the far side of the chamber, Adele slept, a small smile upon her face — perhaps one borne of recollection — a sunbeam caressing her cheek. The letter was on the small table beside her bed. Nelwyna stealthily crossed the floor.

It had been here that Adele had borne her children. Sons, all of them, curse her! Nelwyna had borne four daughters by the time Adele had arrived, four daughters conceived with some difficulty and delivered with even more. Adele had ripened within the season with her first, perhaps because Henry had not been able to leave her be.

Nelwyna had been rid of the first son easily enough. She had aided at the birth, for none suspected the depth of her hatred for this whore, and had offered to check the progress of the babe. She would never forget plunging her hand into Adele's heat, feeling the genitals of a boy, then impulsively easing the slick cord around the babe's neck.

He had been born dead, no one the wiser.

Or so Nelwyna had thought. At the birth of the second, she had been kept from Adele's side by the burly midwife with her suspicious eyes. At Henry's insistence, Nelwyna had been given the infant boy to hold — "her new son" he had said, ever gallant — and Nelwyna had seized a moment to hug him closely. She had pressed the swaddling against his tiny nose and mouth. Only when he wriggled no more had she loosed her hold, and cried out in dismay that something was amiss.

Nelwyna halted beside the bed, glaring down at her competitor with a hatred that was seldom undisguised. The third son had been born here, but Nelwyna had been barred from the chamber, accompanied by Henry to the great hall to wait. No protest had eased his resolve to keep her from joining the women that night, and miraculously, no ale had crossed his lips.

When they put his screaming son into his arms, Henry had tickled the boy's chin and the babe had fallen silent immediately. The small hand had closed around Henry's finger, as if trusting his father to ensure his welfare. Nelwyna still could see Henry, see the awe in his gaze, could hear his voice.

"His name is Rhys," Henry had said with rare vigor, then had raised his knowing gaze to meet Nelwyna's own. "In memory of the Welsh leader Rhys ap Tudur. Already this child has overcome such great adversity that I know he, too, will be long remembered."

He had turned then to address the gathered household. "My wife will never be within three strides of this child, she will not hold him, she will never feed him, she will never be left alone with him. Does every soul understand me?"

That he would shame her so in front of their servants had nigh killed Nelwyna. Henry had no right to speak to her thus!

He had no reason to make the household suspicious of her!

She had hated him from that day forward.

And she had had her vengeance by turning one of the pleasures he loved most against him. Slowly, Henry became accustomed to a slight taste in his beloved ale. That was the only hint of the presence of an herb that addled his wits and shrivelled his intellect.

Nelwyna would have preferred to shrivel another part of Henry and eliminate an entirely different pleasure, but she did not know the potion for that. What she knew had had to suffice.

She laid a hand upon the missive, watching the rhythm of Adele's breathing carefully, then fled the chamber on silent feet.

She would have to return it, but if Adele awakened, all would not be lost. Like many pretty women, like many souls burdened with the abundant blessings of good fortune, Adele was inclined to forget the locale of her treasures. Nelwyna would leave it in the hall, if compelled to do so, and Adele would believe she had left it there.

Nelwyna unfurled the missive impatiently, beside the sole window on the stairs, read in haste, then clenched it in her fist. Rhys had wed!

Adele undoubtedly was wounded that her son had not told her of this news himself, but Nelwyna saw more in the tale. She saw the bride's name and already understood how cunning and thorough Rhys was. Gone was the chance that she could present an imposter as Dafydd's sole surviving daughter.

Nelwyna had waited long for the authority of Caerwyn to fall into her hands fully, she had already seen children dead for her ambition, and she was too aged to wait patiently any longer.

The solution was simple. Rhys FitzHenry would have to die. And if his new bride Madeline carried his child, she would have to die as well. Nelwyna returned the missive to Adele's chamber, then retreated to her own chamber to compose a missive of her own.

It was good, in such times, to have neighbors one could rely upon. Robert Herbert held Harlech, just across the bay, and had made his lust for Caerwyn most clear. It was time, Nelwyna was certain, to secure an alliance with Robert that would grant both of them what they most desired.

Rhys supposed the tavern before them would serve well enough. It was late and

Madeline was clearly tired, though still she rode valiantly without complaint. He would have continued onward, but he suspected they would fare no better.

They would only be more cold and more tired.

This tavern was not located on a main thoroughfare, and it was not one of the larger establishments in town. It was busy, but not too busy, and Rhys was glad to note that none expected to know him here. If they were accustomed to travellers, then they would take little notice of two more.

"I believe the babe is making you ill this night," he said beneath his breath to Madeline, who had not ceased to tuck the bundle of cloth beneath her skirts each day.

"How ill?" she asked softly, with a wondrous lack of argument. That alone showed her exhaustion, to Rhys's thinking. He would do well to provide her with a bed and a warm meal this night, for she must be unaccustomed to such hardship as their journey had demanded.

"So ill that you will be compelled to take to your bed and bar the door." Rhys gave her a stern look as he dismounted in the small courtyard of the tavern. The sound of men enjoying their ale carried from the common room and the creak of masts could be heard in the nearby harbor. The wind was crisp off the sea.

"This must be Dumbarton," Madeline said as he fitted his hands around her waist.

"So it is." Rhys tossed a coin at the ostler, then held Madeline's elbow with care. To his delight, she leaned on him and moaned softly, walking with apparent effort toward the portal. He had thought his ploy a thin one, but Madeline made it entirely plausible.

To Rhys's further delight, she began to complain, as if they had been wed for years and were in the habit of bickering. And her accent changed, her words beginning to rollick and roll with the same vigor as those uttered by the people of the highlands.

Rhys was impressed. He struggled to do as admirable a job of disguising himself as she.

"I fear we rode too quickly this afternoon, my lord," Madeline complained, her tone shrewish. "It was just as I warned you, but did you heed my counsel? Nay, of course not. What need had you of the advice of a mere woman? You and your cursed haste! What rush was there, what need for such a pace?"

"I wanted you out of the rain, lest you be chilled," Rhys answered as if sorely tried by his wife. He exchanged a glance with the ostler, who looked most sympathetic before he ducked away, leading the horses to the stables. The innkeeper came to the portal, taking care to remain out of the rain, while Rhys urged Madeline closer to warmth and a hearty meal.

"So, I am chilled *and* prepared to retch, thanks to your thoughtlessness," Madeline snapped. "It is a foul combination, sir, and one I would have readily forgone."

Rhys pretended to take umbrage at this. "Then you should not have insisted that we had to visit your mother immediately!" He flung out one hand. "You might have been home in your own bed this night but for your own demand. You cannot be warm at home and warm at your mother's abode on the same night!"

The innkeeper bit back a smile at this exchange, and gestured grandly to his humble inn. They stepped through the door and were immediately perused by the dozen or so men gathered there to drink. The smoke stung Rhys's eyes and it was dark, but he did not think he knew anyone in that chamber.

Though it was impossible to be certain that no one knew him. The men glanced up and Rhys was afraid.

Madeline began to behave like a spoiled child. "How could I remain in that unholy place you insist upon calling my *home?* My mother will aid me with this child you have put in my belly, my mother will show me kindness as no one in your cursed household will do!"

"But, my dear . . ." Rhys did not know what to do, much less what a doting husband should do. He glanced to the innkeeper, then to the other men gathered there, all of whom took a sudden and considerable interest in their cups of ale.

Indeed, they turned their backs upon the feuding couple and ignored them.

Madeline burst into tears, so adept at pretending to be a distraught woman that Rhys was discomfited. "All I asked was to visit my mother!" she wailed. "All I asked was to have a good husband! What sin have I committed in my days to deserve this unkind fate?" She pushed him aside and swatted his arm. "You liked me well enough before your own seed made me fat!"

The innkeeper cleared his throat. "Perhaps the good sir would prefer a chamber, that the lady might slumber in privacy?"

"That would be most fitting," Rhys said.

"And a bath!" Madeline cried. "I would sell my soul, sir, for a hot bath." She leaned closer to confide in the innkeeper. "We have only one servant in his abode, and she is the most lazy creature I have ever seen with my own eyes. She is fortunate that I did not insist upon her accompanying us, for my mother would take a switch to her!"

"I have no doubt that a bath can be had for a slightly more reasonable price," Rhys interrupted, feeling some irritation that he was being cast in such unfavorable light. He nodded to the innkeeper. "A cup of ale, a bowl of hearty stew and a piece of bread will go far in restoring my lady's mood, to be sure."

"Of course, sir. I have a chamber at the top of the stairs, which overlooks the street. If you will be so kind as to follow me?"

"One piece of bread?" Madeline snarled as they followed the innkeeper up the narrow staircase. "I could eat *six!* This child has made me ravenous and you, you would save a penny rather than see me granted a decent meal. With such cruelty, I shall end up bearing you a dark child, so shrivelled that even the fairies will not have any desire of stealing it."

Rhys barely kept himself from giving her a shake. "I thought you were too ill to eat much."

The lock upon the door seemed to require every mote of the innkeeper's attention.

Madeline straightened like a queen on the threshold of the chamber and glared at Rhys. "I shall do what I must to ensure the vigor of our child," she said haughtily. "Though you will not thank me for it, to be sure."

Then she turned one of those smiles that left Rhys so dazzled upon the innkeeper, leaving that man blinking as well. "This chamber is lovely," she said warmly. "I thank you for the offering of it and look forward to both bath and meal."

With that, Madeline swept regally into the small chamber, which in truth was barely big enough to accommodate the pallet upon the floor. Rhys did not doubt that a few fleas could be found in the linens.

"A feisty one," that man muttered beneath his breath. "But fair to look upon, if I may say so, sir."

"It is the babe that vexes her," Rhys agreed in an undertone. "I am certain that her sweet nature will return with the babe's arrival."

"That has not been my experience, sir, but I wish you better fortune than mine." The innkeeper leaned closer. "And if you would have a decent night's rest yourself, I would note that among my own wife's skills is that of making a good potion."

"What manner of potion do you offer?"

"One that will ensure your wife sleeps deeply this night." He named a price that seemed quite reasonable to Rhys. Indeed, it would suit Rhys well to know that Madeline slept soundly — remained out of trouble and asked no questions — while he made the necessary arrangements for the continuation of their journey to Caerwyn. His friend's ship would sail south on the night after the new moon, and Rhys intended that they should both be upon it.

"It will not injure the babe?" he asked, knowing that he should do so to maintain their disguise.

The innkeeper shook his head. "Nay, my wife learned it from a midwife."

"I think it a sound notion. Exhaustion does little to aid one's mood, and my lady never sleeps well when we are away from our abode. I thank you for the suggestion."

"Grant me a few moments, sir, and I will return with all." The innkeeper then raised his voice to shout for a brazier for the chamber.

Rhys crossed the threshold and closed the door behind himself with relief. He was utterly unprepared for Madeline to launch herself into his arms, her eyes sparkling with delight.

"Were they not fooled?" she whispered, clearly pleased with her ploy. "There is not a soul who will be able to identify us on the morrow. Did they not look away from us, each and every one of them?"

Rhys smiled at her, unable to resist her delight in her feat.

"They did indeed, *anwylaf*," he acknowledged with admiration. He cupped her jaw in his hand and slipped his other arm around her waist. She leaned against him, a heat kindling in her gaze that made him smile. "And it was all due to your quick thinking." He claimed her lips with his own then, for truly, he could do nothing else.

Chapter Thirteen

In another, much more busy tavern in Dumbarton, Elizabeth was glad to be out of the saddle. The destrier was too large a mount for her. She had known as much as soon as she was lifted into the saddle, though she had not dared to complain for fear she would be left behind. Her knees ached nigh as much as her buttocks, for she had had to clench the steed tightly to ensure that she was not cast into the dirt.

They had ridden for more days than she could count. Elizabeth could not recall having ridden for more than half a day before this seemingly endless journey. She wondered whether she would ever walk with ease again.

She also wondered why Madeline had ever possessed any fondness for James. Elizabeth was certain that she had never met a man so tedious in all her days. She could not imagine that James had any great affection for Madeline, for the man saved all of his admiration for himself.

Elizabeth had the definite sense that

James had only arrived to wed Madeline because his father had thought the match a fitting one, though she knew that was an uncharitable thought.

James plucked at his lute as they sat at the board, more concerned with some tune he had composed this day than Madeline's safety or even the common courtesy of table manners. He had been most vexed earlier this day that Rosamunde had refused to halt their search so that he could ensure he did not forget the tune by playing it a dozen times. He had sulked the remainder of the day, only conjuring a smile now that he had his lute in his hands once again.

Elizabeth would have liked to have destroyed the lute, so sick was she of James's tuneless plucking. The man imagined himself to be far more gifted than he was, in her opinion.

But then, her buttocks ached and she was tired. Perhaps she would have looked more kindly upon him in better circumstance.

Perhaps not.

The spriggan had not been easy company, either. The mischievous fairy had pulled the horses' tails, spooked them in the night, and tied knots in their manes. A skittish destrier was no small challenge, especially for a rider of Elizabeth's size, but the spriggan seemed to care nothing for her convenience.

Additionally, Elizabeth had fished it out of more than one stream and snatched it in the air when it had lost its grip upon one horse or the other. She felt responsible for its welfare, as she was the only one who could see it and she had brought it along, though it had done little to reward her efforts.

At least she knew what it was and that its name was Darg. It talked to her sometimes, and told far better tales than any Elizabeth had ever heard.

She sighed with exhaustion as Rosamunde and Alexander argued about Rhys's intent and watched Darg consider the pottery ale cups on the board. The spriggan would do something, Elizabeth was certain of it, and she only hoped it would not take much effort to set matters aright. She yawned mightily, wanting only a pallet before the fire.

"He means to trick us," Alexander said, dropping his voice and leaning over the table. "He will leave in the night and ride south with all haste. We err in taking our slumber here, especially without knowing his destination within Dumbarton's walls."

"I only hope that Madeline is well,"

Vivienne said with some uncertainty. Vivienne sat opposite Elizabeth, looking as exhausted as Elizabeth felt. "Finding Kerr was horrible! Surely you do not think that Rhys would injure Madeline?"

"I suspect he saved her from injury," Rosamunde said tightly. "I never liked that mercenary Kerr and was glad when your father dispatched him."

"He did?" Alexander asked in dismay. "I did not know of this."

"You should have asked more questions before taking a man into your employ," Rosamunde said firmly. "Tynan likely could have told you more."

Alexander frowned in consideration of this and looked so troubled that Rosamunde laid a hand upon his shoulder.

"I know this has not been easy for you," she said. "You will learn, Alexander, and years from now, you will laugh at your own uncertainties."

"I hope as much," he said and drank grimly of his ale. "It seems all I do turns to disaster."

No one argued with that.

"You could ensure that all ended as well as an old tale," Elizabeth whispered to Darg.

The spriggan laughed, then faced Elizabeth, hands on hips. "A sorry day it will then be, if I should aid a mortal like thee. Fate's sharp needle is meant to prick, no mortal can avoid its nick."

A man at the next table granted Elizabeth a smile that she dared not return. She felt her color rise as she deliberately ignored him, knowing that he probably thought she talked to herself.

She bent over the board, lifting a piece of bread to her lips that she might whisper to the spriggan without arousing curiosity. "You could ensure Madeline's happiness. I saw what mischief you made with the ribbons. You have abilities that I do not."

Darg appeared to be shocked. "An uncommon mortal you might be, if Fate's fine threads you can see." She regarded Elizabeth with suspicion. "The ribbons twine for destined souls, tightly knotted like thorn and rose. Such pairs cannot be rent asunder, come hail or flood or dark or thunder."

It sounded perfect to Elizabeth and she leaned forward in her excitement. "Will you aid Madeline? Will you ensure that her ribbon and Rhys's are properly joined? I liked him when we met and I think she did as well." She refrained from glancing toward James.

Darg grinned. "Her betrothed mortal will soon be, so close that she herself can see." Darg looked pointedly at James then grimaced, not apparently liking the minstrel any more than Elizabeth did.

James crooned to himself as he plucked his tune, nodding with satisfaction at what seemed a most simple and uninspired melody to Elizabeth's ears. He seemed oblivious of the others at the table.

"Dreadful manners," Elizabeth muttered. "Maman would have boxed his ears."

"This mortal's ears are wrought of tin, if he finds beauty in his din," Darg said with disgust.

"Exactly! Madeline cannot be forced to wed him," Elizabeth insisted. "You could ensure that she is happy with Rhys!"

"It is not for me to change her life, to choose for her either wealth or strife."

"That is not true! I saw you knot Rosamunde's ribbons! I do not doubt that you caused the argument between her and Tynan."

Darg shrugged, though its expression was sly and it cast a glance toward Rosamunde that spoke volumes. "Every heart has its own key, the unlocking is not left to me."

Elizabeth gritted her teeth and wondered what she could do to win the stubborn fairy's aid.

"Rhys surely must be planning to sail to Caerwyn," Rosamunde said with conviction, unaware of Elizabeth's conversation with the spriggan. "There is no other reason to have come to Dumbarton. He will not ride further, but arrange passage on a ship. We must keep a vigil and watch the vessels in the harbor." She pointed at Padraig, who heaved a sigh.

"Might I finish this cup of ale first?" that man asked. He looked longingly toward the hearth. "A hot meal would also be welcome, before I spend another night in the rain."

Rosamunde drummed her fingers on the table with impatience, even as Darg climbed to the lip of Elizabeth's cup. The spriggan gave a shout of glee, then bent precariously and sipped of the ale. It drank like a hound, lapping from the surface, though the ale disappeared with astonishing speed.

"I would have you take a count of the ships in the harbor, note their colors and the names of their captains, and then return for your meal. I apologize, Padraig, but we must not lose Madeline when we are so close."

Darg hooted and danced around the rim of the cup while Elizabeth watched. There had to be some way to persuade Darg to help, but Elizabeth could not think of what it was.

Maybe she would be more clever in the morning, after she had slept.

"As you wish." Padraig stood, drained his ale, granted Rosamunde a dark glance, then left the tavern. He drew his cloak around himself, and a chilly gust of wind swirled around the ankles of all as he opened the portal.

Elizabeth shivered, flicked Darg from the rim of her cup, and took another swig of the ale. It warmed her innards in a way that was not displeasing, and even the smell of the peat fire did not trouble her on this night.

Darg meanwhile tumbled across the table, coming to an ungainly halt against Vivienne's cup. The spriggan was on its back, legs askew, a vexed expression on its small sharp face.

"But where is Caerwyn?" Vivienne asked Rosamunde. "Is it a castle with high towers?" The spriggan pulled itself up onto the rim of Vivienne's cup, then drank heartily of that cup's contents.

Could fairies become drunk? Elizabeth was not certain.

Rosamunde smiled. "It has a single tower and faces the sea. When Rhys and I crossed paths before, he was in service to his uncle, who is lord there. He undoubtedly has returned to that abode."

"But where is it?" Alexander asked. "It cannot be on the west of Scotland."

"It is in Wales, in the very shadow of Snowdonia." Rosamunde sipped of her own ale, her gaze slipping over the other people gathered in the tavern as if she assessed a threat. Elizabeth supposed her aunt had become accustomed to always being observant of her surroundings.

"Caerwyn was fortified by the English king Edward I. He defeated the Welsh prince, Llywelyn ap Gruffydd, and made a statement of his suzerainty by building a ring of stone fortresses around Snowdonia and reinforcing the existing ones he captured. Rhys's uncle and the Welsh rebel Owain Glyn Dŵr captured Caerwyn and another keep, Harlech, from the English forces some years ago."

Vivienne picked up her cup and frowned, apparently surprised to find so little ale within it. The spriggan shook a fist at Vivienne for so rudely interrupting its drink, then strutted toward Alexander's cup.

"A fortress?" Alexander sat back and shoved a hand through his hair, leaving it in a dark tangle. "You do not suppose that we will be kept from seeing Madeline, if they reach there before us?"

"Who can say?" Rosamunde spared a dissatisfied glance for James, who had closed his eyes and thrown back his head to listen to his own music. "It would be best if we found them first, would you not say, James?"

Rosamunde had to say his name twice more before James became aware of her voice. "What did you say?" he asked, then scowled at his stilled fingers. "I have forgotten my place in the tune, thanks to your interruption."

"Forgive me for reminding you of the reason for our journey," Rosamunde said tartly. "I had thought you interested in finding Madeline."

Annoyance flickered across James's features and was quickly gone, though not so quickly that the others did not note it. Elizabeth felt Alexander stiffen beside her and saw Vivienne's lips thin. "Of course I am determined to find Madeline," James said and summoned his most charming smile. "She is my betrothed and my beloved."

"You do not seem overly concerned with

her welfare," Alexander said.

"You do not seem fearful that she has been injured, or that she might be unhappy," Vivienne charged.

"Indeed, you seem more besotted with your lute than your betrothed," Elizabeth concluded.

"Me?" James looked between the three of them with astonishment. "I only compose a love song, that I might salute my lost lady appropriately when we are united again." He placed his hand over his heart. "My days have been dark since we parted and I can think of nothing else but seeing her sweet countenance again."

Vivienne snorted. "Then why did you let her believe you dead for the better part of a year? That is no kindness to inflict upon a beloved."

"I thought she knew! I never would have granted her a moment's anguish, had I guessed she did not know the truth!"

"How would she have learned the truth," Alexander asked carefully. "Since every man who fought at Rougemont was killed, but you?"

James colored and averted his gaze. "Oh, I was not the only one. You have heard an exaggeration, to be sure."

Alexander snorted and refrained from

saying more, though it was clear he had more to say.

Elizabeth did not believe James, not at all. She wondered if he had even been at Rougemont. She gave Darg a stern glance, but the spriggan defiantly climbed upon the lip of James's cup. Darg was somewhat less steady on its feet now as it danced around the rim and chortled over the merits of mortal ale.

Alexander picked up his cup, frowned that it was empty, then put it down heavily on the board. "When did you return home from France?" he asked, his annoyance barely disguised. "Where have you been since the battle at Rougemont?"

"Listening to music!" James cried, his eyes alight for the first time. "I heard the music in the cathedrals in France and it was so wondrous that I had to learn more. Madeline will be appreciative of this, I know for certain, for the love of music is a bond she and I share. Listen!" He lifted his lute and plucked his tune again.

Darg put its fingers in its ears and grimaced at the sound. Elizabeth stifled a laugh at the spriggan's antics, for she shared its view. Vivienne and Alexander exchanged a rueful glance.

The spriggan finished James's ale, then

mimicked his crooning manner as it eased closer to Rosamunde's cup. It considered the woman for so long that Elizabeth feared its scheme. She could do little, though, when it climbed to the rim of the cup, then dangled its feet in the ale.

The spriggan kicked its feet with vigor. A spray of ale rose from the cup and drenched the front of Rosamunde's tabard. "What is this?" that woman demanded, unable to discern why the ale was flying. She leapt to her feet, wiping the ale from the rich embroidery. "My garb will be ruined!"

Darg laughed with wicked glee. Vivienne leapt to her feet and wiped at the ale with her napkin, even as Rosamunde tried to brush the wetness away with her hands.

"There must be an insect in the cup!" Alexander cried and reached for the cup. Darg leapt with unexpected agility to the lip of the jug as Alexander lifted Rosamunde's cup, shook it and poured its contents into his own.

James halted his playing and regarded them with irritation. "I beg you heed my song. It is a compelling and beauteous tune that only a barbarian would not appreciate."

Darg laughed so hard and so raucously at this assertion that Elizabeth was shocked none could hear it. The spriggan threw back its head and crooned in perfect mimicry of the lutenist, laughed again, then fell backward into the jug of ale.

The splash made all at the table jump. "Perhaps it is a rat!" Vivienne cried.

"It is in the ale!" Alexander agreed.

"What piteous accommodation you have chosen for us," James said to Rosamunde with a sneer. "Rats in the ale! I have never heard the like of it."

"Then you are welcome to slumber elsewhere," Rosamunde snarled. "I have paid for your bed and bought your food and endured your dreadful music for long enough."

The pair leapt to their feet to argue heatedly about James's manner and Rosamunde's demands. Elizabeth snatched the jug of ale, then poured it on the floor to better reveal the rat. The spriggan fell to the floor with a splat, then coughed and gasped with vigor.

"There is nothing there," Vivienne said, staring at the spilled ale with astonishment.

"It must have leapt out again," Alexander said, peering around the floor of the tavern.

"What manner of heathens are you to cast good ale upon the floor?" the tavern keeper demanded.

"There was a rat within it!" James shouted.

"There are no rats in my abode," the tavern keeper retorted and when James might have argued, he ensured the lutenist's silence with his fist. James fell backward into the rushes on the floor, and did not rise.

The other patrons applauded.

"He is besotted!" the tavern keeper cried to his guests. "There is a man unable to hold his ale, for it is early to be seeing rats that are not there."

The company laughed and resumed their conversations. Rosamunde picked up the lute and set to removing its strings with savage gestures. "At least we will not have to endure his music any longer," she said at Alexander's inquiring glance. She smiled at Vivienne. "Fear not, I would not destroy an instrument of such value. I shall return the strings once he is reunited with Madeline." Then she dropped her voice to a growl. "May we have the good fortune that that should occur soon. I would be certain that my goddaughter fares well."

Elizabeth bent and picked up the spriggan when no one was looking. She hid it in her lap, struck it on the back while it coughed out the last of the ale, then wrapped it in her napkin when it shivered. It sighed and leaned against her hand, then prodded her with its long nose.

"A boon is owed, that much is clear, from me to you for another held dear. To your sister's aid I soon will come, though none can be certain what Fate will see done."

Elizabeth smiled in triumph, at the same moment that the man at the next table caught her eye. She flushed anew, and looked down at her cup, but he did not look away again.

She did not doubt that he was enamored of her wretchedly large breasts and no more than that. Perhaps Darg's spells could be of aid in ridding her of these unwanted curves!

But first matters first. Madeline's plight was more dire, to be certain.

Madeline dreams of a thick fog pressing against the walls of the inn, a fog so thick that it cannot be natural. The fog pours through the shutters and fills the chamber like so much wool. It cannot be halted, but comes at a fearsome pace, growing ever deeper and deeper.

And Rhys sleeps like a dead man, despite her efforts to rouse him.

She closes the shutters, to no avail. She opens the portal, but it flows in from the corridor as well. She turns back and finds Rhys lost to the fog, which now rises to her waist. It surrounds her too, engulfing her to the hips, and as it rises higher and higher, she is less capable of raising a finger against it.

A curious indifference seems to fill her. She feels boneless, weightless, and wonders if this floating sensation means that she is dead.

Madeline does not want to be dead. She is too young to die. She wants to bear Rhys his sons, she wants to hear her husband laugh in truth. She forces her eyes open, battling against the relentless press of the fog.

Rhys stands at the window, looking over the town. He is no longer swallowed by the fog, no longer sleeping, no longer abed beside her. His eyes are cold and silver in hue when they should be dark, as if he has been filled with the fog. The town beyond the window looks different, too, more ethereal, though whether it is simply that Dumbarton lies in darkness or whether they are in another town, Madeline cannot tell.

The night sky is as unnatural as the

fog. It is a wondrous indigo, a dark blue that looks darker because of the swirling silver fog, now only as deep as Rhys's knees. The midnight sky silhouettes her husband's figure, hundreds of stars twinkling in its darkness. They seem to dance around Rhys, as if the very heavens mean to draw her gaze to this man alone.

She might have married worse, to be sure.

Rhys is dressed as he had been that first night at Ravensmuir. Madeline sees the red dragon of Wales upon his tabard. Its eyes gleam at her; it glows upon his dark tabard as if wrought of flame, not the thread of a clever woman's needle.

Rhys smiles the little smile that heats Madeline's blood and she is reassured that he is not changed after all. When he smiles at her, when he caresses her, when he regards her with wonder, Madeline has no doubts of the merit of their match.

She frowns that his cloak is tossed over his shoulders. Was it so before? She cannot recall.

"Sleep with me," she says, the words thick and unfamiliar on her tongue.

"I have been abed," he says gently.

She remembers then, she remembers Rhys's hand upon her breast. She tingles in recollection of the slow caress of his thumb across her nipple. She pats the pallet in invitation.

He shakes his head. "You have slept the night and all the day."

What whimsy! "I never sleep that long," she says, surprised to hear her words slurring together.

"You must have been tired." Rhys bends to retrieve her stockings, then offers them to her. "Come and dress."

Madeline glances at the night sky and cannot stifle her yawn. "Sleep," she manages to say, then nestles back into the bed again. She sighs and pulls up a coverlet wrought of fog, its softness claiming her with lethargy.

"We will not sleep here this night." Rhys sits on the edge of the pallet and tries to push one stocking over her foot. He is awkward with the task, but Madeline is disinclined to aid him. The man wants sons — why does he not come to her bed? "Come, my lady. Aid me in this task."

"Sleep."

"Dress yourself, my lady." Rhys works the other stocking over her calf. They are both twisted, but Madeline does not care. Rhys is cursedly insistent when he shakes her garb before her. "Rise! Don *your kirtle, Madeline."*

"Sleep." Even murmuring the word gives her pleasure.

"We will sleep at our destination. That will be soon enough."

She opens one eye with heroic effort. "Where?"

"You will see when we arrive." He pulls her kirtle over her head and lifts her to a sitting posture. Much as she wants to please him, Madeline's own fingers will not follow her bidding. She cannot fasten her belt around her waist, nor can she don her boots. Rhys is uncommonly persistent, but clearly determined that they will leave.

Madeline shoves a hand through her disheveled braid, too tired to even be annoyed with his characteristic evasiveness. Let him keep his answers. She yawns again, feeling that her jaw will crack with the effort and not caring if it does.

She wants only to sleep.

Rhys pulls her to her feet and wraps his arm around her waist to steady her. His lips are drawn to a thin line, and she touches his mouth with her fingertip, marvelling.

"Vexed," she pronounces, feeling very sage.

He shakes his head.

"Indeed!" she says, thinking he argues the truth of it.

"Vexed indeed, but not with you." Rhys draws Madeline's hood over her hair with a tenderness uncommon to him. He tucks her hand into his elbow as they leave the chamber. Madeline is not surprised to find the fog directly outside the portal. Surely Rhys banished it from their chamber? Surely Rhys means to save her from its potent spell?

The fog swirls up the stairs, as if it will clutch her very ankles and Madeline recoils. This is no small foe. Surely Rhys can see the peril before them?

"Not there," she says, but Rhys only looks into her eyes. She touches the furrow in his brow.

"We go to your mother's abode, remember?" He speaks to her as if she is a mere child. "You wish to bear our babe there."

But he is the one uttering childlike statements. Indeed, the man speaks nonsense! Madeline does not carry a child, either in her womb or in her arms. She regards him with confusion, then looks down and sees the lump on her belly. She touches it and remembers her pledge to Rhys.

She bears his son, in truth!

She looks at him with joy and is confused by his answering frown. The fog drifts around their legs, its chill making gooseflesh rise on her shins. There is fog at the periphery of her vision, fog swirling around her ankles, fog hiding the faces of the men gathered in the tavern's common room.

"Off then, are you?" the keeper demands, his voice so bright and cheerful that Madeline winces.

"Indeed we are," Rhys says. His manner is terse, more terse than usual.

"A bit late in the day to depart, but I suppose the lady slept well." The innkeeper seems to find his comment most amusing, though Madeline does not understand the jest. He nudges Rhys, taking no notice of her. "My wife makes a fine concoction, that you cannot deny."

"Fine is one word for it," Rhys says tightly. "I think it most treacherous to offer such a posset to a woman with child, no less to expect to be paid for it."

"Well, then!" The innkeeper appears to be affronted, but Rhys's tone was harsh. "Value is what we grant here, sir. No cheating on the measure in this inn. I

wager that we will see you, on your return journey."

"I wager you will not," Rhys says. "Mind your wife keeps her posset to herself, or I shall send the bailiff after her. Both witchery and wickedness are against the law of king and church, as any good man knows."

The innkeeper's eyes widen, but Rhys hurries Madeline into the courtyard. His silver destrier solely waits there, though Madeline peers into the shadows for the palfrey. Maybe the horse has become a shadow. Certainly, Arian could be wrought of fog.

Maybe this is what happens to whatsoever the fog claims. Gelert comes to them, half swallowed by the fog himself. Can Rhys not see the danger here?

Madeline opens her mouth to warn him but cannot make a sound. Her tongue is thick and seems unfamiliar; she cannot fashion the words she would have fall from her lips.

Rhys lifts Madeline, quite improbably, into Arian's saddle. She looks about herself, her eyes widening at the distance to the ground, and grips the pommel as hard as she can. Rhys takes the reins and leads the horse from the inn's courtyard. "I sold the palfrey this morning, while you slept," he tells her.

Madeline struggles to make sense of her sudden urge to cry. Has she not lost another horse since meeting Rhys? Will she never be able to have a steed of her own again? She cannot remember and that plagues her.

"The price was too high for taking two steeds. And we do not have need of them both on this journey."

Madeline cannot argue with reasoning she cannot follow. At least the cold fog is withdrawing, or Rhys is leading her away from its clutch. She twists in the saddle and looks back at the faint glow of fog in the inn's courtyard. To her relief, it does not appear to be following them.

She should have guessed as much. She can trust Rhys to take her away from wickedness.

A wind caresses her face, a wind that smells of salt. Has Rhys returned her to Kinfairlie? Madeline's heart leaps at the prospect.

But this sea is unfamiliar. It glitters darkly ahead of them, and a dark promontory of stone rises high on their right. A castle perches on the summit of the great rock, but Rhys leads the horse to the wharves that stretch from the village. They lie like dark still fingers upon the shining water. Ships bob at anchor, lanterns swinging from the rigging of one of them, their masts creaking as the wind rises.

"We sail on this night's tide," Rhys says. "That is why you have no need of a horse for the moment. I could see no sense in paying the passage of a second horse when there are so many at Caerwyn. Had it been Tarascon, there would have been no choice, of course."

But Madeline does not heed his reassurance. He means to take her on a ship! She watches their progress with horror, her lips working soundlessly, as he leads the horse closer and closer to the ships. The vessels dance so innocently on the waves, like a child's toys, but Madeline knows their dark truth.

Ships like these stole her parents. Ships like these bring death. Nausea rises within her. Her parents are lost beneath the waves, stolen from life and entombed in darkness, because they boarded a ship.

And now Rhys takes her upon one of these treacherous vessels.

How can he wish for her to die?

Madeline's stomach churns with sudden violence. She has time only to lean over the side of the destrier before she vomits. Indeed, the purge is so violent that she looks to see if she has truly poured her innards onto the cobbles.

Rhys is immediately at her side, holding her hand, ensuring that she does not fall from the saddle. "It is probably better to be rid of it," he says enigmatically. "I should have thought of that sooner."

Madeline belches like a peasant, then pushes at Rhys's shoulder. He steps aside just in time as she vomits once again. She spits, hating the foul taste in her mouth, and feels a cold trickle of sweat on her back. She thinks of her parents and begins to cry, as if they had been lost to her just this moment. Though she yearns to see them again, she does not wish to die herself. Madeline trembles so hard that her teeth chatter, and she weeps, her tears dissolving the last vestige of the fog.

Rhys swears, then pulls her from the saddle into his arms. He holds her fast against his chest and Madeline nestles closer, grateful for his heat. He is a com-

fort, this unlikely spouse, for all his gruff manner and ferocious guardianship of his secrets.

"We must reach the ship before the tide goes out," he says to her, murmuring against her temple.

"No ship," Madeline whispers, clutching at his tabard.

"They are fast behind us," he says with resolve, and does not slow his pace. The horse and the hound follow. "We must leave this night. The sooner we depart, the sooner we will be home at Caerwyn."

"Home." There is a word that Madeline can savor upon her tongue, even if she knows not where it is.

Home is with Rhys, of course. The realization eases her fear slightly.

"Home," Rhys echoes, sounding as if he smiles a little. "There are two skilled healers there who will ensure this malady is defeated. And the gates can be barred against those who pursue us."

"No ship," Madeline urges again. She wants to explain her fear to him, but words abandon her as bile fills her throat yet again.

"We must take the ship."

"Maman," she whispers, and loses the battle again against her tears.

Rhys kisses her temple with such tenderness that her tears fall with greater frequency. "I will be with you, anwylaf, not your mother. Fret not, for there is nothing to fear."

He puts Madeline on her feet and coaxes her to the gangplank then. The rocking makes Madeline clamp a hand over her mouth. She closes her eyes tightly, willing the contents of her belly to remain where they are.

Rhys grips her hand and stares deeply into her eyes. "Trust me," he says.

And she does.

Madeline nods. She lets Rhys lead her wheresoever he will. The deck of the ship is only slightly more reassuring than the gangplank. She clutches the rail when he returns for Arian, who looks as delighted as she at their next means of conveyance. Gelert leans against her leg, giving consolation with his heat and weight.

She retches over the rail, uncommonly glad to find Rhys's arm around her waist when she straightens once more. He is warm and solid, reliable.

She could indeed have wed worse.

The sailors shout to each other and cast off the ropes, using long poles to push the ship from the wharf. The sails unfurl, snapping in the wind as if anxious to be gone, then billow large as if they mean to swallow the very stars.

Madeline watches the abyss between herself and the shore broaden. She clutches Rhys when six destriers as black as ravens gallop down the wharf the ship has just abandoned.

Black stallions. She frowns as she fights to gather her thoughts. These stallions seem to breathe fire, as if they are the spawn of hell their kin have long been reputed to be. Two rear as they are reined in and the others shake their bridles in frustration.

It is as if they believe they can run across the surface of the waves, no less that they can catch the ship already fleeing on wind and tide.

They are Ravensmuir destriers. Madeline knows they can be from no other stable. The fearsome black of the Lammergeier family's horses is widely reputed, vigorously sought and never replicated — Madeline has been taught this truth from the cradle.

But they are not near Ravensmuir. She eyes the castle on its high stone perch and knows it is not familiar. No, these steeds do not belong here.

Nor does the person riding the fore-most of them. She dismounts, her fiery hair snaring the light of a dozen harbor lanterns. Madeline's breath stops. The woman appears to curse with a familiar gusto, then shakes a fist at the departing ship. The wind snatches away her words, but Madeline knows who she is.

And she understands belatedly what foe chases them.

She twists to find Rhys smiling in what must be triumph. "We flee my family," she manages to say, unable to accept fully what is before her own eyes.

His smile broadens to light his eyes, and his voice drops low. "Perhaps not, anwylaf."

Madeline studies her husband, unable again to make sense of his words. She is not surprised that he declines to say more.

When she turns back to the wharf, it is empty, the stallions and Rosamunde vanished so surely that they might never have been there at all.

"Oh no!" Vivienne cried, even as her aunt uttered a curse far worse. The stallions stamped in frustration, for they were rested enough to run. A couple could be discerned upon the deck of the departing ship, the woman leaning heavily upon the man. He was garbed so darkly as to be swallowed by the shadows, his cloak flicking behind the pair.

"Rhys and Madeline," Alexander whispered.

"I believe so," Rosamunde said.

Elizabeth knew for certain. She saw the two ribbons, one silver and one gold, trailing behind the departing ship, stretching as they did from that shadowed couple.

But something was amiss. Before her very eyes, the ribbons seemed to fray from the tips, as if the wind shredded them beyond repair. They appeared to be newly thin and insubstantial, wrought of mist or broken dreams.

Darg gave a cry of dismay and leapt into the air. The spriggan snatched at the end of the golden ribbon and Elizabeth feared that the fairy would lose its grip.

Or that the ribbon would dissolve and leave the spriggan to fall into the sea.

"Hasten yourself, Darg!" Elizabeth cried, not caring who heard her words. "Run, run, run! You are Madeline's sole chance now!"

The spriggan ran, mounting the swirls of ribbon as if it ran up a staircase that never ceased to move. Elizabeth held her breath, fearing that the ribbons would turn to naught and the fairy would fall into the sea.

But Darg was fleet of foot, swift enough to remain upon the ribbon. The ship sailed onward, vessel and ribbons and fairy swallowed by the darkness of the night, and Elizabeth thought she heard a distant cry of fairy glee.

"We ride to Caerwyn," Rosamunde said firmly, turning her steed as she spoke. "We ride immediately and with all haste."

"You will return the strings of my lute then," James said sullenly.

"I will return them when I see fit and not a moment before," Rosamunde retorted, then gathered her reins in her fist. "Ride on!"

Chapter Fourteen

Madeline was pale and Rhys was uneasy.

He watched her sleep as the ship took to the open sea, and was unable to keep from touching her. He tucked the fur lining of his cloak more thoroughly about her. He felt the cool of her brow, to assure himself again that the malady was past its worst. He felt for the rhythm of her pulse, though he knew so little of healing that whatsoever he felt meant nothing to him.

He hoped so fervently that she would be well that he did not trust his impressions either way. He watched, taut with concern, and feared for her health.

Though Madeline's complexion had always been fair, it was lighter now, as pale of hue as a cloud in a summer sky. There were dark marks beneath her eyes, as if the quantity of her sleep was no indication of its quality. Her flesh had cooled, though now he feared her to be too cold.

Gelert nestled against her, its shaggy head in her lap, and looked askance at Rhys. It was as if the dog knew him to have served his lady false.

He could scarce argue the matter. Madeline's ailment *was* Rhys's fault. He did not cringe from the truth of that. He should have known better than to buy a posset from a healer whose arts he did not know, especially for the sake of convenience alone. He had thought it would be simpler if Madeline slept through the sale of the horse and arrangement of their departure. He had wanted her endless questions to cease, and he had wanted to be certain that she would stay where he had bidden her.

Madeline showed no signs of moving now, and asked no questions, but Rhys was far from content with what he had wrought.

He had thought no further than his own convenience. It was no excuse that he had only known healers of competence, that he had never seen a potion make a person more ill than he or she had been in the first place.

There was no excuse that could compensate for his error.

The ship rocked and creaked. He could faintly hear the sailors shouting to each other on the deck above. The rhythm was not unpleasant and their small chamber was not as bad as it could have been. He could see no vermin, nor any evidence of their presence, and the chamber smelled pleasantly of apples. Rhys knew well enough that a ship's hold could smell far worse than this, but his old seafaring friend was particular about what wares he would haul.

The ship heaved on a swell large enough to indicate that they had gained the open seas. Madeline slumped sideways due to the motion, and the cloak slipped from her neck. Rhys crept to her side and tucked it around her once again. He caressed the softness of her cheek with a fingertip, noting the roughness of his skin in contrast to hers.

He felt the lump in his throat and the tightness in his chest as if becoming aware of it for the first time. He realized that he would do anything to see Madeline hale again. He would sell his soul without a care, simply to see her eyes flash once more, simply to watch her cast an apple at him with deadly accuracy.

He loved her.

Rhys's hand froze at the unassailable truth. Against his own inclinations, he had fallen in love with the woman he had taken to wife. He loved her keen wit, he loved that she was unafraid to take him to task when she believed him to be wrong. He loved her good sense and practicality; he loved that she had adapted to the changes in her life without complaint or tears, and that she was strong and noble and loyal.

He sat back on his heels and watched her, knowing he would never tire of the sight of her, the feel of her against him, the echo of her breath in his ear. It was not her beauty, though that was considerable, it was her spirit that had snared his heart.

Rhys recalled what Madeline had told him about her own heart, and did not doubt that she had told him the truth. She was the manner of woman who would love once and for all time. Madeline was not fickle or reckless with her affections.

It would be James, not Rhys, who Madeline loved until her dying day.

He told himself not to be disappointed, for he should have known not to expect better for himself. Love was not to be trusted or to be publicly confessed. Love was a treasure to savor privately. Should the Fates be so kind as to not steal her away from him now — losing Madeline just as he realized his love for her would be consistent with Rhys's fortunes thus far — he would be the best husband that he could be. He would grant Madeline a good life, he would cherish her. He would find his pleasure in making her as happy as he could.

None of that changed the fact that Rhys knew that the lady was unfairly his own.

He heaved a sigh and frowned. He did not know for certain the name of the lutenist who journeyed with Rosamunde, but he could surely guess.

And what was the merit of his love for Madeline, if he kept from her the sole news that would make her happy?

Rhys sat in the chamber with his sleeping wife and did not like his recollections of how he had treated her. She had asked him for honesty and he had deceived her. She had asked him for his own tales and he had denied her. She had sworn that her heart belonged to one man alone, and he had stolen her away from that one man in order to keep her for himself.

In that lonely chamber, Rhys made a wager with himself. He did not doubt that Rosamunde would find her way to Caerwyn, nor that James would be fast by her side. Though Rhys feared that he might lose his Madeline upon that day, in spirit if not in truth, he had the duration of this journey to make a difference.

He would begin by granting his wife the one thing she had asked persistently of him. He would answer her questions. He would surrender the honesty she desired. Rhys did not imagine that Madeline would like the truth, but he owed her no less.

And if James did come, and Madeline did desire to be with her love, Rhys would not impede her departure. He would yearn for her for all his days and nights, but he would rather lose her and know her to be happy than witness her unhappiness at his side.

He lifted her hand in his and caressed it. No man of honor avoided what needed to be done, simply because it might not proceed in his favor.

Rhys would tell Madeline the truth.

Madeline awakened slowly. Her tongue felt thick in her mouth and her head seemed light. She was hungry beyond belief and her limbs were cramped. Worse, she might have been abed in a cradle, for all around her rocked.

What had happened?

Madeline stretched and opened her eyes, her movement making the hound Gelert abandon her side. The dog stretched, shook, and yawned with a vigor that made her smile, then sat and watched her expectantly. Madeline braced her hands on the floor and discovered that she did not rock — the chamber did.

The walls were wrought of wood. Madeline smelled apples, which made her belly rumble loudly. She was wrapped in

Rhys's dark cloak, its fur lining close against her skin, and her stockings were twisted awkwardly around her legs.

Rhys was slumbering against the portal. The sight of him made Madeline's heart clench. He looked rumpled, and the fact that he had not shaved in several days made him appear more disreputable than she knew he was. There were shadows beneath his eyes and a furrow in his brow, as if all the world's weight sat upon his shoulders.

Madeline stood, clutching the wall to gain her balance, and straightened her garb. She folded Rhys's cloak rather than stand upon it and discovered that her pillow had been Rhys's saddlebag. Much to her delight, there was a comb within it. She combed and rebraided her hair, certain that a morsel in her belly would make her feel fit indeed.

But where was she? She tried to ease past Rhys to open the portal and he awakened with a start. His gaze flew over her, as if he could not believe the evidence before his own eyes, then he scrambled to his feet with uncharacteristic haste. "Are you hale?"

"Well enough." Madeline smiled, for he seemed unusually uncertain of himself. She was surprised that he did not touch her, but his fingers tapped as if he did not trust them to reach for her. "Hungry beyond belief, and unsteady on my feet because of it, but well enough beyond that."

He smiled then, his eyes fairly glowing. "Good. That is good news indeed."

The chamber heaved and Madeline gasped as she lost her balance. Rhys caught her close and braced his feet against the floor. The heat of him was welcome and she leaned against his solid strength. Still she felt a reluctance in him, a reluctance she did not share.

She kissed his throat and he shivered.

"I am glad indeed that you are recovered," he said into her hair. "I erred mightily in buying that posset and I apologize for my folly."

Madeline pulled back slightly to regard him as she assembled her scattered recollections. "You mean the posset that the innkeeper brought after our dinner, the posset that made me sleep."

Rhys shook his head. "The posset made you ill. It was supposed to merely make you sleep."

"You bought a potion to make me ill?" Madeline pulled out of his embrace, but Rhys nodded.

"I did indeed, though that was never my intent. I erred most gravely in trusting the skill of a stranger, Madeline, and ask your forgiveness."

Madeline stepped out of the circle of his embrace, scarce reassured that he had seen fit to buy any kind of potion for her.

"Why would you do such a deed?" She did not expect him to answer her, for Rhys had proven to be adept in avoiding questions, but he colored and stared at the floor.

To her astonishment, he answered her. "I thought it would be simpler if you slept through the morning." He sighed. "I knew you would ask many questions, that you might disagree with me about my chosen course, and that you might not decide to remain alone in the chamber of the inn, even if I bade you do so."

"So you bought me a sleeping potion and deceived me as to its nature." Madeline did not hide her annoyance. "You told me it was no more than hot cider!"

The back of Rhys's neck flushed scarlet, but he did not look away from her. "I did. I thought it best. I was mistaken."

The chamber heaved again, and Madeline was thrown against one wall so heavily that she was certain she would be bruised. She did not reach for Rhys this time, though, so vexed was she with him.

"What manner of chamber is this?" she

demanded irritably. "Where are we that the very floor roils beneath us?" Before Rhys could answer, Madeline gasped in understanding. "We are on a ship!" She clutched the wall as the ship rocked again, then lunged for the portal.

She had to get out of the hold!

Rhys stepped in front of the portal. "What ails you? There is nothing to fear."

"We are on a ship!" Madeline tried to push him aside, though her efforts were futile. "That is reason for fear enough."

"There is no peril here. Our captain is well experienced and the weather is fair. We are not far from shore, yet we are far enough to evade rocks and shallows . . ."

Madeline snatched at the portal again, as she tried to push Rhys aside. "We are on a ship and that is peril indeed!"

Rhys caught her shoulders in his hands. "Have you been on a ship before? Why do you fear it so much?"

"I must leave!"

"Why?" Rhys shook her. "Why, Madeline?"

"Let me out!"

"Tell me."

Madeline struggled against his grip to no avail. She quickly decided that the easiest way to pass the formidable obstacle of her husband was to win his agreement. "My parents were drowned last autumn. Their ship sank and all aboard died."

"Ah." Rhys considered this, taking over-long to do so, to Madeline's thinking. "So that was why you protested our boarding."

"Let me out!" Madeline's breath began to come quickly, so great was her terror that she would share her parents' fate. "I will not linger in the hold and wait to die!" She clutched Rhys's shoulders and tried to shove him out of her way. "Move, Rhys, or I shall go mad!"

He moved, but caught her elbow in a fearsome grip so that she was obliged to remain fast by his side. "Come up to the deck with me and see what a fine day this is."

There was a narrow corridor outside their portal, and a blessed patch of blue sky could be seen far ahead. Madeline hastened toward it and fairly fell upon the ladder.

"I will climb ahead of you," Rhys said in a tone that brooked no argument. "So that you do not lose your footing on the wet deck. Follow close behind me."

"Rhys, hurry!"

He paused and caught her in a tight hug. "We are safe, Madeline. You will see as much shortly." Then he and his reassuring heat were gone, his shoulders blocking the sight of the patch of sky that was keeping Madeline from madness. She scrambled behind him, not caring whether she was graceful or not, and blinked as she lunged into the bright sunlight of a glorious day.

Rhys caught her around the waist and pulled her to one side of the ship, out of the way of the busy sailors. The wind was blustery, and the sails snapped with vigor.

"A beautiful day," Rhys said, his very tone calming Madeline. He braced his feet against the deck and gripped the rail on either side of her, making her feel safe within the shelter of his embrace. He pointed to the shore. "See? There is the isle of Arran, unless I miss my guess. With this wind, we shall be home at Caerwyn in no time at all."

Madeline took a shaking breath. The hills of the isle seemed especially verdant in this sunlight, and she could spy goats or sheep grazing. The sea, when she dared to look upon it, glittered as if its surface was wrought of gems. She did not look down into its dark depths, but across the sparkle of its surface. The air was crisp and cleared the last of the fog from her head.

She turned as the sailors began to sing in unison.

"They sing to ensure that they pull as

one to hoist the sail," Rhys said, anticipating her question. Then he raised his voice and joined the song, his rich voice filling Madeline with an unexpected pleasure. She watched, fascinated, as the sailors hauled on ropes and pulled a massive sail up the mast in steady increments. This second sail swelled in the wind, and snapped alongside the first, and she felt the ship move more quickly.

It was reassuring to have Rhys so fast behind her. His voice steadied her fears, just as his talk had eliminated Tarascon's fear. She found herself leaning slightly against him and told herself that she seemed to be safe enough.

And in truth, there was little she could do about being on this ship. She could not swim and this ship was not directed toward the shore. She took a deep breath. He had spoken aright — it *was* better on the deck than in the cabin.

The song ended and the sailors knotted the ropes, shouting to each other to ensure the task was done well. "Now our speed will be considerable," Rhys said.

"You never sang before," Madeline said and he shrugged, as if discomfited by her attention.

"We have not known each other so long

as that," he said gruffly.

"But you know I am fond of music."

He colored in a most uncharacteristic way. "My voice is a humble one," was all he said, then looked across the sea.

Another detail about their departure from Dumbarton drifted into Madeline's thoughts. "I had a curious dream, courtesy of that posset," she said and knew she did not imagine that Rhys stiffened.

"Aye?"

Madeline tipped back her head to regard him, and noted that his eyes had narrowed. Had there been a vestige of truth in her dream? "I dreamed that those who pursued us, upon the six black destriers, came to the very wharf while we departed."

Rhys's features seemed to set in stone.

"I dreamed that they were not the king's men, but that my aunt Rosamunde led the party. I dreamed that they rode stallions from Ravensmuir."

Rhys's lips tightened.

Madeline dared not fall silent now. She would utter the worst of it, and let him refute it. "And I dreamed that you knew the truth of it all along."

He shook his head with such resolve that she thought he would deny her charge. "I have known only since Moffat.

415

Before that, I too believed the king's men to be fast behind us."

Madeline stepped away from him. "You did know!"

"Indeed, I did."

Madeline considered this. Her family gave chase, but why? Rosamunde had been the only one to endorse Rhys — she must ride in pursuit to rescind her support.

Something had made Rosamunde change her thinking about Rhys.

In face of that, Madeline felt new suspicion of Rhys's motives. His easy confession was most uncharacteristic. "Why are you admitting to this deed? It is unlike you to answer my questions so readily."

Rhys's smile was almost a grimace. "I resolved that it was time I answered your queries. I have served you poorly, Madeline, both with the posset — though I never imagined it would be so potent — and in refusing to tell you what I know. You asked me for honesty, and I have made a poor task of granting that to you." His manner was so sincere that Madeline's annoyance with him faltered. "I would do better, if you would grant me the chance."

Madeline turned to face the sea, both hands grasping the rail. "You *knew* that my family pursued us, yet still you fled onward."

416

Rhys nodded as he turned, taking a place alongside her.

"Do you know why they pursued us?"

He braced his elbows upon the rail and rubbed his chin with one hand. He shot a quick glance her way and his eyes were bright. She had the definite sense that he was uneasy. "I can guess."

"Then, I would ask you to do so."

Rhys pursed his lips, as if seeking the words. "First you should know that I doubt that they are your family, or your blood kin."

He could not have uttered another thing more astonishing to Madeline. "How can this be?"

Rhys held up a finger for her silence, then turned to face the sea as he told his tale. "Once, many years ago, I was witness to a wedding. Dafydd ap Dafydd saw his sole surviving daughter wed to a knight named Edward Arundel." Madeline watched a smile touch Rhys's lips in recollection. "They were a most happy pair. I remember their laughter. She wore a coronet of daisies in her dark, dark hair."

Madeline felt slightly uneasy with this detail, her own ebony braid flicking in the wind behind her.

Rhys glanced at her. "The bride was well

known as a rare beauty. She had eyes of the clearest hue of blue, so blue that they were oft compared to sapphires. Her name was Madeline, Madeline Arundel."

The uneasiness within Madeline grew.

"Despite the couple's happiness, theirs was a match that suited their families' desire for alliance. Dafydd was intent in securing the new Welsh alliance with the Earl of Northumberland. Edward was the son of a prominent knight in the Earl's household."

"But that was the alliance that saw Henry Hotspur, the Earl's son and heir, charged with treason and killed."

"Nay, Hotspur was killed later, in 1403, though all was rooted in the same unrest."

Madeline tried to forge a link between Hotspur and the charge against Rhys and failed. "You were too young to have fought even then."

"But not too young to have seen the damage." Rhys pursed his lips as he stared across the sea. "Many men died trying to regain the sovereignty of Wales in those years of warfare and strife. Villages were razed and much damage done in retaliation for the rebellion. I was raised in a land that echoed with absences, with the silence of those who should have been there. Last winter, even Dafydd ap Dafydd passed this earth, his dreams of a sovereign Wales turned to disappointment."

Madeline leaned closer, intrigued despite herself. "But Dafydd ap Dafydd's death must have left his daughter's husband, Edward Arundel, as his heir."

"It would have, if that couple had lived longer than the old man himself."

"They are dead?"

Rhys nodded. "I followed them, all these years later, to Northumberland. Madeline Arundel lived but a year, her husband a few years longer."

So that was why Rhys had been so far from home! He had been seeking his family.

"Then the holding reverts to the crown, does it not?"

"In England, it would. But in Wales, the blood in a son's veins is of more import than the marital state of his parents. A bastard can inherit lands under Welsh law."

"You are talking about Caerwyn," Madeline guessed. "Caerwyn must have been Dafydd ap Dafydd's holding. Are you Dafydd's bastard son?" She knew Rhys would not answer such a personal query and was astonished when he did.

"I am his nephew. My father Henry was Dafydd's younger brother. He had four daughters by his wife and one bastard son by his concubine." Rhys met her gaze as he tapped his finger upon his own chest.

"But I would wager that you can inherit Caerwyn only if you are the last of your kin," Madeline guessed. "You said that your sisters were dead and that Dafydd had only one daughter. Did Madeline Arundel have no children?"

Rhys smiled and regarded her so warmly that Madeline was confused. "She had one. Madeline Arundel died in childbirth, but the child lived. That child was a girl." His gaze was steady. "My cousin bore her babe at Alnwyck and died in so doing, though the name of her child is not recorded."

Madeline gripped the rail even tighter beneath his steady gaze, for she guessed what he meant to imply. "Alnwyck is near Kinfairlie," she said. "You think I am that daughter."

"Madeline's babe was born in 1398."

"As was I!" Madeline stared over the water herself, stunned by what Rhys suggested. What if her kin were *not* her kin?

He leaned down and murmured into her ear. "It was writ at Edward Arundel's funeral in 1403 that the Lady of Kinfairlie took the deceased's daughter to raise as her own."

Madeline felt suddenly dizzy. It all made treacherous sense.

"Why else would your kin be so ready to be rid of you that they would sell your hand at auction, as one would sell livestock? It is clear that they meant to save the expense of a dowry upon one who is not of their lineage."

Madeline clutched Rhys's sleeve as she turned to face him. "Then why did you wed me?"

He studied her, his expression wary. "You have wits enough to guess."

"You wed me because if I am that daughter, then I am the sole other claimant to Caerwyn. I would be the only person who could keep it from your hand."

Rhys inclined his head in agreement and anger roiled within Madeline. His motive was so cold, so calculated. She would have been more relieved to learn that he had wedded her out of lust.

"So, you wed me for Caerwyn, no more and no less."

"That is true."

"Though you believe me to be your cousin's child! Surely such a match is sinful!"

Rhys shook his head. "Not where I was raised."

"Barbarian!" Madeline cried.

Rhys turned to appeal to her, his very manner so guilty that she knew he did not even find himself so innocent as he would have her believe.

That infuriated her as little else could have done. "You bought me, to ensure your claim to the keep you so love. And you would plant your seed in my belly solely to ensure that your legacy passes through your lineage."

Rhys sighed. "Madeline, not solely for that . . ."

She had no desire to hear his excuses. "You need not try to soften the truth with pretty words, Rhys FitzHenry!" She might have stepped away, but Rhys claimed her hand.

"Nay, I mean that this is not the worst of it."

Madeline clutched the rail, uncertain what else he might confess. "Tell me."

"I saw the party in pursuit of us in Moffat. Four people I recognize travel with Rosamunde, and one other whom I do not."

Madeline caught her breath.

Rhys counted on his fingers. "There is

Rosamunde, there is Alexander, there is Vivienne, there is your youngest sister who sees fairies . . ."

"Elizabeth."

"There is another man I spied in Ravensmuir's hall, a swarthy man who wears a gold earring."

"Padraig. He sails with Rosamunde."

"And there is another man." Rhys's expression turned somber, his gaze piercing. Madeline feared what he would say. "He is fair, his hair an uncommon blond, and he carries a lute upon his back."

Madeline raised her hands to her lips in astonishment. She could never have prepared herself for that revelation! "Do you know his name?"

"I could guess." Rhys's tone was rueful. "Indeed, the return of your betrothed might explain why they pursue you with such haste."

James. James gave chase.

James!

Madeline raised a fist to her chest, shocked by what Rhys had told her and even more by his deception. "But you knew, you *knew* this and said nothing. You guessed that James gave chase since Moffat," she said, not hiding her dismay.

Rhys inclined his head in acknowledgment.

The wretch had lied to her! She had trusted him, she had surrendered to him, she had done all she could to ensure that their match had a chance, and Rhys had lied to her.

No less, he had lied to her about the one thing that might have changed her regard for him.

"You guessed as much, and yet you continued to flee their pursuit," she said, needing to hear the indictment from his own lips. "You kept me from my one true love, and you did it by choice."

Rhys nodded. "I did not say that I was proud of what I had done."

"You faithless knave!" Madeline stepped away from her husband, fury consuming her and choking the angry words that rose in her throat. Tears glazed her vision. She had wed the wrong man, and had lost her true love by but a day!

"Madeline, I am sorry. I know that I erred . . ."

"Do not try to explain your crime!"

"In truth, I am not certain of the identity of the lutenist. We but guess, Madeline. Remember as much."

"It could be no other lutenist," she insisted. "There would be no other reason for Rosamunde and the others to give chase."

Rhys grimaced at the truth of that. "I am sorry . . ."

"No!" Madeline took a deep breath and spoke with a calm that surprised even herself. "An apology will not make this come aright. Words will not suffice."

"Then what would you have me do? Though it is belated, I grant you the honesty you desire."

"I believe there is but one thing you can do. You had best make haste in finding yourself a mistress," Madeline straightened and held her husband's gaze. "You will never be between my thighs again and I understand that you have need of a son."

"But . . ."

Madeline interrupted him, her words as sharp as a well-honed blade. "I was prepared to wager with you, Rhys. I was prepared to make an arrangement that we could both find amenable. But you have lied to me and you have deceived me, and you even admit to all the wrongs that you have committed. You have ensured that an amiable marriage is no longer possible between us."

"But we are wed, and our match is consummated . . ."

"And if I am your cousin's daughter, then we are too closely related to be wed by the laws of the church. Our marriage can be annulled for cause of consanguinity."

Rhys looked so shocked that Madeline's conviction wavered for a heartbeat. Could she do Rhys such injury?

But surely he only deceived her anew. Surely he only meant to change her will to suit his own? Surely he had anticipated this protest from her?

Surely he fought only for precious Caerwyn?

"Not in Wales!" he insisted with rare anger. "We acknowledge no such injunction against consanguinity! A man cannot wed his sister or his mother, but his cousin is well enough, if the match suits."

Madeline stepped away, for if he touched her, she knew she would be lost. She was too susceptible to his potent caress. "We were not wed in Wales, Rhys. We were wed by the priest in your aunt's convent, a priest who answers to the Archbishop of Canterbury."

Rhys seemed to be stunned by this prospect, but Madeline warned herself to not trust whatever appearance he gave. "But that cannot matter . . ." he said, doubt in his tone for the first time since Madeline had met him. He spun and considered the horizon, his brow furrowed. "But you would not annul our match," he insisted, his gaze searching hers. "You could not do so."

Madeline smiled tightly. "Why would I remain? What reason have you granted to me, Rhys FitzHenry, to find myself gladdened to be your wife?"

His mouth worked for a moment, and she feared that he truly was surprised. "We meet well abed."

"Marriage must be more than that, especially as you already vowed to me that I could not rely upon you to be faithful to me alone. You may have need of sons, but I am not certain that I have need of a spouse. Find yourself a whore, Rhys, and she may keep you content."

Leaving her husband staring at her in annoyance and astonishment — and fuming more than a good bit herself — Madeline marched away from him. Her fears of the ship were forgotten for the moment, so severe was her anger.

How could Rhys have so betrayed her trust?

Madeline made her way back to the cabin, her tears only spilling when Gelert welcomed her with such enthusiasm. She sat with the dog and tried to summon her memory of James's beloved face.

To her horror, Madeline could not remember what James looked like. Indeed, another man's grim visage filled her thoughts. Madeline tried to recall the sweet magic of James' voice.

She could not hear him, not in her memory. Instead, she heard the lilt of a deeper voice, one that recounted a tale with humor and passion.

Madeline desperately sought some recollection of her beloved James, her fear easing only when she envisioned his slender fingers upon the strings of his lute. She smiled and closed her eyes, knowing all would come aright. James would come to her at Caerwyn, for Rosamunde knew Rhys's destination. Rhys himself had supplied the detail Madeline needed to have their marriage annulled.

Something twisted deep within her, for Madeline knew she had become fond of Rhys. But he himself had sworn that he had no intent to love his spouse. He desired Caerwyn and sons, no more and no less. His wife would be a vessel, no more and no less.

James was the man for her, Madeline knew it well.

They would be united soon, and they

would be together for all eternity. Rhys, she suspected, would not even miss her. Against all odds, Madeline's sole desire would be her own.

How curious then that her heart did not sing in anticipation. Madeline remembered the gift from her mother, then, and her fingers shook as she unfastened the velvet pouch around her neck. She poured the Tear into her hand and was reassured by the sight of the gem.

A fierce light burned deep within the stone, brighter than the glimmer she had seen before. It was a golden light, a vigorous glow that told her that all finally came aright.

Her tears must be tears of joy, and only fell with such enthusiasm because of her hunger. Madeline told herself as much, time and again, and stared at the bright star in the stone.

But she could not believe it and she did not know why.

Chapter Fifteen

Rhys had little to lose. At this point, he told himself, his marriage with Madeline could only improve.

Unless, of course, it ended.

Rhys was not quite prepared to face that prospect, not without fighting for the lady's favor. In his view, he had the duration of this journey to win her heart, and he had no intent of losing a moment granted to him.

How could he have forgotten the differences in consanguinity laws between the Welsh church and the Roman one? How could he have erred so soundly? How could he have wed Madeline within a chapel that answered to Canterbury and never seen the flaw in his choice?

He was losing his wits in the presence of this woman. And worse, he did not want to be without her, at any price.

Rhys fetched two bowls of the stew the sailors had made with salted cod, two tankards of ale and a loaf of bread. When a man tried to take issue with Rhys's portion of bread — of which there would be no more before they reached another port — Rhys gave him such a glare that the man slunk away like a whipped hound.

Rhys marched down the lurching corridor, carefully balancing his burden, and acknowledged that he was more fearful of what he might face in the small cabin ahead than any battle he had faced in all his days.

He rapped upon the door, though Madeline did not answer.

Rhys had not truly expected her to do so. He thought he could discern the sniffle of tears, and cursed himself for granting his lady such injury that she wept.

It was his duty to see her smile again, if nothing more. He braced his feet against the rolling deck and cleared his throat, for he knew just the tale to recount to her.

"Once there was a man whom all believed to be blessed with keen wits. His wife thought him the most clever man in all their valley, though soon she was to be proven wrong."

Rhys heard a little sniff of laughter from behind the door, which was better than the tearful sniffle he had heard earlier. He dared to be encouraged.

"This man was not only clever — at least

in the estimation of his friends and neighbors — but he dearly loved to see others merry. So, his heart was good, if his wits were soon shown to be somewhat less so. This man befriended a group of fairies, who lived beneath a hill near his home. It is told that he had done them some favor, though I do not know its nature. Suffice to say that the fairies felt inclined to indulge him and offered him his heart's desire."

The ship was obviously struck by a swell, Rhys lost his footing slightly, and some of the stew went over the lip of the bowl. The pain where it landed upon his hand reassured Rhys that the meal was not yet cold, though he winced until the burn's sting subsided.

He knew that Madeline would be afraid of the ship's motion, and he continued his tale with haste, hoping to distract her from her fears.

"And so, this man thought about his friends and neighbors, and how much he liked to see them merry, and he asked the fairies for a harp that would play of its own accord. Those who loved to dance in his valley had long complained of musicians who grew tired before they did, and he thought this a fitting gift that would make all merry. He was sufficiently good of heart to wish to share his good fortune.

"The fairies bade him go home, and when the man awakened the next morning, he found a harp beside his hearth. He knew from a single glimpse that this was no mortal harp — it was wrought of gold and the strings shimmered even when they were still — and he was delighted. That very night, his friends and neighbors gathered to see the marvel, and the man laid his hand upon it. No sooner had he touched the strings than the harp began to play a merry tune. Every soul gathered there could do naught else but dance."

Rhys juggled his burden again, hoping that Madeline was listening to him, and further that she would find favor with his tale. "The music from the harp was so merry that the people danced with uncommon vigor. They leapt and spun, they stamped their feet and clapped their hands, they danced until they swore they could dance no longer. But they could not halt, not so long as the harp played. Their feet were enchanted by the music, so they danced and danced and danced.

"When they cried that they could dance no longer, the man lifted his hand from the harp. It fell silent then and only then, and all agreed that it was a marvel. The wife

433

thought that her spouse was a rare prize, for not only had he won his heart's desire, but his desire had been one to make more merry than simply himself.

"And so it went that the friends and neighbors came calling when they had need of a dance, and the man brought his enchanted harp to every gathering in the valley. All enjoyed the music, all benefited from this gift of the fairies, all danced as they had never danced before. All thought the man wondrous, but slowly, he began to doubt that he was invited to join festivities for his own sake. He began to believe that people asked him only so that he would bring his harp. He began to think that his friends only feigned friendship, that their true affection was for the fairies' gift. He began to think his friends and neighbors unappreciative that he had shared his good fortune. This shadow seized hold of him and would not relinquish its grip.

"And so one night, he laid his hand upon the harp strings as so many times he had before. His friends and neighbors danced, for they could do nothing else, and they danced and they danced and they danced. But when time came that they were tired, and they called out to him to halt, the man pretended that he had not heard them.

"The man let the harp play on and on. He coaxed it on without remorse, and he compelled his friends and neighbors to dance endlessly. So deep was his conviction that they invited him solely for their own pleasure that he resolved to grant them their fill of dancing. The older and the weaker began to collapse in exhaustion, but the man did not heed them. Even the virile began to weep that they could endure no more, but the man only laid his hand more firmly across the strings. When the dawn touched the sky, the man finally let the harp fall silent.

"He looked up, seeking his vindication. To his horror, his friends and neighbors had not only fallen to the floor, but some of them were dead. Many more were nearly so. There were holes in the leather of their shoes from the force of their dancing, and even those who were alive could scarce move. His wife was among those who had died in the mad dance.

"The man was sickened by the folly of his deed, his heart weighted like a stone." Rhys paused to lick his lips and juggle the bowls again. He could hear Madeline's breath beyond the door, as if she anxiously awaited his next words.

"And the following morn, the morn of

his wife's funeral, when the man awakened, there was no golden harp upon his hearth. He never saw the harp again, and he never had the chance to aid the fairies again. He had no friends after that trick, and his neighbors distrusted him. Not a one of those who had danced on that fateful night ever danced again.

"The man was alone. He missed his wife sorely, far more than he missed the harp. He lived very long, though he did not prosper. Too late he learned that he was neither so clever nor so good as his wife had believed him to be, too late he learned that his heart's desire had been his all along."

Rhys finished his tale and considered the stew. It was cooling, the steam no longer rising from the bowls with such enthusiasm. There was silence behind him, a silence that told him that he had failed in his first attempt to soften Madeline's anger with him.

Then she opened the portal. Her eyelids were puffed and reddened, her lips tight. Her lashes were dark spikes, still wet with tears. Her flesh was pale, a reminder of the posset that had so weakened her and her distrust of ships, and her fingers seemed to tremble upon the door. Rhys was certain that she was the most beauteous woman that ever he had seen. He knew himself a knave for having so deceived her and knew his tale to be a poor offering.

It was the only one he had, beyond himself, and he knew Madeline could not desire so little as that.

"Is that by way of an apology?" she asked.

"It is meant to be but a start," he said, hardly daring to hope.

Madeline studied him, though Rhys could not guess her thoughts. "You tell many tales of people losing all they hold dear. Do you think then that no good fortune can endure?"

Rhys frowned, for current evidence seemed to confirm that possibility. "I have oft believed as much, for that has been my experience."

"But?"

"Perhaps the lesson is that one should savor whatsoever one is granted, for one cannot say how long any goodness will last."

She smiled then, though her smile was sad, and she rubbed the hound's ears as if only Gelert could grant her solace. "Can a person not hope for better, instead of fear that matters must become worse?" Her eyes were bright and she watched him, as if anxious to know his answer.

Rhys licked his lips, uncertain what she wanted him to say, wishing desperately that he knew the correct answer. "That would be a fine skill to learn."

She tilted her head. "What have you endured, Rhys, that you hope for so little?"

"No more than most," he said with a shrug.

Tears filled Madeline's eyes then and she averted her gaze. Rhys feared that she would close the portal and he spoke before he could consider the wisdom of what he offered.

"I will confess to you what you have asked of me time and again," he said abruptly, making a pledge to her before he could swallow the impulse. Madeline met his gaze, her own eyes bright. "I will tell you why I was named a traitor."

She said nothing, though her eyes widened. Rhys could not understand her mood and he feared that he would err again if he said more.

Perhaps she did not wish to know his tale any longer.

Perhaps she did not care.

Perhaps he deserved no less for the wound he had granted her.

"Are you hungry?" Rhys offered the stew

and ale, the bread being tucked beneath his elbow, and the hound stretched to its toes to sniff the food. "It is humble fare, but it is yet a little warm."

Madeline's glanced at the bowls of stew. "I am hungry, as must you be. We had best eat it, afore the hound finds all of it upon the floor." She studied him with rare intensity. "And then I will have your tale, if you are still inclined to share it."

Rhys nodded, words abandoning him utterly for the moment. Madeline smiled then, a sight to warm him to his toes. She stood back and let him enter the small chamber, and Rhys' heart thundered fit to burst.

The lady granted him a chance, and he meant to ensure that she never had cause to regret it.

Rhys FitzHenry had vowed to confide in her. Madeline could scarce believe it. She would have more readily believed that this was another man, one who resembled Rhys in appearance only. It was so unlike Rhys to share his own tales, no less to volunteer to do so.

Madeline wondered why he felt so compelled. She was curious, though. She barely tasted the stew he had brought, though it put a satisfying heat in her belly. Madeline was not so annoyed that she could not admit herself glad of Rhys's company. She felt safer with him beside her, for even if the ship foundered, Madeline believed that Rhys would not abandon her.

There was much to be said for a man who could be relied upon.

They ate in a companionable silence, the hound glancing up when Rhys ran the last bit of the bread around the inside of his bowl.

"I thank you for bringing the food," Madeline said. "I was more hungry than I had believed and I feel much better."

Rhys nodded. "One's fears are always less when one's belly is full."

"I suppose that is true enough." Madeline said no more, merely waited, for she was not truly convinced that Rhys would keep his promise. It was as much against his nature to share such secrets as it was a part of his character to keep his vows.

If he did confide in her, she wanted it to be because he chose to do so, not because she had entreated him.

So, she sat in silence, showing a patience she had not known she possessed.

It took him some moments to compose his thoughts, then Rhys lifted a finger. His own memories were entangled in the greater history and he wanted to recount a coherent tale. "You must know already Owain Glyn Dŵr, and his dream of Welsh sovereignty."

Madeline nodded at his sidelong glance. "Hotspur was allied with him, and thus named a traitor."

"Indeed," Rhys agreed, appreciating that his wife was not witless. "Owain Glyn Dŵr and his allies meant to replace Henry IV with Edmund Mortimer as King of England. Further, they intended to divide England between them — Scotland and the north to the Earl of Northumberland, Wales and the west to Owain Glyn Dŵr, and the rest to Mortimer. The scheme failed, of course, for it was too bold and Henry IV was too wily."

"It is bold to try to unseat the king."

Rhys chuckled. "Though Henry IV had done much the same. He himself deposed Richard II in his own favor."

"If one succeeds, there is no charge of treason."

Rhys nodded and sobered. "At any rate, Owain Glyn Dŵr came oft to my uncle's abode, filling the air with his dreams of what Wales might be, for they had fought side by side and were old comrades. Owain knew all the history of our people, he could recount all the old tales. He had a rare charisma and a resonant voice, and people listened to his words.

"There is a tale that Arthur and his knights are but sleeping within Eryri, and that they will awaken to aid the true prince of Wales. It was said in those days that Owain was that one, the man chosen to reclaim Welsh independence. It was whispered that he was a sorcerer, so potent was the spell that he cast over his audience. He cast a potent spell over me, to be sure."

Rhys looked to the lady beside him and was startled to find her watching him, listening avidly to his tale. He looked away, unable to hold her bright gaze.

"I should begin sooner, the better for you to understand. Wales has been a kingdom for ages beyond recollection, though oft it has been without a prince. The Normans were but the latest to try to claim the land of Wales: they enslaved the Welsh, or kept us in fetters, or reduced our status to serfdom, but their suzerainty was never assured. Rebellion was constant.

"Llywelyn ap Gruffydd was our last

leader, acknowledged as Prince of Wales by the English kings until Edward I declined to make such acknowledgment. Llywelyn withheld tribute in protest, was declared a rebel, and killed in 1285."

"Edward I made few allies in Scotland either," Madeline murmured.

"He was a king determined to unite the isle beneath his hand, one can say that much for him at least."

"At least," Madeline agreed, and they shared an unexpected smile. Rhys felt a tenuous bond between them and he dared to take her hand within his own.

She did not resist. Indeed, her chilled fingers curled around his own, as if taking comfort from his heat. She was finely wrought, this wife of his, as delicate and beauteous as a spring blossom. He thought of losing her and hastened on.

"Llywelyn's head was carried in triumph to London; his only daughter was confined to a nunnery; his nephew Owain was imprisoned at Bristol; his brother was dragged through Shrewsbury, then hanged, drawn, and quartered. The crown's message was clear: There would be no more seed of Llywelyn ap Gruffydd, no more rebellion, no more Princes of Wales.

"And lest anyone doubt his intent, Edward had fortresses built around Eryri, a circle of iron and stone that reminded all of his suzerainty and his power. Caernarfon, Aberystwyth, Harlech, Conwy, Beaumaris, Flint, Rhuddlan. Even the few Welsh keeps there, like Caerwyn, were captured and fortified in the English king's name. Every child learned the names of those Norman castles, every child saw their pennants, ornamented with the English king's insignia, snap against the sky. Every Welsh child learned to resent what they represented."

"Foreign authority, tithes and taxes sent abroad."

"More than that." Rhys smiled that Madeline was no fool. "Towns grew behind the high walls of these fortresses, towns occupied solely by English men and women. There were ports, served by English ships, which sold goods to English merchants in those towns. Welshmen were not allowed to enter the towns, much less to live there or make their trade there; we were not allowed to hold title to land. With every issuance of military forces and plague through those fortress gates, Welsh discontent grew."

"No man of sense could have predicted otherwise," Madeline said softly. "That is a harsh hand laid upon the land."

"Further, on the line that had once been the border with England, lands had been granted to Anglo-Norman noblemen. These Marcher lords, their holdings upon the Welsh March, owed little suzerainty to any king."

"They could do whatsoever they desired," Madeline guessed and Rhys nodded. "We have such lords upon the Scottish March, as well," she said ruefully. "The crown is dependent upon them for whatever peace they keep. I would wager that between the March and that ring of fortresses, the Welsh were allowed to build a few baronies."

"Indeed they were, though the English judges and English law seldom ruled against their own. And so it was that Owain Glyn Dŵr, Lord of Sytharch, a man of some comforts and a Welshman besides, knew that his boundary dispute with a neighboring Marcher lord would never be resolved in his own favor. He took up arms against the offending neighbor and against all expectation, he won."

"Ha!" Madeline cried.

Rhys smiled fleetingly. "Flush with triumph, he called himself Prince of Wales and swore that he would recapture the independence of the land he so loved. His army swelled with each passing day and each victory. They ultimately drove the English from all lands between the Marcher lords and the sea. They even captured Harlech, which Owain made his own, as well as Aberystwyth, and Caerwyn."

"And Caerwyn became your uncle's holding."

Rhys nodded. "He and Owain had fought together and Caerwyn was his spoil. Owain established a royal court at Harlech. He put the red dragon upon his pennant, he sent emissaries to the Pope and to the French king. He resolved to found a university, the better to educate the priests for the Welsh church, which would be loosed from the bounds of Canterbury. He dreamed boldly, and he dreamed the dreams of a thousand Welshmen. He called himself 'the mighty and magnificent Owain, Prince of Wales'."

"He was not lacking in modesty!"

"Not he! He was embraced by Fortune, charming, the closest to a king any of us had seen. His court was filled with musicians and poets, seers and sages, beautiful women and bold knights. It seemed that the old Wales of tales had been reborn beneath his hand. There was a time, in 1405 or a little later, when it seemed that all Owain touched would turn to gold, that naught he touched could go awry."

"And then it did," Madeline prompted, then smiled. "It is my sister Vivienne who always guesses the next part of the tale. I apologize, for I know it to be an irksome habit."

"I am not irked," Rhys said, enchanted with the sparkle of her eyes. "But you speak aright, for then matters did go awry. The tide turned slowly but surely against Owain, and his forces lost more often than they won. His son was captured in 1406, his brother killed in the same battle at Usk. Sytharch was razed, and the English seized Harlech in 1408. Worse, Owain's wife, two of his daughters and three of his grandchildren were taken to the Tower of London to die. Those of his men who survived became mercenaries, either travelling to France to fight against the English, or begging in Wales. They were known as *Plant Owain*, and the Welsh people treated them with kindness, for all knew they had tried to make a change."

"But what happened to Owain? I would wager little good."

Rhys shrugged. "No one is certain. He was offered a pardon by the king in 1415, but he never revealed himself. There are those who say he died in Dunmore in 1414, others who say he surrendered his life on hearing of his wife's death — still in captivity — in 1413. Some insist he lives with another of his daughters in Herefordshire. I never saw him again myself, not after that rout at Usk."

"But Owain could yet be alive," Madeline said. "It was not that long ago."

"That is what the seers say. There is a tale . . ."

"There is always a tale, when you are speaking!" she teased. Rhys felt his neck heat. He made to apologize for his tendencies, but Madeline laid her other hand upon his arm. "I like that you tell tales, Rhys. You have an uncommon talent for it. You should sing more oft as well, for your voice is fine."

His neck heated in truth then, and it seemed his words stumbled from his lips. "There is a tale that Owain fled the battle of Harlech, devastated that he had lost all that he had gained. He was burdened with remorse that his wife and kin had been captured, certain that he could not have failed them more. And as he climbed into the mountains, unknowing where he went, he met an abbot. It was early in the morn, the sky still dark, so when the abbot greeted him, Owain said 'You are too early, Abbot'. And the abbot smiled and shook his head and said 'Not I. It is you, Owain Glyn Dŵr, Last Prince of Wales, who have arrived too soon.' "

Madeline shivered, then considered Rhys. "You did not see him after Usk, you said. Did you fight for him?"

Rhys smiled ruefully. "All men old enough to swing a blade fought for him. I had the good fortune to survive my youth."

"You fought with Thomas," Madeline guessed.

"We fought in the rear guard. It was at my uncle's insistence, for I had seen only fifteen summers, and it was the reason we survived."

"You were able to flee when the battle was lost."

Rhys nodded. "Thomas and I lost count of how oft each had saved the hide of the other in those years. There is no other man to whom I could better trust my back. We were young, we took foolish chances, but we had both bravado and Fortune at our sides."

"That was why you were named a traitor?"

"Nay. It was later, in 1415, that I earned

that charge." He held up a finger. "But let me tell you first of my uncle. Despite his alliance with Owain, Dafydd did not lose Caerwyn when Owain lost all."

"But how could that be? Did he change loyalty to the king?"

Rhys nodded. "Some say that Owain lost because my uncle withdrew his support, others say that Dafydd perceived the direction of the wind and acted in his own best interest alone. I cannot say what compelled him, but he sought an audience with Henry IV and secured his own future with a pledge of fealty in 1407. He was permitted to keep Caerwyn as a feudal grant from the English king. If Owain Glyn Dŵr had ever crossed the threshold, however, Caerwyn would have been immediately forfeit."

"Would he have come?"

Rhys rolled his eyes. "It would be safe to say that they two, once such fast friends and allies, had become estranged." Rhys looked down at his hands. "I argued with my uncle then, the sole time ever. I was certain that he had betrayed all that I thought he believed." He fell silent then, reliving that heated exchange. He had been so young, so rash, so certain he was right.

"What did he say?"

"*Poni welwch-chwi'r sŷr wedi'r syrthiaw?*" Rhys whispered, his voice hoarse.

Madeline leaned against his side. "It sounds so beautiful, like music in words. What does it mean, Rhys?"

"It is from an old poem, writ when Wales was lost to Edward I. 'Do you not see the stars fallen?' " Rhys took a deep breath. "It is a lament, an elegy for the lost majesty of Wales. The last line of the verse is *Poni welwch-chwi'r byd wedi r'bydiaw?* 'Do you not see that the world is ended?' "

"Oh!" Madeline seemed to be fighting her tears.

Rhys continued grimly. "My uncle said that he believed the time for rebellion had passed, that we could not defend Wales against England and win. The power and the wealth of the English crown was too great, and we could best preserve what we loved of Wales by ceding suzerainty."

"How?"

"He said that paying tithes and ensuring order would sate the English king, and turn his eye away from us. Dafydd said that then we could teach our children, and train them for the king's own posts, and gradually gain more wealth than ever we would win with war."

Madeline pursed her lips. "It seems a most

pragmatic course. Were you persuaded?"

Rhys laughed shortly. "Nay! I thought he made a tale that excused his own betrayal, and I told him as much. But then I left Caerwyn, and I journeyed through Wales, and I witnessed the devastation left by the war. Crops failed, plague raged, and the English merchants had left the towns in Wales, taking their coin and their trading agreements with them. More people died after the war of starvation than had been killed in the battles."

Rhys frowned and let his thumb slide across the softness of Madeline's hand. "But I was sufficiently young to believe that all of our woes had been inflicted upon us by the cursed English, not that our own deeds had had any part in shaping our misfortunes. When Henry IV died in 1413 and Henry V succeeded to the throne, it appeared that the son was the very mirror of his sire. He declared that no less than all of France should be his inheritance, and planned to reinvigorate the war with the French crown."

Rhys sighed. "We had all been taxed and tithed beyond belief in the name of these ambitious kings. When I heard that there was again a scheme to place a Mortimer upon the English throne, I pledged my aid.

I thought to see the madness halted, for the Mortimer clan had a blood claim to the crown and surely could not be so lustful for power and wealth as the spawn of Henry of Bolingbroke.

"The Earl of Cambridge, Lord Scrope of Masham, and Sir Thomas Grey of Heton were the trio at the heart of the scheme, though there were many of us. We aimed to sink the king's ship upon his departure to France."

"You were caught."

"Upon the very eve that the plan was to be enacted."

"But you must have been betrayed!"

Rhys nodded slowly. "Indeed we were."

"You know who betrayed you."

Rhys met her gaze steadily. "I alone broke our vow of silence. I only confided in one other soul, for I believed that he would aid our cause. He had clung to the bright dream of Owain Glyn Dŵr and it was rumored that he alone knew the location of the old rebel's abode. He swore to keep my secret, but he lied."

"Your father!" Madeline breathed, her grip tight on his hand.

Rhys nodded. "We were snared when we gathered on the wharf. Thomas and I escaped in the darkness, though the others named us and a price was put upon our heads. The three leaders were executed, and their blood is upon my hands. Thomas took his monastic vows and was forgiven." Rhys inhaled deeply. "I had no intent to become a monk."

"But you were never caught?"

"In Wales, I am safe enough."

"You have been nearly captured in England," she guessed. "Why did you risk the journey to Northumberland?"

He might have imagined the lady to be concerned for his fate, but Rhys knew that he saw only what he desired to see. Madeline had great compassion for all, he knew this well. Rhys looked away from her concern and spoke gruffly. "I had to be certain of my cousin's fate."

"You had to secure Caerwyn, at any cost. Oh, you are a fool to risk your hide for a title!"

Rhys kept his gaze averted, not wanting to know for certain whether she was scornful of his ambition or concerned for his life. "Henry pardoned the others a few years past, and I had hoped that my name would be cleared. Perhaps that day yet will come. Perhaps the king has forgotten me."

Madeline snorted. "No English king forgets any man who raises a blade against him. Do you truly believe that Henry will grant you suzerainty of Caerwyn?"

Rhys met her gaze, letting her see the steel of his determination. "It is not my intent to grant him a choice. I trust you have the wits, even if you are my cousin's daughter, not to challenge my suzerainty either."

Their gazes held, a shimmer of will in the air between them, and Madeline straightened beneath his gaze. "You have never been granted your desire, Rhys, but I can change this detail. I cede all claim to Caerwyn, and I will sign a deed to that effect. I know that Caerwyn is the sole dream you hold within your heart. You have treated me kindly. This will be your compense."

She told no lie, Rhys knew it well, yet his triumph was as dust in his hands. He felt no need to shout in victory, he felt no satisfaction that he had achieved his goal.

Instead, he watched Madeline turn her back upon him and felt that, yet again, he had erred.

"I will sit vigil while you sleep," he said, knowing there was little else he could offer her.

"I will not sleep in this place," she argued, though her exhaustion was clear.

"You have need of sleep, my lady, to heal from that potion. I will remain with you, and remain awake. I pledge to you that I will ensure your safety if ill fortune befalls the ship."

"Why?"

"Because, for this moment at least, you are my wife."

"And thus, your duty?"

"And thus, my concern," he corrected with some annoyance. "I do not wish you ill, Madeline. Can I not grant you some courtesy without suspicion?"

The anger melted out of Madeline's shoulders as she regarded him. "Of course you can." An unexpected smile lifted the corner of her lips. "I thank you, Rhys."

Though it was a pale shadow of the dazzling smile she could offer, still it rendered Rhys mute. He silently offered his cloak to her and Madeline wrapped herself in its generous fullness, even as she yawned. She tried to make herself comfortable opposite him on the chamber's floor, and he watched her for a moment, before lifting her into his arms. He braced his back in the corner, setting a finger against her lips when she might have protested.

"I would have you be warm," he said and wrapped his arms around her. She sighed in capitulation and laid her cheek against his chest, her one hand furled like a new leaf within his own. In but a trio of heart-beats, her breathing had slowed and the lady slept.

Rhys was content, smelling her sweet scent and the lingering perfume of apples, Gelert nestled against his leg and Madeline curled in his lap. He was so content that he wished they would never arrive at their destination.

He recalled the moral of his own tale, and he savored the gifts granted to him, knowing all too well that Madeline might soon be gone.

Chapter Sixteen

They sailed southward for four days and nights. Rhys assured Madeline that the sea was particularly calm, though she started at every ripple on its surface. She preferred to be on the deck, and mercifully, their journey was blessed with such good weather that she could remain outside.

Madeline stood at the rail by the hour, the sun warming her hair and Rhys bracing his hands on either side of her. His voice was always in her ear, his tales and his songs enchanting her utterly. Every rock seemed to remind him of a song; every bay, every cliff, every tower prompted him to tell her a story.

There was an urgency about Rhys, though Madeline believed it was because he drew near to his home. It was proximity to Caerwyn that brought a tremor to his voice, it was love of this land that brightened his eye. It was the prospect of seeing Caerwyn that made him shout on the fifth morning as they rounded a point.

They dismounted, Madeline finding herself infected with Rhys's anticipation. Arian was clearly pleased to have hooves on solid ground again. Gelert shook as Rhys bade the captain farewell and the men shook hands. Madeline found herself anxious to hasten onward but for a different reason than Rhys, for surely Rosamunde and James had reached Caerwyn by this time.

She made no protest when Rhys lifted her into the saddle, then swung up behind her. He clamped a hand around her waist and touched Arian's sides with his spurs. They galloped, all intent upon making haste to Caerwyn.

They reached the summit of the point of land that jutted into the sea, and the glittering bay spread before them made Madeline catch her breath. The water was a deep blue hue, the sunlight making it look to be cast with thousands of gems. The cliffs around it rose steeply from its surface, the hills behind were verdant. Far above them all loomed Eryri, its flanks the hue of slate, a crest of snow still on its highest peak.

Directly opposite them, a fortress with four square towers seemed to rise from the very sea, its towers apparently hewn from the stone cliffs. Pennants snapped in the wind above those towers.

"Harlech," Rhys murmured, following her gaze. He pointed to another fortress, so much further down the coast that it was barely visible. "Aberystwyth." It all seemed so familiar to Madeline, for she remembered Rhys's tales, and she half expected to see the old rebel Owain step out of the gorse to greet them.

Rhys indicated a keep below them and to the left. It was more humble than the others, a fortress that could be overlooked by a hasty gaze. A high square wall encircled a single tower. The gates were open, and a small village clustered outside the fortress walls. Madeline could see the harbor and faintly hear the bell of the chapel ringing.

"Caerwyn," she guessed.

"Caerwyn," Rhys agreed. He shouted and spurred the horse. Gelert barked, Arian surged down the hill, hooves thundering. Madeline laughed, savoring how delighted they all were to be home. She twisted to see Rhys, for she loved to see his smile.

"Home," he said, an odd sadness in his eyes, then he kissed her so soundly that Madeline understood she would never taste him again.

She would leave him at Caerwyn and he knew it. Madeline knew she should have rejected his salute, but she could not turn away. She could not resist Rhys's kiss, could not imagine being without it, for he awakened a yearning within her that she feared no other man could sate. Madeline turned so that she could wind her arms around his neck, she pressed herself closer to him and made this last kiss one she would never forget.

Later Madeline would realize that that kiss had betrayed them. Later she would realize how unlike Rhys it was to ride un-prepared, his helm in his saddlebag and his sword sheathed. Indeed, he could not draw his sword, much less swing it, with her seated before him and his arms wrapped so tightly around her.

Later, she would see how fully they had erred.

They were within the village before Rhys spied the trap.

His head spinning from Madeline's sweet kiss, he had wondered where the villagers were as they had drawn near to Caerwyn. He had puzzled over the relative silence of the surrounding hills. There should have been shepherds tending their flocks, there should have been fishermen mending their nets, there should have been women emptying slops and trading gossip.

But there was not a soul abroad.

Arian galloped into the village with such

fury that none could have missed their arrival. Rhys heard a whistle, feared deception, then mercenaries erupted from all sides.

They were surrounded in no time at all.

Gelert barked furiously. Arian reared and whinnied. Madeline screamed. The destrier was useless in such close quarters, for it could not be turned. The sole advantage Rhys saw was that his attackers were not mounted.

He knew what — or who — they wanted.

Rhys leapt from the saddle in a smooth leap and only stumbled slightly. He unsheathed his blade before he found his footing fully, swung and killed a mercenary.

"Rhys!" Madeline screamed.

"To the hills!" Rhys shouted the command to Arian in Welsh. The destrier's pace faltered and it hesitated to obey. Rhys had never dispatched it without him before, and Madeline was pulling the reins, trying to turn the horse back. Its nostrils flared at the chaos surrounding it, and Rhys thought it could probably smell the blood.

He dispatched another pair of mercenaries to meet their Maker, and glanced back to find Madeline trying to urge the reluctant steed toward him. She kicked a mercenary in the face who tried to grasp her, and spat at another.

Doubtless his intrepid wife would try to save him, given the chance! Rhys ground his teeth and struck another telling blow. There was sweat on his brow already, and the mercenaries were yet spilling out of houses and the fortress gates. He could not hold them back for long, but he would not grant them the chance to despoil Madeline.

Rhys shouted his command again, swinging his blade with gusto against his assailants. Gelert understood Rhys's command and snapped at the horse's legs. Arian shied, uncertain whom to obey, fought the bit and kicked a mercenary fool enough to try to grab the reins. The dog snarled and leapt, Madeline granted a wound to an attacker with her small eating knife.

To Rhys's relief, the destrier suddenly decided that the dog was the most insistent threat, and that the best plan was to evade Gelert's teeth. Arian turned tail and galloped into the hills beyond the village, Gelert snapping at its heels. To Rhys' relief, no one else pursued the steed. He heard Madeline shout in frustration, but knew she would not be heeded.

He roared to draw every eye to himself and fought with new vigor. The mercenaries fell upon him, his shoulder was cut and his thigh was nicked. Rhys fought until he could no longer hear hoofbeats, until he knew for certain that his Madeline had escaped Caerwyn.

Then Rhys cast away his blade and held up his hands, letting himself be captured. They could do whatsoever they desired with him now. He knew Madeline had been saved.

The destrier was a crazed beast.

Arian galloped as if the hounds of Hell were behind it, although only Gelert was in pursuit. Madeline pulled the reins, she stood in the stirrups, she shouted and begged, but the horse did not heed her any better than it had previously. It ran up the path to the mountain, away from Rhys and Caerwyn, and over the crest of the first hill without slowing its pace.

A stranger urged his smaller horse off the road ahead, out of the path of the racing steed. The man seemed surprised and Madeline thought he had never seen a steed like this warhorse of Rhys's. She waved madly at him, hoping he might have some scheme to halt the horse.

The man whistled and the horse halted so abruptly that Madeline was almost cast over its head. She fell back into the saddle with a resounding thump. Arian stood, ears twitching and sides heaving, then nickered at the other man.

"You vexing beast!" Madeline cried and the stranger laughed. He was a dark-haired man, tall and slender, though he carried himself with some authority.

Madeline knew, though, that he must be Rhys's friend. Only Thomas, in her experience, had been able to command Rhys's steed. Gelert trotted to the man's side, tail wagging, the dog's response also calming Madeline's fears.

This man looked to be slightly older than she, and the gaze he cast over her was appraising. "And how did an English maiden come to ride the horse of Rhys FitzHenry?"

"I am from Scotland." Madeline dismounted and cast the reins over the destrier's head as she strode to the other man. "You must be one of my husband's friends," she said. "He has been beset in the village at Caerwyn, and I fear he has been captured. We must aid him!"

Instead of making haste down to the village, the other man frowned. "I feared their scheme was as much. I thought to waylay him on his ride homeward." At Madeline's confusion, he gestured to the road behind them. "This is the best passage through the hills, and Rhys oft uses it."

"We came by ship," Madeline said and the man nodded, though he was clearly not reassured.

"Ah, forgive my manners!" he said suddenly and forced a smile. "I am Cradoc ap Gwilym. I am sheriff of Caerwyn."

"But you are Welsh. I thought only the English could hold offices in Wales."

Cradoc smiled. "And so they could, until Dafydd ap Dafydd chose to make the best of what would be, and so they were, until Rhys FitzHenry argued for a place for me. I owe him much. You call Rhys husband. There are those who will lose a wager when that man takes a wife."

Madeline almost smiled. "Nonetheless, he has taken one. I am Lady Madeline, born of Kinfairlie and now Lady of Caerwyn." As she claimed her title through Rhys for the first time, she felt her chin rise with a measure of his pride.

Cradoc smiled and bowed. "May God in his grace grant you many sons and many years of happiness."

Madeline understood that this must be his customary blessing for married couples, but still she sobered. "God can do no such thing if Rhys is killed by his assailants. Who are they?"

"They came from Harlech just days past and evidently came to await Rhys's return. They have hidden themselves and those bold enough to protest their presence have disappeared."

"But surely they would have arrested the sheriff?"

Cradoc grinned. "They would have had to catch me first." He gestured farther down the road. "I invite you to accompany me, my lady. Now that we know their intent, perhaps we can reason how better to foil their scheme."

Madeline whistled to the dog, cautious about proceeding to some more private place with a man she did not know.

Cradoc surveyed her so thoughtfully that she wondered whether he guessed the root of her hesitation. "There are others hidden over the crest of the hill, already. I halted them on this road this very morning. You may know them for they, too, came from the north."

"Who?" Madeline demanded, even as her heart began to pound in anticipation.

"Madeline?" Vivienne cried and Madeline spun to find her siblings racing toward her. They surrounded her with noisy enthusiasm and Madeline smiled to see them all again.

"Are you hale enough?" Alexander asked.

"Were you injured?" Vivienne asked.

"Darg!" Elizabeth cried. "Darg is on your shoulder!"

Alexander caught her close and spun her around. Vivienne kissed her cheeks and hugged her tightly. Madeline picked up Elizabeth in her turn.

"Tell me that Kerr had no chance to hurt you," Alexander insisted, his gaze intent.

Madeline smiled and kissed his cheek. "I was safe all along," she said with surety. "I was with Rhys."

Rosamunde forced her way into the tight circle of siblings. There was a suspicious shine in her eyes and her embrace was uncommonly forceful. "Did I not tell you as much?" she whispered into Madeline's hair.

"I told you the lass was as strong as good Toledo steel," Padraig said roughly. This faithful cohort of Rosamunde's winked at Madeline, the way he shifted his weight telling her that even he had been fearful of her fate.

Then her family stepped back, so that Madeline could see the last member of their company. James was taller and slightly broader than he had been, his smile was more ready and his tan was darker. Madeline waited for her body to respond to his presence, but she had felt more relief in encountering Rhys's friend Cradoc than in her betrothed.

"Well met, Madeline," James said, then bent low over her hand. He kissed her knuckles and Madeline felt nothing at all. Not a shiver was awakened by his touch and no heat awakened in her belly. It was all too easy to recall Rhys's suggestion that James had never kissed her as Rhys had done.

No less to find it true.

It was shock that slowed her response, to be sure.

Madeline deliberately closed her fingers over James's hand and forced a smile to her lips. "It is good to see you, James."

He laughed. "Only good to see me? I think it wondrous to be in the presence of your beauty yet again. You are as lustrous as I recall, my Madeline, as luminous as the moon." He made to strum his lute, glancing across the company to ensure that all watched him, then grimaced when his fingers coaxed forth no sound.

Vivienne laughed. "Rosamunde has yet to return the strings!"

James sneered. "Any soul is a heathen, clearly, who cannot appreciate a fine tune."

"James had more interest in his music

than your safety," Alexander said grimly. Madeline watched her siblings turn against her betrothed, their opinion of the man more than clear.

"Would it not have been fitting for me to greet Madeline with a love song, composed only for her?" James demanded, taking affront at their manner. Madeline noted that their reserve did not melt. "An ode to Madeline's spectacular beauty would have been a fine greeting, but I have no such offering to make, thanks to your interference."

Madeline was beginning to find his references to her beauty annoying. "What is of import in this moment is how we shall aid Rhys," she said firmly, then told the others that Rhys had been captured.

"These are sorry tidings," Rosamunde said, then turned to Cradoc. "You feared that something dire was afoot."

"They came from Harlech. Robert Herbert, the lord there, has long tried to prove himself the heir of Owain Glyn Dŵr, if not by blood than by deed. He hungers after all of the fortresses held by Owain, including Caerwyn."

Rosamunde frowned. "But how could he have known when to expect Rhys's return?"

"A runner came days past, bringing a missive from Lady Adele's sister," Cradoc said. "She is an abbess near York."

"Miriam!" Madeline said and the sheriff nodded. "We were wed at her abbey, over her protest."

"But who is Lady Adele?" Vivienne asked.

"She must be Rhys's mother, the mistress of his father," Madeline said.

Cradoc nodded. "There are only the two women left at Caerwyn, Henry's wife and his mistress. One of them must have sent word, perhaps even inadvertently, to Robert."

"They may all be imprisoned," Rosamunde mused and the group looked as one at the crest of the road. They could not see Caerwyn but Madeline felt as if a shadow had slipped over her.

"Surely no one will injure Rhys?" she said.

"There is no heir to Caerwyn after him," Cradoc said.

Madeline barely kept her hand from stealing over her flat belly. Could she carry Rhys's son already?

Would Rhys be pleased if she did?

Madeline dared not think of that. She turned to her aunt, needing to know the truth. "Rosamunde, I would ask you to recall my birth, if you could. Rhys said something most strange to me, and perhaps you can recall whether it is true."

"What is that?"

"He thought me to be the child of his cousin Madeline . . ."

"The daughter of Rhys's uncle, Dafydd ap Dafydd, who wed Edmund Arundel and went to Northumberland," Cradoc cried. At Madeline's nod, he became more animated. "Any surviving child of that union could challenge Rhys's suzerainty of Caerwyn, for Dafydd was the last lord and his other children have all died."

"Madeline Arundel died in childbirth with her first and only child," Madeline said and Cradoc crossed himself with some sadness.

"She must have been Catherine's first choice to be your godmother," Rosamunde said to Madeline. "I knew that I was your mother's second choice, for her dearest friend had recently died, though I did not know more of that friend."

Madeline nodded, for this made sense. Rosamunde never asked for more detail on any matter than she was granted, perhaps because she herself tended to confess to others only what they needed to know. "Madeline's husband, Edward, died five years later, in 1403. Rhys said that my mother took Madeline's child back to

Kinfairlie, for the child had been orphaned."

"And he thought you might be that child." Rosamunde guessed, then shook her head. "It seems unlikely. I attended your christening, after all, and you were only days old."

"But you must recall Ellyn," Alexander said with sudden urgency. His eyes were bright.

Madeline turned to him, a ghost stirring in her memory. Ellyn. The utterance of that name made her vaguely recall another child, a quiet, small child.

Rosamunde shook a finger at him, evidently remembering the matter as well. "That tiny child! She was so sickly, and of an age with Madeline. I teased Catherine that she had brought home a changeling, not a mortal child, and that the fairies would steal her back one night." She shook her head. "I had forgotten all about poor little Ellyn."

Alexander grinned. "And she would never play with us, remember?" He nudged Madeline. "I probably granted her more attention than any other soul at Kinfairlie, so convinced was I that she should join our games. You were not even five summers of age, Madeline, and you, Vivienne, were younger still. Malcolm was a babe."

"I do not recall her," Vivienne said with a shrug.

"I think that I do . . ." Madeline admitted.

"You preferred to play with Vivienne," Alexander reminded Madeline, then sobered. "It was only later that I understood that Ellyn did not play because she was ill."

"She died very shortly after her arrival at Kinfairlie," Rosamunde said. "Hers was a short sad life."

Alexander nodded. "I remember Madeline Arundel as well, for she and mother rounded at the same time and oft visited with each other." He shook his head, seeming snared by some fond memory. "She was a kind woman. She always brought candied angelica because I loved it so and no one at Kinfairlie knew how to make it. She would feign surprise when I found it amongst her embroidery. I remember how Maman wept when she died."

"She *was* a kind woman," Cradoc affirmed. "I remember her well. And such a laugh! She lightened hearts wheresoever she went."

"I think Maman was still round with you when we had word of Madeline Arundel's death," Alexander said. "I recall Papa arguing with our castellan about telling Maman some dire news so close to her time. He insisted that she must know, while the castellan said it would only do her injury." He tapped a finger on Madeline's shoulder. "You must have been named in memory of Maman's friend."

Madeline liked the notion well, whether it was true or not. "But Ellyn died?"

Alexander nodded, his manner sad. "There is a stone in the churchyard at Kinfairlie for her, a small one with a cherub upon it. Maman used to pray there in memory of her friend and little Ellyn, as well."

Cradoc shook his head. "Ah, I recall Madeline and Edward's nuptial feast. You never saw a happier pair. They were so smitten each with the other, so glad to face life together. It is sorry indeed that they had so few years together."

"Perhaps they savored each moment fully," Madeline suggested softly and the others nodded at that prospect.

The company stood in silence for a moment, grieving for the lost couple and their child. Madeline imagined that the wind even took a mournful tone. When next she was at Kinfairlie, Madeline resolved she would visit the stone laid in memory of

Ellyn, the tiny quiet child she had almost forgotten, and she would say a prayer for all of them.

Rhys's captors were rough, but they did not do him much injury. He suspected that he was wanted alive for some purpose, though he could not guess what it was.

A good twenty mercenaries surrounded him and marched him through Caerwyn's gates, which he supposed was a compliment to his fighting abilities. He was not surprised that he was forced down the ladder to Caerwyn's dark dungeon, nor was he surprised that he was shoved into its one cold chamber. He was not surprised when the oaken door was slammed behind him, and the cell plunged into darkness as the key was turned in the lock.

He was surprised when a voice cleared behind him.

Rhys jumped and pivoted, his hand falling to his empty scabbard and closing upon no weapon at all.

"Rhys?" his mother asked, her voice trembling. "Rhys, is that you?"

"Mother!" Rhys stepped into the murky darkness, hands outstretched. His mother made a sound suspiciously akin to a sob, clutched his hands, then fell into his embrace. She was smaller than he, still soft and perfumed as always she had been.

But she was shaking, shaking to her very marrow, and she wept as he had never heard or seen her weep before. Rhys held her tightly and said nothing, for there was little reassurance he could grant.

Rhys knew this cell well enough to know that there was no escape from it, that the sole way out was through the portal, that the lock was doughty. He knew that they would remain here until it pleased their captor to release them, and he understood enough of people to guess that any release would not be a merry event for himself and his mother.

The door would be unlocked because they were dead, or because they were to face their execution. His sole consolation was that Madeline had been spared this fate.

Perhaps she would be happy with James.

Perhaps he should not torment himself with such thoughts in what were likely to be his final hours.

His mother, however, had other ideas. She straightened finally, sniffled, then poked him in the chest with an imperious finger. "You were married! And I had to learn the truth of it from my sister!" Adele made a sound of disgust in her throat.

"How could you have done this to me? You know how she loves to know all about everyone, how she savors holding some morsel of news that others have not yet heard. How could you have failed to send me a missive yourself?"

"The matter was complicated," Rhys said. "And it may not be of import, after all."

"What do you mean?"

"Madeline seeks an annulment." He felt his mother's shock, could imagine her expression as she pulled back slightly.

"This cannot be true! My son has not consummated his match?" Adele shook her head with such vigor that Rhys felt her gesture. "You are hale enough, Rhys, and you like women well enough. Surely there can be no reason for her to find fault."

"I suspect she is the daughter of Dafydd's daughter, Madeline Arundel. That was why I wed her."

"You wed her to secure Caerwyn," his mother guessed. "That was why I had no warning of it! You did not even tell me the nature of your quest when you left. Hmmm, Miriam does not know that detail."

"But if it is true, my Madeline and I are too closely related to be wed by the consanguinity laws of Rome." Before his mother could scoff that such laws had no sway in Wales, Rhys laid a finger upon her shoulder. "We were wed in Miriam's abbey, by a priest answerable to Canterbury and thence to Rome. She will gain this annulment with ease. I erred in forgetting the difference in ecclesiastical law, and now I will lose my wife."

"You must indeed have been blinded by love to have made such an error in your determination to be wed with haste. It is unlike you, Rhys, to omit any detail from a scheme."

Rhys felt his neck heat, for he had been a fool and could have done without his mother's agreement on that point.

Adele made a sound of disgust. "What use to you is a wife who does not see your merit?" She patted his shoulder. "Is the girl blind? Is she witless? You are a valiant warrior, you are easy to look upon, and you possess a holding that will see her fed . . ."

"Mother, we are in the dungeon of that holding," Rhys felt obliged to note. "It seems unlikely that I will ever be its lord in truth."

"It is unfair!"

Rhys could feel his mother fuming at the injustice served to her only son. Indeed, her protectiveness made him smile, for it was not all bad to have some soul think well of him.

"It is all the fault of that witch Nelwyna," she said with vigor.

"Father's wife?" Rhys frowned. "She is responsible for this? I always thought her most amiable."

"Hardly that! Every soul in this keep thought her so sweet and kind, but I oft saw her looking at me with malice in her gaze. I never liked her, but I was polite for your father's sake. He seemed to think her deserving of compassion, and here we stand, reaping the fruits of that compassion! He should have spurned her when she granted only daughters, he should have cast her out when my first two sons died . . ."

"What first two sons?"

"You had two older brothers, but they died young. One came dead from my womb, strangled by the cord. At the time, the midwife said something foul about Nelwyna being of no aid, but Henry bade her bite her tongue. And then the second boy died, while Nelwyna held him, just moments after he had come screaming from my womb. Even Henry could make no argument then, and he ensured she was not in the chamber when you were born."

"I had no knowledge of this," Rhys said in astonishment.

"No one was certain, no one but the midwife. Henry was cautious, and protective of you. I only believed the truth years later." That finger rapped him on the chest again. "Do you recall when you were injured as a boy, when you fell from the saddle?"

"Of course. It was of no import."

"Ha! That was what she wished all to think! There was a thorn beneath the saddle of the horse chosen for you to ride." His mother tapped his chest again. "Do you recall being ill after we celebrated the victory of Owain and Dafydd, when first we gathered at Caerwyn and made it our home?"

"I was young to drink so much ale," Rhys noted. "Of course, I was ill."

"You were ill because you were given tainted ale! We discovered the truth only when you slept overlong and a woman in the kitchen confessed her part to Henry. She had thought she partook in a jest, and feared she would be party to a murder. She named Nelwyna, but Nelwyna denied all."

Adele fairly growled in her vexation. "And Dafydd said he could not act upon the testimony of a serving wench who had probably sampled too much of the ale herself. Nelwyna was known to be unkind to the women in the kitchens, and Dafydd thought this indictment an attempt at feminine vengeance." She shook his tabard. "But again, you almost died! Praise be to God that you have the vigor of my family!"

"Again, I knew nothing of this."

"Henry did not wish to poison your thoughts. It was the sole matter upon which we argued, for I felt you should be warned." She tapped him on the chest once again. "Then there was the accident during your training, when that marshal used a real sword against you while yours was only wooden."

"I thought it a test."

"He had been bought," Adele spat. "Though I dare not say with what. Dafydd forbade him to return to Caerwyn and had a discussion with Nelwyna. He also sent you away to fight with Owain Glyn Dŵr, for finally the threat she posed was understood."

Rhys was astonished, for he had never guessed the peril that had faced him in his youth. "And Nelwyna is also responsible for our imprisonment?"

"I thought her improved since Henry's death, for always I believed that jealousy of my time with him was at root. But then Miriam sent her letter, and when I awakened from my afternoon sleep, it was not where I had left it. I guessed that she had read it, for she shares Miriam's love of gossip."

Adele sighed. "I did not guess that there was greater import than that, not until Robert Herbert and his knights arrived at our gates." Adele swallowed. "And she welcomed him, with open arms and open thighs." She spat into the corner of the cell. "And she calls me the whore!"

Rhys mused over this revelation. "It makes some sense. Herbert has always desired Caerwyn. She must have told him that if he acted in haste, it could be his own."

"And she has always wished to be Lady of Caerwyn, so she told me when I was imprisoned here. They have made a bargain, those two villains, and to see their ambition achieved, you must die." Adele clutched Rhys's tabard again, and her fear echoed in her voice. "But we will not die, will we, Rhys?"

Rhys held his mother more tightly, for he dared not lie to her. He could not see how they could avoid dying, not without aid, and he could not guess who might aid them now.

His mother understood the import of his

silence, and he whispered nonsense to her as she began to weep anew. Never had he felt so powerless before. Never had he faced such despair.

The sole consolation was that Madeline had not been captured as well. By spurning him, she had saved her own hide from Nelwyna's ambition, and for the first time, Rhys was glad that Madeline had chosen to pursue that annulment.

It seemed he would not have long to mourn her absence, after all.

"What care have we of these people's woes?" James said with sudden impatience, then claimed Madeline's hand. "Caerwyn and Rhys FitzHenry are not our concern, not any longer."

"Rhys is Madeline's husband!" Vivienne reminded the other man with impatience.

"I am her betrothed." Curiously, James's claim awakened no response in Madeline.

Cradoc snorted, there obviously being no doubt in his thinking which role had superior claim.

"You never contacted Madeline to tell her that you were yet alive," Elizabeth said, then put her nose in the air. "I cannot even *see* your ribbon and Darg has just spat upon you. You are fortunate that my manners are rather better."

James gave the girl an odd glance, then smiled at Madeline. "You are rid of a husband this way, Madeline. Our fate lies north, in my father's abode."

"In your father's abode?"

"He has promised me a stipend, upon wedding you." James winked. "He likes you well, and I like the notion of an annual stipend even better." He laughed, but no one shared his jest.

"But what will you do?" Madeline asked with care.

"I will create music." James smiled a winning smile.

Madeline considered him, recalling Rhys's assertion that every man must fight one day to protect what is his own. She was beginning to understand the impulse of her heart, to see clearly what she should have guessed long ago. "Surely you learned to do battle in France, and have some hunger to continue to do so?" she asked politely.

James laughed merrily. "Me? I managed to evade my father's men at the earliest opportunity. I spent my time in France in the churches, listening to their heavenly music."

"Then you were not even at Rougemont,"

Alexander said, his voice cold with accusation.

"Why else do you imagine that I yet breathe?" James asked, his manner scathing. "I am not in such haste to die for coin and land."

"Though you welcome the assets brought by both," Madeline said quietly. James granted her a sharp glance and she straightened. "And what shall I do in your father's abode? Your mother has enough ladies-in-waiting and daughters underfoot."

James seized her hand as if he would lead her into a dance. "You shall sit and be beauteous. You shall smile upon the company, and all shall bask in the splendor of your beauty. You shall inspire me. You shall receive odes and poems from me, and if you feel such necessity, you will embroider some frippery or other." He waved his hand dismissively, then smiled anew. "You, Madeline, will be my muse."

It seemed a rather thin prospect, compared to Rhys's dream of building prosperity for those beneath his hand, for ensuring that all had justice and sufficient food in their bellies. Madeline was certain that his wife would have greater responsibilities than choosing a piece of cloth for embroidery.

"We could have a child," James suggested, apparently seeing Madeline's lack of enthusiasm. "After all, I am certain that you are still a maiden, are you not, my beloved?" His manner became more anxious. "There will be no doubt as to the paternity of any child you bear, will there? Will there?"

"I am no longer a maiden," Madeline said calmly, watching James all the while.

He averted his gaze and cleared his throat. "But surely you cannot have conceived a child already? It has been only a few days." He seemed reassured by his own reasoning. "Why, you must have only met abed the once! All know that a maiden cannot conceive when first she is sampled."

"Of course she can," Rosamunde said with a laugh. Cradoc and Padraig covered their smiles with their hands and looked across the hills with feigned fascination.

James colored and his lips set. His gaze was hostile now. "How many times have you coupled with the wretch?"

Vivienne and Elizabeth listened avidly, their eyes wide as if they knew they should not heed Madeline's words but could not bring themselves to do as they should. Madeline felt her own color rise, for this was not a matter that should have been discussed before so many souls.

"My husband and I met numerous times abed, so many times that I lost the count," Madeline said, feeling a stubborn urge to witness how James faced the truth. She had done nothing wrong in treating her legal husband with honor! "Rhys is most anxious for sons. We were wed. How could I deny him his nuptial due?"

James blanched and released her hand. He stepped away, his hand upon his brow, clearly distressed by these tidings.

"Had you been so concerned with my maidenhood, you might have troubled to send word to me that you yet lived!" Madeline turned her back upon James. She found herself trembling, so great was her anger. Vivienne slipped a hand into hers, then gave her fingers an encouraging squeeze.

Rosamunde stood with Cradoc, her brow furrowed. "I will aid Rhys, if it can be done, before my departure," she said. "I owe him a boon, for he ensured that my name was never linked with the failed coup in 1415. I would never have been permitted to drop anchor in many ports without that surety."

"Aye, that is true enough," Padraig said with a nod. "Our necks are not stretched thanks to his silence. I, too, will help."

"I will aid Rhys, as well," Elizabeth said with uncommon resolve for her age. "He is the get of fairies," she said when the others regarded her in surprise. "There may not be much I can do, but I will do whatsoever I can."

"Do not forget me!" Vivienne said. "I will not stand aside while a man who can tell such stories is cheated and killed."

Alexander smiled at Cradoc and then at Madeline. "My blade is in Rhys's service." He tapped a jingling sack of coins upon his belt. "Let us see him hale first, then I will return his coin and win your annulment, Madeline."

Madeline regarded the sack of coins with horror. Now that the prospect of annulment was imminent, it did not seem so desirable after all.

Chapter Seventeen

Cradoc and Rosamunde conferred, then crept to the crest of the hill to watch the proceedings far below. When they returned long moments later, Rosamunde looked resolved and Cradoc seemed skeptical.

"The sole unguarded path into the keep will be through the drain," Rosamunde said, speaking in a tone that allowed no argument. She flicked a glance between those pledged to aid Rhys. "Someone must enter the fortress through the sewer that leads to the sea, then open the gates for the remainder of us."

"I will do it," Alexander said. Vivienne and Elizabeth protested, but he shook his head. "It is too dangerous for either of you and I am more slender than Padraig. Cradoc must remain with the rest of you, for he alone knows who is friend and who is foe."

"He speaks good sense," Cradoc said to Rosamunde.

"It happens on occasion," she agreed with a wink for her nephew. The company turned to climb to the crest of the hill, but

James seized Madeline's elbow and held her back.

"I see no reason why we should risk our own hides," he said sourly. "Let us flee now, Madeline, let us make haste to my father's abode. Leave your siblings to resolve this matter, if they insist upon it. The horses are unguarded, we could be gone before they could halt us."

The very idea of abandoning her family after they had come so far to aid her, no less Rhys, was utterly abhorrent to Madeline. "I thought you only desired a maiden for your bride," she reminded James, pulling away from his grasp.

James nodded, then shrugged. "True, but a man must make some sacrifices to ensure his father's favor. I will still wed you, though you are soiled."

He could not have chosen a worse word.

"I am not *soiled!* I have been saved from the folly of wedding you!" Madeline turned her back upon the astonished James and ran after her family. She caught Rosamunde's sleeve in her hand. "Rhys loves nothing more than Caerwyn. I would see it safely in his keeping. I am smaller yet than Alexander. Let me take this task."

"But, Madeline, it is too dangerous!" Alexander protested.

"I can hold my breath longer than you, you know it well."

Alexander colored at Cradoc's confused glance. "I used to sneak into the bathing chamber and dunk my sisters while they sat in the tub. Madeline learned to hold her breath and remain so still that I oft feared I had killed her."

"Then Papa near killed him for so tormenting us," Vivienne said.

Cradoc smothered another smile and Padraig chuckled openly.

"It is not amusing, if the prank granted her a useful skill," Rosamunde said. "I say that we let Madeline do this deed." The others nodded, but before they could speak, James interjected.

"Madeline! You cannot do this thing!" He snatched at her arm, as if he would forcibly restrain her.

Madeline removed her arm from his grasp. "Rhys saved me from Kerr's assault. I owe him no less than to reciprocate in kind." She granted her former suitor a cool glance. "You desire me only to ensure your own leisure, but what will happen when your father dies? What will you do if he ceases to admire your music? Do not say he will never do so — how else did you find yourself in France? It has happened

492

before and it will happen again."

Madeline turned her back upon James and met her aunt's approving gaze. She removed the velvet sack from around her neck and kissed it before passing it to Rosamunde. "I would ask you to take this in safekeeping for me."

"It is warm," Rosamunde said as she fingered the velvet.

"It probably carries my own heat," Madeline suggested but Rosamunde shook her head.

Smiling, Rosamunde loosed the cord and let the stone fall into her palm. The entire company gasped in awe at the magnificent stone. Madeline could not believe how it had been transformed. It could have been a drop of sunlight. Indeed, the gem was so radiant that no one could look directly upon it.

Rosamunde laughed. "It was like this upon your mother's wedding day," she said, her voice husky.

She dug in her purse and removed something gold. It was a setting for the stone, wrought of golden wires that caught the stone in a fine cage. Rays extended out like beams of light, spreading from the glowing stone. The whole pendant hung from a fine golden chain, which Rosamunde put around Madeline's neck. The stone nestled in the hollow of her throat, its heat warming her through.

"You need have no fear of losing this now," Rosamunde said, "for its radiance will light your path and its chain is short enough that it cannot slip away."

"But the chain could break," Madeline whispered, fingering the stone as she feared losing such a prize in the sewer of Caerwyn.

"These bonds are stronger than you can guess." Rosamunde kissed Madeline's brow. "You have chosen aright, child. The Tear declares as much more clearly than can be spoken. It is time to aid Rhys."

Madeline was terrified.

She and Alexander crept down the steep hillside, so that they could slip into the sea unobserved. With every step she was certain that they would be spied, that some archer would dispatch an arrow with deadly accuracy and their quest would be lost.

But they reached the shore with no more than scratches on their hands and knees. They left most of their clothing hidden on the shore, each wearing only a chemise. Alexander insisted that they each keep their belt and a small knife.

"You must move quickly," he counselled, concern furrowing his brow. "We do not know where the drain will end, though likely it will be in the lower realms of the keep."

"In the dungeon?" Madeline guessed.

Alexander grimaced. "We shall hope that it is not within a cell."

Madeline shook her head, though she was far from certain. "It cannot be, for then prisoners could easily escape."

"Unless there is a grille fixed atop it." Alexander's frown deepened. "There should be air within the drain, for it must run level with the ground to come from the keep to the sea. Remember to turn your face upward, if any water comes rushing down the drain."

"Will it?"

"Who can say?" Alexander caught Madeline's shoulders in his hands. "I wish I could do this. I wish that you were not to be in such peril."

"But the way may be narrow, and I may have to hold my breath long . . ."

"I know, I know." Alexander forced a smile. "I wish also that you did not make such good sense, Madeline." He hugged her tightly and his words were hoarse. "Be safe. Be swift. Be blessed in this task."

Alexander took Madeline's hand before she could answer him, this brother who could easily make her chest tighten with the vigor of her love for him. He led her into the sea, the waves pulling and pushing at them as they waded ever deeper.

They kept only their heads above the surface, though the waves oft deluged them. They clung to the rocks of the coast like barnacles upon the hull of a ship. Madeline hoped that their dark wet heads, if any noted them, would look sufficiently like those of otters or seals that no alarm would be cried.

They had only to follow their noses to find the opening of the drain. Turds bobbed on the ocean surface, closer together as they drew near to the gaping dark hole. It was bored into the cliffs and unobstructed by any grille.

"It must have been wrought by the Romans," Alexander said with awe. "Papa always said they were more plentiful in Wales, for they mined metals here." He slid his hand along the stone, admiring how it had been chipped away. "Caerwyn must be old."

Madeline nodded. "Rhys said as much."

At the mention of her spouse's name, the siblings looked at each other. "Are you certain?" Alexander asked. "The hole here is large enough for me."

"It will not remain so," Madeline insisted. She kissed his cheek, knowing that her effort might be doomed to failure. "Father taught you more than you realize," she said softly. "Kinfairlie, and our siblings, are safe in your hands, Alexander. Be well."

Madeline plunged into the dark tunnel, before her brother could say something that might make her weep. Her breath came quickly already, though she knew that she would have to control it to find success. Her heart thundered in her chest, so loudly that she feared the sentries would hear its pulse carried through the dirty water in which she moved.

The tunnel closed more tightly around her with every step, the smell of slops assaulted her, the water moved less vigorously and thickened to a slurry. It was up to her knees and it was cold, though she supposed it would have been more revolting had it been warm. She could not hear the sea any longer, she could not spy a glimmer of light. There was only the smell of the water and the gentle incline of carved stone beneath her feet.

And the impetus that was Rhys tugging her onward. The stone around her neck cast a faint glow, a ray of light that kept her from madness. At least she did not proceed blindly.

Madeline's fears remained at bay until the tunnel narrowed abruptly to the width of her shoulders. She stood hunched in the larger corridor and considered the hole from which muck spilled. There was no other way onward. She reasoned that this must be beneath the keep itself, for she felt she had walked forever. Perhaps the type of stone had changed here. Perhaps the hole narrowed even more farther ahead.

She refused to consider that she might become stuck. She had to help Rhys. Panic would serve them both poorly. Madeline climbed into the hole, stretched out supine. She half-dragged herself, half-writhed, the stones digging into her back, and somehow she made progress. She was not certain how far she moved or how fast, the darkness assailing her as it had not before.

Madeline began to be afraid.

Water rushed suddenly over her, water smelling of urine and dirty pots. Madeline grimaced and clung to the stones, holding her place as it washed over her with a vengeance. Her heart raced, she thought of her parents trapped beneath the darkness of the sea. Had their last moments been like this? She feared to drown, she knew that she would never be found, that none would aid her . . .

And then she recalled Rhys, telling her tales aboard the ship. She thought of his conviction that they were safe, and she was reassured. She heard again the rhythm of his voice and the memory made her smile.

Indeed, she could have wed worse. She could have wed James.

If she and Rhys saw their way through this challenge, if still he desired her as his wife, Madeline knew that she would remain gladly by his side. Perhaps one day, he would come to love her. Perhaps she should appreciate the man's deeds and his valor more than any sweet words he could offer.

Perhaps she should see the merit of what she had been granted and savor it.

She closed her fingers around the stone that her mother had worn and found strength in its glorious heat. Madeline realized that she had misunderstood its earlier portent.

The stone had been dark at first, because she had already decided to flee Rhys. The Tear must have predicted Kerr's assault.

The Tear had lit with a glimmer after Rhys had saved her from Kerr. She and Rhys had been wed then, the first step in sealing their fates together.

The star had brightened within the gem when Rhys had confessed his errors to her. Could it be that Rhys had realized then that he held her in some affection?

Was the Tear's current radiance a sign of the growth of Rhys's regard for her? Or did it indicate her own love for him?

Perhaps the stone shone most brightly when a pair loved each other with uncommon vigor, because that love would light their united path ahead.

Madeline had to reach Rhys to know for certain.

Encouraged, she found a grip on the stones overhead and pulled herself onward. Madeline recounted the tale of the man with the fairy harp to herself, though she knew she had forgotten some of it, though she knew that she could never tell it as well as Rhys. She kept her eyes closed, not wanting to see all that floated around her, and pulled herself onward despite the ache in her arms.

Suddenly, Madeline bumped her head. She bit back a curse, tipped back her head to see the offending stone, then gasped aloud.

The tunnel turned straight up, stretching above her head to a circle of flickering light. That aperture did not appear to be far away, perhaps a distance akin to the height of two men. There were handholds carved in the stone on one side, as if boys might have to climb down the drain to clear it on occasion.

And there was no iron grille across the opening.

Heart aflame with hope, Madeline pulled herself around the bend in the drain. Her hands shook, but she forced herself to think clearly. There would be a challenge ahead, of that she had no doubt. She took a deep breath, then climbed with newfound purpose.

She reached the top of the drain and peered over the lip.

The drain opened into a stone chamber. The chamber was dark, the only light coming from a lantern upon an unsteady table. Madeline guessed that the room was beneath the earth, or beneath the tower of Caerwyn. The stones in the walls looked large enough to be foundation stones.

Indeed, a wooden ladder ascended to a patch of light at the far end of the chamber. There was a solid wood door to her left, one with such a fearsome lock upon it that she thought she knew what it was.

She could see only one person. A plump bald man sat upon a bench beside the flickering lantern, his mouth open as he snored softly.

Madeline eased silently out of the drain, slops dripping from her sodden chemise.

She grasped her knife as soon as she stood free of the drain, her gaze fixed upon the sleeping man. The air was cold here and she shivered, even as she moved closer to the man. A ring of keys was cast upon the table, alongside a sword that Madeline recognized as Rhys's own.

The man was of considerable size, Madeline saw, and she realized that she would have only one chance against him. If he but raised one of those heavy hands against her, he could fairly kill her.

Surprise, and perhaps her wits, would be her only asset. Madeline took another step closer, her knife shaking in her grip. The water dribbling from her chemise seemed to make a fearful amount of noise as it fell upon the stone floor. A thousand doubts plagued her.

What if Rhys was not locked behind that portal?

What if Rhys was asleep there?

What if Rhys was dead?

What if there was no one to aid her? What would this man do to her once he subdued her? Madeline could guess that she would not enjoy whatever happened if she failed. She took the last step and closed her hand over the keys.

They were heavy, wrought of brass, and

there were two of them upon the ring. She had to choose the right one, as well! She pulled the ring off the table and it jingled slightly. Madeline caught her breath and froze in place.

The man frowned, then continued to snore. Madeline exhaled in relief, shivered suddenly in the chill, and sneezed.

The man was awake and on his feet in a heartbeat. He roared and reached for the hilt of his blade. Madeline seized the only chance she had and jabbed her knife into his eye.

He bellowed in rage, then swore. He staggered backward, blood streaming from his face, and Madeline nearly lost her grip upon the keys.

"Who is there?" Rhys shouted from behind the locked portal. "What happens out there?"

Madeline heard him pound upon the portal in frustration. She snatched up Rhys's sword and threw herself across the chamber. "Which key?" she shouted.

"The longer one," a woman replied.

The jailor lunged after Madeline, blood streaming down his face. She shoved the key into the lock, turned it hard, and jumped out of the way as Rhys flung the door back on its hinges.

"*Anwylaf!*" he said in evident amazement,

then took one glance across the chamber. He seized his blade from Madeline's hand, and drove it into the jailor's chest just as that man leapt toward them.

The jailor's blade clattered to the floor.

Madeline leaned against the wall in her relief, astonished to find her knees shaking. Rhys grimly ensured that the other man was dead, then turned to face her. A light danced briefly in his gaze, and Madeline stared at him, her heart bursting.

If only he would say something, if only he confessed himself glad to see her, then she would know she had not done this deed in vain.

But Rhys clearly could not make sense of her presence. He even frowned when his gaze danced over her. He pulled his tabard over his head, then cast it in Madeline's direction, his manner so dismissive that she flinched.

"You had best cover yourself, Madeline, lest all think you offer more than is your intent," he said, then pivoted to study the chamber anew.

Madeline realized then that her chemise clung to her flesh so wetly that she might as well have stood naked. She sneezed again, then pulled his thick tabard over her head. It hung to her knees and was warm with Rhys's heat. She wrapped her arms around herself and shivered, even as she watched Rhys pace the chamber. He stood at the base of the ladder and listened.

"*Anwylaf*," a woman mused. Madeline glanced up to find an older woman in the portal to the cell. She looked amused, her one brow arched and her lips curved in an affectionate smile as she surveyed Rhys.

He ignored her.

"You did not say that Madeline was your *anwylaf*," the woman teased. The back of Rhys's neck turned an unmistakably ruddy hue.

"It is scarce of import," he said gruffly.

"He always calls me as much," Madeline said. "For I am his wife."

The woman chuckled and offered her hand with grace. "As I am his mother, Adele. I am delighted to meet you, Madeline." She drew closer to Madeline. "But you are mistaken, my dear. *Anwylaf* does not mean 'wife'. How curious that Rhys did not make the distinction clear." She laughed lightly then, as if not finding the matter curious at all.

Rhys pointedly ignored this discussion. Indeed, he seemed intent upon listening to some noise from above that Madeline could not discern.

Madeline was confused. "But what does *anwylaf* mean, then?"

"It means 'dearest one'." Adele's smile broadened. "In my family, we use it only for our beloved. You must understand, my dear, that I am even more happy to meet you, now that I know my son calls you his beloved."

Madeline could not halt the answering smile that curved her lips. She had desired a sweet confession from Rhys, unaware that he had been making it all along.

There had to be worse things than having his mother surrender the secrets of his heart to his wife — who was determined to have their marriage annulled — but in this moment Rhys could not think of what those things might be.

He had no time to ponder such whimsy, and truly, there would be no need to ponder it if they three did not survive.

Madeline sneezed, drawing his gaze to her sorry state. She was soaked and she smelled, but there was a stubborn gleam in her eyes that made him proud. She was a rare treasure, this woman with a valor to match his own. They suited each other well, to Rhys's thinking, and he knew he had perceived as much when first he glimpsed her at Ravensmuir.

506

She watched him and he dared to hope that she had returned for more than duty. "I pledged to open the gates for the others," she said.

"How many?"

"Only five. Cradoc ap Gwilym, the sheriff, met Rosamunde on the road and kept her from riding on to Caerwyn. He was trying to warn you, for he feared the intent of Robert Herbert."

Rhys nodded. "Cradoc is a good man and a fair fighter. Then there is Rosamunde and who else?"

"Alexander, Vivienne and Elizabeth." Madeline smiled a little at his disappointment. "Unless you count the fairy that only Elizabeth can see, whom she calls Darg."

"It is no small thing to have a fairy on our side," Adele said with favor. Her tone did not dispel the fact that odds were decidedly against them.

"What of our own men? Were they captured, or killed?" Rhys asked.

"They pledged to serve Robert," Adele said, "for they declared their loyalty was to Nelwyna."

"Do you think it true?"

Adele smiled. "No one is truly loyal to Nelwyna, Rhys. They lied, the better that they might be able to aid you. Robert guessed as much, for he has separated them and scattered them amongst the ranks of his own company."

"But they might take your side, given the chance," Madeline said, before she sneezed again.

There was nothing for it. They had to leave the chill of the dungeon, and do their best. Rhys pulled Madeline's blade from the jailor's eye and wiped it on the man's tabard. He handed it back to her, then spoke quickly.

"I will lead. Mother, you will follow close behind me. Madeline, you must guard my back. We must endeavor to remain together, for if we are separated, I will not be able to defend you both. We must capture Robert and Nelwyna, and hope that will cool the ardor of the others for battle."

"They will be in the solar," Adele said, crossing her arms across her chest. "Nelwyna spoke bluntly of what she offered to Robert, and I have heard the men complaining that he never leaves her bed."

Rhys nodded. One excellent thing about Caerwyn was the simplicity of its design. There was one staircase which clung to the inside of the tower's wall. The hall was immediately above the dungeon and filled the ground floor. Above were two chambers, one facing inland, which had been that of Nelwyna and his father, one facing sun and sea which had always been his mother's. Crowning that was the solar, Dafydd's chamber, which filled the uppermost floor of the tower.

There were few places to hide in Caerwyn's tower, which would make it easy to find Robert and Nelwyna.

It might also work against Rhys, for there would be no refuge once they were spied.

"What about the gate?" Madeline asked.

Rhys shook his head, unable to see how he could achieve this, as well. He did not want to hurt her feelings, but he doubted the others would provide much aid against the dozens of mercenaries. "We shall see what we can do." He nodded once to the women, then climbed the ladder with no small trepidation.

Rhys had had no notion of how much time had passed in the dungeon, so he was surprised to find the hall dark. Night had fallen and the smell of meat told him that the men had eaten. They slumbered, stretched out on pallets that nearly covered the hall floor, while half a dozen torches burned fitfully on the wall.

He had time to hear his mother exhale in surprise, then he spied a flicker of movement. Adele strode away from him with purpose, lifting her skirts carefully as she crossed the room. She winked before she opened the portal to the courtyard, then slipped out of view.

Rhys gaped after her. Surely there must be sentries afoot? But there was no sound, no hue and cry, no alarm. He imagined his mother striding across the bailey, lifting the key from the sleeping gatekeeper's hand and opening the gate.

Madeline seemed to be fighting a smile. Rhys shrugged, then turned for the stairs, thinking this might prove more readily won than he had dared to hope.

After all, no one knew that he had been loosed from the dungeon. Perhaps his fortune changed! He leapt onto the bottom step, reaching back with one hand to ensure that Madeline was close behind him.

They reached the second floor and stood back to back in his mother's chamber, circling slowly while they both sought signs of life. There appeared to be no one in the chamber, though the light was more dim here than in the hall below. The gem on

Madeline's breast glowed, illuminating a little space around them.

Their gazes met and Rhys saw Madeline's nose twitch. He snatched at her, covering her mouth with his hand and burying her face in his chest just as she sneezed again.

They froze as one, but there was no movement beyond the racing of their own hearts. Rhys exhaled, caressed Madeline's cheek, then indicated the door to Nelwyna's chamber. She lifted her blade grimly and nodded agreement.

The door was unlocked and swung open silently. The chamber beyond was dark, too dark for Rhys's taste. He thought he could hear breathing, as if someone slept in the shadows beyond. He stepped cautiously into the room, his blade held high, and his mother screamed from far below.

Rhys glanced over his shoulder in fear. In that heartbeat, he felt motion beside him. Madeline lunged forward and stabbed her knife into the assailant who had been lurking in the shadows. That man's blade was mere inches from Rhys's throat.

The man was only stunned, but Rhys swung his blade and ensured he would surprise no one again. The man fell. Rhys pivoted to face the chamber again and his heart sank to his toes. The light from Madeline's gemstone was reflected in the blades of a dozen men who had leapt to their feet. They drove as one toward him.

"Stay fast behind me!" Rhys bellowed, as if he meant to leap into the chamber. Instead, he leapt back and slammed the portal into the chamber. The men fell heavily against it and several swore.

Madeline smiled at him, then she sneezed again. Rhys seized her hand and fled toward the stairs to the third floor. They were not so quiet now, for they had need of speed. They were only halfway up the stairs when the men tore open the door of Nelwyna's chamber and roared at the sight of Rhys.

A sentry was awakening at the summit of the stairs, but he was not quick enough to evade the bite of Rhys's blade. Madeline's gem revealed the man to be a stranger, probably one of Robert's most trusted men.

Rhys lifted Madeline's knife from her grip, bent and slit the man's throat. There was a gurgle, no more, then he was still and silent. Rhys wiped the blade and returned it to her, then kicked open the portal.

Another dozen men roared for blood

and leapt at Rhys. They were trapped between the two groups. Rhys bellowed and charged into the chamber, Madeline fast behind him. Rhys swung his blade and felled two men so quickly that they seemed astonished, even in death. He bent to finish the deed.

"On your left!" Madeline cried and Rhys straightened with his blade swinging. He heard her grunt as she drove her own blade into some sorry soul, then she pressed the hilt of a knife into his left hand. They fought well together, for though she could not match his strength, the gem ensured that she could see more.

A mercenary leapt at Rhys, swinging his blade with such fury that Rhys had to jump out of its path. Footsteps pounded on the stairs, but he dared not glance that way. He circled the mercenary, Madeline fast behind him, and heard the clash of blades on the other side of the chamber.

With each success, the battle became more complicated. There were many bodies and the light was not good. The floor was slick with blood and Rhys had to use care not to lose his footing. He dispatched a mercenary with a grunt, then realized he had lost something else.

Madeline was no longer at his back.

Rhys spun, seeking her, and found instead the glimmer of light from her gemstone. None other than Robert Herbert was lit by the stone's glow, the blade of his sword glittering against Madeline's throat. He wore no more than his chemise, his feet were bare, and he held Madeline by the hair. He stood beside the curtained bed.

Rhys froze. He straightened and spread his hands in surrender, letting his blade dangle from his hand. He did not drop it, though, for he saw Alexander easing ever closer to Robert. It must have been Alexander's arrival he had heard earlier, and the younger man who was responsible for killing some of their foes.

"You can have Caerwyn," Rhys said. "I know that is your desire. I ask only that you release the lady."

Robert sneered. "You have nothing with which to bargain."

"I bargain with my life. Kill me instead of her." Rhys put the tip of his blade against the floor and leaned both hands on the pommel. "Unless you are the kind of man who is only confident in the killing of women?"

"I have not lived so long because I am fool enough to rise to such bait," Robert said smoothly. He let the tip of his blade slide down Madeline's throat. "Perhaps I have another scheme for the lady, one that does not require her demise."

"You would not!" Nelwyna shouted from the bed. "You made a pledge to me, you wretch!"

She leapt from the bed in naked fury. Robert turned, and Rhys knew he would have to see Alexander. Indeed, Robert shouted then swung his sword at Madeline's brother. Rhys leapt across the chamber, fearing he would be too late to save the younger man. Alexander raced toward Nelwyna, perhaps hoping to use her as a shield.

Madeline guessed Rhys's plight. She jumped upon Robert from behind, and wrapped her arms tightly around his face.

He cried out in dismay and stumbled. "The stench! I cannot breathe! Get off me, woman!" Only then did Rhys recall that Madeline's chemise was soaked with sewage.

Her diversion granted Rhys the time he needed.

Rhys flung Madeline behind him and struck Robert across the face with his fist. That man staggered, then swung his blade at Rhys's groin. Rhys danced out of its path.

The battle erupted on all sides again, and Rhys realized that all of the others were here to aid him. On the far side of the chamber, a fallen mercenary lifted his head and surreptitiously reached for his blade.

Vivienne cried out a warning then struck that man in the head with a poker. Elizabeth swung a pair of flaming torches, setting fire to the garb of any man fool enough to come close to her. Rhys watched as she drove one torch into a man's face despite that man's screams.

"These Lammergeier women are wrought of stern stuff," Rhys muttered, even as he backed Madeline into a corner. She chuckled, then sneezed, so he knew where she was without risking a glance her way. She must be growing tired, after her ordeal of this day, and he was determined to ensure that she had no more need to fight.

Robert fought like a man half his age, and Rhys was glad of Elizabeth's torches. The pair dodged and feinted, nicking each other with cursed frequency. There was blood on Rhys's hands and a cut on his brow that was determined to bleed into his eye. Their blades clashed again and again, neither willing to cede, each well matched to the other.

Alexander and Nelwyna struggled on the far side of the chamber. Nelwyna's generous size and her anger made their battle a more even match than it might otherwise have been.

"Men!" Nelwyna cried. She looked as if she intended to wrest Alexander's head from his shoulders. "You are all liars and scoundrels, louts one and all. You think of nothing beyond your pricks and your ambitions and your ale!"

"Ow!" Alexander shouted, and kicked her in the knee.

"Ow!" Nelwyna cried, and kicked him back. Alexander darted backward and lifted his blade against her.

"You will not kill a woman old enough to be your grandmother, will you?" Nelwyna crooned. She stooped so that she looked older and more feeble than she was. Alexander's blade wavered. "I am old and wrinkled and you are too honorable a knight to kill an old woman devoid of defenses."

"So long as you have your tongue in your head, you are scarce defenseless," Robert muttered.

Nelwyna turned, hatred in her gaze. "You cursed vermin! I offered you my all . . ."

"And it was precious little, for it had been well savored afore."

"Oh!" Nelwyna gasped in outrage. She dived toward Robert and Rhys saw his moment. He jabbed his blade into Robert's gut with such force that the tip of the blade might have erupted from Robert's back. Rhys pulled out his blade and Robert staggered, though he did not fall.

He turned and gave Nelwyna a savage blow across the face. "I should never have heeded your lies," he spat as she lost her footing. "I should have guessed that Caerwyn could not become my own that easily." Then he fell to his knees and Rhys struck him again. Robert landed facedown amidst his fallen mercenaries, though Rhys kept his blade pointed at him.

Nelwyna stumbled from the impact of Robert's blow, her hand raised to her face. Alexander straightened behind her and lifted his sword. He swung the blade so forcefully that his blow should have been fatal.

Or it would have been, had it struck the older woman.

Nelwyna clearly tripped. They all saw her trip, although none of them ever agreed later as to what could have tripped her. The floor was barren there, but she stumbled all the same.

Alexander's blade whistled past her and

the weight of the blow buried it in the wooden floor. Rhys heard a strange gleeful cackle, and saw Nelwyna's expression of horror as she tumbled over the sill of the window and disappeared from sight.

Nelwyna screamed as she fell to Caerwyn's bailey, and then she screamed no more.

"Ha!" Rhys smiled at the sound of his mother's triumphant cry in the bailey. "Now, there is a deed well done!"

Rosamunde could be heard to laugh along with Adele, those two women obviously hale enough.

Rhys backed Madeline further into his corner, staring all the while at his fallen foe. He dared not lower his blade or avert his gaze, not until he knew for certain that his avaricious neighbor lived no more.

He did not trust Robert, and half-expected that the man only feigned death. Rhys dared not expose Madeline to another threat, not until he could be fully certain that she was safe.

But the lady leaned against him, her chest against his back. He felt the wet of her chemise soak his own garb, felt her curves against him. He felt her sigh of relief, he felt the trembling that still claimed her. Her hands slipped around his waist, as if he alone kept her upright, and she held fast to him.

Rhys hoped she wanted more from him than warmth. Some tension eased out of Rhys when Alexander confirmed that Robert was truly dead. Madeline whispered Rhys's name and the exhaustion in her voice tore at his heart.

Rhys claimed Madeline's left hand with his own, and interlaced their fingers. His ring still graced the middle finger of her hand, the silver ring he had taken from his own smallest finger all those days ago at Miriam's abbey. The sight of it, the fact that she had not removed it and cast it aside, granted him hope.

After all, she was here.

Rhys held Madeline's cold hand captive against the pounding of his heart, flattening it beneath the heat of his own palm. Perhaps she truly would remain by his side.

She sneezed, then leaned her cheek against his back with a sigh. The fingers of her other hand knotted into his own chemise, as if she would hold him fast.

"Anwylaf," she whispered and a lump rose in Rhys's throat.

With that one word, Madeline told him

all he had need of knowing. Rhys understood not only that she would stay at
Caerwyn, but why.

He lifted her hand to his lips, intending
to kiss her palm, then recoiled at the smell.
"*Anwylaf,* you have need of a bath," he said
sternly. Madeline laughed, then sneezed
three times in rapid succession. Rhys
caught her up in his arms and bellowed for
hot water. He would not lose her through
illness now!

"I have no maid," Madeline said, her
eyes dancing with mischief.

"I shall see you well served," Rhys retorted, then grinned down at her. "You
need have no fear otherwise."

The lady laughed and curled against his
chest. "I love you, Rhys FitzHenry," she
said, her eyes shining.

"And I love you, my Madeline." Rhys
tightened his hold upon her, more relieved
than he could declare in words. "It seems
that we have much to celebrate this night."

"Sons," Madeline said with resolve. "We
have sons to conceive this night."

And Rhys FitzHenry laughed aloud, for
the first time in years, much to the evident
delight of his wife.

Epilogue

Rhys had called for a feast, for all those abiding at Caerwyn and his neighbors besides to meet his new wife, but it took a fortnight for the feast to be arranged. Of course, there were tales to be shared, for Rhys had not known about Ellyn and everyone had to share the tale of their adventures on the journey from Kinfairlie, as well as of their role in the recapture of Caerwyn.

There were funerals to be planned, for Robert Herbert and Nelwyna. The mercenaries also had to be buried and there was some consultation between the priests of Caerwyn and Harlech as to the spiritual status of those fighting men. In the end few were buried in Caerwyn's consecrated ground.

The neighboring lords had to be invited to the festivities and arrangements had to be made for the feast itself. There were friendships to be formed and Caerwyn itself to be explored. Alexander and Vivienne and Elizabeth went hawking and hunting with Rosamunde and Adele, accompanied by an extensive party of Caerwyn's men. The feast was the excuse for their hunt, for the kitchens had need of meat, but they had a merry time. Alexander resolved to tell his uncle, the Hawk of Inverfyre, that falcons would be a fitting gift for the newly wed couple.

Madeline had continued to sneeze throughout that first night at Caerwyn, for she had been chilled to her very marrow. Rhys had undertaken her care himself, and they had remained locked in the solar for six days and nights. Rhys had opened the portal only to receive food and had made an enigmatic comment about sons.

The others oft heard him singing or the pair laughing. Adele had reported that both looked hale enough when she took them a meal, but no one was inclined to oust them from the solar.

There was a further delay when they finally rejoined the company, as Adele insisted upon fussing over Madeline's garb for the feast.

To the great relief of all, an old missive was found within a trunk of Nelwyna's. This missive had been dispatched by King Henry V in 1416 — it declared that Rhys had been pardoned, along with his fellows, on the condition of future loyalty to the crown. Only Nelwyna had ever laid eyes upon the missive, for she had hidden it away, though all of Caerwyn rejoiced to know Rhys to be safe from the king's wrath, after all.

Rhys himself dispatched a missive to the crown regarding the suzerainty of Caerwyn, and the response came with astonishing haste. The king, it seemed, had heard tell of Rhys's competent stewardship of Caerwyn beneath his uncle's direction. The king considered Rhys to be reformed and laudable, and well deserving of Caerwyn's seal.

Madeline suggested that the king was busy with other matters and that Dafydd had spoken aright. Prompt payment of tithes and a lack of rebellion had indeed turned the king's eye to other concerns.

In commemoration of Rhys's title, Madeline and her sisters insisted then upon modifying his insignia. He had worn only the mark of his homeland for years. It was time, Madeline insisted, that Rhys have colors to call his own.

He did not protest overmuch.

And so it was that the moon was waning on the night that all gathered at Caerwyn. They came to celebrate Caerwyn's new lord, who was familiar to them, and to meet Caerwyn's new lady, who as yet was not.

A new banner hung over Caerwyn's high tower and the same insignia graced the dark tabard of Caerwyn's new lord. The red dragon of Wales now emanated golden rays on both tabard and insignia, not unlike the rays that surrounded Madeline's precious Tear of the Virgin. The rays were similar, as well, to the glowing orb of Kinfairlie's insignia. The sisters' clever needles made it look as if Kinfairlie's orb had slipped behind Wales's red dragon, much as the setting sun will slide behind a ship upon the seas.

"Mingled insignia for mingled blood," Madeline had said with a smile, her hand sliding over her flat belly. Her sisters had not known whether she but hoped for a child, or whether she knew already that she carried one. Vivienne and Elizabeth agreed, however, that Rhys would make a fine father.

Rhys stood at the foot of the stairs on this night of nights, all in black save for the brilliant insignia upon his tabard. Alexander stood beside him, hands folded behind his back, the colors of Kinfairlie upon his tabard. Rosamunde stood alongside, resplendent in her own uncommon garb. They waited for the other women to descend. The entire company was on their feet and wearing their best garb. The musicians played a winsome tune, though James had returned to his father's home.

Alexander thought that the preferable arrangement, and it had been he who had encouraged James to leave.

Now, Alexander cleared his throat and spoke softly. "I would have a matter resolved between us, Rhys."

Rhys granted the younger man only the barest glance of acknowledgment. "Indeed?"

"I brought your coin with me on this journey, for I thought to repay you the auction price if Madeline wished to wed James," Alexander said with haste. "I thought it would be unfitting for you to have paid for a bride who abandoned you."

Rhys shrugged. "How fortunate for both of us that Madeline did no such thing. You have a fat purse to keep, as was initially your hope, and I have the bride who was my initial hope." He turned back to watch the stairs.

"But I have changed my thinking."

Rhys did not apparently hear this comment.

Alexander seized his host's sleeve. "Rhys, I know that I erred. I know that I should not have auctioned Madeline's hand."

"Matters ended well enough," Rosamunde interjected.

"If you mean to apologize, I would suggest you apologize to Madeline," Rhys said, with that same infuriating calm. "She is the one who was done a disservice."

"I mean to return your coin!" Alexander said in frustration, and was rewarded by Rhys's look of surprise. He took his host's hand and placed the sack of coin heavily within it. "Here! I will not have mere coin between us. Let us be friends and allies, let us be brothers."

Rhys considered the sack of coin, apparently astonished. "Are you certain of this course?"

"I can do nothing else to remove the stain I put upon our family's name."

"I thought you had need of the coin."

"No one can need coin so much as to put a barrier between himself and new kin." Alexander did not know what he would do about the crop that would surely fail, but there had to be another solution than this one. In truth, he was glad to be rid of the weight of the coin.

Rhys smiled slowly and put his hand

upon Alexander's shoulder. "You become a man before me." His gaze was steady and Alexander was relieved to see no censure in those dark eyes any longer. "If ever you have need of a loan, Alexander, come to me. You will find my terms more readily met than those of a moneylender."

Sadly, Alexander did not feel it appropriate to beg such a loan immediately. He nodded and inclined his head. "I thank you, Rhys." Then he pointed to the summit of the stairs. "Look! The women finally join us!"

Every eye turned to watch the ladies arrive. Elizabeth descended first, her face more red than ever Alexander had seen it. She tripped on her skirts on the bottom step and Rhys caught her elbow with ease. She thanked him and her blush deepened even more as she scurried to Alexander's side. "How hideous," she whispered. "Why could I not simply wait here with you?"

"Because you are the sister of Caerwyn's lady," Alexander reminded her.

"Rosamunde is her aunt," Elizabeth retorted.

That woman smiled. "I have made my own rules for so long that I forget there are others. Do not be so quick to step away from the expectations of others, Elizabeth.

I would not change my choices, but you might if you made the same ones."

Alexander could think of little he might say to add to that. He looked back to the stairs.

Vivienne, in marked contrast to Elizabeth, clearly savored the attention of the company. She smiled, and her hips swung as she descended the stairs with grace.

Vivienne was followed by Rhys's mother, Adele, who positively beamed in her delight. Adele kissed Rhys and pinched his cheek when she paused beside him, a familiarity that Alexander would have found unthinkable.

Yet more incredibly, Rhys not only endured it, but smiled.

"Grandchildren," Adele said with mock solemnity, patting Rhys's cheek as if he were a small boy. "I desire many grandchildren and I desire them soon."

"I shall see what can be done, Mother," Rhys said, then winked at Alexander. Alexander was shocked. His response must have been clear, for Rhys chuckled.

Then Madeline halted at the summit of the stairs. Her hair was covered by a veil, her face framed in silk. Her beauty, though, was more astonishing than ever, for she glowed with a new happiness. She wore a kirtle of a rich red hue, the same hue as the dragon in Rhys's insignia, and it was thickly embroidered with gold at the cuffs and the hems. The Tear of the Virgin hung at her throat, shining with unrivalled brilliance.

"That gem is astonishing," Alexander murmured.

Rhys grinned. "Aye, there is no treasure so fine as the Jewel of Kinfairlie." He moved to the foot of the stairs, offering his hand to his lady wife. He kissed Madeline's hand when she met him there and the pair seemed oblivious to all others in the hall.

"But there is no Jewel of Kinfairlie," Alexander said.

Rosamunde laughed beside him. "Is there not, Alexander? Show me a more radiant gem than your sister."

In that moment, Rhys and Madeline turned, the Lord of Caerwyn holding his wife's hand high. "I bid you all welcome my lady wife . . ."

"Your *anwylaf*," Adele interrupted with satisfaction.

The couple laughed and Madeline flushed. "My *anwylaf*," Rhys agreed easily, and the crowd chuckled in their turn. "Lady Madeline of Caerwyn!"

"He will kiss her, of that you can be certain," Vivienne said with delight. "It is simply too perfect of an ending to their tale."

"It is only a beginning," Elizabeth said, which made both sisters smile.

The happily wed pair exchanged a smile, oblivious as they were to all other than each other, then Madeline cupped Rhys's jaw and kissed him with vigor before all the men and women of Caerwyn. The assembly applauded, then began to stamp their feet. Alexander found himself hooting with all the others, so well pleased was he that Madeline had found the happiness she deserved.

"Woho!" roared some merry soul and every person in the hall turned to look.

A portly man, who looked to be a monk by his garb, grinned at the assembly with pleasure. He led a horse by its bridle, that beast swishing its tail as its ears flicked.

"We look to have timed our arrival well," he said to the horse. The beast nuzzled him and nibbled at what remained of the monk's hair, as if in agreement. "A feast is no small welcome, especially for such humble travellers as ourselves."

"Thomas!" Rhys shouted with obvious delight, and much of the company echoed his greeting.

"Tarascon!" Madeline cried, then picked up her skirts to hasten across the hall. Alexander realized belatedly that it was indeed his sister's palfrey that followed the monk into the very hall.

The lord and lady greeted the new arrivals with much merriment, and the assembly closed around them, clamoring for the tale. Alexander smiled as the monk exchanged hearty greetings with many in the company: This Thomas was clearly well known here and held in great affection.

Alexander's smile broadened as he watched his sister Madeline, her features alight. Rosamunde had spoken rightly. However poorly this marriage had begun, it could not have ended better. He need not fear for Madeline's future, not with Rhys by her side.

He could not have asked the Fates for more.

Well, perhaps he could have asked for a measure more coin in Kinfairlie's treasury, but he would find a solution to his woes somehow.

Only Elizabeth saw the spriggan skip over the heads of all gathered there that day. Only Elizabeth saw Darg seize the blue ribbon that seemed to flow suddenly from Madeline. Only Elizabeth saw Darg braid that ribbon with the gold and silver ones already twined together behind Madeline and Rhys. They were long ribbons, every one of them, and Elizabeth was glad to know that this Madeline would have many more years with her true love than Madeline Arundel had savored.

But Elizabeth hugged the secret to herself. Let all the family wait nine months to know the truth of what — or who — Madeline and Rhys had wrought. Darg winked at her from across the hall, and Elizabeth winked back, content to keep the fairy's confidence.

For now.

Dear Reader,

I hope that you enjoyed Madeline and Rhys's adventure. Rhys's tales are all Welsh folktales; however, the tale of the dog Gelert is known in many versions in many cultures. It has been traced to India by folklorists, and it even forms part of the legend behind a medieval French saint, which was originally a greyhound credited with healing sick children.

This family at Kinfairlie is proving to be a lively group. Next will be the story of Vivienne, the sister who most loves a romantic tale. Will she be able to forgive a man who tricks her into believing he is who he is not? And will that man, so anxious to see only earthly advantage, ever be convinced that there is more to life than what meets the eyes?

Of course, Alexander still has a few things to learn about responsibility . . . and you must have guessed that Rosamunde is not about to leave matters as they stand with Tynan. There is a lot afoot at Ravensmuir and Kinfairlie, so please join Vivienne and me for *The Rose Red Bride*, coming later this year.

Don't forget to visit my Web site for the latest news, covers and review quotes — and to enter Chestwick's biweekly contest. My virtual home is at http://www.delacroix.net, so drop in for a cup of mead.

Until next time, happy reading!